THE FINAL ROUND

ERNEST DEMPSEY

138 PUBLISHING

ALSO BY ERNEST DEMPSEY

Sean Wyatt Archaeological Thrillers:

The Secret of the Stones

The Cleric's Vault

The Last Chamber

The Grecian Manifesto

The Norse Directive

Game of Shadows

The Jerusalem Creed

The Samurai Cipher

The Cairo Vendetta

The Uluru Code

The Excalibur Key

The Denali Deception

The Sahara Legacy

The Fourth Prophecy

The Templar Curse

The Forbidden Temple

The Omega Project

The Napoleon Affair

The Second Sign

The Milestone Protocol

Where Horizons End

Poseidon's Fury

The Florentine Pursuit

The Inventor's Tomb

Adriana Villa Adventures:

War of Thieves Box Set

When Shadows Call

Shadows Rising

Shadow Hour

The Relic Runner - A Dak Harper Series:

The Relic Runner Origin Story

The Courier

Two Nights In Mumbai

Country Roads

Heavy Lies the Crown

Moscow Sky

The Adventure Guild (ALL AGES):

The Caesar Secret: Books 1-3

The Carolina Caper

Beta Force:

Operation Zulu

London Calling

Paranormal Archaeology Division:

Hell's Gate

Guardians of Earth:

Emergence: Gideon Wolf Book 1

Righteous Dawn: Gideon Wolf Book 2

Crimson Winter: Gideon Wolf Book 3

For my friend, Neil Joyce. Say a prayer at the cathedral on the hill for me.

PROLOGUE
10 YEARS AGO

"This has been excruciating to watch."

Tyler stared at the television, unable to pry his eyes from the drama unfolding on the screen as the two golfers marched up the fairway.

It was the final round of the open championship at White Oak National Golf and Country Club, and even though he was only eleven years old, Tyler Knox understood the gravity of what he was watching.

"I don't think we've ever witnessed a collapse like this, Bob. Not in the last thirty years, anyway," the color commentator said.

"Certainly not, Kip," the play-by-play man agreed. "It's truly monumental, and in more ways than one. If you're just tuning in, boy, you've missed a final round for the ages here at White Oak National. Graham Sullivan led by four strokes at the turn. But that lead evaporated after a series of miscues, and now he stands one stroke back on the leaderboard as the two men make the long walk up to the eighteenth green."

"You can't help but feel for Sully," Kip said. "He did everything right for three and a half days. Just an incredible display of skill he put on through most of the tournament."

"That's right, Kip. He was at the top of the leaderboard at the end of *day one and never relinquished that lead until a few moments ago with a bogey on seventeen."*

"Too many mistakes, Bob. But to be fair, Jamie Winthrop has played lights out on the back nine. Coming into the final round it looked for all the world he wouldn't catch Sullivan through the front."

Tyler remained glued to the television. Sullivan, a forty-eight-year-old man with thick brown hair tucked under a white Puma Golf baseball cap, trudged up the hill next to his caddie. The latter focused on the notepad in his hands, silently assessing the layout of the green. Sullivan, however, kept his head down. He looked like a man defeated, unable to come to grips with how he had blown one of the biggest leads in major tournament history.

It wasn't the only thing torturing him.

The television network had detailed the tragic story of the recent death of Sullivan's twenty-year-old son, Mackey.

Details about the car accident spread across the golf world like a wildfire in a field of dry grass.

The fact Sullivan had been able to compete at such a high level since then had been nothing short of incredible, but he'd yet to capture that elusive first major.

Golf, it seemed, was a microcosm of his life—one tragedy after another.

The less publicized subtext in Sullivan's odyssey was the divorce just three months after his son's death.

His wife, unable to cope with the death of their son, had found comfort with another man. But that story was one the networks didn't discuss—not on air, at least.

Tyler had heard the story, but as an eleven-year-old kid he didn't fully understand the details of the divorce.

His parents had never split up, though they certainly fought enough to warrant it. No matter how much they worked, they always struggled to put food on their rickety, hand-me-down table. Tyler was surprised the roof on their single-wide trailer didn't leak, considering how old it looked from the outside. It wasn't much better inside.

He'd taken to golf just over a year before, at the young age of ten, when his father took him out to a driving range near their house.

The range was little more than an old cow pasture next to the interstate, converted for golf by simply putting up a big net along the road and setting up signs in the uneven, undulating field.

His father was friends with the range owner, an old, skinny man named Jim Crawford, who sported a thin rim of gray hair around his shiny scalp. That gray hair was about as much color as the old man could muster at his age.

Jim had been kind enough to let Tyler use a set of rental clubs for free, though that price was probably too much for the crappy old set.

Still, they were good enough for a kid who'd never played before, and Tyler took an immediate interest in the game after his first flush shot with a child-size driver.

Ever since, he'd been completely enamored with the game of golf and begged his parents to let him watch the major tournaments when they were on television.

Neither seemed to care since both of them worked six days a week and were too tired to do anything else when they were home.

With no siblings, golf became Tyler's companion and his teacher, and when he wasn't watching it, he spent time in the backyard near the field, swinging the 5-iron that Jim had let him take home from the range.

"You only need two clubs to be a scratch golfer," Jim had told the young boy when he turned eleven. "The pros might be able to do it with a six-iron and a putter. But for you, I'd say a five is probably in order. It'll give you a little more distance until you're bigger."

Tyler recalled that as he'd watched Sullivan strike a 6-iron to within ten feet of the pin on 18, giving him a makable shot for birdie. His opponent's shot sat twenty feet away with a bending run at the cup. Winthrop's putter had been on fire that day, especially on the back nine, but that one would be more difficult, and with the pressure of the tournament yoked across his shoulders, it seemed all but assured he would two-putt for par, placing all the tension on Sullivan to make his birdie putt and force a playoff.

"Even after that incredible approach, he just looks like a man defeated." The television announcer's assessment perturbed Tyler, even if he knew it was correct.

"Can't say I blame him. He's been on this ride before."

"That's right, Kip. Four times a runner-up to a major title. The old bridesmaid line comes to mind for sure. But this one is really going to sting if he can't recover."

"Don't listen to 'em, Sully," Tyler said to the television. "You got this. Make the putt. Win it in the playoff."

The sun dipped low in the Northeastern Tennessee sky over White Oak National. The cameramen panned shots of the rolling hills, lush with leaves on thick branches, tall stands of pine, and rhododendron in the undergrowth, blooming pink in the shade. The camera shot cut to a scene of the crowd gathered around the 18th green, and more fans as they applauded the two gladiators on their march up the hill.

Winthrop waved to the cheering fans, soaking up the moment of what he appeared to be certain was an inevitable triumph.

"An incredible comeback by Winthrop today," Kip said in his distinct English accent. *"Well-deserved applause."*

"He certainly seems to be enjoying himself, Kip."

"Can't say I blame him," the Englishman said. *"This will be one of the greatest comebacks in golf history."*

"Shut up," Tyler snarled. "Sully isn't out of it yet."

Graham Sullivan had been Tyler's favorite golfer since the first time he saw the man play on television. He'd spent hours watching his online tutorials for beginners, and had honed his swing to look almost identical to Sullivan's. As close as a kid could get.

"Well, he still has some work left to do. That putt is anything but a gimme. And if he leaves it too low, it could find its way down to the bottom of the green."

"Wouldn't that be a wild turn of events?"

"Indeed."

Winthrop strolled up to the fringe, his signature red shirt flapping in the warm Tennessee breeze though still tucked into gray golf pants. He raised his black Titleist baseball cap and waved it at the crowd.

Tyler stewed at the arrogant display. "He's acting like it's already his," the kid sneered.

Sullivan split away from his opponent to go to the other side of the green. His caddie followed, setting the bag off to the side of the fringe as he studied the lie. Sullivan stood atop a rise on a patch of grass between the fringe and the bunker and eyeballed the line for his putt.

"Winthrop's got his work cut out for him on this one," Bob said through the television speakers.

"Yeah. We've seen several people leave it low this week on this hole, and more than once they ended up sucking on a bogey for their trouble."

"Leave it low," Tyler said, inching forward on the tattered sofa in what passed for their living room. He rested his bony elbows on bare knees sticking out from holes in his jeans, unable to lean forward far enough.

He couldn't imagine how nervous he would be if he were one of those guys on the green in that moment.

Winthrop stalked around his ball like a tiger hunting its prey. He crouched behind it, tilting his head to the right to assess the angle of the green. He looked up at his caddie and said something. The caddie replied, but Tyler couldn't hear the exact words.

The golfer stood and paced back around to the right-hand side of the green, then crouched down again, analyzing another angle.

The caddie pointed at something on the green, and Winthrop nodded.

Tyler's gut tightened with the tension of the moment. He pressed his hands together in a praying fashion, steepling his fingers up to his forehead as he watched on in anxiety-stricken wonder.

The camera switched to a shot of Sullivan, who also shifted his position and squatted down to get a clear look at the line to the hole. His caddie crouched just behind him, looking over his shoulder and whispering something about the speed or bend of the putt.

He stood up and stepped back onto the fringe to allow Winthrop to putt first, being the farther man out.

Neither golfer said a word to each other.

"Winthrop looks like a predator out there," Kip said. *"Look at the way he stalks around the ball. His confidence is absolutely brimming right now."*

"It sure is." Bob's voice grew silent as Winthrop stepped up to the ball. *"This is for birdie, and the Tour Championship."*

"Miss it," Tyler prayed. "Miss it. Miss it. Miss it."

He couldn't watch, but he couldn't look away either.

Winthrop addressed the ball, placing his feet evenly around a foot away. He did a toe tap, as if to get a feel for the green, then lowered his putter to a few inches above the ball. He hung it there for a moment, glancing over at the hole, back to the ball, to the hole again, and the ball once more.

Then he swung the putter forward and back a few times in a smooth, fluid motion to gauge the tempo he'd need.

He lowered the putter down to the tight Bermuda surface. He exhaled, paused, and then swung the club.

The face of the putter struck the ball purely in the center. Tyler stood up and neared the television as the ball rolled toward the hole.

"That looks good," Bob said. *"This one's got a chance."*

The crowd cheered, louder and louder by the second.

Tyler rubbed both temples as the ball neared the cup. He held his breath.

The ball slowed down. Then it hit the edge of the cup and rimmed out, rolling mere inches past.

"Oh my, that was close."

Tyler yelped loudly at the near miss. He raised both fists in the air.

The crowd groaned at the nearly perfect display of skill. They followed their disappointment with immediate applause.

Winthrop glanced over at Sullivan still standing on the rise behind his ball, arms crossed as he watched.

Sullivan gave a curt nod, a polite gesture to allow the closer man to finish out the hole before taking his putt.

Winthrop stepped up to the ball, this time with a more casual approach, lined up the putt, and tapped it in.

"*Par for Winthrop,*" Bob announced. "*And fourteen under for the tournament.*"

Winthrop pulled his ball out of the cup and shook hands with his caddie before walking off to the side to clear the way for Sullivan.

"*All the pressure now is on Graham Sullivan. Four-time runner-up. Has never won a major. You have to start to wonder: Is this his last chance?*"

"*Once you're over forty, the window starts closing,*" Kip added. "*I certainly know a thing or two about that.*"

"*That's right. But you had one major at forty-one.*"

"*I was lucky.*"

The men chuckled quietly as Sullivan took one last look at the putt.

"*This one is makable for a great putter like Sully,*" Kip said. "*Other than the back nine today, he has been like a man possessed on these greens here at White Oak.*"

Tyler held his breath as Sullivan stepped up to the ball.

The golfer glanced over at the hole. He looked back to the ball, then the hole, then lowered his putter.

"*Graham Sullivan for birdie, to tie and hit minus fourteen... and to force sudden death.*"

Tyler remained glued to the screen as Sullivan took the putter back then swept it through the ball.

"*This one looks good,*" Bob said, teasing the audience to heighten the drama.

The ball rolled toward the cup. The crowd could barely contain themselves.

Then the ball slowed down a foot away from the hole and dipped to the left.

"*He's got the read right on this one,*" Kip said.

Tyler couldn't take it. It had to go in. It just had to.

"Come on, Sully. One time."

The ball neared the cup. It seemed for all the world as if it were going straight into the heart.

At the last second, though, it turned slightly and rolled just past the bottom lip of the cup.

The crowd gasped in disappointment.

The camera focused on Sullivan, who stared in disbelief at the ball sitting less than four inches away from the cup.

"Absolute heartbreak again for a man who knows it all too well."

The camera switched over to Winthrop, whose caddie stood behind him looking giddy. Winthrop himself appeared to be reservedly happy about it all.

Tyler watched in sheer devastation as Sullivan walked over to the ball, leaned over on one foot, and tapped it in.

"Graham Sullivan with par, and thirteen under. But we have our first repeat champion here at White Oak National in over fifty years. An absolutely incredible performance by Jamie Winthrop. Our 2012 Open Championship winner."

Tyler switched off the television before he could hear or see any more.

The obvious heartbreak of Graham Sullivan shaking hands with the winner, then with the caddies before walking off the green, was one that Tyler never wanted to experience for himself.

1

PRESENT DAY, CHATTANOOGA, TENNESSEE

"You're never going to make that, Jack," Todd taunted from across the green, his smirk as wide as the massive green he and the other three golfers stood upon.

Tyler Knox stood on the fringe, surveying the scene with the calm focus of a seasoned caddie, though he was but a young man of twenty. He raised the white visor and scratched his scalp under matted, dirty blond hair. Slender and athletic, with an ease of movement honed by countless rounds under his belt, he wore the responsibility of his role like a second skin. The banter, the stakes, the tension of the moment—none of it seemed to touch him as he stepped forward, eyes narrowing as he assessed the lie.

The air, warm and thick with the scent of freshly cut grass, hummed with anticipation. The golden glow of the late afternoon sun bathed the 18th hole of the Green Mont Golf and Country Club, a jewel nestled among rolling hills and dense forests. The course, renowned for its beauty, design, and degree of difficulty, wound its way through the landscape, each hole offering its own unique challenge, culminating in the 18th—its green a masterpiece of subtle dips, rises, and wicked slopes along the lightning-fast surface.

The membership dues here were astronomical, as was the initiation fee. But beyond that, potential members also had to prove themselves. This club wouldn't just let any hacks in. Requirements in the bylaws stated players had to pass an assessment by the club director, which meant playing a round with him to prove they weren't going to desecrate the course with abhorrent play.

Tyler's charge, Jack Henderson—a stocky man with a love for loud golf attire that was as unmissable as his boisterous laugh—waited beside the ball, putter in hand. Tyler wondered if the astronauts on the International Space Station could see his neon green shirt with the naked eye. No satellite imagery required. His caddie counterpart and close friend, Justin Bennett, had joked between the two of them earlier that if he were ever stranded on a deserted island, he hoped it would be in a shirt that color so he could be found and rescued quickly.

"Well, Tyler?" Jack said. "What do you think it's going to do?" Tyler thought his voice betrayed a hint of nervous apprehension. "You haven't steered me wrong yet today."

Tyler didn't answer immediately. Instead, he stalked the perimeter of the green, the gaze from his blue eyes never leaving the firm ground. He'd walked this green hundreds of times over the last few years. He knew every curve, every undulation like the freckles on his face.

The surrounding hills and dense forests watched in silence—their slopes and valleys a testament to the timeless location of this beyond-exclusive course. The nearby woods, a dense thicket of evergreens and deciduous trees, stood as silent sentinels, their branches whispering secrets only the wind, or maybe Arnold Palmer, could understand.

The green itself was a thing of beauty and treachery. Masterfully designed by a genius and insidious architect who had eventually drunk himself to death for fear he'd never design another course like Green Mont, it demanded respect and precision from all who dared challenge it. Tyler's eyes traced the subtle breaks, the slight incline that could turn a confident stroke into a humbling hard lesson learned. The long shadows cast by the late afternoon sun added another layer of complexity to the read.

Finally, after a minute of checking multiple angles, Tyler stopped, crouched, and squinted. He could see it now—the path the ball needed to take, a gentle arc that would use the slope to its advantage, a dance with gravity and geometry. He stood, returned to Henderson, and pointed. "Aim just outside the left edge," he advised, voice steady. "There's a break about halfway you can't see from here. Trust the slope; let it carry the ball in."

Henderson gave him a sidelong glance, as if daring to question the read. Then he grinned. "You make it sound so simple, Tyler. You sure you don't want to putt it for me?"

Tyler grinned back. "No, sir. You've done the work to get here. Now it's time to get the glory."

The statement stretched the smirk on Henderson's face to a full smile. "Well, all right then, son," he said in his Southern accent.

Mr. Lee, one of the opponents, a tall man with an air of quiet confidence and dressed in the crisp whites of a golf traditionalist, chuckled. "It's a shame he can't putt for you," he quipped, drawing a round of laughter from his partner. Henderson's partner snorted but kept his composure—for the most part.

Henderson nodded at Tyler, a silent acknowledgment of their shared understanding. Gripping his putter, he addressed the ball, the weight of the moment settling around them like a cloak. The silent tension was nearly as dense as the humidity, broken only by the distant call of a bird, unseen but felt, a reminder of the life teeming just beyond the manicured perfection of the course.

After a deep breath and an exhale, Henderson pulled back the putter head and then swept it forward in a smooth, even motion.

On a quick green such as this, it didn't take much to get momentum. The ball rolled, true to Tyler's read, curving gracefully as it approached the cup. Time seemed to slow, the world holding on pause as the white sphere bore down on its goal—the empty cup.

The opponents craned their necks, leaning forward as they stared at the rolling ball drawing closer and closer to the hole. For a second, everyone held their collective breath—even the caddies.

The ball slowed down slightly as it inched toward the cup. For a moment, Henderson must have believed it didn't have enough gas to get there. But at the last second, it dipped a little farther and disappeared straight into the center of the hole.

The cheer that erupted from Henderson and his partner was matched only by the groans of their opponents. Their whoops and hollers echoed into the forests, off the hills, and back in what was usually a somber place of quiet reverence.

The bet, a friendly yet fiercely contested wager, was settled on the dance of a golf ball across a green canvas.

"Great putt, Jack," Lee said with a wide smile. "That was awesome." He reached into his pocket and fished out a wad of bills as he walked over to his opponent. The two shook hands, and then Lee planted the money into Henderson's palm.

"Thanks, Grant." He cast a wayward look over at Tyler, who stood next to Justin, watching the men shake hands in the traditional way to end a round. "Couldn't have done it without my caddie."

Lee followed his stare and nodded. "Yeah, you better tip that boy well. I'd say he deserves half of that money at least."

"You're not wrong," Henderson agreed with a chuckle. He counted out several bills, folded them, then pressed the money into Tyler's palm with a not-so-subtle handshake.

"Thank you, sir," Tyler said gratefully.

Lee turned and reached into his pocket to fish out another set of bills for Justin. This stack was shorter than the one he'd given Henderson, but it was above the club minimum for tipping the caddie.

He thanked Justin, handed him the money, and started back toward the clubhouse. His partner did the same, with the assurance from Justin that he would have their clubs cleaned and waiting for them at the front of the clubhouse.

As the group made their way back, the hills and forests their silent witnesses, the moment lingered.

Tyler waited beside Justin, watching the men slap each other on the back and talk about who was buying the first round at the bar.

Once the men were off the green, Tyler and Justin stuffed the money in their pockets without counting it and picked up their assigned bags. They knew better than to count the cash with the men still in view. All the caddies knew to wait until they were back in the caddie shack before checking their spoils.

As the sun dipped lower, casting the two young men's shadows over the Bermuda grass, Tyler and Justin made their way back toward the clubhouse. Their shoulders were sore from the burden they carried—a heavy bag on each side. Both of them thought those style of bags were for show more than practicality. Sure, they could carry a ton of things—range finders, umbrellas, more balls than even the most novice of golfers would need, but so could smaller bags like the ones most of the caddies used. Minimal in design, those slender, more lightweight models had everything the big bags did except for maybe a built-in cooler.

Tyler adjusted the bag on his right shoulder. The move only provided a few seconds of relief before the cushioned strap resumed digging into his muscles.

"Great read back there," Justin said as they passed through the cool shade of an ancient magnolia. The old tree stood just outside the clubhouse's back entrance where the men had just disappeared.

"You saw it too, I'm sure," Tyler said.

"Yeah. Of course." The words didn't match his obvious lack of confidence in the answer.

Tyler chuckled at his friend. "I'll be glad to get these bags off."

"No kidding. I think Mr. Lee has a dead body hidden away somewhere in his."

Nestled amid the rolling hills and lush fairways of the picturesque Southern golf course, the clubhouse stood as a testament to rustic elegance and timeless charm. Its façade, a blend of natural stone and weathered wood that flowed across the building, whispering stories of the land's rich history and the countless footsteps that had meandered its paths down through the ages.

The two caddies approached the spacious porch that was connected to the bar in the back. A counter ran along the wall beneath an open window to the bartender so members could sit and have their mint juleps outdoors. A line of welcoming rocking chairs and lazy ceiling fans across the covered porch offered a prelude to the warmth that lay within. It was a place where time seemed to slow, inviting visitors to sit, rock gently, and bask in the tranquil views of the sprawling greens and azure skies.

A pair of heavy wooden doors sat to the right of the outdoor bar. Inside, dark, polished wooden floors contrasted with the rugged beauty of exposed beams overhead, creating a cozy, cabin-like atmosphere that felt both grand and intimate. The air was perfumed with the scent of aged wood and the faint, comforting aroma of a crackling fireplace that served as the heart of the communal space.

Within this sanctuary, every corner and crevice was meticulously designed to cater to the needs and comforts of its guests. The pro shop, a treasure trove of golfing essentials and fineries for those who could tell the difference, promised the thrill of new discoveries. The locker room, with its sturdy wooden lockers, offered a private respite for golfers to refresh and regale in the day's triumphs and follies.

The clubhouse's lounge was a haven of relaxation, where plush leather sofas and chairs invited weary visitors to sink in and unwind. Here, the camaraderie of the game continued, with tales of near-misses and spectacular shots echoing amid laughter and clinking glasses.

Meals in the clubhouse were an experience unto themselves. The dining area, with its large windows, framed the golf course like a living portrait, allowing diners to feast not just on the sumptuous Southern cuisine but also on the breathtaking vistas. The ambiance, enriched by the gentle glow of lantern light and the soft melodies of a distant piano, wove a spell of enchantment that lingered long after the meal had ended.

Tyler thought about all of this as they passed the porch, walking around it toward the front of the building where the bag drop and pickup was located.

They rounded the corner where huge azalea bushes—their pink and white blossoms gone for another year—stood amid rhododendron and sculpted boxwoods. Beyond the drop-off loop in the front, a wide parking lot cut into the surrounding forest. To the right, a few golfers hit balls on the driving range, sneaking in a little late afternoon practice. Some of them were probably trying to correct problems they'd experienced from a round earlier in the day.

That was often the worst thing a golfer could do—trying to fix things that went wrong on the same day. Tyler found that sometimes stepping away from the game, even if for only a day or two, helped exorcise those demons. He knew some guys who went months without lifting a club and then showed up to play lights out. They, of course, were exceptions to the rule, but the game of golf was, and always would be, a fickle shoe that didn't fit every foot the same way.

Jeff, the guy running the drop-off and pickup for the day, heard the jingle and clanking of clubs as the two caddies approached. He was just under six feet tall, with tousled ginger hair, and probably ten times more freckles than Tyler. While the caddies were required to wear the standard white coveralls, the guys in the pro shop and out at the bag drop wore dark blue polos with the white club crest over the left breast, along with white pants.

"What's up, guys?" Jeff greeted. He sounded way too cheery to Tyler.

"How does he stay so happy all the time in this sweltering heat?" Justin whispered.

"I imagine that big umbrella over his podium helps a bit."

"Did y'all just finish up with Mr. Henderson's group?" Jeff asked, pressing on with the conversation despite it being one-way traffic so far.

"Sure did, Jeff," Tyler answered.

"Who won?"

"Who do you think?" Justin answered as they neared the podium. He and Tyler stopped and shrugged the bags off their shoulders, then eased them onto the green wooden rack next to the driveway.

"Henderson?"

"Bingo."

Tyler thought Jeff seemed proud of himself for having guessed correctly. "Knew it."

"Why? Because Tyler was on his bag?"

"No..." Jeff couldn't hide the lie, and he didn't try hard to.

"It's okay, Jeff. Tyler is the best caddie out here."

"It's not a competition," Tyler interjected. "We're all on the same team. Speaking of—" He reached into his pocket and pulled out the wad of cash. He peeled a twenty-dollar bill off the top, stepped over to Jeff, and pressed it into his palm. "Make sure those clubs shine," he said with a wink.

"You don't have to give me that much," Jeff insisted, his mouth open.

"It's cool. We're all on the same team here."

"I appreciate it, Tyler."

Justin sighed and took a twenty out of his stack. He handed it over to their younger counterpart.

"Thanks, Justin. That's too much money for cleaning some clubs, though."

"I agree," Justin said, half joking. "But I can't let Tyler make me look bad. Besides, I'm sure our group took good care of us too." His comment sounded more hopeful than truthful.

Tyler neither confirmed nor denied. "Just make sure those clubs shine," Tyler said with a wink. "See ya later, Jeff."

He turned toward the driving range and the caddie shack beyond it. Justin joined by his side, and the two made their way past the thinning group of golfers tweaking their swings. One of the men was hitting his driver, and every time he struck the ball, the accompanying boom echoed through the trees.

Tyler and Justin had caddied for many of the members at the club, and they'd built up a good reputation as being solid caddies. But neither of them knew the men hitting on the range and so walked by casually without saying a word.

The caddie shack was built to mirror the exterior of the club-house but to a much smaller scale. It featured the same rustic design that hearkened to the sense of nature all around the course. The building would have been mistaken for a cabin if not for the proximity of the golf course and driving range.

Tyler stopped at the outside edge of the covered patio and reached into his pocket again.

"How much did Henderson give you?" Justin asked. "It looked like a lot." He fished his tips out of his coveralls and started counting too.

"More than the minimum," Tyler answered with a grin. He split up the stack and handed the two bills over to his friend.

"Whoa. Two hundred each?"

"Yep."

Justin handed a hundred back. "Lee gave me two hundo. That's a sick day of work."

"Too bad they aren't always like that," Tyler quipped. "Could you imagine making that every day?"

"Wouldn't need to go to college with that kind of coin. That's for sure."

"Yeah, but I don't necessarily want to be schlepping people's golf bags around the rest of my life. No matter what it pays."

"What about those caddies on the pro tour? They make like ten percent of their player's prize money."

"True," Tyler agreed, folding the money and stuffing it into his pocket. "I suppose if you're making that kind of dough, it wouldn't be so bad. Plus, you're only on one bag instead of two."

"Not to mention the travel," Justin added. "I bet you get to see some pretty amazing places on the pro tour."

Tyler saw the daydream unfolding in his friend's brown eyes. He figured Justin was imagining the immaculate courses, the exotic locations, the parties after every round, the famous people he could hang out with, and probably a girl or two he could hit on with his infamously terrible game.

"Well, if I win next week, you'll get a taste of it at least."

"Don't think I haven't considered that. Actually, I've been able to think about almost nothing else. I can't imagine how you must be feeling."

Tyler shrugged and looked out at the driving range. Stray rays of light speared through the treetops on the western edge of the forest, tracing across the manicured grass and onto the trees on the opposite side.

He leaned against one of the wooden posts supporting the porch roof. It was his turn to daydream, but he cut those visions short. The odds of success were stacked against him, and he knew it.

Then again, the odds had never been on his side.

He'd grown up in a poor working-class home less than fifteen minutes from here. His parents had worked hard to keep food on the table, clothes on their backs, and a roof over their heads.

When Tyler's father died suddenly from a heart attack a few years ago, things only got more difficult for his mother and him. Fortunately, he was old enough to start working and had immediately auditioned for a caddie position here at the club.

The course was closed on Wednesdays, which was dubbed "Caddie Day." The caddies were allowed to play the course as much as they wanted on Wednesdays, and Tyler took every advantage of it he could. He even signed up for the dreaded early morning classes on Wednesdays just so he could get to the course by lunchtime and squeeze out a quick eighteen to thirty-six holes before dark.

"I know you can do it," Justin said, interrupting the string of not-so-pleasant memories.

"It's a tough field," Tyler countered.

They were referring to the open tournament final round coming up the following weekend. The tournament winner would get the opportunity to play in the open championship at White Oak National in three weeks. Only four people nationwide qualified at four different regional events.

"It's good luck for you they're playing the regional final here. You should have an edge on everyone else. And no one reads the place better than you."

"That's a shame," Tyler joked.

"Why's that?"

"Because you're going to be on my bag."

"Maybe you're second best at reading the course then," Justin added.

The laughter between them died down, and a somber air returned.

"You nervous?" Justin asked.

Tyler nodded. "Of course I'm nervous. You'd have to be a robot not to be." He continued staring out at the range. One of the men picked up his bag and started back toward the parking lot. "I wish my dad was here to watch it. He got me into the game. Whenever he watched me, I felt more confident with every swing."

"I'm not going to say anything cliché like your dad is still with you in your heart or anything like that. But I will say this: You have one of the sweetest, most natural swings I've ever seen. You've won the Caddie Cup twice in a row. And you made it through the first three qualifying rounds for the open championship. You can do this, Tyler. I believe in you."

"Thanks, man." Tyler offered an appreciative grin.

"Besides, I really want to go to the open championship. Way I see it, you're my only ticket in."

2

Tyler parked his car in front of the apartment building and turned off the engine. He sat there for a moment, thinking about his conversation with Justin at the caddie shack.

The last dying rays of daylight faded over the horizon at Missionary Ridge and Lookout Mountain beyond.

Their apartment complex wasn't the nicest in the city, but it was situated on top of a hill near the mall. Tyler would park there sometimes and just watch the sun set, taking in the quiet time to reflect on where he was in life, on where he wanted to go. He'd heard people say to dream big dreams, to never stop believing in yourself—the usual cat poster clichés. But that didn't stop him from doing it anyway. He spent hours visualizing what it might look like, how it might feel to be on the pro tour, surrounded by fans, eating amazing food, staying in fancy hotels, and most importantly, giving his mother a better life.

The conversation with Justin hadn't calmed his nerves regarding the upcoming tournament the following weekend, no matter how much they may have laughed in the process.

There was no way on earth Tyler could keep his mind from

wandering to a dangerous place where hopes and dreams dared to fly. Life had taught Tyler that hoping and dreaming could be dangerous.

Still, the lure of what Tyler felt he was born to do drew him in with thoughts of escaping. Winning the qualifier to get into the White Oak National Open Championship could be a life-changing moment.

He didn't have any misgivings about winning *that* tournament. But a good showing might put him on the map, and perhaps even give him an opportunity to get on one of the lesser tours. After that, who knew what could happen?

"Who am I kidding?" he said. "Thinking like that is not healthy. No sense in getting your hopes up, Tyler."

But the nagging thoughts continued to pepper his mind.

He'd wanted to be a professional golfer for as long as he could remember, but as time passed and he learned more about the game, the bitter reality of the sport's nature loomed over him like an executioner's blade.

He heard the statistics and the odds of actually getting the tour card to be a pro golfer. Mathematically speaking, it was easier to get into pro football, and those were extremely long odds.

In golf, the margins for success were thinner than a blade of Bermuda.

Tyler had spoken often to one of the private coaches who worked at the club. The guy had spent years trying to carve out a professional career, hitting the lower circuits to try to work his way up into the big league. He'd managed a couple of near wins in a few tournaments, but the money at that level was barely enough to pay the bills, much less take care of all the travel and accommodations.

Most of the golfers in the minor tours had to work as instructors to supplement their winnings, and most of the time that was just to keep things afloat.

Even when one of them made it to the top tier and earned their tour card, that was no guarantee they'd remain there. Guys lost their cards every year, and were forced to work their way back into the tour again.

It was a grind. Tyler knew that. But he still dreamed of doing it.

He'd never wanted to do anything else, even though he was working his way through college to earn a degree in computer engineering.

Tyler had always had an affinity for computers, but that skill had never been allowed to grow due to financial constraints at home. He managed to pick up old computers and change out the parts. Learning bits of code here and there, he was able to build functional computers and learn a lot while doing it.

In some ways, his financial handicap actually turned into a positive because he was forced to do things that people who simply bought computers from a store could not.

He took a breath, got out of the car, and removed his clubs from the back. Tyler never left his golf clubs at the apartment during the days he was gone, and he didn't dare leave them in the car overnight.

The thievery epidemic had grown over the last four years, seemingly nationwide. Car break-ins, especially at places like this, were increasing by the month. And while no one had yet tried to break into a home here at the apartment complex, it had happened in other places nearby. Tyler knew it was only a matter of time until someone was brazen enough to come here.

It wasn't as if his clubs were a valuable commodity. But that didn't always mean anything to someone looking to make some quick cash. Even his old clubs could fetch a few dollars at the local pawn shops or secondhand sporting goods store.

He slung the bag over his shoulder and closed the trunk. The license plate rattled when the lid shut, just like it always did—a permanent reminder that the nine-year-old Honda he drove was barely hanging on.

The car had gotten him where he needed to go for the last three years since he saved up enough cash to buy the thing. And he counted himself lucky that it only needed a few minor repairs along the way, mostly things he could handle with the aid of Justin's toolkit and his father's garage. Still, he'd often get looks of sympathy from fellow drivers.

He walked across the parking lot to the white apartment building and into the stairwell leading up to the second floor. The black railing along the stairs looked freshly painted, as did the white exteriors of the apartments. It had been an effort by the property owners to make the place look newer, more appealing to potential renters.

In truth, the place had been a massive upgrade for Tyler and his mom, made possible with some of the money Tyler made from his job as a caddie.

He climbed the stairs up to the second floor, turned left around the railing, and walked over to the door. Even outside he could smell the odors of dinner cooking in the kitchen. He smiled, detecting the overpowering scent of onions, garlic, and roasting potatoes. The faint smell of freshly baked bread also caught his attention.

The instant he walked in, the smells from the kitchen overwhelmed him, washing over him like an aromatic tidal wave.

He closed the door and saw his mother at the stove. Her curly brown hair with streaks of gray jiggled as she busily stirred a wooden spoon in a cast-iron skillet.

Molly Knox was a pretty woman. In her mid-fifties, she somehow concealed her age and the crappy hand life had dealt her with smooth skin and a kind demeanor. Even the circles under her eyes had an almost chic look to them, like badges of honor from going to rock concerts or raves in the 1990s and not coming home until the sun peeked over the eastern horizon.

"Hey, Mom," he said with a bit of forced cheer.

She turned around and smiled at him, but the eyes didn't lie. Those dark circles hung under them, and it looked as if she hadn't slept in days. He knew that wasn't too far from the truth. She'd picked up extra shifts at the local distribution center the last couple of weeks in an effort to build up a little safety net in savings. He'd tried to tell her he could help more, but she was stubborn and had always been a hard worker.

Just like so many, it seemed no matter how much she worked, getting ahead was ever the elusive target.

"Hey, honey."

No matter how tough her day may have been, Tyler saw that she always put on the disguise as if nothing was wrong. To Tyler, his mom was like a soldier, never stopping, always gutting it out. He respected that about her although it broke his heart to see her work so hard without a break for herself.

"How was your day?" she asked, as usual.

"It was good."

"Whose bag were you on today?"

"Mr. Henderson and Mr. Dougher."

She cast him a grin as she tossed the thin potatoes in the rich garlic butter. "Do I have to ask if they won?"

He smiled back sheepishly and shrugged. "Yeah, they won."

"No surprises there." She looked back at the pan. Satisfied the potatoes had been stirred enough, she pulled open the oven door and slid the skillet in. "These just need ten more minutes."

"All good." He walked over to their rickety aluminum table in the corner near the kitchen and took out the money he'd made. He placed two of the hundreds down on the surface and kept one for himself.

She turned around in time to see the act and immediately planted both hands on her hips. "What is that?" she demanded with her head cocked to the side. Tyler wasn't sure if that look in her eye wasn't one of disapproval.

"I made a little extra today," he confessed. "My tuition is already paid up for the month. And with the rest of what I made, I'll have my gas money covered for the next couple of weeks. You need that money more than me, Mom."

"Tyler, I can't let you do that."

"Yes, you can, Mom. Please. Just take it. You already work so hard. And you never do anything for yourself. Maybe go treat yourself to something. Like a spa day, or buy something nice."

She shook her head, tears welling in her eyes. She walked over to him and wrapped her arms around him. "You're so sweet, Son. You really are."

He hugged her back.

"But I can't use that money for a spa day. Heck, I don't even know what that is." They both giggled at the admission. Her eyes fell to the weathered gray golf bag propped up on a bipod stand just inside the door. The clubs had seen their best days twenty years before, and were probably as old if not older than him.

"You really need new clubs."

"Two hundred isn't going to take care of that. Besides, these are still good. Good enough to get me into the qualifier for the White Oak National Open Championship. Seriously, Mom. Do something nice for yourself. Or put the money in the bank for a rainy day."

She let him go but placed her hands on either side of his face and peered into his eyes. "Well, those we got plenty of." She shook him for a second then released him again. "Go get cleaned up. Supper will be ready soon."

He did as she said and walked back into the hallway toward his room on the right. He paused in the doorway and looked back toward the table where she stood, staring down at the money, shaking her head.

She picked it up, slowly, and stuffed it in her pocket. She kept her head down and didn't look his way.

The act softened Tyler's eyes, and for a few seconds, he felt a twinge of pride as he stepped into his modest bedroom and out of sight.

He washed his hands, then splashed some water on his face, rubbing his eyes and cheeks.

Tyler never showered at the caddie shack. He preferred the privacy of his own bathroom and always bathed just before going to bed at night. Being clean before bedtime was one of the little luxuries in life he truly appreciated. He doubted any of his friends felt the same way. Like so many things in life, they probably took it for granted.

Tyler had learned to feel grateful for every moment, every breath, every tiny, good thing in his life. He and his mom had so little. Complaining didn't seem to do anyone any good.

He took a hand towel off the rack to his left and dried his face.

After hanging the towel up again, he planted his hands on the sink and stared into his own blue eyes. He was nearly twenty-one years old, with his birthday coming up the following week.

He knew he wasn't old, despite many of his friends thinking they'd seen and done it all in life. Still, there was an impending sense of pressure mounting in the back of his mind.

The qualifying tournament was his shot, his moment to change his stars, and finally get a chance at something amazing.

Up until this point, he and his mother hadn't been living. They'd been surviving. And Tyler was tired of that. More for his mom than for him.

He promised himself that when, not if, he made it onto the pro tour, the first thing he was going to buy was a new house for his mother. And a car to go with it. And as many spa days as she wanted.

Tyler had spent more nights than he could remember lying awake in his bed, visualizing that scene—of what the house and car would look like, the utter expression of disbelieving joy on her face, and the gratitude and pride he would feel in that moment.

"It's coming," he said to the young man in the mirror. "It's already there for you. All you have to do is take the swings."

He heard the sound of plates and silverware rattling from the kitchen, a signal that dinner was ready.

Tyler walked out of the bathroom and back through what passed for their living room—a small space with a modest 32-inch television on the wall opposite a secondhand couch and a single mismatched chair.

He found his mother placing the plates and forks down on the table. She'd already set glasses of water in their respective spots.

They always sat in the same places, seemingly reinforcing the rut that their lives remained perpetually stuck in.

He eased into his seat across from her. They both bowed their heads, and Molly said a quick blessing over the food, just as she'd always done since Tyler could remember, and then picked up their forks.

He shoveled a piece of potato in his mouth a closed his eyes slowly as the garlic and butter tantalized his taste buds.

"So good, Mom," he said. He forked a piece of roasted broccoli and stuffed it into his mouth. He eyed the mac 'n' cheese but wanted to save it for last. His mother made it from scratch, and it was so much better than the stuff in boxes.

"I'm glad you like it, honey." She chewed for a few seconds, then took a drink of water to wash it down. "So, tomorrow is Caddie Day at the course. Last chance to get ready for the big dance."

He blushed and nodded, keeping his eyes on the plate of food in front of him.

"Well," she said, "I'm sure you'll do great. No one knows that course better than you."

"I guess so. They let the rough grow out deeper into the fairway, so the landings are going to be tighter than usual. And I'm sure the pin placements will be difficult, definitely different from tomorrow."

He played with a piece of macaroni, twisting it with his fork in a little circle on the plate.

"Tyler," she said, staring at him with her head cocked. It was a look seemingly every mother on the planet knew how to use to get their kid's attention. He lifted his head and met her gaze. "You don't need to be nervous. You're a great golfer, Son. Nobody works harder at it than you."

"But what if I don't win?"

She shrugged. "Then nothing changes. It's all good."

He shook his head. "But that's just it. I want things to change. You deserve a better life, Mom. You work too hard just to get by."

"Tyler," she interrupted, "I am fine, Son. We have everything we need. We've never gone hungry, never been without shelter. I'm grateful for that. So don't you worry about that tournament. You play free, like it doesn't matter. Just like you've always done."

He did his best to reflect her easy smile, but deep down the knots in his stomach tore at his emotions. He'd never felt this way before about a tournament, or any round of golf. It had always just been fun for him. But now, he felt the weight of his future bearing down on him.

"Just remember, Son, everyone else you're up against is feeling the same thing. They're all people, just like you. Let them put the pressure on themselves. You just go out and hit the ball the way you've always done, and you'll be fine no matter what happens."

They finished the meal with little conversation. Tyler asked about her day, and she ran through the usual stuff about the things going on at the distribution center and how the bosses were pushing to meet quotas. Tyler noticed her voice was as tired as her eyes.

When they were done, Tyler stood and picked up his plate, walked over to the sink, and started rinsing it off.

"I'll do that."

"Mom, it's the least I can do," he said with a playful warning in his eyes. "You relax."

He went back to the table and picked up her empty plate, then returned to the sink.

"You're a sweet boy."

"I'm almost twenty-one. I don't think I qualify as a boy anymore."

"You'll always be my boy. No matter how old you are."

She'd said that line a million times if it was once.

"I know," he replied as usual.

His phone buzzed in his pocket. He pulled it out and looked at the text message.

A smile crept across his face.

"Who's that?" Molly asked.

He twisted his head a little too quickly to look at her but didn't immediately answer.

"You look like the cat who ate the canary," she added.

His cheeks reddened.

"Let me guess. Lucy?"

"Yeah," he relented.

"What does she want?"

He checked the text again. "It's nothing. Just wanting to hang out."

Molly shrugged. "So? You got all your assignments done for tomorrow morning?"

"Yeah. But—"

"Then what's the problem? She's a nice girl, Tyler."

"I know."

Lucy was a nice girl. She came from a good family—a wealthy family. They'd become friends over the last few years at the university, having met in some of the elective classes they'd chosen.

Their friendship had never grown into anything more, which Tyler knew was his own fault. He'd never been good at reading what girls were thinking, even if his few friends pummeled him with encouragement.

"She's into you" was the one Justin seemed to use nearly every day.

If Tyler could have taken a step back and objectively looked at the situation, he'd have probably reached the same conclusion. But he couldn't get beyond his own shortcomings, the things and events that had occurred throughout his life that kept him where he was—just a poor kid from the wrong side of town trying to make something more of himself.

That last part was the biggest hurdle with a girl like Lucy. She wasn't like him. Her family wasn't like his either.

He'd convinced himself that even if she was into him, it could never work out because her parents wouldn't approve of the relationship. He'd seen the types before. Heck, he'd caddied for those types.

Deep down, though, the truth was Tyler didn't believe he was good enough for Lucy. He didn't have money, a nice car, a nice house. He felt fortunate they'd been able to upgrade to a decent apartment a few years ago after his father died, but even that seemed inadequate for a girl from her background.

"Soooo?" Molly said, cutting into his thoughts. "You going to go meet her or what?"

It felt weird to him to have his mom coaxing him to go meet up with a girl, but the night was early. "Yeah, I guess so."

"That's the spirit," she said, with a little laugh.

He shook his head at her and smiled.

"I'll take care of the dishes, sweetie. You go on and have some fun. You don't do that enough."

"I don't mind. I can do them real quick."

She stood, walked over, grabbed him by the shoulders, and physically moved him out of the way and toward the door. "Get out of here. Go see that nice girl."

"Okay. Okay," he said with a laugh. "I'm going."

3

CHARLESTON, SOUTH CAROLINA

"You sure about this, Sully?" Max Cromwell stared at Graham Sullivan after he asked the question. "Lots of guys older than you keep going."

Graham's eyes were focused on the media room beyond the curtain. There weren't many reporters there: a few locals from nearby Charleston and a couple from regional tour magazines and PR teams. There was one from a national sports channel, but he looked annoyed to be in attendance.

"You got plenty of other horses in your stable, Max. Most of them can run faster than me now."

Max, the founder of the Cromwell Sports Agency, had several high-end, and a few more mid-level, clients he represented. At one point, Sullivan had been his top dog, and in some ways still was depending on the demographic.

While the sponsorship deals weren't rolling in like they did at the beginning of Sullivan's career, he still pulled seven figures from a catalog of endorsements.

"That's not why I'm asking, Sully," Max countered. He looked over at his client standing by the wall just behind the half-open black curtain.

Graham had been a figure of seasoned distinction on the golf course. His tanned, freckled skin was a tribute to his years of experience. But the fight had left him long ago; evident in his stance and in his vapid gaze. His hair, once a uniform shade of dark brown, had matured into a distinguished palette of the original color but now streaked with gray and silver, each strand cut in a style that spoke to a practical, straightforward approach to life.

At fifty-eight, his physique bore the robustness of an active life, shaped and maintained through years of swinging clubs and traversing fairways. Though time had subtly shifted his game from the vigor of power to the virtue of strategy, his resilience and strength remained undiminished. His hands, marked by calluses and lines, were the silent narrators of his journey through the game, telling tales of triumphs, challenges, and the sheer love of golf.

His attire was always a reflection of the sport's smart-casual ethos —a crisply pressed polo shirt paired with trousers that matched the weather's demand, and sturdy golf shoes that had trod countless courses. The accessories he chose—a wristwatch for timing, sunglasses against the glare, and often a cap or visor to shield his eyes —were not merely functional but also indicative of a man who had curated his life with the same care he applied to his game.

His posture, upright yet relaxed, was the perfect balance between the confidence of experience and the humility before the game's ever-present challenges. This was a man who had learned the art of patience on the green, a golfer whose every move was a lesson in the grace of aging without fading, in the quiet confidence of knowing the game as deeply as one knows oneself. The lines etched around his eyes were testimonies to countless hours spent squinting under the sun in pursuit of perfection, yet these same lines deepened with warmth and approachability whenever he smiled.

Those smiles were rare, though, seeming to occur only as often as the seasons changed. His life had been a series of utter disappointments—a tragic, lonely existence.

It was a strange thing. He had fans all over the world. People lined up to meet him and get autographs at every event he attended. But outside of a few friendships, including the one with Max, Graham felt completely alone.

The loneliness tortured him the most when he returned home from a match, or even from practicing on the range at the club where he lived.

Sometimes, he would just drive around for a while to avoid going back to the house. His fans didn't see that side of him, nor did the sponsors. Graham knew Max saw it, but he was the only one. He'd been there through every heart-wrenching loss, including the worst one—the death of his twenty-year-old son in a car wreck.

A few months after the accident, Graham's wife, Linda, had left him, claiming he'd buried himself in golf and that he hadn't been there for her when she needed him the most.

That part didn't fool him. He knew she'd been cheating on him with, of all people, his nemesis, Jamie Winthrop. Being several years younger than Graham, she was closer to Winthrop's age, but Graham doubted that was the reason.

Linda had always wanted to be with a winner; she'd told him exactly that during one of their last fights. She'd confessed she loved the spotlight, the VIP parties, the supercars, the yachts, the exotic locations—all the trappings of a lifestyle of the ultra wealthy.

Graham was wealthy by nearly any standard, but he didn't live that kind of life. Sure, he had a house on an elite golf course, in one of the best neighborhoods in South Carolina, but he drove an ordinary sedan, didn't travel much, rarely attended parties, and preferred to keep a low profile.

He turned to his agent and offered a rugged grin. "I know, Max. You've been a good friend all these years. But what am I doing?"

"Playing the game you love, man. I know it hasn't panned out like you would have wanted, but you get to golf for a living. Doesn't get much better than that."

"We discussed this before. Golf isn't everything, Max." He peered out to the empty table sitting in front of the thin crowd of reporters.

"I've spent my entire life working on my game, countless hours practicing. Sure, I've made a lot of money along the way, had some great experiences. But I just don't have it in me anymore."

Max gave a nod. "I know. I just had to make sure you were really sure this is what you want to do." He chuckled. "Of course, you can always come out of retirement."

Graham allowed a muted laugh and shook his head. "You are a stubborn son of a gun, Max."

Max smiled wide, showing off his bright white Hollywood teeth. He flattened his navy-blue blazer and straightened his tie, checked his watch one more time, and then stretched his neck in both directions. "Okay. Showtime."

He walked out into the press room, his smile beaming at the collection of journalists. Graham followed behind him. They stopped at the two chairs and took their seats behind the microphones. One photographer in the back of the room snapped some pictures, but Graham saw that his expression suggested he didn't care about the assignment. Another man with a video camera on a tripod perked up a little as the men entered the room. Several other reporters were using their phones for video, all positioned on smaller tripods on the edges of the room.

Max leaned forward as Graham adjusted his black blazer and shifted in his seat.

"Thank you all for coming today," Max began. "I really appreciate it. I'm sure you all are wondering what's going on, so I'll step back and let Graham do the talking."

Graham gave a nod and leaned forward. "As Max said, thanks for coming here today. I know there are probably other places you'd rather be than sitting here with an old mid-level golfer like myself. So I'll make this brief." He paused, folding his hands in front of the microphone stand.

A pain that had tormented him for years crept up in his gut, then snaked its way into his chest. Tears pushed at the boundaries of his eyes, but his will wouldn't let them pass.

"I've been golfing most of my life," he began. "Started when I was eight years old. I remember the first time my daddy took me out to a little par-three golf course about ten minutes from our house in the suburbs. It was nothing more than an old cow pasture some guy had converted into a course." He smiled faintly, recalling the condition of the place. For what it was, the man who owned it did a good job keeping the greens cut short and the fairways in decent condition.

"That course was where I fell in love with the game. It was an instant addiction. The feel of the clubface hitting the ball, the sound it made on contact, and watching that white sphere fly was such an amazing experience every single time—except when I duffed the ball."

The crowd laughed at the joke.

Graham gave it a moment and put on a somber expression. "I don't have to rehash my life story. You all know it. Heck, a lot of you helped write it for the world to see. Some of you did a terrific job of documenting my biggest chokes." No one made a sound, and a few shifted uncomfortably. "Oh, that's not an accusation. It's okay. I was the one who choked. You just wrote about it."

He glanced down at the table for a second.

"Golf is a crazy game, sort of like life. You work hard, do your best to achieve your goals, but most of the time you fall short. But you keep going. I heard an analogy once about a gold miner who was digging for gold in a piece of property he'd bought. He dug for months, never finding that vein he was hunting for. Eventually, he gave up and sold the property to some other sucker who thought, as he had, they might find the mother lode somewhere in the mountain. The new miner, instead of starting a new mine, went into the one started by the last fella. He started digging and couldn't believe it when, after only a few minutes, he broke through into one of the biggest gold veins in history. The other miner had been so close but given up mere inches from generational wealth."

Graham exhaled slowly as he recounted the first time he'd heard that story. Then he looked up, panning the room of empty chairs and the few sets of eyes there to hear him deliver his announcement.

"I always thought if I just kept going, kept digging, I would finally reach that mother lode. Heaven knows I put in the time. I know you've all heard about the idea of ten thousand hours to reach success and expertise. Well, I've put in way more than that on the range, the putting green, and on the course. But I can't do it anymore. It's time for me to sell the mine. Maybe a few years ago I was only inches away from that lode. But now, at fifty-eight, I don't think I can dig much longer. So today, I'm announcing my retirement from the game of golf."

A hushed gasp fluttered through the room.

Graham was caught a little off guard by the reaction. *What had these people come here expecting to hear? A new endorsement deal with a fiber supplement company?*

"The upcoming open at White Oak National will be my final competition," Graham continued. "So, I'll open the floor to questions if any of you have some."

He leaned back a little and waited. A young man in the front raised his hand, and Graham nodded toward him. "Go ahead, Tim," he said.

"Thanks, Graham. So, does this mean you won't continue playing on the senior tour too? Or is White Oak just going to be your last major?"

"No, I'm retiring from the game altogether. White Oak won't just be my last major. It will be my final competition."

A blonde woman in a red suit a few seats away raised her hand. "Sarah," Graham said.

"So, is this due to an injury?"

"No," Graham shook his head. "I've been pretty fortunate regarding my physical health over the years. I owe a lot of that to my personal trainer for keeping me pretty fit, except I never did get those six-pack abs I always wanted."

The small group laughed.

"But I'm fine. No knee or back pain. Shoulders are good, except for a little tightness in the early morning. But that's normal, all part of getting older, I suppose. That's what they tell me, anyway."

Another man in the back of the room, this one a little closer to Graham's age, raised his hand. Graham pointed to him.

"Do you think at some point there might be a chance of a comeback? You know, maybe coming out of retirement if you're feeling good?"

Graham chuckled into the microphone. "Jeez, Frank. The body isn't even cold yet."

The room erupted with laughter again.

His easy Southern manner and keen sense of humor had always helped Graham in rooms like this. People seemed endeared to his personality, even if there weren't many of them in attendance.

"In all seriousness, though, Frank, I don't think so. Sure, anything is possible, but I'm tired. I had some good times, and I got to do something most people would dream of doing for a living for a really long time."

Frank nodded and made a note in a little black journal.

Sarah raised her hand again. After he acknowledged her, she cocked her head to the side and arched her right eyebrow. "So, the White Oak National Open Championship is going to be your last tournament and your last major. But you've never won a major."

The sting from that fact had long since blunted in Graham's heart. It was a nagging irritation, but he'd made his peace with it. At least, that's what he told himself. There were times that regrets popped up, about things he could have done differently—a change of clubs, adjusting for the lie, or maybe just playing a shot safer than he had. But he couldn't alter the past, no matter how much he wanted to.

"Is there a question in there, Sarah? Or are you just trying to make me feel good?"

Everyone laughed again.

"Sorry. Yes," she said. "What I was going to ask is, do you think you have a shot at winning it? You haven't placed in the top fifteen in a major tournament in over two years. The oldest player to ever win one was fifty years old. You're fifty-eight now."

The room fell silent. The question stumped him, although it probably shouldn't have. He hadn't anticipated someone asking that.

Graham's lips parted in a broad smile. "Thank you for the reminder, Sarah. I'd forgotten my age." More laughter interrupted the presser. "My swing is still good. I haven't lost much power in the last dozen or so years. My putting game and short game are still really strong. But, like you so delicately pointed out, I've struggled in majors for the last few years. Can't say why, honestly. Going into every one, I felt good. But to answer your question, of course I think I can win it. Any golfer who doesn't think they can shouldn't be playing in the tournament to begin with. That's the point, right? If you want to play for fun or for the love of the game, go play a local course and give some younger gun a shot. So yeah, I'm playing to win it. And I'm going to give it all I got. May as well go out on top, right?"

The answer sent smiles across the faces in the room.

One more hand went up. It was an older gentleman in the back wearing a white blazer with matching pants, and a dark blue tie. His long nose and slender face made him look like a bird of prey.

"Hey, Sam," Graham indicated.

"Hey, Sully. So, I have to ask, of all the tournaments, and the majors, why this tournament? Any particular reason you chose White Oak? There are still several other tournaments to play before the year ends."

"Yeah, it's a good question, Sam. It's pretty simple, actually. White Oak has always been my favorite tournament. I never made any bones about that. Not only is the setting one of the best in the world for a golf course, but I also love the format of the tournament. Anyone can get in if they qualify. It's a chance for amateurs to earn their way into the big dance for one shot at glory. If they do well enough, they get invited back the next year, which I think is really cool."

"But some of the players—"

"I know some of the pros don't like that concept because they spent so much time and hard work earning their tour cards, but I don't see it that way. Just go out and be the best golfer for four days. If you get beat by an amateur, then they were better than you. Who cares if they have their card or not? I know that will upset some of my buddies on the tour, but that's the beauty of White Oak. Anyone can have one shot at the title, then after that the tour goes on the way it always has. Doesn't mess with anyone's livelihood."

Everyone seemed to appreciate the thoughtful answer, Graham thought.

Sam continued. "Do you think we will ever see an amateur win it, considering it's never happened in the history of the tournament?"

"Sure. Why not? The tour is composed of the best golfers in the world based on aggregate performance, which results in being rewarded with your tour card. But like they say in football, any given day an underrated team can beat the best in the world. It'll happen one of these days, I'm sure. And when it does, I'm certain all of you will have an amazing time writing about it."

More laughter ensued. When it died down, Max surveyed the room for a few seconds. No one else raised their hand.

"Well," he said, leaning forward again, "if that's all your questions, I think we will end it right here." He waited a couple of seconds. "Okay. Thank you all for coming out. We really appreciate it, and I'm sure we'll see some of you at the tournament in a few weeks."

He stood up, and Graham did a moment after. They walked back behind the curtain into the green room as the reporters finished making their notes, and started exiting.

Once the two men were out of earshot, Max turned to Graham. "I thought that went well. You really are good at these things."

"They're just people doing a job like anyone else," Graham said.

"More like a pit of vipers. And they'll bite you the second you make a wrong move."

"So don't make a wrong move. Simple enough."

"Those types lambasted you over the years. You heard what that one said about never winning a major. Like you need the reminder."

"It's fine, Max. Take it easy. Pretty soon, this will all be over, and you can go back to worrying about all your other clients."

"I am taking it easy," Max replied, pulling out a packet of gum from his pocket. He unwrapped a piece and popped it into his mouth, offering the packet to Graham, who declined with a wave of his right hand. "They should just show a little more respect. That's all."

"They were great. I didn't mind any of it. Just keep your eyes open at the tournament."

"Eyes open?"

"For new talent. I'm sure one of the amateurs at the event might be worthy of the old Max Cromwell eye."

4

CHATTANOOGA

Tyler parked his car outside Lucy's house along the street. The sprawling white mansion towered over him from its perch on the hillside overlooking the fairway of the 17th hole. A gas lamp hung over the doorway between the columns supporting the portico, its flame flickering in the darkness and casting an eerie orange-and-yellow hue across the white façade and black door.

Just standing there on the street next to the mailbox, he felt small and insignificant in the shadow of the massive home. Tyler couldn't guess how many square feet it was, but it was easily ten times the size of his economy apartment.

He could see the giant crystal chandelier inside the foyer through an arched window over the doorway. Beyond that, a spiral staircase led up to the second floor. Lights were on in several of the windows, one of which he knew was Lucy's—the one on the far left.

He'd been in the house several times, never feeling comfortable while there. He did his best to fit in, to say the right things to Lucy's parents and act like he belonged. But Tyler knew the truth. He didn't belong, no matter how much he wanted to.

To their credit, Lucy's mother and father were always kind and welcoming to him. They asked about how things were going in school, and her father always inquired about his golf game.

Joe Park was a member of the club where Tyler worked, though Tyler had never caddied for the man. He'd been on an opponent's bag once or twice, so Joe knew what he could do from the caddie's perspective.

Lucy's mother, Anna, didn't seem to care much for the game, instead opting to spend most of the warmer days at the club's pool.

Tyler hesitated a few more seconds. He steadied his nerves and started up the driveway. He only made it a few steps before the front door swung open and Lucy appeared in the doorway.

She wore a tight black tank top and gray leggings. Her black hair draped over her bare shoulders. She beamed a gleaming smile at him from the top of the steps and waved excitedly.

Even from forty feet away, she was the prettiest girl he'd ever laid eyes on. A full-Korean-American beauty, her parents had emigrated here in mid-1987 during the fall of the Fifth Korean Republic, a dictatorship that aimed to crush creativity and free-market enterprise.

Lucy was a different kind of beautiful than most of the girls he'd known. Just the sight of her stirred something in his chest—her black hair, her pale skin, her slight frame and delicate features—and he forced himself to choke back the nerves as his palms began to sweat.

He knew he shouldn't be nervous. They were friends and had spent hours together every week. But things had been building up, and something told him their relationship was about to change.

In truth, he wanted it to. He wanted her to be his girlfriend. But Tyler was terrible at reading women. He'd barely dated in the kiddie pool that was high school, and since landing in college, that hadn't changed much.

To his credit, he was always busy working or completing school assignments. There'd never been much time for more than that. He'd made time, though, to hang out with Lucy.

From first sight, he'd wished she would take a romantic interest in him, but being too shy and lacking confidence, he never pushed the issue.

Lucy closed the door behind her, tucking the blanket in her hand under one arm and descending the steps to meet him.

The warm evening air carried the scent of her perfume into his nostrils and straight to his brain. It was intoxicating in a way that made him want to grab her and kiss her, and hold her until the sun peeked over the forests beyond the fairway.

"Hey," she said, cheerfully to his ear. "Glad you could make it. I was worried you might be too busy."

Tyler shook his head. "I'm never too busy for you," he said and immediately regretted the cheesy line.

Her smile disarmed his concerns instantly. "You are so sweet."

"Your parents home?"

"No. They're down at the clubhouse having some drinks with friends."

"Still seems crazy to me they're members at Green Mont. How does your dad have enough time for that much golf?"

She shrugged. "He doesn't. But he likes to have a little variety."

"Ah." He looked down at the rolled-up blanket under her arm. "What's with the blanket?"

Lucy smiled up at him. "I thought I mentioned we were going to look at the stars."

"You did."

"Well, come on then. Let's go look at the stars."

She grabbed him by the hand and dragged him around the left corner of the house. The second her hand touched his and began to pull, Tyler felt his heart going right along with her. His palms started to sweat—again.

"Where are we going?" he pressed.

"The best place to look at the stars out here." The brief response was all he'd get, apparently, and so he left his fate to her whims.

Lucy led him around the back of the house, to the huge multilevel deck jutting out from the wall. A hot tub simmered on the lowest landing, and for a second he wondered if that was where she was taking him. He quickly dispelled that theory. *Why would she bring a blanket for that?*

They walked across the back yard and into a thin strip of trees that lined the 17th fairway. The canopy loomed over them, blocking out the sky save for a few patches where the limbs and leaves had never filled in.

On the other side of the trees, the two stepped out into the thick rough next to the fairway. Tyler hesitated, pausing for a moment.

Their arms stretched out until Lucy felt the tug. She turned and stared. "What's the matter?"

"Couldn't we get in trouble for coming out here at night? Isn't it trespassing?"

She smiled at him again. "Yeah, I guess. But no one comes out here at night. The rangers are all gone for the day. You trust me, right?"

He nodded that he did.

"Good," she said. "Come on."

She pulled him forward out into the tight, firm grass of the fairway.

When they reached the center, she stopped and unrolled the blanket, spreading it out on the ground.

"Good thing it hasn't rained in a week."

"Yeah, and they don't run the sprinklers until the morning." She plopped down on the blanket, kicked her legs out, and propped herself upright with her hands. Then she patted the spot next to her. "You going to just stand there, or are you going to sit next to me?"

The invitation alone was enough to shake his insides like an earthquake.

"Yeah. Of course. Sorry." He eased down onto the blanket, careful not to get too close but also not so far away that it seemed like he was trying to avoid her.

Glad I took a quick shower after dinner, he thought, reflecting on the decision to rinse off the sweat and grime from a hard day at the club.

He followed her gaze, staring up at the stars.

"I was never really very good at spotting all the constellations," he confessed. "I mean, some of the easier ones, sure."

"Yeah, I don't pay much attention to that either. I just like looking at them. I know some of the planets and stars, but I think it's more fun to look at them and wonder what is going on there right now. You know?"

"Same. Although the light we're seeing from those stars is millions, and sometimes billions of years old. So really, we're kind of looking into the past from here."

She rolled her head to the side and stared at him. "I never really thought about it like that before. But you're right. It's like a time machine looking glass. Shame we can't see more detail."

He twisted his head to the side too. For an instant, he met her gaze, and a tingling sensation crept across his entire body. He quickly averted his eyes and looked back up at the sky.

Her gaze lingered for a few more seconds before she returned to staring at the stars. "Are you nervous?"

"What?" He blurted the response a little too quickly.

"About the tournament next weekend," she clarified.

He'd shown his hand, and he knew it. So he tried to play it cool. "Yeah, I mean, a little. You'd have to be crazy not to be, I guess. But I think I have as good a shot as anyone else."

"I do too. You're a good golfer, Tyler. At least from the little I've seen, and from the scores you've told me about. And no one works on their game more than you. You're going to do great. I know it."

He wished he had her confidence. His previous comment had been more his mother's thoughts than his own. Tyler knew he posted good scores. Being a scratch golfer put him into the upper echelon of millions of golfers worldwide, but even so, there were still plenty of people better than him out there.

"Thanks. I appreciate the support."

"And I'm going to be there to cheer you on," she added.

"Really?" He turned to face her again. This time, she maintained her position, staring up at the twinkling night sky.

"Of course, silly. I wouldn't miss it. You're like my best friend, after all."

In the course of two seconds, he went from the highest peaks of hope to the bottom of Death Valley. There was that word—*friend*. And not only that; she'd used the term *best friend*.

It was a death knell to any chance he thought he might have had at something more with Lucy. His mother, he figured, had been wrong about her assessment of the situation.

"Thanks," he managed, fumbling for the word that didn't come close to expressing his disappointment.

He did appreciate the fact that she was going to come support him and watch him in the tournament, even if that only added to the nervousness he felt in his gut. But now he felt like he'd been dropped squarely into the center of the dreaded friend zone.

Lucy rolled her head to the side and peered into his eyes. "You sound disappointed."

He quickly shook it off. "No. It's really cool you'd come out to watch me play next Sunday. Seriously. I appreciate it. You don't have to do that. You're a great friend."

He looked up at the stars once more, trying to avoid her stare.

"I can be more than a friend if you want me to be, Tyler."

For a second, he wasn't sure he'd heard correctly. One minute, he'd plummeted from the stratosphere, only now to be lifted there once more by a single sentence.

He looked over at her. Even for someone as romantically inept as him, there was no mistaking the desire in her dark brown eyes.

He swallowed back a gulp of fear. His lips trembled, but he saw that hers did too.

"I... would love that."

"But?" It was like she was reading his mind.

"But... I'm not like the other guys in your neighborhood, or the ones you grew up around."

She smiled with a subtle snort. "Yeah, I know. That's one of the things I like most about you. You aren't like them. They're all stuck up rich little brats who had everything handed to them in life. And despite that, it's still not enough. Most of them are fake, and all of them think they're God's gift. You, on the other hand, are real." She inched closer to him. It was an almost imperceptible move, but he noticed. "You're sweet and kind, and you appreciate the smallest things in life."

His heart raced, and he wondered if hers was doing the same.

"I don't have money, Lucy. And what about your parents? How would they feel if—"

"If what? I chose who I wanted to go out with? They're not prison wardens, Tyler. I can date who I want. And besides, they like you."

"They like me as your friend."

"And they would like you as my boyfriend too."

The mere sound of the word *boyfriend* sent a jolt through his body.

"I like you," she continued. "I always have. Maybe you didn't notice."

"I'm not good at reading signals."

"Clearly," she laughed and moved another inch closer to him.

He tried to keep looking up at the stars, but now her perfume overwhelmed him like a galaxy all its own, drawing him tight inside, unwilling to let go.

"Do you really think—" He turned his head toward her, but before he could utter another word, she shifted closer, wrapped her hand around his head, and pulled until their lips met.

They were soft and full, and felt like nothing he'd ever touched before. He closed his eyes and looped his arm around her to hold her tighter.

After a few seconds, they parted and stared into each other's eyes.

"I've wanted to do that since the moment we met," she admitted.

He swallowed against the nerves, his charging heartbeat, his shaking fingers. "Me too."

She smiled wide. "Took you long enough."

"Yeah, sorry about that."

"Stop apologizing and kiss me again."

"You're sure your parents are—"

Lucy pulled him close again and shut him up.

5

CHARLESTON

Graham sat in front of his television. His favorite baseball team, the Atlanta Braves, were up 3-1 in the top of the eighth inning.

He loved watching baseball. It was one of the few things that took his mind off the past, and off golf. It was a weird place to be to need something to take one's mind off golf. Usually, golf was the thing that took most people's minds away from the rest of life. But when it became life—well, that's when the joy could get sucked out of even the things that sustained and enhanced that life itself.

He picked up the glass of whiskey next to him on the end table and took a sip as the batter lined out to right field.

Tonight, even baseball seemed unwilling to give him an escape from reality.

He'd seen the headlines regarding his retirement scroll by on the bottom line at least a half-dozen times since the first pitch.

Every time the chyron displayed the news of his retirement, Graham grew a little more nauseated. The whiskey helped a little, at least to numb the pain.

He'd pretended that everything was fine when Max asked him if he was sure about it. And the act he put on was worthy of an

Academy Award. His longtime agent couldn't see beyond the mask. Not that it mattered. Like Graham told him before the presser, Max had plenty of other clients, most of whom were pulling in more money than him at this point.

Sponsors weren't lining up to sign him like they used to, and that was okay. Back when he was in his twenties, Graham had felt like the end would never come, that he was immortal and could play at an elite level forever.

He thought that despite the warnings from some of his mentors— older players on the tour who'd already peaked and were now on the downslide of their performance curve.

"Nothing lasts forever," one of his mentors had once said.

The man was the same age then as Graham was now.

Graham had blown off the clichéd statement. He'd heard it before a million times growing up. Older people always said stuff like that. But he would be the one who was different. He would push well beyond the boundaries of age and science.

Now, sitting in his chair in the living room, watching baseball alone, he knew he'd fallen prey to the greatest fallacy of all—that youth was wasted on the young.

He'd played aggressively in his prime, like a man with nothing to lose, he roared into the tournaments without fear, and he treated every shot the same way.

Big risk, big reward, he'd always said. But time after time, with every gambling shot he took, every momentous swing, he'd fallen short when it mattered most.

What had once been a shining star on the horizon of a promising career, had proved to be nothing but the lights of a low, rickety flying airplane coming in to land.

He won a few smaller tournaments during his run, but no one would ever remember that. He'd made millions of dollars from both his winnings and his endorsement deals. He would never lack for money or security. And if he had any heirs, they wouldn't either for at least a few generations if they were smart.

But he didn't have an heir. His son had died in a horrific car crash more than a decade before, his life snuffed out by a truck driver who'd swerved into the wrong lane at the wrong time.

Graham took another sip as the batter for the visiting team struck out on a hanging curve ball. The crowd cheered as the score plastered across the screen and the announcer read the three batters coming up in the bottom of the inning. Then the channel went to a commercial.

Just when Graham thought he couldn't feel worse, Jamie Winthrop's face popped up on the screen.

"You gotta be friggin' kidding me," Graham muttered, reaching for the remote to mute the commercial.

Winthrop was hawking a new line of golf shoes, talking about how comfortable they were.

He'd been Graham's biggest rival since the younger golfer appeared on the tour at the age of 23. Now, nearing fifty himself, Winthrop still showed no signs of slowing down. Somehow he'd continued playing at a high level despite his age, even winning one of the majors earlier in the year. That made six for him so far, and the media frenzy over his persistent chase for lucky number seven was enough to make Graham want to throw up his whiskey.

The man defied the odds, playing extremely well into his forties —better than most in their thirties.

He was a nagging splinter that Graham couldn't pluck no matter how many times he tried.

They'd been paired in final rounds four times, three of those in major tournaments. Graham lost every single one of those, and in the three majors in epic, catastrophic fashion.

Only one of those times had he gone into the final round trailing Winthrop. And the last one, ten years ago now, was one that had haunted Graham without end.

He'd gone into the final round at White Oak National with a huge lead over Winthrop. This was going to be it. He could feel it—taste the trophy as his lips finally pressed against that bitter metal he'd longed for his entire life.

He had slept well the night before, as he did before most tournaments. After what must have been millions of swings throughout his life and having hit every shot imaginable, he was as prepared to win as any golfer on Earth.

He'd woken up the next morning at 6:30 as he usually did, gone downstairs to the hotel coffee bar to get his morning cup, and made his way out to the course with his caddie, Mackey. Their usual routine had gone fine—hitting balls on the range, getting a feel for the pace of putts on the practice green, and chipping for fifteen minutes.

Winthrop was there too, working on every facet of his game. The two didn't say much except for polite, gentlemanly good mornings. But Winthrop had one passive-aggressive jab as the two stalked the putting green.

"You think this is going to be the one, Sully?" Winthrop had asked.

There was a tone to the question, a sharpness to his words. Winthrop wasn't rooting for him. He wasn't his friend. The man had been anything but ever since their first encounter. He was young, cocky, and carried himself with an air of invincibility that Graham wished he could knock down a peg—or six.

"I guess we'll see," Graham had answered, keeping his temper under wraps.

His caddie, Jason, hadn't missed the barb, and Graham could tell he was stewing under his standard blue baseball cap that all the caddies at the tournament wore. The thing might have blown off his head if they lived in a cartoon.

Graham could never be sure in the years since, as he'd contemplated his future during scores of dark nights of the soul, but he always wondered if that exchange on the putting green had altered his mindset. If he'd let Winthrop two-step into his head.

The first nine holes had gone fine. He'd even added to the lead by two strokes, widening the margin. The lead he had over Winthrop going into the back nine was a veritable canyon. Only a monumental collapse would lose the tournament at that point.

Graham took a deep breath as he recounted the events, the chain of incredible and horrific circumstances that unfolded one after the other.

He raised his glass and pulled a long sip of whiskey into his mouth. He held it there for a few seconds, absorbing the flavors before swallowing. He exhaled to ease the burn, and enjoyed the oaky aftertaste.

After the fire in his throat subsided, he was left with a numbness that he wished would permeate his entire body. But that was how people went overboard. They'd keep drinking until they couldn't feel anything anymore. Graham knew that, in reality, what they wanted was to feel something again that didn't hurt—not to feel nothing.

The types of people who hit the bottle for comfort weren't just trying to escape their pain. They were trying to feel some sense of joy again, a feeling of peace that defied understanding, perhaps taking them back to a time when all the world was right.

But a drink couldn't do that. Graham knew it all too well. He'd watched it destroy lives, more than a few on tour. So he always restricted himself to one, and stuck to that hard-and-fast rule since the time he could buy it for himself.

It was a discipline few possessed. Unfortunately, that skill wouldn't win him any awards, and more importantly, any major tournaments.

He gripped the glass with a firm hand, his fingers tensing around it tightly.

The thoughts of that lost major at White Oak squeezed him like his fingers on the tumbler.

He wondered for the trillionth time what he could have done differently, what swing change might have happened on the back nine that caused the first slip, then the second, then the third. What did he alter in his putting stance, or in the way his putter struck the ball? His caddie's reads were perfect, as they usually were. Graham simply missed putts he'd been making all weekend, and indeed most of his life.

A sigh escaped his lips, and he looked down at the glass resting on the chair's armrest, his fingers now gripping it with white knuckles.

He knew he hadn't changed a thing in that tournament. His process, how he addressed the ball, his swing tempo—it had all been the same as before. Only one thing had been different: the thoughts roiling in his mind.

Winthrop, intentionally or not, had gotten in his head with that one subtle comment on the putting green before the tournament. "You think this will be the one, Sully?"

Sitting there in his armchair, he felt the same anger that had tormented him for years whenever he reflected on the brief interaction with his rival. But over the years, his ire had shifted focus.

Initially, in the aftermath of the collapse and the biggest choke job in golf history, Graham had blamed Winthrop for the loss. Graham was convinced the man had made the comment to get in his head, a little psychological warfare before the final round.

Over time, however, Graham realized that it wasn't Winthrop's fault at all. That simple sentence, the question whether he'd be able to finally win a major, was just words. They had no power unless Graham allowed them to. And he had. Not at first. But as he drew closer and closer to that beautiful finish line with his greatest triumph in sight, something mounted in him he'd felt too many times before—pressure to not blow it.

He'd lost leads In tournaments long before White Oak. Sadly, it had become his calling card—the guy who comes up small in big moments.

His solution to this was to immerse himself deeper into the game, spending more and more time practicing, working to hone his craft. It became more than just a job, more than something he had once enjoyed as a young man. It morphed into an obsession.

Then his son had died.

It was the worst loss of his life, orders of magnitude more painful than any stupid golf tournament had ever, or could ever, make him feel.

The day Mackey died, a piece of Graham died too.

Regrets haunted him.

He'd wished he had spent more time with his son, but traveling on the tour took him to a new city, and sometimes a new country, every week of the year. Visits home were infrequent and short, more like quick stopovers in the middle of a longer, more important journey.

Mackey had enjoyed golfing with his father. Graham often recalled the first time his son had ever swung a club. He was only five years old. Graham had an old driver he'd cut off and regripped so it would be the right size for a child.

Graham wished more than anything he could have had more time with Mackey. But the tour constantly pulled him away from his wife and son. For what it was worth, Mackey didn't seem to resent that. He attended school, getting good grades all the way up until he was in college.

He made the high school golf team and earned a scholarship to the University of North Carolina in Chapel Hill.

Graham shuddered as he recalled the events of the night he got the call, and he raised the glass to his lips, holding the rim there for a moment before taking another drink.

"Mr. Sullivan?" the cop on the phone had said.

After that, everything was a blur. Terrible pain racked Graham's chest as he listened to the officer tell him what happened. An 18-wheeler had veered into Mackey's lane on the freeway and cut him off —plowing him off the road and into the end of a guard rail.

The horrible timing of the accident was uncanny. Had the truck veered into Mackey even ten feet farther down the road, his vehicle would have simply glanced off the rail with nothing more than cosmetic damage. A hundred feet farther back, he might have been able to stop in time, or at least minimize the impact.

His wife, Linda, was inconsolable.

When she eventually left Graham a few months later, he wasn't surprised, nor did it shock him when she ended up with another man only weeks after that, ironically, turned out to be Winthrop.

The blame she placed on him for not being there for her after

Mackey's death was a deflection from her own inner turmoil. Graham knew that, and while losing his wife didn't feel good, that part of the ordeal didn't hurt all that much. It was more about the loss itself rather than losing her, specifically, from his life.

Linda had shown her true colors. She wanted attention, money, fame—all the trappings of a house built on sand. She drank all the time, sometimes starting off the day with a shot of vodka after waking up at 10:00. Graham knew she'd leaned into pills as well, though he wasn't sure about the frequency of that abuse.

She'd used their son's death as an excuse to gaslight Graham, casting blame where there was none. All the while, she'd been seeing Winthrop behind Graham's back.

Loneliness was something Graham had come to accept as a part of his life like the cup of coffee he drank every morning. It wasn't that he wanted to be alone, or even enjoyed it. He simply accepted it.

There'd been a few women who piqued his interest here and there, but those never panned out. His schedule didn't allow for much dating, and as the years went by, the ladies showing up at VIP events and tournaments grew less and less interested in him. There weren't many that wanted a guy his age, much less a pro who had failed so miserably so many times. The only ones that entertained the idea were easy for him to identify as gold diggers looking for a sugar daddy—a disturbing trend he'd learned had exploded thanks to the advent of cell phones and a slew of sites designed solely for that purpose. The rise of social media had merely poured gasoline on what had long been a raging cultural trend.

He knew plenty of men on the tour who cheated on their wives with the use of dating apps, digital singles bars where people could find a quick hookup with no strings attached.

Graham didn't have the energy for that.

Deep down, he did want to find someone—but it seemed people of substance were a rare breed.

He looked up at the framed picture on the mantel beneath the television, offset to the right. It was an image of him and his son, Mackey. It was taken the day Mackey turned eighteen. They were standing in front of a new SUV—a gift Graham had given him for his birthday.

Graham refused to give him a new car for his sixteenth birthday, insisting that Mackey first drive an old beater of a truck to get his feet wet. It had proved a reasonable decision since Mackey put more than a few dents in it along the way. But once he'd rid himself of being accident prone, Graham happily bought him the new ride.

It was in that SUV Mackey had died in that tragic night a decade before.

Graham had considered putting the picture in storage. It was a painful reminder of the worst night of his life, iced by being the worst year of his life.

The game came back on, and Graham blinked away the tears to refocus on baseball—one of the few things that took his mind off the bad stuff that filled his thoughts. He turned up the volume with the remote and allowed himself to fall back into the distraction of the national pastime, fully aware that once the game was over and he went to bed, he'd be lying down with all those demons once again. Not even the Atlanta Braves could keep them at bay.

6

CHATTANOOGA

Tyler arrived at the course earlier than usual on Wednesday morning. Typically, he would show up around nine and play a few rounds. But today was different.

He'd found it difficult to sleep the night before. His nerves kept his stomach in knots, and he hadn't been able to shut down the thoughts racing through his mind.

Lucy's perfume had lingered on him when he'd gone home after their romantic evening in the fairway under the stars. He could still feel her soft lips against his, and he wanted to keep feeling that as long as possible.

Tyler thought back to the hours before when he lay in his bed. He recalled the feel of her hair between his fingers—silky, black strands that flowed with a life of their own. He wanted to hold her all night and dared to hope that perhaps, someday, that dream might become a reality.

Tyler opened the door to the caddie shack and stepped inside. Unsurprisingly, he was the first one there.

He left his clubs against the stand outside the door and walked into the little building, making his way over to the kitchenette to the left, where he found a half-full bag of ground coffee.

After setting up the coffee machine and pressing the brew button, he walked over to the living room area, where a brown leather couch and two matching club chairs sat around a television that hung over a gas fireplace. The place was small but packed with charm, and memories.

Tyler had appreciated the caddie shack ever since his first time setting foot inside. It was like a home away from home, and in many ways much nicer. His apartment didn't have a fireplace or a leather couch. This felt like the kind of place he would love to hang out if he had money.

He and the other caddies played poker in here sometimes after their workdays were over, and they'd even spent time watching football, baseball, and the conclusion of big golf tournaments in here.

It was a rare moment when he had the place to himself, and while he enjoyed the camaraderie of having the other guys around, it was nice to have some quiet for a change.

The coffee machine bubbled and dripped from the corner of the kitchenette—the only noise that filled the room other than the muted sounds of songbirds in the trees outside.

He picked up the remote and plopped down on the couch on the left side, then turned on the television.

The screen lit up with a scene of a golfer hitting a ball in dramatic fashion. The swing was in slow motion, and the camera zoomed in on the ball at the last second to emphasize the brand.

Tyler had seen the commercial many times before. "Sure would be nice to get an endorsement deal from that company," he mused, dreaming of how it would feel to get paid to play with the best golf balls in the sport.

He watched the screen change back to the channel's main content with a former pro and a sports anchor sitting behind an anchor desk.

"Welcome back and good morning," the anchor on the left said. His smile was as white as his button-up shirt, and his quaffed dark blond hair didn't move as he spoke and moved his head. "In case you missed it, there was big news in the world of golf last night as

Graham Sullivan has decided to step away from the game at the age of fifty-eight."

Tyler's breath caught. Had he heard correctly? He leaned forward, digging his elbows into his knees as he watched.

"Allen, what do you think about this turn of events for a guy who still has some great golf left in him, particularly on the senior circuit?"

The anchor looked to the former pro. His gray necktie nearly matched the thick hair on his head.

"Yeah, Mack, this one caught me off guard, and I think a lot of people around the golf community are also feeling surprise, shock, and a whole lotta sadness. He might not have the trophies of a Tiger or a Nicklaus, but a lot of golf fans love this guy."

"In case you're just tuning in and hadn't heard the news, here is a clip from last night's press conference on Kiawah Island, where Sullivan has a home."

The screen flipped to the scene from the night before at the press conference.

Tyler watched as his childhood hero announced his retirement, and that the upcoming open at White Oak National would be his final tournament as a professional golfer.

Something tightened in Tyler's chest at seeing and hearing the man tell the world that he was hanging it up.

The television switched back to the news desk again.

"Strange time to call it quits, wouldn't you say, Allen?" Mack asked.

"Yeah. I mean, he's been playing some quality golf lately. A couple of top-five finishes on the senior tour. I understand he hasn't placed in the top fifteen recently on the main tour, but you have to accept that as you get older. Things don't work the same way they do when you're a young buck."

"He didn't mention anything specific regarding an injury. Do you think there might be something in that regard that's causing this abrupt retirement?"

"Hard to say, Mack," Allen shrugged. "I know the injury thing was why I left the game in my mid-fifties, but I don't know of anything major that Sully has had to deal with in the last five or six years."

"The timing is certainly unusual as well, wouldn't you say?"

"It is. There are still some tournaments left in the season. Makes you wonder if he's just getting tired or if he has the will to keep going."

"Good point. Of course, everyone knows Sully's story by now—the tragedy of his son's accident just over a decade ago, and the improbable collapse at White Oak just a few months after."

Tyler shook his head. "Why do they always have to bring that up?"

"Right," Allen said. "Maybe calling it quits after that tournament is his way of getting closure on more than just golf, but I'm not going to speculate on that. It's his life, and I suggest everyone, us included, respect his decision. I know from personal experience that it couldn't have come lightly."

The television switched to highlights from Sullivan's career, starting with his first win at a minor tournament in Arizona, another in Dubai, and then moving on to the first of his epic losses at a major.

"Truly, a great golfer and a terrific person whose professional career was marred by a series of unlikely collapses," Mack said. "It will be interesting to see how he performs in his final tournament. Do you think he makes the cut?"

Allen paused for a second to consider the question. "Hard to say. There are a few guys who make the cut that are around his age, but it's going to be tough. The field is looking pretty strong this year, and Sully has been playing some quality golf lately, as we said, but will it be enough? You never know. Maybe he has a little magic left in him to get through to Saturday."

"I think I speak for all of us when I say I'd love to see it."

"Definitely."

"And let's not forget: The White Oak National Open Championship is a special tournament. This coming weekend, the four final qualifying rounds are going to be played around the country, which means four amateur golfers are going to get the chance of a lifetime to play in a major tournament with professionals from all around the world."

"It's a great tournament, Allen," Mack said. "And like you said, it provides an incredible opportunity for four amateurs to win their way into the open."

"Right now, there are four golfers out there in the four corners of the country who have a chance to change their stars and have a once-in-a-lifetime opportunity to play with the world's best. It's got to be a lot of pressure, especially for an amateur."

"Yeah, it is, Allen. You're right about that. But everyone left in the field has played through a few rounds to get here, so you're talking about battle-tested players, regardless of their amateur status. These are guys who know how to play, and play at a high level. But there's nothing like standing over a must-make putt to win a tournament for a shot at the big time. I can only liken it to when I got my tour card. It came down to me and another guy, both with the same score going to eighteen. I made the putt for birdie. His lipped out. Of course, he made the tour a few months later, but the pressure for something like this is immense. Most of these guys aren't trying to get their tour cards. They haven't gone through qualifying school. Some have, sure, but the majority are club pros or just really good players at their respective clubs."

"Well, it will certainly be interesting to see who comes out of the four qualifiers. You never know, maybe one of them will get paired with Graham Sullivan for a round. Wouldn't that be something?"

"A chance to play with a legend like him, in his last tournament, that's the kind of thing you tell your grandkids about."

Deep down, Tyler felt a real connection to that last bit of the conversation. The channel switched over to another series of commercials. He muted the television and stood up. The coffee pot beeped, signaling that the morning brew was ready.

As he walked over to the kitchenette, he found himself wishing for the chance to play with his hero, Graham Sullivan.

The odds of that happening were extremely thin, even if he won the qualifier this coming weekend.

He opened the cabinet above the counter next to the sink and removed his coffee mug. It was black with the words *Coffee Nation* on it with three beans below the text feathered out like a blooming flower. Beneath the beans, the text read, Death Before Decaf.

The mug always made him smile even before the much-needed brew spilled into his mouth.

He picked up the coffee pot and filled the mug with the steaming, dark brown liquid then replaced the pot and walked back over to the couch. He set the mug down on a leather coaster atop an end table and stepped over to the fireplace and switched it on.

As he returned to the couch and sat down, the gas ignited with a whoosh. The fire flickered steadily in the hearth, its rhythm casting dancing shadows around the floor just in front of it.

Tyler loved being here at this time of day. It was still mostly dark outside. The moon still hung low in the sky above the trees on the slopes of the nearby hillside. But sunlight encroached across the darkness—nature's changing of the guard.

This place may have just been a caddie shack to the other guys that worked here, but to him it was a fortress, a retreat from the worries of the world. It represented something he could look forward to at the end of a long day of lugging heavy bags around, a sort of man cave where he and the other caddies could unwind and tell stories about the rounds they guided, or joke about some of the horrific shots they saw by golfers who believed they were better than they were.

And in rare cases, on mornings like this, the caddie shack was Tyler's temple. It was meditative, peaceful, and renewed him with a sense of energy and purpose. And on a day like today, it was the perfect place to help him focus.

The television's program switched to a replay of the tournament from the weekend. That was what Tyler wanted to see. He kept the sound muted but watched each tee shot, every approach, chip, and putt with rapt attention.

He'd heard that many pros spent time before a round meditating or visualizing. This was based on research that suggested seeing one's success before it happened helped make it happen.

Tyler believed in all that, but as someone with an attention deficit, he chose to take a different tack. Sitting and meditating with his eyes closed, trying to focus on future outcomes of shots, putts, and even entire rounds was difficult for him. He'd get two or three minutes into the process, and then his mind would wander, taking him to a daydream state where he was on a roller coaster, or on a boat, or at the beach, or kissing Lucy.

He smiled as that thought reentered his mind again and had to recenter his mind on the television and what he was trying to do.

Instead of trying to see himself accomplishing the things he wanted to in a round, he watched the professionals, but not as a fan or a casual observer. Tyler absorbed what they were doing—the fluid motion of their backswings, the slight pauses at the top, the momentum changes, the way their hips drove their arms forward like trebuchets generating immense power. He watched the way their clubs struck the ball, and the way the players finished. Some of them had high extensions with their arms as they turned and completed the swing. Others kept the club lower, more parallel with the ground.

Tyler didn't discriminate with his viewing visualization technique. He often watched female professionals too because, like he always said, a good swing is a good swing. Didn't matter if they were a guy or girl. In fact, some of his favorite swings to watch on Instagram were female golfers, along with a guy out of Japan who had an astoundingly casual approach to his swing.

He raised the mug to his lips and smelled the fresh coffee. He loved the aroma. It was one of his favorite smells in the world. Every time he walked into a coffee shop, he paused for a second to appreciate it.

He took a sip of the hot coffee and winced. "Little too hot still," he muttered, setting the mug back on the end table.

Tyler continued watching the tournament replay, taking in every detail he could.

He'd learned this technique when he was sixteen, watching one of the major tournaments on the pro tour. Before then, he'd simply been a fan of the sport. It was, like for so many others, just a benign pastime.

But something changed that year. Instead of merely observing, he began to realize that some of the guys on the tour weren't any bigger than him. They didn't possess any sort of superhuman strength or abilities. They'd simply honed their skills to the point that they were better than most of the players in the rest of the world.

This mindset shift changed everything for Tyler.

He'd been a good player before, usually hitting in the low 80s or high 70s. Once he made this single alteration in how he watched tournaments, he began to take on the physical characteristics of the swings he observed.

He once heard a coach say that athletes are athletes. The man claimed that a great basketball player can be a great soccer player, and a great quarterback can be a great pitcher. Their minds, he said, were electrically connected to physical skills. The guy called it kinetic intelligence.

Tyler knew a kid in his high school like that. Justin had been a good basketball player, but one season the soccer coach needed players and asked him to come out. He'd never played the sport before but took to it immediately and ended up scoring multiple goals by the end of the year.

For Tyler, he simply watched the best in the world and applied what he saw to his own game.

The change had been astounding.

His scores had dropped immediately, taking him down into the scratch range and beyond. He started shooting under par with incredible regularity. His distances for every club went up by significant percentages, and his putting game developed more consistency.

When his buddies, Justin included, asked him how he got so good so fast, he told them he simply tried to mimic the pros. He watched what they did, and it imprinted on his mind.

Tyler even got a few of them to test it out for themselves, but none of them ever caught on to the concept. Maybe it was simply that they didn't understand how to apply what he was saying.

He took another sip of coffee and continued watching the replay. He fast forwarded through the commercial breaks, trying to get in as much viewing time as possible in as little time as possible.

Fifteen minutes in, he heard the jingle of clubs near the door.

Tyler checked his watch. The other caddies would probably not be showing up for another thirty minutes, but Justin had promised to be there early to get a head start on the day.

This, for them, was not going to be an ordinary Caddie Day at the club.

The door opened, and Justin appeared in the door. He looked over at Tyler, who was craning his neck to look back. Then Justin glanced at the television.

"You're doing it again, aren't you?" he asked as he closed the door behind him.

"You know it. Seems to be working out so far."

"Yeah, well, I wish it worked for my game." He made his way over to the coffee pot in the kitchenette, removed his red mug with the Tennessee state flag on it, and filled it with hot coffee.

He walked back over to the living room area and sat down in one of the club chairs, looking up at the screen. "When do you want to get out there?"

"When we finish our coffee," Tyler answered without so much as a sideways glance at his friend. "Would be good to get a couple of loops in today."

Justin frowned. "You sure you don't want to take it easy? No sense in wearing yourself out six days before the big tournament."

Tyler grinned, prying his eyes from the television. "We're going to wear ourselves out caddying all week."

"Against my advice, I might add."

"I need the money. Besides, I don't work on Saturdays, so that'll give me a day to rest up before the tournament."

"I still think you should take the rest of the week off, but what do I know."

Tyler understood what his friend was saying. But there was nothing he could do about it. His mother needed help with the rent, the groceries, and the utilities. Things had gotten expensive the last few years. Inflation was up, wages were down, and every extra dollar he could pull in took a little more weight off his mother's shoulders.

He didn't think Justin fully appreciated that.

He wasn't wealthy either, but he had two parents—both pulling in enough money so that Justin could focus on his studies and work only when he needed to. That didn't change the fact that Justin had big dreams of his own, as he'd made clear to Tyler on more than one occasion.

He was always talking about making more and more money, but for luxury items like cars or vacations. Tyler couldn't help but feel like his buddy wasn't just viewing this as an opportunity for one but for both of them to climb out of holes they'd been assigned early in life.

Justin stared at his friend for a few seconds.

"What?" Tyler asked, staying focused on the television.

"You seem different today," Justin said. "I can't put my finger on it. It's something... brighter. Like, you're happier than usual. Less tired."

Tyler shrugged. "I don't know what you're talking about."

Justin didn't break his gaze. "No, there's something in your words. And in your facial expressions. What's going on?"

Tyler twisted his head and looked over at his friend. "I don't know. Nothing changed. Well, except that I kissed Lucy last night."

Justin had just raised his mug to his lips and started taking a sip when he heard the words. He spewed coffee across the top of the cup in a fine mist, barely able to contain the accident to a minimum.

"What?" he blurted.

7

The sun dangled in the partly cloudy sky over the mountain to the east. It was getting close to lunchtime, and the two friends' stomachs grumbled to remind them they needed to eat soon.

They'd picked up a couple of snacks from the snack bar at the turn but had yet to eat a full meal.

Tyler held off eating until late in the morning, opting for an intermittent fasting approach to his daily caloric intake. It was, he claimed, why he had a slender but muscular physique. Everyone over forty he told that to just nodded and assumed it was because he was twenty.

Justin, on the other hand, hadn't eaten yet purely because he'd gotten out of bed late and run out of time in his hurry to get to the club for the early round.

Tyler walked up to his ball sitting on the edge of the fairway next to the first cut and propped up his bag on its two legs.

"That's a nice lie," Justin said, stopping next to his friend's bag. "What are you thinking here?"

"You're the one who's going to be caddying for me on Sunday," Tyler answered. "What do you think?"

They stood on the tightly cut Bermuda fairway of the 18th hole, staring toward the green perched on a slight rise bordered by two massive bunkers on either side. The slightest hook or slice would send the ball into the sand, and with the steep banks on the back edges leading up to the fringe, getting out was a tricky proposition.

"Yeah, but you've been calling your own shots all day."

"And I hope you've been paying close attention."

Justin chuckled. "Not sure why you even need a caddie. You're a caddie! You should just carry your own bag."

"Okay, first of all, the rules state you have to have a caddie. Can't carry your own bag. Second, I thought you would enjoy being on a real golfer's bag for a change."

"Ha! You mean other than when I'm on my own bag?"

Tyler pulled a 7-iron out of his bag and walked over to his ball. "No. I mean in general."

"You're hilarious."

Tyler laughed and winked at his friend. "You know I'm just messing with you. You've got a great round going right now, man. What are you, two under?"

"Even par right now," Justin answered. "Two bogeys, two birdies, and the rest were pars."

"That's solid."

Justin didn't act like it was all that great. "It's a boring round, man. You're parked here on eighteen at six under. I don't know how you do it. The course record is eight under."

"So, you're saying I need to hole this one out to tie the course record."

"You're a funny guy. You know that, right?" Justin cocked his head to the side and eyeballed the club in his friend's hand. "What do you have there? Six-iron?"

"Seven."

"From this distance?"

"It's felt good today. Hitting the ball a little harder than usual. Normally, I could go with a six here. Make sure to put that in your notes."

Justin shook his head as he laughed. "I'm barely on the green, and I had to hit a five to get there."

"Yeah, but you were fifteen yards behind me."

"Oh, sure, rub it in."

Tyler stepped up to the ball and spread out his feet. He dangled the club over the ball for a second then began whipping the face back and forth in a loose motion, breaking his wrists with every pass.

It was something he did before every shot that wasn't a putt. It helped him relax and stay loose so he wouldn't try to swing too hard. That was the downfall of so many golfers worldwide. They'd swing out of their shoes on drives and approaches, when they only needed to loosen up a little.

It was a technique he'd learned from a coach he found on YouTube, as well as from a video clip he'd seen on the site from a pro working with a couple of novices.

The pro had told the two students to only try to hit the ball three-quarters of the distance they needed to hit their target. So, if they were two hundred yards out, only try to hit the ball 150 yards.

He couldn't believe the results. Both the golfers, a male and a female, increased their distance by ten to fifteen yards per club, exceeding the target every time. This told Tyler that swing mechanics and ball striking were far more important than sheer strength. It was a principle that reflected in guys with slim builds crushing drives over three hundred yards on the pro tour.

After a couple more whips of the club over the ball, he lowered the face down to the grass and focused on the right side of the dimple-covered sphere.

Some golfers hesitated a long moment at this point. Not Tyler. A second after the club's edge touched the ground, he began his back-swing, taking it up and over his shoulders while turning his hips until his left shoulder pointed down at the ball.

Then, with the iron nearly flat and pointed at the target, he paused for a nanosecond before bringing the club back around, starting the motion with his hips.

The club snapped through the air with a perfect arc, the face striking the ball with a sound only golfers would call beautiful.

The two watched the ball take off like a rocket, launching into the air with incredible speed. It arched high into the sky, aligned almost perfectly with the pin sitting in the back-right corner behind a bunker.

"Man, that looks really good," Justin said, holding his breath. "That one's gonna have a chance."

The ball reached its zenith and then started to descend. A gentle breeze picked up, brushing across the fairway and tickling the two friends' skin.

"Come on," Justin said.

Tyler didn't utter a peep. If he said anything, it was only through subtle movements of his lips, and only for himself to hear.

The ball dropped like a bomb onto the green, bit, and then backed itself up toward the pin.

The young men's eyes widened as it bore down on the hole.

"Disappear," Justin pleaded. "Disappear!"

The ball rolled until it was—from their vantage—only a few inches away from the pin. Then it stopped.

"Aww, man!" Justin exclaimed. "That was so close! You nearly eagled the hole to tie the course record."

Tyler nodded. "Yeah, that was a pretty good one."

"Pretty good? Dude, that shot was amazing. You really did almost tie the course record with an eagle."

"You mentioned that."

Justin raised his hand for a high-five. Tyler grinned sheepishly and slapped it.

"Great shot, buddy," Justin said.

"Thanks."

Justin arched an eyebrow at his friend as Tyler retreated to his bag and slid the iron back into its place. "You don't seem excited. You're going to shoot seven under par on an extremely difficult course. This is your best round here so far. And it's the week of the qualifier to get into the White Oak National Open Championship."

"Maybe I should have saved some for the tournament," Tyler joked.

"Yeah, no kidding. I hope you can do that again this weekend."

"You and me both, buddy."

Tyler picked up his bag and slung it over his shoulder.

"I still can't believe you do all this with those old clubs," Justin said, shaking his head as he glanced at the bag. "I can't imagine what you would do with a proper set of clubs with the latest tech built in."

"Doesn't seem to be helping you all that much," Tyler jabbed.

"You're an idiot."

The two laughed as they marched toward the green.

"You had a little something extra behind that," Justin commented.

"Yeah. Like I said, everything just felt a little stronger today. I don't know why. Some days are just like that, I guess."

"Right. Or maybe it's because you made out with Lucy Park last night."

Tyler snorted, trying to disguise both his embarrassment and the truth. "Nah. And we didn't really make out."

"You said you two kissed. On a blanket. On the fairway. Under the stars. I don't need all the gory details. Personally, I'd rather not hear them. But come on. You made out with her. Didn't you?"

Tyler's cheeks burned. He lowered his head and stared down at the grass under his feet as they neared the edge of the green on a narrow patch of landing strip between the two huge bunkers.

"I mean, yeah. We made out a little. It was really nice, man. I haven't felt that kind of connection with a girl before."

"You've made out with a girl, though, right?"

"Sure. I mean, a little. But last night felt different."

Tyler set his bag down just outside the fringe and plucked his putter from its slot.

Justin offered a grin to his friend. "Yeah, I bet it was. Lucy is smokin' hot, man. Well done."

"No. It's not like that. I mean, yes, she is. But she's different from the other girls."

"You got that right. Her parents are loaded. She's definitely a keeper, buddy. Don't screw this one up. You could be set for life if you end up with her."

Tyler didn't like the sound of that. Something stirred in his gut, and he forced himself to squelch the fire.

"I honestly haven't even thought about that, J. I'm my own man. I earn my way. I don't want to be a parasite off someone else's money, or their parents' money?"

Justin laughed and walked over to his ball.

"I'm just messing with you, Ty. I know you're not like that. But you have to admit, it would be a nice perk. You know, a little icing on the cake."

"Let's just drop it, okay? I don't like thinking about it that way. That's not why I'm into her. And it's not just her looks either. She's really cool, and we have a good time together."

"Okay, okay. Relax, pal. I got you. You're into her. And she seems like she's into you, which, by the way, I called, if you don't remember."

"Yeah, yeah. I remember."

Justin stepped up to his ball and squatted down to get a look at the line. "So, I just need to hear a couple of little words out of your mouth."

"Which are?"

"You were right, Justin."

"That's four words."

Justin nodded. "True." He stood up and took a step back, still analyzing his putt. Tyler loomed ten feet behind him, tilting his head to the right as he also sized up his friend's line.

"What do you think?" Justin asked. "About two feet outside the cup to the right?"

"Few inches less than that," Tyler answered.

He walked around Justin and over to his ball, where it was sitting only eight inches from the hole. He marked the ball with a dime he kept in his pocket, and then repaired the crater the ball had left ten feet away.

"Dude, that one's good. You don't have to mark it. Just pick it up." Justin said.

"No way, man. In the tournament, you have to putt everything out. I gotta play this the right way. No gimmes in the qualifier, or in the open."

"I like where your head is," Justin replied. "You're sure about that read?"

"Pretty sure. But you're a caddie too. Trust your gut."

"Seems like I heard that somewhere recently."

Tyler rolled his shoulders with a laugh. "Yep."

"Okay. Here goes nothing."

Justin walked up to his ball, tapped his feet a few times, and then gave the putter three practice swings before lowering it behind the ball. He exhaled and swung, striking the white sphere in the dead center of his putter's head.

The ball rolled—fast at first—as it screamed up the slight rise. Then it started bending, just as he'd thought it would. "Come on," he muttered.

"Pretty good speed," Tyler said.

The ball continued bending its run toward the cup, curving dramatically on the green slope.

Then it started running out of steam, slowing as it neared the cup. It stopped six inches to the right of the hole. Justin sighed in disappointment and looked up to the sky as if it could offer some sort of consolation.

"Ugh. I can't believe that. It was so close."

"Great putt, man," Tyler offered. "Nice par."

"Yeah, but it would have been nice to sink that birdie."

"That wasn't an easy putt. You're like twenty-five feet back over there."

"I'd call it thirty, but whatever."

Tyler laughed. "Did you take your line or mine?"

Justin pressed his lips together and clenched his teeth. He inhaled and then grumbled, "Mine."

"Oh!" Tyler boomed. "Man, I told you."

"You also told me to trust my gut." Justin walked over to the ball, leaned down, and tapped the putt in for par.

He bent down and took the ball out of the cup then stepped back to allow Tyler to replace his ball.

Tyler stepped back to his ball mark, set the ball down, and removed the coin, slipping it back into his pocket. He didn't need to take a look at the line here. It was straight in, and at that distance, even a poorly struck putt would probably go in.

He tilted his head at an angle to give it one quick assessment, then addressed the ball and stroked it into the cup.

"Outstanding birdie, Ty," Justin said, nearly shouting at his friend. "You almost tied the course record."

Tyler reached into the hole and removed his ball, inspecting it for a second as if checking for scratches.

"Thanks, buddy," he said, turning to his friend.

Justin extended his hand, and Tyler gripped it firmly.

"You want to go another round?" Justin asked.

"I thought you said I need to take it easy this week."

Justin's grin widened. "I did. But that was before you kicked my butt. I can't go down like that."

"The next round could be way worse."

"That's true."

The two laughed as they walked back to their bags. They slid their putters back in the slots and hefted the bags over their shoulders.

"Let's see how we feel after lunch," Tyler suggested.

8

CHARLESTON

Graham Sullivan parked outside his usual coffee shop and let the car idle while he finished listening to a YouTube video about three words of wisdom from some fiction author based in Texas.

He wasn't sure he'd heard of the guy before, but he enjoyed the content. When the video finished, he hit the Subscribe button and the Thumbs-Up, then killed the engine and stuffed the device in his pocket.

Graham stepped out of his black Lexus sedan and looked around for a second, taking in the sights of Charleston. Then he glanced down at the hood of his car. He'd washed it earlier and was happy to see the autumn pollen hadn't overtaken it yet.

His sedan was technically a luxury car, but it wasn't like some of the vehicles other pros drove. Lately, everyone had been on a big Maserati kick, though some of the higher rollers had a Bentley or two in their garages.

Flying in that air had never been Graham's thing. He just wanted a nice car with a strong yet reliable engine.

He'd had the same vehicle for five years and had considered trading this one in, but it had the feel of a worn baseball glove to him.

It was comfortable, and he could always count on it to be there when he needed it.

The microcosm of that line of thought as it pertained to his life in general wasn't lost on him. He didn't need to see a psychiatrist to tell him that, even though he had been to one regularly for the last decade.

It wasn't some suppressed childhood trauma expressing itself in his choice of car. That problem was out there in the open, and he understood it quite well.

His father had died when he was young, leaving him and his mother a significant amount of money, which his mother spent reck-lessly on luxury items and the latest trendy things. Fortunately for Graham, half of the money was left in his name, safely protected in a trust until he turned eighteen.

Because of his mother's lack of frugality, he'd learned to be smart with his money—saving and investing at a young age. The one luxu-rious thing he bought for himself in his younger years was a new set of golf clubs at the age of nineteen.

He'd taken to the game his eighth-grade year, then played for the high school team after that.

Graham was a natural, with a swing as smooth as butter and a deadly accurate putt. He quickly rose up the ranks on the team and even led them to a state title.

In college, he'd been even more successful and had finished in the top ten as an amateur in a major.

The sky was the limit back then. Sports magazines featured him as the next golden child of golf, a rising star that would take over the game for the foreseeable future.

To his credit, he'd never let much of that go to his head—not in an egotistical sense. But with every article, every interview, every prediction, the pressure mounted inside him. Despite all his early success as a young man, Graham felt an impending sense of doom hanging over him, perpetually waiting for the other shoe to drop.

He'd pondered it for the last thirty-plus years of his life: Why a golfer who was so good, and even came up big in clutch moments as a younger man, could somehow fall apart once he hit the pro tour.

He wondered if part of it was due to the unexpected death of his father, or if it had more to do with the way his mother blew through her inheritance afterward. She'd ended up being completely broke within two years of his passing and ended up finding another man to leech on for sustenance.

Graham loved his mother, but after the death of his father, they grew distant, and even more so when she ended up marrying the new rich guy.

Already in college, Graham was grateful he didn't have to engage with his stepfather, except for holidays. Even then, it was purely out of necessity and decorum.

By the time Graham finished college, his mother had divorced the guy and moved on to the next greener pasture—this time a man two years younger than her.

While Graham didn't cut her off completely, he also didn't go out of his way to spend time with his mother after that.

She called now and then, but it was usually with the same angle —needing money.

He helped her, of course, but always felt like he was enabling her issues.

When she passed away five years ago, he had felt almost relieved, though a little guilt riddled him over that sentiment.

Graham washed the memories out of his mind with a deep breath and a smile at his sedan parked along the curb in front of the coffee shop.

He walked up to the door, opened it, and stepped inside as the aroma of fresh coffee and pastries crashed over him like a wave.

The place was locally owned and seemed to be doing well despite being pitted against national chains just a few blocks down the street in either direction.

He'd noticed the phenomenon in many places—this innate desire by people to support locally owned establishments. They could get consistency at big chain restaurants and coffee houses, and maybe that was why those places did so well. But local artisanal businesses had risen from the ashes over the years due to new customer sentiment, and places like this were thriving because of it.

The line at the counter was four people deep, all of them in their early twenties and looking to fuel up either before a day at work or a long study session at the local university.

The workers behind the counter took orders and scrambled as they made lattes, chai teas, cappuccinos, mochas, and the occasional black coffee.

Graham enjoyed the pace of it all, and the simple interior design of the shop. Exposed air ducts and vents hung from the ceiling over an exposed, cracked concrete floor.

The building had been a mechanic's shop in its past life, with the new owners converting it to a coffeehouse after significant renovation. The garage part was perfect for days like this when the morning air was warm. The proprietors opened the garage door to provide an open-air setting for several tables. Down in the well where oil changes used to take place—they'd turned that into their roastery.

Graham didn't have to look at the menu written on a chalkboard behind the counter. He got the same thing every time he came here—a large black coffee and an egg-and-cheese croissant.

At this point in his life, consistency was the only thing he had left, though now and then Graham wondered if a change was due. There was such a thing as growing old and calcified, and those were the last adjectives Graham wanted people to use to describe him.

He turned his head to the left, sweeping the room full of younger people sitting at tables with their laptops in front of them. Still more were perched on stools at a counter that ran along the windows that made up the exterior wall all the way to the front corner and to the back left of the building.

Graham's eyes fixed on a woman in the corner. Her brunette hair was pulled back in a ponytail that stuck out through the black baseball cap she wore on her head. She was in the same uniform as the other workers behind the bar, red apron included.

She was reading a book—a novel of some kind from the looks of it—and Graham assumed she must have been on her break.

But she looked older than the rest of the workers in the shop, probably mid to late forties by his estimation. He found himself staring at her, captivated by her appearance. She was beautiful, and he wondered how long she'd been working here since he'd never noticed her before.

Graham noticed movement out of his periphery, and realized he'd missed another move toward the counter.

He glanced back over at the woman in the corner, unable to rip his curiosity away from her. She turned the page of her book and then picked up a cup of coffee sitting on the counter in front of her. She held the cup for a few seconds before taking a sip, keeping her eyes focused on the pages the whole time.

"Can I take your order?" the young woman behind the counter asked.

Graham realized it was his turn and shuffled forward. He hoped the girl at the register hadn't noticed him staring at her coworker. It wasn't like him to do that. But there was something striking about the woman in the corner, and a ball of nerves tightened in his gut.

"I'll have a large black coffee and an egg-and-cheese croissant," he said.

"Going with the usual again?" the girl asked with a cute grin.

He smiled back at her, a little embarrassed though he didn't know why. "Yeah. I guess I'm sort of predictable."

"All good. It's nice to have something predictable in a world that usually isn't."

"I like that," he said, producing his credit card from his money clip.

She gave him the total, and he tapped the card on the screen, added a couple bucks for a tip, and then took his receipt.

"Number two-twenty-two," she said. "Enjoy your breakfast."

He thanked her and moved down the line toward the pickup area at the end of the bar. Graham wasn't surprised she remembered his order. She'd seen him in here dozens of times, if not more.

He stopped in front of the espresso machine to wait for his order while the barista behind it fiddled with the cups, the grinder, and the buttons to froth a cup of milk. The machine sizzled and hissed, sounding like some kind of nineteenth-century steam contraption. It even looked the part, clad as it was in a boggling swirl of chrome, tubes, and pipes. Under his breath, he wished the barista good luck.

Graham found his eyes wandering back to the brunette woman in the corner again. She looked up from her book and turned her head in his direction. He immediately shifted his feet and averted his gaze to some nonspecific spot outside the building. A red sports car was the first thing that caught his eye, and he remained fixed on it until she went back to reading her book.

He gulped a dose of fear down his throat and turned away from her, looking over the counter at the workers as they danced in a peculiar, worker-bee rhythm to prepare the breakfast orders.

One by one, the other customers received their orders, leaving Graham next in line at the counter in the back corner.

He stood there at an angle so he could still see the brunette with his peripheral vision. *What was it about her?* He didn't know, but an urge he hadn't felt in a long time began to swell inside him.

Should I go over and talk to her? Doing so would be foolish, or so he told himself. He hadn't done something like that in longer than he could remember. And what would he say, anyway?

He tried to shove away the ridiculous notion as he waited for his order, but his mind kept turning back to her.

What are you worried about, Sully? You walk over, strike up a conversation, and be friendly. That's it. See where it goes. Don't hit on her. Just be nice. But don't be a creep either.

The self-talk in his mind did little to settle his nerves. He'd seen a million women, and most of the time he didn't think anything of it. What made her different? Why was today different from all the other days?

He didn't know, but he decided he had to find out.

"Number two-twenty-two," the barista said, setting down a brown bag with the owl logo printed in black on the front. He placed the large coffee next to it.

"Thanks," Graham said to the young man.

"You're welcome, and have a great day."

"Well, we'll see how that goes," he replied under his breath as he turned away from the counter.

He worked his way around a couple of tables and then along the patrons sitting on their stools until he stopped at an empty one catty-corner to the brunette.

He swallowed, took a breath, and stepped past her, setting his bag and cup down on the counter.

She looked up at him from her book, her blue eyes hooking him instantly. She smiled and then returned to her text, turning the page before reaching over for her cup once more.

Graham glanced at the book cover. He didn't know the author, but it looked like some kind of an adventure.

"Any good?" he asked, easing into his seat.

The woman looked up again, this time making more eye contact with him. Thankfully, she didn't seem annoyed or suspicious that the strange man was talking to her. He noticed her name tag on the apron and made a silent note. *Alicia.*

"It is, actually," she said, a smile he hoped was curious stretching across her face. "Do you like archaeological thrillers?"

"You mean like a treasure-hunt-type story?"

She nodded. "Yeah."

"Sure. Who doesn't? Some of my favorite movies are those kinds. But I've only read a few books like that."

"Well, there are a lot of them out there now. From a ton of different writers."

"I'll keep that in mind." He lifted his coffee off the counter and removed the lid, setting it down next to the bag. Steam trickled up from the hot liquid, evaporating in the air. "You work here?"

She raised both eyebrows. "What gave it away?" she asked, sounding dry to him.

"Sorry. Stupid question. Obviously, you work here. I just... I come in here a lot, and I've never seen you before."

She tilted her head to the side. Graham saw she wasn't annoyed, necessarily, but also maybe uncertain as to where this was going. He felt the same way.

"I usually work afternoons. They needed some extra help this morning, so I came in. I'm on my break."

"And I am interrupting that. I apologize." He turned away and started opening his bag.

"It's okay," she said. "I still have ten minutes. Do you make it a point to know everyone at every coffee shop in Charleston?"

He blushed but also chuckled. "No. Just this one. I come in here most mornings. Do that enough times, you get to know who works here when."

"So, this is your regular spot for morning coffee, huh? You have good taste."

Her comment disarmed his nerves a little, and he found himself getting more comfortable with the conversation. That's all it was, a conversation. With a total stranger. Who happened to be a beautiful woman who worked in his favorite coffee shop.

He forced those thoughts aside and forged ahead. "Yeah." He looked around at the interior of the shop. "I like the feel of this place. Mornings like this, I usually sit out there in the garage area."

"Why not today?" she asked, glancing through the window at the area he mentioned.

"I don't know, actually. I just felt like sitting here this morning."

"Any particular reason?"

He felt like she was trying to draw the truth out of him, and if he confessed, he'd immediately look like a weirdo.

"No. Sometimes I just like to mix it up."

He hoped the lie sounded convincing. Mixing it up was the exact opposite of how he lived his life.

"You never want to get stuck in a rut. That's where fun goes to die."

Her words struck him in a way he hadn't expected. How long had it been since he'd had fun, like real, honest, fun? He sat there thinking, trying to recall the last time he'd laughed hard at something, or taken real pleasure in an activity. He appreciated the bourbon he drank now and then, and tried to be thankful for his home, his bed, his car, the money he had in the bank.

"You okay?" she asked, twisting her head a little as if making sure he wasn't having a stroke.

"Oh. Yeah. Sorry," he recovered, realizing he'd drifted off into his own questions. "I was just thinking about what you said. I do need to mix it up more. I think I've been stuck in a rut for way too long in life."

She closed her book and set it aside, then picked up the coffee cup sitting next to her and held it while she peered into his eyes. "That sounds painful."

He huffed. "Yeah. I guess it does, huh." He raised his cup to his mouth and took a careful sip of the hot coffee.

"What do you do for a living?"

He nearly spit out the drink, but managed to keep it in long enough to choke it down.

"You okay?" she followed up, curious at his reaction.

"Yeah. I'm good," he said, wiping his lips with the back of his hand. "Sorry. Was a little hotter than I expected."

"We do make it that way here. Always two hundred degrees."

"The way it should be. Extracts all the oils and flavors from the beans."

Her eyebrows lifted again. "I'm impressed. Not many people know about that. Are you a coffee nerd?"

"Not really. I just like good joe. And this shop makes the best in Charleston. Actually, some of the best I've ever had. And I've had coffee all over the world."

"So, you travel a lot?" she took a sip from her cup.

He bobbed his head. "You could say that. Yeah."

Then she dropped the question again that he didn't want to answer. "So, what do you do?"

9

Graham loathed to tell her. One of the reasons he loved this coffee shop was that few golfers came here. It was more of a local young professionals' hangout, or a place for free-lancers to congregate. If any of them were fans of the sport, none had ever paid him any attention. Maybe it was because he was older, and beyond his prime. He didn't catch the headlines like he used to, and his face wasn't plastered on billboards or television commercials anymore.

There was something about this woman that made him want to know more, to go deeper into who she was, and what her life was like —her passions, interests, habits, all of it. Her eyes were kind and full of a warmth he hadn't seen before.

Most women he met on the tour were only after two things— the fame and money that came with being attached to a pro golfer. That fact made him feel self-conscious about telling her the truth.

What was he thinking? He'd just met this woman, and they hadn't even introduced themselves. And here he was worrying about her getting attached to him for his status.

"I'm going to be retiring in a few weeks, actually," he stalled.

"Oh, congratulations. That's great. You don't look old enough to be retiring. I guess business was good?"

He offered a humble smile. "It was okay. I..." He faltered, but she leaned forward an inch as if to draw it out of him. "I'm a golfer."

Her expression puzzled him. Was she put off guard? Confused? Apparently, neither.

"That's cool. I don't really know anyone who plays, except my brother Alex. But he's not very good. You look like you're dressed to play today." She noted his gray polo and light blue trousers. "How often do you play golf?"

He lowered his eyes to the coffee cup, realizing she didn't understand. "I'm a pro golfer," he clarified.

Her eyes widened. "Oh, that's cool. So, which one of the local clubs do you work at?"

Graham laughed at the response.

"What's so funny?" she demanded with a smile. He loved it when she smiled. It was intoxicating, and he felt his chest warming every time he looked at her.

"No, not that kind of pro. I'm a professional golfer. You know? On the tour?"

The answer dropped her jaw. "I. Am. So. Sorry. I didn't realize that's what you meant."

"Don't apologize. It's fine."

"Wow. That is so cool. You get to play golf for a living. Have you ever won any tournaments?"

There it was. He'd worried it might get to this. After that came the insincere groveling, and if it didn't, there was no way he could gauge if she was into him because of money or because she actually liked him. This factor alone was the biggest reason he'd remained single ever since Linda left him.

"A few," he said, his voice dropping. "None of the majors. But I've done okay in my career."

"Why are you hanging it up? You seem like you're young enough to keep going for a while."

"I'm fifty-eight," he confessed, certain that was going to end the conversation, or at least any chance he might have of seeing her again in the future. "There are golfers still playing that are older than me, but I just feel like the time is right to move on."

"Do you enjoy it?"

He shrugged. "Sure. I guess so. I always loved playing golf, but it's like anything else. Once you do it for a job long enough, that's what it becomes: A job. I'll keep playing after I retire, just not in big tournaments anymore. Would be nice to visit some new courses around the world and play without the pressure."

"How interesting," she said. "I've never met a professional golfer before. Or any pro athletes, come to think of it. But you're right. Anything can become a job. Then again, I'm fifty-two and still trying to figure out what I'm going to do with my life."

It was his turn to be surprised. "Wait a minute. You're fifty-two?"

She giggled, her cheeks reddening slightly. "Yeah. Why? Do I look older?"

"No." He said it a little too quickly. "No, I mean. Definitely not. You look much younger. I was going to guess at least ten years younger than that. You've aged very well." He realized how he must have sounded, and tried to reel it back. "I'm sorry. I didn't mean to—"

"Thank you. You're very kind. And you should also get your vision checked."

He shook his head. "My eyes work just fine." He took a breath and realized he'd maybe just made it awkward, but he held her gaze. "So, you were saying that you're still trying to figure out what you're going to do with your life?"

"Right," she said. "Yeah, I mean, I've been working here for the last few months. Before that, I was working in retail. Got laid off. So, now I'm here, trying to figure out my next move. I've bounced around from job to job like that most of my life. I guess I just sort of fell into that mode after college."

"What's your degree in?"

"Communications. I worked for a company for five years after college, then I quit to travel the world. By the time I came back a few years later, everything had changed. Social media had taken over, and

I had fallen behind the times. Didn't feel like I could ever catch up, so I took whatever jobs I could find to pay the bills. It's not a glamorous life, but I still think something better is coming. Although, it's hard to think that way when you're in your fifties."

"I know what you mean," he said.

She scowled. "You just got done telling me you traveled all over the place, and you play golf for a living."

"Yeah." He took a longer sip of coffee this time, unwilling to counter her point.

"But it's not all it's cracked up to be. Is it?" she asked. "Everything always looks great to everyone else on the outside. But when you're on the inside, it's a very different reality."

Her words stabbed deep into his chest. She'd touched a pain he'd kept hidden from everyone—the media, his sparse collection of friends, and the rest of the people he knew on tour.

"I'm sorry," she offered. "I didn't mean to—"

"No. Don't apologize. It's okay. But you're right. More right than anyone I've ever spoken to."

She looked down at her watch. "My break is over in a few minutes, so I better get back there." It felt forced and unnatural, awkward to him. "It was nice chatting with you, though."

"Graham," he said, extending his hands. "Graham Sullivan."

"Nice to meet you, Graham. My name is Alicia. Maybe you should change things up and come in during the afternoon sometime." She collected her book and her cup and stood.

"Maybe I will." He smiled at her, hoping he didn't look like a moron.

"You do that. If you come in during my break, perhaps we can pick up our conversation again."

"I'd like that."

She turned and walked back to a door marked Employees Only in the corner that led back behind the counter. She disappeared through it, and Graham swiveled around to face the window.

His heart pounded in his chest, and his mind went wild with a million thoughts. Some of them were hopeful, daring him to dream of seeing her again and continuing their discussion. Other thoughts were less encouraging. Doubts swam to the surface like sharks looking for an easy meal. They smelled the blood of past failures, both personal and professional. They fed on his lack of self-confidence, and on every insecurity that disappointment had forged inside him.

He hadn't felt like this in more years than he remembered. It was like he was in high school again, his false sense of bravado completely destroyed by a beautiful creature.

Graham suddenly realized he didn't want to eat his breakfast here after all. It seemed strange to have his back to her, munching on a croissant while she toiled away behind the counter.

His self-consciousness took over, and he quickly folded the top of the bag back to its original form, grabbed it and his coffee, and made for the door. He only risked a quick glance back over his shoulder at Alicia as he reached the exit. She stood with her back to him, busy with something behind the counter. Whatever she was doing, he couldn't see due to the view being blocked by the espresso machine.

It didn't matter. He had to get out of there. He pressed on the rounded metal bar on the glass door and shoved it open, stepping back out into the warm South Carolina morning. He turned on the sidewalk and walked briskly back to his car.

What would have normally been a simple series of steps to return to his car felt long and drawn out, each movement dramatic as if drawing unwanted attention from the woman behind the counter. He was exposed out here trying to make a clean getaway.

He sat behind the wheel, placing his cup in a cup holder in the center console. Graham still held the bag in his lap as he stared through the windshield and into the coffee shop.

"What are you doing, man?" he muttered. He cursed himself for being such a basket case. "Real smooth, *Capitan*. Real smooth."

He shook his head, cursing himself for acting like such a fool. He saw her through the glare of the coffee house windows. She moved with the grace of a ballerina as she filled cups and stirred beverages. Maybe that was just his imagination glamorizing her.

Graham thought again on how many women he'd met in his life. Even his wife hadn't struck him the way Alicia did. Why, he didn't know. There was an energy about her that transcended her outer beauty. And it wasn't as if she was the most beautiful woman he'd ever seen. Hers was a simple, natural grace, an easy demeanor that magnetized the air around him and kept him stuck to his car seat in the parking lot, still holding the warm brown bag in his lap.

He shook himself out of it and pressed the ignition button. The engine growled to life, and he set the bag down on the black leather passenger seat.

With one last look and a long sigh, he shifted the car into reverse, checked the rearview mirrors, and backed out.

10

CHATTANOOGA

Tyler set his bag down outside the caddie shack, propping it up on a patch of grass in the shade next to the riverstone pathway leading to the front door.

"Incredible," Justin said, setting his bag down next to Tyler's. "I still can't believe you nearly tied the course record."

"Yeah. Pretty wild." Tyler's response was subdued, but that didn't keep his friend from going on about it.

"I mean, the caddie record was four under. You destroyed that."

Tyler chuckled. "I set that one."

"I know! You're going to kill it this weekend at the qualifier." Justin's expression turned to what looked to Tyler like concern. "Wait a second." He looked at Tyler with heightened intensity. "You're going to need a caddie in the open. Are you going to—"

"I think you're putting the cart before the horse a little, buddy. Let's just see how this weekend unfolds before we start worrying about things like that."

"Yeah, but let's just say hypothetically. If you were to win and make the open, would you get a pro caddie? Or would you take me?"

Tyler laughed, shaking his head at his friend as he lumbered toward the door. "You are so funny. Fine. Hypothetically, if I win the tournament this weekend and qualify for White Oak, you're going to be my caddie. There. Happy?"

Justin lingered behind for a few seconds, his head hanging low as he stared at the ground. The sudden realization hit him like a bag of bricks to the head.

"I'm going to need some new clothes."

"What?" Tyler asked, stopping at the door to turn around.

"Nothing."

Tyler scowled with suspicion, then opened the door and stepped inside. The television was on, and two of the other caddies sat on the leather couch, each munching on a bag of chips. One had a can of Coke on the end table, the other a Dr Pepper. Both turned around as Tyler and Justin entered the room.

The air conditioning doused the heat radiating from their skin, cooling the perspiration to the point it almost felt chilly.

"Hey, fellas," the guy on the left side of the couch said.

"What's up, Dawson?" Tyler answered, making his way over to the refrigerator while Justin closed the door.

"How'd you do in your prep round for the big qualifier?"

Dawson was a little shorter than Tyler and Justin, and a good fifteen pounds heavier. He got plenty of exercise from walking the course all the time with a pair of bags slung over his shoulders, but he also loved eating, as evidenced by the bag of chips in his hand and the empty one next to the can of Coke to his left.

"I did fine," Tyler answered, looking into the fridge to decide which beverage he was going to choose.

"Fine?" Justin blurted. "Fine? You nearly tied the course record."

"What?" the other guy on the right-hand side of the couch asked. "No way."

"It's true, Mitchell," Justin retorted. "And he dang near slammed home an eagle to do it on eighteen. Missed by six inches."

Mitchell shook his head in disbelief. The thick, wavy brown hair on his head shimmied with the movement. He had freckles on his slender face from all the time spent out in the sun. He was the youngest of the four of them, but had a natural disposition for skepticism.

"Come on. You expect us to believe that?"

"I believe it, Justin," Dawson said through a mouthful of chips. He picked up his cola and washed down the snack. "Didn't you have the caddie record anyway?"

"He beat it by three shots today," Justin reminded.

"That's amazing."

"There's no way he shot seven under," Mitchell continued, turning his attention back to the television. "I'll believe it when he does that this weekend."

Tyler and Mitchell had never gotten along. Mitchell came from a wealthy family. His parents were members here at the club, which was why the other caddies knew he was here "working" in the first place.

He'd complained about it a few times, referring to a conversation about his parents telling him he needed to learn some responsibility and start working. Mitchell's response was to question why he needed to start working when he had all the money he would ever need in his trust fund.

Tyler didn't judge kids with trust funds. He hoped someday he'd be able to build up one of those for his own children. Having one didn't make a person good or bad. It was how they acted with it. And in Mitchell's case, he acted like an ass.

"Maybe you should come out and watch, then," Tyler offered, never taking his eyes off the contents of the fridge.

"What?" Mitchell asked, tearing his eyes away from the television to look over at Tyler.

"I said maybe you should come out and watch this weekend."

Still, Tyler kept his eyes on the decision laid before him.

"Why would I waste my Sunday to come out and watch you choke in the biggest moment of your life?"

"Should I pick the red or the blue," Tyler mumbled, trying to decide which flavor of sports drink he'd choose.

"What was that?" Mitchell demanded.

"Sorry. I was trying to decide between red or blue. Think I'll go with red." Tyler reached into the fridge, pulled out a bottle, and closed the door. "Biggest moment of my life?" he asked, twisting the lid off the bottle as he turned toward his inquisitor.

Mitchell faced him, his body twisted, his arm draped over the back of the couch. Tyler could tell Justin wanted to say something, to stand up for his friend, as well as for all the other people out there who were born into blue-collar families. Tyler thought Justin simply hadn't yet figured out that wealth did not equal wisdom.

Tyler glanced at Justin just standing there stewing, trying to cook up something clever to say on Tyler's behalf, probably.

"Yeah. And you're going to choke."

"Right," Tyler said, raising the bottle to his lips. He took a couple of gulps while holding up his left index finger, signaling his counterpart to wait for a second while he drank. He let out a refreshed "ah" and screwed the bottle cap back on. "So thirsty. Warm one out there. So, yeah. You said something about me choking in the biggest moment of my life."

Mitchell nodded, a grim, stern expression on his face as though he were trying to intimidate Tyler.

"Well, first off, maybe you're right about half of it."

Mitchell's face twisted in confusion.

"The part about me choking," Tyler clarified. "There are going to be some good golfers out there this weekend. Top one percent of players from this region. So yeah. It is highly unlikely I'll win, much less be able to go out there and perform like I did today."

Justin stared at Tyler with what looked like more befuddlement on his face than Mitchell's.

"But," Tyler continued, "it isn't the biggest moment of my life. Not by a long shot."

Mitchell blew air through his lips. "Like you ever had something bigger than this happen in your life."

"Oh, I wasn't referring to the past. I was talking about the future. I know that even if I don't win this weekend, something bigger is waiting for me. Maybe I'll fail in that moment too. But I'm going to do the best I can."

"Good luck with that" was all Mitchell could say. He turned back around to watch the television. It was a tournament going on in Dubai, and one of Justin's favorite players was teeing off.

"Who's winning?" Justin asked.

"Your guy, Williamson," Dawson answered.

"Nice." Justin looked over at Tyler, who was watching the television.

It was as if the engagement with Mitchell had never even happened. And now Tyler was watching the pros swing again, studying their every move, every detail that he could sear into his muscle memory to use later.

"Tyler," Dawson said, "dude, you should be celebrating or something. What are you doing?"

Tyler grinned, casting a momentary glance across the room. "What I always do. I watch the pros. It helps me sort of meld what they do with my own game."

"He absorbs what he sees them do," Justin said. "At least, that's what he told me." He turned his attention to Tyler. "I just hope you saved some for the big tournament."

Tyler didn't respond, but he had a feeling he knew what Justin was thinking. They'd talked about it before—more Justin than Tyler —about what getting into a professional tournament could do for their lives.

Justin verbally expressed his pipe dreams on more than one occasion. And he was right. Getting into one of the majors could change their life trajectory. But that was the wrong thing to focus on.

Tyler knew the only way to win was to concentrate on each stroke, one at a time.

The rest, he hoped, would take care of itself.

11

CHARLESTON

Graham pulled into a parking spot at the club and shifted the gear into park. He knew Brandon, the kid working the bag drop-off, would be walking down the parking lot soon to offer to take his bag to a cart.

Still, Graham lingered there in his vehicle with the engine running.

He couldn't shake the encounter with Alicia earlier that morning. And he had no idea why.

It was as if she put some kind of spell on him—unconsciously— while reading a novel in a coffee shop, minding her own business.

Graham popped open the trunk, killed the engine, and got out of his car. No sense in sitting around dwelling on it. He'd probably never see her again.

He walked around to the back of his car and removed his golf shoes. Brandon, as predicted, was walking toward him.

"Good morning, Mr. Sullivan," Brandon said, tipping his white cap as he approached.

"Morning, Brandon."

"You want me to take your bag to a cart?"

"No, I'm just hitting the range today."

"I can take it to a spot on the range if you like."

"No, thank you, Brandon. I'll carry it. Besides, I see Mrs. Chamberlain is pulling up. She'll be glad to have your help."

Betty Chamberlain was known around the club for flirting with the boys who worked there. It didn't matter to her that she was in her seventies and they in their late teens or early twenties. Her husband had died five years ago. Now, she was living her life like she didn't care what people thought.

Brandon turned around and saw the woman's silver Mercedes G Wagon driving down the street toward the club.

"Better hurry," Graham teased.

Brandon nodded. "Hit 'em good, Mr. S."

"I'll try, Brandon."

The young man trotted back up the parking lot to the umbrella-covered podium at the bag drop. Graham grinned and shook his head as he sat down on the edge of the trunk and slipped out of his street shoes and into his golf cleats.

When he was done, he stood, lifted his bag out of the cargo area, and closed the lid. Slipping the two straps of his carry bag over his shoulders, he took off toward the range beyond the near corner of the clubhouse.

It was after lunch, and from the looks of it, the outdoor bar area had cleared out before he arrived. A few of the guys hitting the turn sat at a table, eating turkey sandwiches and munching on potato chips.

They waved to Graham as he marched by.

For the most part, the members here didn't bother him too much. They were friendly in a cordial, social convention kind of way. But Graham knew they also felt a little trepidation in approaching the old pro. They weren't ignoring him. They just treated him like any other member around here, and he appreciated that.

Every now and then, a guest would be on site for a round and want to get a picture or an autograph. Graham was never bothered by it and always spent a few minutes asking the guest about themselves. It made people feel good when someone they deemed famous asked personal questions. Graham didn't think of himself as anything special. He was just another person, and on the golf course everyone was there for the same reason—escape from reality.

Graham passed the end of the clubhouse and crossed the cart path leading down to the pro shop located downstairs from the outdoor bar.

He passed a section of dogwoods planted near the chipping green and kept walking up over a little rise and then down the other side, where the driving range opened up. The tee box stretched eighty yards from left to right. The range itself opened wider, cutting a huge swath amid the forest on either side.

Four men and two women occupied six of the stalls. Graham kept walking, greeting the players with a kind smile and polite hello, or "How are you?"

He kept going until he reached the end of the strip then set his bag down against the metal stand. He removed his golf glove out of the lowest pouch and fit it onto his left hand. Then he pinched a few tees from the same pouch and stuffed one under the rim of his cap just behind his right ear. He'd never seen anyone keep tees there, but for him it was just natural.

He tipped over the full bucket of balls sitting to the right of the tee box, dragged one away from the pile, and nudged it onto a clean patch of grass. Graham stepped back and looked out across the range, taking in the setting around him.

The sounds of clubs smacking into golf balls mingled with the serenity of the forest, of birds chirping, a babbling creek that ran along the right-hand side behind a tall net, and the rustle of the wind through the forest canopy.

Graham closed his eyes and took in the sounds. They were one of his only semblances of peace he found in this world. The sight and sounds of the ocean were another. The third was in the woods. He'd grown up camping with his friends in high school. Their parents went often and always invited him to come along since Graham's parents weren't into that sort of thing, particularly his mother.

He learned to love nature because of those camping trips, and he viewed golf courses as an extension of nature.

He'd heard various comedians talk about what a waste of land it was to be used for a ridiculous game, but what they didn't mention was how golf courses served as a sort of protected area for wildlife. Out here, animals could roam free—and that included the occasional alligator in the water hazards.

If there was one species he could leave off that protected list, it was those frightening reptiles. He'd never had a close encounter with one, but they were always present in the low country courses such as this.

Graham inhaled the warm air. It smelled of cut grass with a pinch of salt from the ocean a few miles away. Soon, it would take on a different scent, one that hinted at autumn begrudgingly giving way to winter—not that it got super cold down here. It was one of the reasons he'd chosen the area to call home.

He exhaled, clearing his thoughts, and opened his eyes. It was a routine he'd adopted long ago when he was in college. Just taking a few seconds to clear all the junk out of his mind and focus on a few simple, good things around him seemed to make his body relax.

Graham stepped up to the ball, spread out his feet, and whipped the wedge around a few times to loosen his wrist and get a feel for the weight of the club. He'd done it a million times in his life with the sport. But every day was different, every outing to the range or in a round presented new and often unexpected challenges.

It was why his father once told him that was why it was the perfect game, because it could never be mastered no matter how good you got. Graham had laughed at the comment, and in his youthful arrogance hadn't understood its meaning.

It was one of the standout conversations he'd had with his father during his youth, probably because not long after, his father had passed away.

Graham didn't beat himself up for lost time, or for things he wished he'd said. His father had spent most of his time in the corporate world, eventually working himself into an early grave. The doctors had tried to tell him to lower his stress levels, but Bill Sullivan wouldn't hear of it. He'd worked hard to get where he was in life, and he wasn't about to slow down due to a little stress.

He always claimed that the anxiety helped propel him every day, that it energized him to do what needed to be done with his company.

The one positive Graham took from his father's death was that it taught him not to live life that way. He refused to let stress get to him. In fact, it was one of the reasons he'd gone all in on golf. There was something about swinging a club and striking the ball that, even when done incorrectly, still felt good.

He addressed the ball, positioning the wedge behind, and then took a swing.

The clubface clipped through the ball with a clean click, launching the ball high into the air toward the target—a small green 125 yards away. Graham watched as the ball reached the peak of its flight, then dropped down onto the green, rolling to a stop about five feet from the pin.

He smiled, satisfied with the first shot of the day.

Graham always began with the smaller clubs first then worked his way up to the driver. No one had ever told him to do it that way. He just figured it made sense to warm up with the lighter, shorter irons.

He dragged another ball over to a nice patch of thick Bermuda and looked out at the range again. Thoughts of Alicia seeped into his mind.

"Nope," he said, turning away the distraction. "Not right now, brain. Focus. Big tournament coming up in a few weeks."

He shook his head and stepped up to the ball again. He swung again, but this time the ball carried just to the right of the green and dribbled off over the side.

Graham sighed. "Come on, Graham. Focus."

He pulled another ball out of the pile and locked all of his attention on it. But something in his gut kept gnawing at him. It was a little voice that usually warned him about trouble, a sort of fight-or-flight instinct that occasionally made him tense up and worry.

Now, though, it was telling him something else—something he'd never heard from that voice before.

"Ask her out, moron," it said.

He shrugged off the thought and dragged another ball back into position. This time, he looked sideways into the field and maintained focus on the pin. Then he looked back down at the ball, addressed it, and swung.

The ball rocketed off the clubface, but it pulled hard to the left, landing on the opposite side of the green from the one before.

He glanced down at the scuff in the grass as if that was the culprit for the inaccurate shot, shook his head, and walked back to his bag. He slammed the wedge down into its slot, and pulled the Velcro patch on his glove.

He stuffed the glove back into the pouch, along with the tee in his hat, and zipped it shut.

Under normal circumstances, Graham would stay out here for an hour or so just honing different shots, but today was different for some reason. And the only thing he could pinpoint was the brunette who kept sauntering into his mind's eye.

It was no use. He couldn't pull his thoughts away from her.

"She was just being nice to you, Graham," he muttered, trying to convince himself there was nothing to it. "She's nice to all the customers."

He couldn't understand how a woman he'd never met had exacted such control over his thoughts and feelings after one chance meeting.

He had to know more.

Maybe he'd start drinking more afternoon coffee.

12

CHATTANOOGA

Tyler parked the car outside his apartment building and let out a long sigh.

He was glad there'd been no classes in the morning, thanks to the school being out for an extended weekend. He wondered what his round might have looked like had it begun around noon when he finished sessions for the morning at the university.

That thought loomed in his mind, carrying him into the future, to a far-off dream he shouldn't have dared to even wish to be true.

Final round pairings started in the afternoons, when all the other golfers had swept the dew from the fairways.

"Don't even think about that," Tyler muttered to himself. But he couldn't help it. His imagination whisked him away to the final round of the White Oak National Open Championship. He saw himself in the final round, walking up the fairway to the 18th green with a chance to win the tournament and become the first amateur to clinch a major championship since 1933. On top of that, an amateur had never won at White Oak. Being the first to accomplish that feat would not only be a massive accomplishment but would change Tyler's life, and his mother's, forever.

He shook his head and refocused on the upcoming weekend. That was where his mind needed to be. Actually, it should have been on finishing his assignments for the next day's classes, but he'd done most of the work ahead of time and only had a few things left to button down before he turned it in.

His mind kept tugging him back to the upcoming tournament at Green Mont, his chance to change his stars and get an opportunity to play with the biggest golfers on the planet. From there, he'd have to be on the radar of sponsors, if he wasn't already.

He'd played for his university golf team for about a year, before he'd had to quit and work at Green Mont to help his mom with bills.

"Stop it," he said. "You're going to drive yourself crazy thinking like that. You're a college student. Focus on what's in front of you, Tyler."

He closed his eyes and turned his attention back to the things he could control—schoolwork, every swing, and his job as a caddie.

No matter how hard he tried, the qualifier the upcoming weekend kept popping back into his thoughts.

For most of his classmates, the weekend was a time to blow off steam at big parties. He'd never been much into the party scene. He'd gone to some, both in high school and now while attending college, but getting plastered wasn't his thing.

Plenty of friends and even random strangers always offered him booze at the shindigs, but he preferred to keep his wits about him and also not test the limits of driving after having indulged.

The main reason he'd remained sober was that he wanted to keep as many brain cells as possible because golf required extraordinary focus. If he maintained a sharp mind, the body would respond, and so would the scorecard.

Tyler turned the key in the ignition. The engine died, and he sat there for another few seconds, thinking about what the weekend might hold.

In a few short days, he'd be playing in the biggest tournament of his life for a chance to play with the best in the world at the White Oak National Open Championship.

He'd seen the list of players who were in the qualifier earlier that week. He didn't know many of them, save for another local named Parker Rathman.

Parker was a pro at another club in town and had plowed his way through the qualifying rounds to reach the last one. If Vegas ever set odds for the open qualifiers, Tyler figured Rathman would be a heavy favorite.

Tyler had never seen the guy play, but he'd won a few city tournaments and had done well in the member-guest tournament at Green Mont on numerous occasions. That didn't matter. None of the other players mattered. Tyler knew that.

There was only one thing he had to worry about—himself. Golf was sold as a game played by a field of players, all pitted against each other. But the reality was that it was a game of one—a single golfer against themselves, and the course.

He opened the car door and stepped outside. Dark gray clouds churned in the darkening sky to the west.

"That's not a good omen," Tyler mused. Then he chuckled to himself and closed the car door, opened the back, and took out his school backpack.

Compared to the bags he carried at his job as a caddie, this bag felt like it was full of feathers.

He slung it over one shoulder the way the cool kids did in the 1990s, closed the back door, and started toward the stairs.

The apartment complex seemed unusually quiet, though it was nearly 7:30. He supposed most of the tenants had been home for a few hours and either already gone out to eat and returned or were still at some of the local restaurants.

His phone buzzed in his pocket, and he fished it out, expecting to see a text message from his mother. Something along the lines of "When will you be home? Supper is ready."

Instead, he was pleasantly surprised to see the message was from Lucy.

"Hey, you," it read. "How'd your practice go today?"

He smiled, and if someone had seen him standing there with that stupid grin illuminated by the light of his phone's screen, he might have felt like an idiot. Or maybe he wouldn't have cared.

He quickly tapped out a response on the little keyboard and hit the Send button.

"It went well," he answered. "I missed tying the course record by one stroke."

Tyler stood there for a moment, waiting for her to reply, and then decided to keep moving.

He walked up to the stairs, and just as he started his ascent, the phone vibrated in his hand.

"That's incredible," she said. "But I'm not surprised. I know you're great. I just hope you know how great you are."

He felt his cheeks burn at the kind words. No one had ever spoken to him like that before. Then again, he'd never spent as much time with a girl as he had with Lucy, and even then, he thought they were just friends.

Now, they were way beyond the boundaries of the friend zone.

He kept thinking that things were moving so fast now that it had gone from them just hanging out and having fun together to suddenly making out on a blanket under the stars in the middle of a fairway.

But the truth was it had been a couple of years coming, and nothing had changed until Lucy had been brave enough to confess how she truly felt.

The relief he experienced after that admission was immense. He'd been keeping the same feelings pent up inside since the first week they met. But now, it was all out on the fairway, so to speak.

Tyler's only concern was that he didn't want things to change between them, how they treated each other, and the fun times they shared.

"You're amazing. I hope you know that," he replied quickly. Then added, "How was your day."

He climbed the stairs, imagining her smiling as she read the message.

He turned at the landing and continued toward his apartment, his thoughts a muddy mixture of what his mother had prepared for dinner and where his girlfriend was right now, what she was up to, even what she was wearing.

The thoughts of her returned the scent of her perfume to his memory, taunting him, making him wish she was next to him right now.

Tyler reached the apartment door, fiddled with the keys, then finally got it inserted into the keyhole and unlocked it.

He pushed the door open, lumbering into the room as he dragged his bag behind him. Right away, he noticed the stark absence of the smell of food cooking in the kitchen. Usually, when he got home around this time, his mother had been preparing something for the two of them to eat for dinner.

His eyes darted to the kitchen, which he found empty. No pots sat on the stovetop, and nothing warmed in the microwave, or in the oven.

He looked over into the living room next, but she wasn't there either.

Tyler closed the door behind him and locked the deadbolt, set his golf bag off to the side next to the television entertainment center, and hung his keys on the hook by the doorframe.

"Mom?" he called out. "You home?"

He'd seen her car out in the parking lot in the usual spot, so he knew she had to be here.

At first, he thought maybe she was in the bathroom taking a shower after a long day at work. But he didn't hear the shower running. He passed his bathroom on the right and then at the intersection at the end of the hall, turned left toward his mother's bedroom.

He saw the door was halfway open. A dim light shone through the doorway, indicating one of the nightstand lamps must be on.

Tyler thought maybe she was lying in bed, reading while listening to music. Or just the latter.

He stepped inside and found his mother lying on her back, head propped up on a pillow. Her face was pale and moist, her hair matted with sweat.

"Mom? Are you okay?" He rushed over to her side and bent down, placing the back of his hand against her forehead.

She smiled up at him weakly. "I'm okay, just a little tired."

"Tired? Your head feels like it's on fire. You have a fever."

"It's nothing. Just a cold. You know, whatever is going around right now."

Tyler frowned at her downplaying the condition. "Mom, there isn't anything going around right now. No one is sick."

She laughed feebly. "Something is always going around, Ty."

"I'm going to get you a cold washcloth."

"Don't worry about me, honey. I'm good."

He shook his head, ignoring the order, and rushed into the master bathroom. He found a washcloth at the top of a stack on a shelf and turned on the faucet. He soaked the rag in the cold water for a few seconds, squeezed it out, and then returned to her side.

Tyler folded the washcloth in half and laid it on her forehead. "There," he said. "That feel better?"

She nodded. "Yes, but please, don't worry about me. I'm fine."

"Did you take something for the fever?"

"Not yet. I just got home a little while ago from work."

He sighed, frustrated by her stubbornness. His phone buzzed in his pocket, but he didn't feel like responding to Lucy at the moment. He had more pressing issues.

"I'll get you the ibuprofen," he said.

Tyler disappeared back into the bathroom and opened the top drawer under the sink where his mother kept most of her meds. He rifled through a few prescription bottles, then found the one he was looking for, twisted the cap, and dropped three gel caps into his palm before replacing the lid.

He set the bottle down on the counter and returned to the bedside. "Here," he said, holding out his hand with the pills. "You'll need to sit up."

She grinned at him and shook her head. "I know what to do,

honey. I'm the mom. Remember? I've taken care of you plenty of times when you were sick."

"And now it's time for me to return the favor."

She shimmied up a little on the pillows stacked behind her head. Tyler picked up a bottle of water she'd left sitting on the nearest nightstand and removed the cap then handed her the bottle.

"Thanks, Ty. You're a good kid." She popped the first pill into her mouth, chased it with a gulp of water, and then repeated the process until she'd swallowed all three gel caps.

"You're working too hard, Mom," he said, looking down at her with pity in his eyes. "You need to rest."

She chuffed at the statement. "I'm fine. I'll feel better in a few hours, and I'll be as good as new tomorrow."

"I know you think you have to work all the time to pay the bills, but you don't. I'm making good money this season at the club, and I want to help out more."

"No," she snapped. "That money is for your future. You already help out more than you need to as it is."

He recalled the wad of cash he'd given her the other day after getting way more in tips than he planned.

"Whatever. You need to take it easy. I don't want you going to work tomorrow. Okay? If I have to call your boss, then so be it."

"Tyler, honey, I'm fine."

"You look like the guy in Monty Python in the scene where the dude is shouting for people to bring out their dead."

She arched an eyebrow. "Thanks a lot."

"I'm just saying, I can tell you're feeling worse than you're letting on. I'm going to go make some soup for you. And you're going to call in sick tomorrow. Understand?"

Molly stared up at him with a mixture of indignation and admiration in her eyes. "Okay, Tyler. I'll call in sick tomorrow. But you don't have to make me anything to—"

"Chicken noodle or minestrone?" he asked, cutting her off. "I've seen both in the pantry."

She rolled her eyes at his intrepid, stubborn demeanor. "Chicken noodle. Please. Thanks, sweetie."

"You're welcome. You just take it easy. Drink plenty of that water."

"I'm the parent here, remember?"

He ignored the statement as he walked back out into the hallway and toward the kitchen.

He'd never seen his mother look so wretched before. She was always a rock, an impenetrable fortress of immunity that never allowed a virus or infection into her system.

Tyler had heard that when people with strong immune systems got sick, it often looked far worse than normal folks simply because it never happened.

He found a pot down in the cupboard below the coffee machine and set it on the stove top. Then he took a can of chicken noodle soup out of the pantry, checked the date on it, and then peeled back the lid before dumping the contents into the pot.

Then he switched on the stove, set it to a low-medium heat, and stepped back.

Finally, he took a few deep breaths to recenter himself. He'd gone from worrying about a stupid golf tournament to finding his mother looking like she was on death's door.

He doubted that was the case, that she had anything so serious it could kill her, but she certainly looked the part, and deep down it scared him.

Tyler's phone buzzed again in his pocket, and he remembered he'd been in the middle of a chat with Lucy.

He took the device out and saw he had two messages—one from Lucy, and one from Justin.

He tapped the one from her first and read it.

"I knew you weren't like the other guys. You make me feel good. I can't wait to see you again. Maybe tomorrow night?"

The feeling in his chest wanted to say yes, but his mind was stuck on his sick mother in the master bedroom.

"Maybe," he replied. "We'll see." He sent the message and immediately wished he could have had a better response.

Accepting it was done, he moved on to the text from Justin.

"Great round today, bro. You're going to light it up at the qualifier this weekend. And just think, in a couple of weeks, we're going to be hobnobbing with the best players in the world."

Tyler grinned at the statement. "I hope you're right," he texted back and hit the arrow button.

He returned to the text from Lucy and noticed she hadn't responded. It had only been a minute, so she probably hadn't seen it yet, but insecurities tugged on his mind, riddling it with guilt about not having given a deeper explanation.

Then again, he didn't want to worry her either. His mom probably just had a cold, like she'd said. In a day or so, she would be back to her usual self.

The pan on the stove began to sizzle, and he quickly stepped over to it, took a spoon out of a nearby drawer, and stirred the soup. He turned the heat down and continued stirring for another minute.

Then he picked up his phone again, and started typing another message to Lucy. "Sorry. I just got home. But yeah, text me tomorrow. I always like hanging out with you." He hit Send again, and set the device down on the counter.

Tyler was only mildly satisfied with his messages to her, and with every second that passed, he wondered if he was sounding too casual, or not casual enough.

He shook his head to clear the insecure doubts from his brain and raised the spoon to his lips.

The meat-and-noodle infused liquid steamed and filled his nostrils with the salty scent of herbs and broth. He blew on the soup to cool it, then took a sip.

It was already hot. "That didn't take long," he realized.

Then he retrieved a bowl from the cupboard, filled it halfway with the soup, and set the spoon in the hot liquid to return to the bedroom.

He carried the bowl back down the hall, then turned into his mother's room expecting to find her sitting up on the pillows.

"Soup's ready, Mom," he announced. He bit his tongue when he saw her turned over on her side, eyes closed, breathing in a steady rhythm.

She'd fallen asleep.

He sighed and walked over to the nightstand, set the bowl down, and picked up the damp washcloth that had fallen off her head and onto the pillow.

Tyler looked down at her with genuine sympathy. He hated that she worked so much, hated that she never got to do anything fun in life or have anything nice.

He saw the women at the club, what they wore, what they bought. He heard them talking about their extravagant vacations to exotic places, or about the brand-new luxury cars they just bought—often replacements for models they'd just received a year or so prior.

It wasn't that he loathed them for having money, or for how they spent it. He just wished he could give that life to his mother.

If anyone deserved it, it was Molly.

She worked tirelessly, and never complained, always had something good for him to eat on the table when he got home from his long days, and wore a perpetually comforting grin that told him everything was going to be okay, even on days when he felt discouraged about his life's trajectory.

He bent down and turned off the lamp, casting the room into darkness, then picked up the hot bowl of soup. After one last look at her, he turned and left the room, closing the door behind him.

Deep within him, something stirred. It was an emotion that called to him, more than ever.

He needed to play the round of his life this weekend.

13

Tyler barely slept that night.

He dozed off multiple times throughout the course of the evening and early morning hours, but something would wake him up, and then the thoughts returned.

At first, it was worry about his mother. She'd looked rough the night before, and he wanted to make sure she was okay. Those paranoid musings led to other things—visions of him screwing up in the big tournament this weekend, or finding out that Lucy wasn't all that interested in him after all.

He tossed and turned, his will working overtime to try to purge all the negative premonitions. But every time he roused from his sleep, they returned.

Normally, he slept well at night. Attending classes in the day and working a loop at the course in the afternoon was enough to exhaust even the most energetic of people.

Around three o'clock, he got out of bed and tiptoed down the hall to his mother's bedroom and cracked the door open. He peered inside and found her still sleeping, with her head turned the other way.

He noticed the steady rhythm of her breath, and relief settled over him. Tyler considered going in and checking her temperature but decided against it. She obviously needed to rest, and interrupting that might cause more harm than good.

He just hoped that she was going to take the next day off from work. Other than weekends, his mother hadn't taken a day off in months. Maybe longer.

Tyler ended up going back to bed without a more thorough check on his mom, and spent the rest of the night in a state of half sleep.

He finally rolled over at seven, checked his watch on the nightstand, and dragged himself out of bed to get ready for class.

The first thing he noticed was the usual grayish light of day seeping through the curtains of his bedroom window, partially illuminating his darkened room. Then he detected the smell of coffee, which was typical on days when his mother went to work, but today she should have still been in bed.

He pulled on a pair of shorts and shuffled over to the door. He nearly bumped into the dresser to his left, but luckily avoided it and the painful stubbed toe that could have resulted.

Out in the hallway, he found the lights from the kitchen radiating into the corridor. Opposite his bedroom, his mother's door was open.

He shook his head, ventured over, and peeked in to have a look. As he suspected, the bed was empty.

"Mom?" he said, thinking maybe she was in the bathroom. But the door to the bathroom was open, and the lights within were off.

He turned around and made his way down the hall and into the living room and kitchen. The place was empty.

Tyler sighed, exasperated. "I told you not to go to work today," he mumbled, spotting the coffee pot still on in the corner. The pot was half-full of dark brown brew, just as it always was. His mother made sure to make enough for the both of them, knowing he typically woke up about thirty minutes after she left for the day.

He noticed something on the counter next to the machine. He walked over to the counter and found a note written in black ink from his mom.

"Hey Ty. Thanks for taking care of me last night. I feel much better today, so I'm going to work. Please don't worry about me. I'm fine. Just a little headache is all, but nothing concerning. I'll see you home later for dinner. Have a great day. Love, Mom."

He shook his head and set the note back down on the counter. Even if she was feeling better, he wished she'd have taken the day off to rest and recover. Whatever had ailed her the night before wasn't good. That much he knew. She looked like a ghost, and with the fever, he figured she'd caught some kind of virus.

She was a grown woman, though, and stubborn to a fault. He couldn't make her do anything she didn't want to do.

Resigned to defeat, he took a mug out of the cupboard and filled it with coffee to allow it to cool while he put on his regular clothes.

Class started in an hour, and he needed to go over his notes for a test they were supposed to take.

He wasn't worried about the exam. He'd prepared for it on top of all the other things going on in his life. But test taking was easy. He never stressed out about it like so many of his classmates in college, or even high school. Today's test was going to be multiple choice with an essay component, both of which fit right in his wheelhouse.

With his coffee poured, Tyler returned to his room to get dressed.

He slipped on a pair of jeans and put on his deodorant and replaced the T-shirt he'd worn to bed with a fresh one. After getting into his shoes and socks, he returned to the kitchen to retrieve his precious cup of joe before sitting down for one last pass through the content for the test.

As he sipped the hot drink, sitting at the kitchen counter, he struggled to maintain focus. Thoughts of the upcoming tournament loomed in his mind, wrestling with other thoughts of Lucy, what she was doing right now, and when he could hang out with her again. They were in the same class this morning, so he knew he'd see her then, but he also knew their interaction would be quick since they both had other classes to get to after the test.

Not getting a good night's sleep didn't help with his unexpected lack of focus. Normally, he woke up energized, ready to take on the day. He didn't like this new thing. He felt groggy, as if his mind were in a thick, Southern fog.

He sipped the coffee greedily, and when the mug was two-thirds empty, he returned to the machine for a refill. Maybe it was a good thing his mother had gotten up to make the coffee after all.

Tyler finished covering the few gaps he thought he might have in his studies, packed up his things, and left the apartment.

The hilly back roads to the university offered sweeping views of densely forested ridges on either side and rolling fields in the valley through which the road dipped and weaved.

He'd been driving these roads since getting his driver's license. It never got old, no matter how monotonous the rest of his daily routine was.

The quiet road also offered him a chance to collect his thoughts for the day, to focus on the tasks he needed to complete, and to do a little visualization for the upcoming tournament.

Today, however, seeing the future he wanted, the round he wished to play, was more difficult. Fatigue marred his effort, and concern for his mother kept pushing its way back into his mind. Then there was Lucy. He wanted to play it cool but not freeze her out.

Tyler shook off the fog of worry. It would be nice to not have to worry about classes or work ever again.

He wanted his job to be on the pro tour, as one of the top golfers in the world. He knew the odds of that happening were low for anyone who dared to dream of it, but that didn't stop him from hoping.

Now, he had more than hope. He had one round to prove himself worthy to play with the best in the world. One shot at glory. Once he was in the open, anything could happen.

Fifteen minutes after leaving his house, he pulled into the parking lot outside the liberal arts building and killed the engine. He noticed Lucy's car a few spots down and smiled.

She was already here, twenty minutes early.

He peered into her vehicle's tinted windows but didn't see her silhouette inside. He figured she'd gone into the building, probably to go over a few last-minute details about United States history she might have skipped during her preparation.

He grabbed his book bag and made his way down the sidewalk to the brick building. It was three stories tall, with darkly tinted windows to protect its south face from the morning and early afternoon sun that beamed down from the sky over the hills to the east.

He climbed a set of stairs to the entrance and walked inside, immediately spotting Lucy on one of the cushioned gray sofas to the left, where a few other students pored over books.

She looked up at him and smiled happily, then stood and set her books down in her seat.

He grinned back at her as she hurried over to him, threw her arms around him, and planted a kiss on his lips. Then she pulled away a few inches and looked up into his eyes.

"Good morning," she said.

"That's definitely a good way to start the morning I could get used to."

Her teeth shone as her smile widened. "Are you okay? Our conversation ended a little abruptly last night."

He nodded. "Yeah. I'm good. My mom wasn't feeling well, so I was trying to take care of her."

"Oh, I'm so sorry. Is she okay?"

"Yeah. I think so. I told her not to go to work, but she did anyway. Left me a note saying she was fine."

She lowered her arms and motioned to the sofa. "I saved you a spot. Are you ready for the test?"

He nodded. "As ready as I can be," he answered.

Lucy's smile dimmed. "You look tired, Ty. Are you okay?"

"Yeah. I'm good. Just didn't sleep great. No big deal." He decided to turn the questions to her. "You ready for the test? Anything you're worried about?"

She shook her head as she led him over to her spot on the couch. "No, I don't think so. I'm not sure about the essay part. You know how Dr. Burns is with those."

Professor Burns had a laundry list of eccentricities, most notably his unusual practice of walking up the steps on the sides of the class-room as he lectured. Multiple times, he'd turned and started shuffling through full rows of students only to stop in the center in front of an empty seat, and continue his speech.

His essay procedure was just as unique. The students were required to study for three essays, but would only have to write about two of them, depending on a flip of the coin he performed dramatically before the exam.

"He's an interesting guy, I'll say that," Tyler said.

She sat down and cleared space for him. He joined her on the firm cushion and set his bag down.

"I don't know how you can think about school with the big quali-fier coming up this weekend," Lucy said. "I know I wouldn't be able to think about US history, or any other college class for that matter."

"Yeah. I mean, it's hard not to think about it."

"I'd say that's an understatement. You feel good about it, though, right?" She looked over at him with her kind, dark eyes. They comforted him in a way he hadn't even considered possible before. He'd always thought her beautiful, but now that sentiment was deeper; it had more meaning.

"The test? Yeah, I'm ready."

She frowned. "No, silly. I mean the—"

"I'm kidding," he laughed. "Yes, I'm good with the tournament too."

"I'd hope so. You nearly broke the course record at Green Mont yesterday."

He shrugged off the accomplishment. "Tied," he corrected. "Nearly tied it."

"Still. That's insane." She paused, mindlessly flipping pages of her book with her thumb. "It's cool if I come watch, Sunday, right?"

He nodded. "Of course. If you want, I mean. I don't expect you to do that just because—"

"Because I'm your girlfriend?"

One of the other students in a chair nearby looked up from his cramming session, then quickly returned his eyes to the pages in his lap.

Tyler smiled. "I didn't want to impose, or whatever. But that's what you want?"

"To be your girlfriend?"

"Yeah. I mean, for us to be a thing."

"Isn't it what you want?" A fleeting look of concern flashed across her face.

He melted it with an easy smile. "Definitely. And yes, I would love for you to be there Sunday. I'll need all the help I can get."

"Not sure how much help I'll be, but I'll always be there for you, Ty. Now," she said, turning the pages of her book more deliberately, "tell me about the presidency of James K. Polk."

14

CHARLESTON

Graham sat in his car, gripping the steering wheel as if it were the only thing separating him from a thousand-foot drop to his death.

He stared through the windshield at the coffee shop as the wipers swiped back and forth, throwing sheets of rain off to the left. Dark clouds churned in the sky overhead, as if Mother Nature herself was trying to stand in his way.

Graham hadn't come to the coffee shop this morning, which wasn't out of the norm. Even though the workers there considered him a regular, he didn't visit the place every day when he was in town.

This morning, he'd taken his coffee at home, sipping it in the breakfast nook overlooking the green in front of his home. He'd watched a few of the dew sweepers come through shortly after the sun cracked through the cloudy sky to the east.

He imagined those guys never got to finish their round. It had been raining like this for the last four hours.

He also knew he wasn't going to get in any practice unless he went to one of those golf simulators.

Graham loathed those things. The technology had come a long way in the last several years, getting more accurate with their estimations of distance and trajectory, but it still felt unnatural to him, like vaping or paying taxes.

He preferred to skip the morning session and relax. None of it mattered anyway. If he spent every waking hour of the day working on his game, or watching reruns of his favorite eighties movies, the results were still going to be the same. Maybe he'd make the cut at White Oak; maybe he wouldn't. He'd stopped caring.

That was a stance he wished he'd taken much earlier in life. Perhaps it might have changed some things for the better. Or things could have been far worse. Graham didn't know that, but he did know that he was starting to care a lot less about the little things, the everyday stress, the emotional bric-a-brac of life.

Not caring also meant he didn't lament about the past. He didn't blame himself for his ex-wife leaving him, or for the tragic death of his son, no matter how much the dark figure of guilt tried to wedge its way into his mind.

He'd been a good father, as good as he could have been while on the road most weekends of the year. And he was always a loyal husband.

Graham shook his head. He'd been down this path of thinking more times than he cared to recall. Regret wasn't his friend. It did no good to allow it to tempt him.

And right now, those needling thoughts were taking his mind away from the moment. So much for caring less.

He peered through the glass, but it was difficult to see into the coffee shop with the pouring rain outside.

He'd just have to go in and see if she was there.

Alicia had mentioned she usually worked in the afternoons, though he'd failed to ask what time her shift typically began.

"Well, old man, you're just going to have to walk in there and find out," he said to himself. "And if she isn't there, you just order a coffee, and be on your way."

Of course, the plan either way was to order a coffee. He couldn't just walk into his usual coffeehouse, look around, and then leave. People would think he'd lost his mind.

He took a deep breath, turned off the car, and climbed out. He pulled the rain jacket hood up over his head as he slammed the door shut and hurried to the awning over the building's entrance.

In the four seconds it took him to get out of his car and under shelter, his pants got soaked from the knees down to his shoes.

At least he'd worn weatherproof shoes today. One of the things Graham hated the most in life was having wet socks, and he'd endured that plenty in his younger years on the golf course.

He shook off some of the water from his jacket and opened the door to the coffee shop. As always, the smell of fresh coffee smacked into him and warmed his soul.

He stepped inside and pulled back the hood to his jacket, quickly surveying the interior. Fewer people were there than in the mornings when he typically visited, but that was to be expected. This time of day, people were more apt to start drinking other types of beverages with less caffeine in them, save for the addicts who seemed shackled to a coffee mug no matter the hour.

The sound of the rain pattering against the tin awning and matching roof echoed in his ears like a million ticking clocks, as if telling him time was running out, to hurry up and make his move.

Graham realized he was loitering at the entrance when a young woman in a lavender raincoat turned sideways to get around him and stepped to the door. She held a drink carrier loaded with four to-go cups in one hand.

He moved aside and held the door for her as she passed, then after two more lengthy seconds of hesitation, took a step away from the entrance and paused next to a long shelf. Varieties of neatly packed bags of coffee lined the lower three shelves. The upper three contained T-shirts, hats, and coffee mugs that showed off the shop's branding.

Graham peered behind the counter and immediately saw her.

Alicia was working close to the pickup end of the bar. There was no line at the counter, and only a half-dozen customers sitting around at the tables behind laptops, perusing their phones, or reading books.

Graham suddenly felt a wave of pressure crash into him. He'd played in international pro tournaments most of his adult life, with huge cash prizes on the line, as well as his legacy as a golfer. Millions of people around the world watched him play, on top of the tens of thousands in attendance at the events. He'd done countless television interviews and press conferences, appearances on shows, and even released a series of tutorial videos on a smooth golf swing.

None of those things made him feel as nervous as he felt at this moment.

Despite his epic failures when it came to winning a major tournament, he still felt at home on a golf course and with a club in his hand. It was a safe space where nothing could touch him.

Here, he was out of his element.

He'd been seeing a psychiatrist for years, ever since his wife left him.

Graham didn't think he was crazy or that he had some kind of repressed childhood memories, but thought it was the prudent thing to do. He'd heard of other athletes using sports psychiatrists, and while he wasn't sure that would help him with his game, something deep inside him told him it was a healthy process, especially after the death of his son.

Standing here now, staring at the barista he'd come to talk to, he questioned that assessment of his sanity. A crazy person would stand here and stare at her like a creep.

Go order a coffee, moron, the little voice in his head commanded.

As if on their own accord, his legs started moving, carrying him to the register. He stopped at the counter and smiled awkwardly at the young woman waiting to take his order.

"Hey, what would you like today?"

"Um," he fumbled for the words. "I'll take a small black coffee, please." He reached into his pocket and pulled out his money clip, removed the credit card he always used, and prepared to pay.

His eyes wandered to Alicia behind the espresso machine to his left. She moved gracefully as she cleaned the machine and its various parts.

"Okay, one black coffee," the girl at the register said. "Anything else?"

"No, thank you," he said, shaking his head.

She gave him the total and asked for his name.

"Graham," he said, and held out the card, ready to tap it on the reader. Once the screen changed and displayed the amount owed, he tapped it.

The word *Approved* showed up on the screen, and the girl smiled up at him. "You're all set. You can pick up your order at the end of the counter."

He took a deep breath, replaced the card in his money clip, and thanked her.

Graham felt like his feet were stuck in concrete boots. His muscles were unresponsive, as if his entire body had locked up and refused to move. His palms sweat, and he felt his heart racing.

Just move, man.

Somehow, he managed to take a step to the left, then another. Finally, he reached the pickup area and waited, watching Alicia as she turned, picked up a cup from a stack near a double coffee machine, and pressed down a lever to extrude the dark liquid into the cup.

She filled it to the top, capped it with a plastic lid, and then slid a sleeve around the container before spinning around to face him.

Their eyes met, and for a second, a blank expression covered her face.

She doesn't remember me, he thought. Disappointment rippled through him, sucking the air out of his lungs.

Then, suddenly, her face lit up as she remembered him. "Hey, stranger." Her tone sounded genuinely glad to see him.

"Hey back," he replied, smiling sheepishly.

"Black coffee for Graham." She set the cup down on the counter. Instead of turning around and going back to her tasks from before, as was the norm, she lingered there, planting her hands on the hips of her black pants.

"Thanks." He felt like a moron. Here he was, with the woman

he'd come here to see standing right in front of him, and he couldn't think of a thing to say.

He always had a plan. It was part of his process whenever he played golf. Every shot had a clear intention, and he had backup plans in case things didn't go the way he thought they would.

Here, he'd just walked into the shop without having a clue what to say to her. Instead of being precise, meticulous, he'd just burst into the coffee shop expecting her to be enamored with him.

Maybe not that far, but those were the exaggerated thoughts burning in his brain.

"How you doing?" she asked, as if tugging him into a conversation with a rope.

He nodded as he pulled the coffee toward him. "I'm good. How are you?"

"Can't complain. Just working my usual shift." Her expression changed to one of suspicion. Her eyelids narrowed, and she cocked her head to the side in an accusatory manner. "I think this is the first time I've seen you in here during the afternoon. Decided to change things up?"

He choked on her question and nearly knocked over the coffee. *Get it together, man. You're a world-class golfer. You deal with more pressure than this week in and week out.*

"Yeah," he managed. His voice nearly cracked. "I just thought I could use a little afternoon pick-me-up."

"The post-lunch coma is real," she said.

"Oh, I haven't eaten lunch yet." He realized he was actually starting to feel a little hungry. "Actually." He paused, uncertain how to continue.

Her eyebrows lifted as she waited in anticipation for what he might say next.

"I... um." He couldn't do it. It was too difficult. Graham didn't know why he was feeling so cowardly, so weak. Sure, it had been a long time since he'd asked a woman out, but this was ridiculous.

You're losing her, man.

"I was wondering," he said, "if you would, um—"

"Sure." She smiled at him.

"What?" Confusion smacked him in the face.

Alicia leaned her head forward, giving him a look as though it should be obvious. "You were going to ask me out, right? Because if not, now I'm going to feel like an idiot."

"No," he said quickly. Too quickly.

"You weren't going to ask me out? Okay then." She started to turn away. "I guess I will definitely need to find another place to work."

"Yes. I mean no. Don't do that." He found himself tangled in a word pretzel and couldn't seem to get out. "Sorry. What I meant was, yes, I was going to ask you out. And no, please don't find another place to work. I really like the coffee here, and if you go work somewhere else, I may not like theirs as much."

She grinned. Her eyes squinted with the smile, lighting up her face.

"Well, we can't have that, can we?"

He shook his head. "No. I... don't like change much."

"And yet here you are, standing in a coffee shop in the middle of the afternoon, asking out a woman you just met."

The realization dropped onto him like a yoke over his shoulders. He had just done that, and survived to tell the tale. Not only that; she said yes. His brain quickly formed the next words.

"So, dinner? I know it's cliché, but food is good, and good conversation with it is even better." He surprised himself. That actually sounded pretty good.

"When?"

Another customer entered the building and walked over to the register. She'd have to work on their order soon, so time was against him once more.

"When do you get off?" Graham couldn't believe he was being so bold.

She arched her right eyebrow. "Six. But if you're wanting to do tonight, I'll need to go home and change clothes."

"Sorry. Is tonight too soon? I... I'm not very good at this."

Her smile disarmed him. "You're doing great, actually. You got the yes out of the girl. That's the hardest part, isn't it? Let's do tonight at seven." She turned and stepped over to the register, found a pen and paper, and wrote something on it. Then she returned to the pickup area, and handed him the paper. "That's my cell. Text me, and I'll send you my address."

He bit his lower lip. "Okay. I will." Graham smiled back at her. "Thanks for the coffee," he said. "And for saying yes."

"You're welcome. And thanks for asking. I'll see you tonight."

Graham nodded, and she turned away to get back to work. He spun around and walked toward the door, clutching his coffee in one hand, and the more valuable prize in the other. He stuffed the phone number into his front-left pocket to keep it from getting wet in the deluge outside.

He couldn't stop smiling as he pushed through the door and back out into the rain. Graham didn't care how wet he got now. He felt like he could part the clouds in the sky overhead.

Good job, Graham, he thought. *Now, where am I going to take her?*

15

CHATTANOOGA

Tyler knew there was going to be trouble the second he saw Mitchell's smug face. It would have been harsh to call Mitchell his nemesis—accurate, but harsh.

Ever since the moment Tyler introduced himself to the other caddie, Mitchell hadn't tried to hide how he felt about the guy from the wrong side of the tracks. He'd gone out of his way to make Tyler feel that he didn't belong in this world, that he was, and always would be, an outsider.

Mitchell stood to the right of the door going into the caddie shack. Two other guys were positioned opposite him, leaning up against the wall, fiddling with their phones.

Tyler didn't recognize them but assumed they were friends of Mitchell, probably there to see if they could score a caddie position for the remainder of the year. Judging by their colorful polos and shorts, and expensive shoes, Tyler figured they came from money—just like Mitchell. They looked about the same age as Mitchell, who was a few years younger than Tyler, but both guys were strong, bearing the look of a couple of high school varsity football players.

"What's up, Mitchell?" Tyler said, lacing his voice with the friendliest tone he could muster. It was a feeble attempt to hide his suspicion. The fact that none of the three guys were sitting in the rocking chairs in the shade, instead opting to stand up, suggested they were up to something.

"What's it to you, Knox?" Mitchell said with a tone of utter contempt. Even the way he used his words were an attempt to make Tyler feel beneath him.

Tyler rolled his shoulders. He wasn't going to let Mitchell get to him today. He'd just aced a test, by his account anyway, had a good day of classes, got to see his new girlfriend—that still sounded new and amazing—and now it was a beautiful day out to walk a loop on the course.

"Where's Justin?" Tyler asked, trying to diffuse whatever Mitchell was playing at.

"He's on a couple of bags. Mr. Jenkins sent him out with Thomason and Smith earlier."

"Oh."

It wasn't unusual for Justin to start the workday ahead of Tyler, especially on Tuesdays and Thursdays, when Tyler had classes until 1:30 in the afternoon.

"Yeah. You and your boyfriend got split up today. You think you're going to be okay to do a loop by yourself?" He looked over at the other two stooges, who both cackled as if on command. It was easy to see who was pulling the strings with these two yes-men.

Tyler rolled his eyes as he approached the door. He stopped and looked over at Mitchell. "I think I'll manage," he answered, not falling into the trap Mitchell so clumsily laid.

Mitchell leaned close, near enough for Tyler to smell the pungent body spray he'd used way too liberally, and seemingly over his entire body. "Don't hurt yourself out there. Would be a shame if you couldn't compete in the tournament this weekend."

Something in his tone carried more than just a benign curse. Tyler wasn't sure what it could be, but he wasn't going to stay out here and tempt fate. He needed to get changed into his coveralls, check the roster, and get ready for his loop.

"Thanks" was all he said in response and opened the door to the caddie shack and stepped inside.

The door closed behind him, and the air-conditioned room cooled down his temper. *What is with that guy?*

Tyler took another step deeper into the common room, moving toward the hall in the back that led to the locker room. He scanned the area, noting it was empty, and continued ahead, down the short corridor and through the door in the rear.

He let the glossy, stained door close behind him and stepped into the caddie locker room. There was a bathroom with multiple toilets, as well as three shower stalls through a door to the left. To the right, two rows of lockers and benches with dark brown leather cushions occupied the space.

Tyler walked over to the second row, then to his locker in the back corner. He opened it, then pulled out one of two pairs of coveralls he kept hanging in there. It smelled fresh and clean, just as it always did.

The club maintenance manager always did a great job with their uniforms. It had to be a thankless job, but Tyler made sure to tell him thanks whenever they bumped into each other.

Tyler didn't like the idea of someone doing his laundry, so he thought of it more like a football or baseball manager that washed the team clothes. Considering it that way didn't make it seem so weird.

He slid his feet through the legs and was about to pull the top up over his shoulders when he heard the door to the locker room open with a slow, eerie creak. He stuffed his hands through the short sleeves and shrugged himself into the rest of the coveralls, turning to the sneakers he kept in the locker.

Out of the corner of his eye, Tyler caught a slight movement accompanied by the sound of fabric swishing.

He twisted his head and looked to the end of the row. Mitchell stood between him and the exit, along with his two cronies behind either shoulder. They all wore menacing expressions on their faces, firing silent threats Tyler's way.

"What do you want now, Mitchell?" Tyler propped up his right foot on the bench and started unlacing his shoe.

"What I want, Knox, is for you to go back to whatever hole you crawled out of."

Tyler frowned. He usually had good control of his emotions. He wasn't quick to anger, unlike his friend Justin, who was a real hothead. Keeping his wits about him was one of the reasons Tyler was such a good golfer. When he made mistakes, they didn't linger long in his mind to spark future ones. That was how players went on tilt. One error led to another, until their entire rounds were completely destroyed.

He'd watched his hero, Graham Sullivan, do that multiple times, though it was unclear if it was Sully's emotions or just bad luck that caused his catastrophic chokes.

"Sorry, Mitchell. I can't do that right now. I have to get to work." He took off his shoe and tossed it into the locker, removing the sneaker in its place. He slipped his foot into it and began tying the laces.

"You don't get it," Mitchell snarled. "You don't belong here, trailer-park boy. You're not one of us. And you'll never be one of us." He took a threatening step forward.

Tyler finished tying the laces and removed the other shoe, half-tempted to fling it at Mitchell's face. Instead, he put on the other sneaker and tied it, doing his best to defuse the situation by ignoring the threat.

Tyler knew how to fight. But he preferred not to resort to violence, and had only been in a few actual fist exchanges back when he was in high school. One of those times had been with a friend, after which they immediately laughed about their bruises and black eyes.

That was a different situation, a moment when tempers flared between friends. It was what guys did now and then. They needed to blow off steam or work out some aggression. More often than not, there was a handshake and a bygones left to float away.

Tyler could take down Mitchell if he had to. He doubted his spoiled counterpart had ever been in a fight before, or would even know what he was doing if he had been. Hence the two henchmen he brought along today.

It was clear now that this had been an ambush the entire time, a coordinated attack by Mitchell.

Tyler had never done anything to piss him off, other than being a better caddie, and a better golfer. He figured that last part was what had set Mitchell off. The silver-spoon kid had never encountered someone like Tyler before, a guy who grew up poor, playing with an old set of clubs, dominating the game.

Nearly setting the course record earlier that week must have been the spark that lit Mitchell's fuse.

Tyler turned to face him, finding that the three guys were standing shoulder to shoulder, effectively blocking off any escape Tyler might have attempted.

"What is this, Mitchell? Some kind of a threat?" Tyler closed his locker and started toward the door, disregarding the human blockade.

He tried to slip between Mitchell and the guy on the left, but neither budged, and Mitchell raised his right hand and shoved Tyler backward.

Mitchell wasn't strong enough to move him much, but it was the intent behind the assault that told Tyler all he needed to know.

"Seriously, Mitchell. Enough screwing around. I need to get out there and hit my loop. I don't want to keep the players waiting. You know how Mr. Rawlings gets when we're late."

The caddie master was a stickler for being on time, and for good reason. Golf course tee times weren't just a suggestion at Green Mont. They were law.

"Oh, I'm counting on you being late for your loop today," Mitchell said, taking a step toward Tyler. He balled his right fist as he approached.

"Mitchell, come on, man. What did I do to piss you off so bad that you want to fight me here in the locker room? You realize we could both get fired, right?"

Mitchell shook his head. "Oh, they won't fire me. My dad's a member here. Stern talking to? Maybe. But I'll be fine. You, on the other hand? Is your dad a member here?"

Tyler felt his fingers tightening into a fist almost unconsciously.

"That's right," Mitchell continued. "Your dad is dead. And your mom is probably working under a bridge somewhere right now."

Tyler's self-control disintegrated in that moment. The insult about his father and the utter disrespect of his mom, the woman who birthed him, who worked so hard every day so he could have a chance at a better life, a woman who had never done anything dishonorable, was too much for Tyler to contain.

His eyes narrowed as the rage coursed through his veins. He no longer felt concerned about losing his job as a caddie, or the larger implications for his life. It was time to put Mitchell in his place.

16

Even with the fury of hell raging inside Tyler, he wasn't going to throw the first punch, no matter how much he wanted to. He still had that much self-control.

If this was going to go down, he'd at least have the excuse of self-defense.

"Come on, Trailer Park," Mitchell goaded. "What are you waiting for?"

"I don't want to do this, Mitchell."

"I bet you don't. I've been waiting to kick your ass for a while now."

"Waiting to grow a few more inches?"

Tyler knew the second he flung the insult, it would send Mitchell over the top. He was a good five inches shorter than Tyler, so the reach factor in a fist fight would be a huge advantage for Tyler. But Mitchell had numbers on his side, and Tyler wasn't sure he could take all three of them on.

"You think you're funny?" Mitchell snarled. "Let's see how funny you are with a broken nose."

He lunged ahead, rearing his right fist back in a clumsy, uncoordinated way. If he had plastered the attack on every billboard in the county, he couldn't have telegraphed the punch more.

Mitchell fired his fist toward Tyler, who took one step back, planted his foot, and drove his own fist forward.

Mitchell's arm overextended, his elbow straightening to its max, eliminating what little power might have been behind the attack.

Tyler, on the other hand, had plenty of force behind him. He swiped his left hand to the side, knocking away Mitchell's impotent attempt, and plowed his knuckles into Mitchell's jaw just as he turned his face to avoid the punch.

Tyler's fist snapped a few inches behind the target, rocking Mitchell's head back and to the side.

The assailant's momentum hadn't helped him, only making the blow that much worse. His legs gave out underneath him, and he crumpled to the floor. He clawed at the carpet to try to retreat, but his movements were clumsy, uncoordinated. Tyler knew he'd nearly knocked him out in one shot, but the fight was far from over.

"Get him," Mitchell blurted through a bloody lip.

The other two guys stepped forward at the same time, both wearing vengeful expressions on their faces, their eyes narrow, their skin red with anger.

The one on the left was closest to Tyler, so he made that guy the first target. This one was skinnier than the other, and taking him down would even the numbers, even if the third guy had more bulk.

He waited until the last possible moment, then quickly jumped up to the right, planted a foot on the bench, then used it as a vault to leap over to the row of lockers to the left. The back-and-forth movement confused the attacker for a second, and he halted his advance, adjusting his position with both fists raised.

Tyler's left foot pushed against the lockers, and he jumped forward, driving his heel into the guy's nose before he could coordinate a defense.

Tyler heard and felt a satisfying crunch.

His momentum drove the attacker back and down to the floor, where he ended up landing on top of the guy.

Tyler raised his right fist like a hammer and was about to bring it down in a flurry of painful shots, but the third goon grabbed his wrist and pulled him off his prey.

An instant later, Tyler felt a thick arm wrap up and under his left armpit in a full Nelson. Tyler tried to wriggle free, but the guy's other arm looped around his neck and squeezed.

Mitchell stood up, looking dazed from the punch he'd absorbed, but now with more menace in his eyes. The other guy who took the shoe to the face struggled to his feet, his face and colorful shirt a bloody mess from nostrils that oozed red.

"You're going to pay for that, Trailer Park," Mitchell sneered.

Tyler tried to wriggle free from his captor's grasp, but it was no use.

Mitchell rushed forward, and drove a fist into Tyler's abdomen.

The blow sucked the air out of his lungs, and his body instinctively attempted to double over. But the guy holding him from behind wouldn't allow it.

Mitchell swung again, this time striking Tyler across the jaw.

Tyler's vision blurred. Though Mitchell clearly didn't know how to fight, even a novice like him could do significant damage with a contained target.

Mitchell delivered another shot, this time to Tyler's left eye as he desperately turned his head to avoid a direct blow.

His head snapped back, bumping into the face of the guy holding him.

That gave Tyler an idea.

He lowered his head while Mitchell prepared to deliver a knockout punch. Then Tyler whipped his head back as hard as he could and felt his skull make solid contact with something soft behind him.

The arms around him loosened just enough for Tyler to wriggle free and duck beneath the punch. Mitchell couldn't stop now, and his fist met his friend's chest just below the neck.

Tyler grunted, and drove his shoulder forward, hitting Mitchell in the midsection like a pro linebacker.

Mitchell let out an "Oof!" as Tyler kept churning his legs until the two of them hit the floor, Mitchell's back taking the brunt of it.

Tyler raised his right fist, ready to mete out more punishment, when the door burst open.

"What's going on in here?" a familiar voice shouted.

Tyler stood up just as the caddie master, Mr. Rawlings, stepped around the row of lockers.

Rawlings surveyed the area twice, trying to come to grips with what was happening in his locker room.

The man was in his mid-sixties, with gray hair combed over to one side, and piercing blue eyes framed by wrinkles etched by his decades on the fairway. He'd been at this club since before the boys were even born.

"Tyler? What is the meaning of this?"

Mitchell clambered to his feet and pointed an accusatory finger. "He attacked me, Mr. Rawlings. I always knew he didn't fit in here. He's nothing but a trailer park thug."

Tyler labored to catch his breath. His abdomen still hurt from the first blow, not to mention the stinging radiating from his left eye, or the throbbing in his jaw.

"So, you're telling me that Tyler here tried to jump all three of you guys?" Rawlings asked, clearly not buying the story. His eyes fell on the other two. "And who are you two? Are you members here?"

"No, they're guests of mine," Mitchell explained.

The other two guys said nothing.

"You two, get out of my caddie shack. Caddies only in here."

He jerked his thumb toward the door. "And don't let me see you back here at this club again. You hear?"

The two looked at each other, as if questioning whether the old guy was serious.

"I said get out!" Rawlings shouted.

Mitchell's friends reluctantly left the room, the stockier one making sure he delivered one last shoulder barge to Tyler as he passed.

"That's enough," Rawlings warned, stepping closer to the guy to usher him out of the room.

Once they were through the door, the caddie master turned his attention back to Mitchell and Tyler.

"Now, I don't know what is going on here, but this is unacceptable. You two are both employees of the club here. My caddies are all on the same team."

"Mr. Rawlings," Mitchell started, but the old man wasn't having any of it.

"Shut up, Mitchell."

Rawlings put his hands on his hips. He visibly worked through what he needed to do with this situation. It was clear he'd get no truthful answers from Mitchell, and Tyler wasn't saying much.

"Are you going to tell me what happened, Tyler?"

"Why are you—" Mitchell cut in.

"Boy, I am warning you. One more peep, and I'm calling your father."

The threat seemed to silence Tyler's nemesis, but for how long was unclear.

Tyler finally caught his breath, though the anger burning inside him only dimmed to smoldering embers.

"Mitchell," Rawlings said, "go wait in the common room."

"But—"

"Boy, you better go now, or you are really going to regret it."

Mitchell looked back over his shoulder at Tyler, glowering at his rival. It was a scathing glance that seemed to say *This isn't over.*

He slunk out through the door, and when it closed, Rawlings turned and faced Tyler again.

"You gonna tell me what happened, son? This isn't like you, Tyler."

"I think it's pretty clear what happened, Mr. Rawlings," Tyler said. "Obviously, I decided to pick a fight with Mitchell and his two buddies here in the locker room." He looked around the area as if sizing up the tactical advantage of being cornered by three other guys.

Rawlings let a laugh escape his lips but immediately returned his face to a stern, irritated expression.

"You definitely got wit, kid. And from the looks of it, you can handle yourself in a fight. Although you're going to need to put some ice on that eye, or it'll swell shut."

Tyler shook off the suggestion. "I'll be all right, Mr. Rawlings. I need to get to my loop."

Rawlings' head turned back and forth. "First off, you're in no condition to do that. You got blood on your uniform."

"My spare is clean, sir. It'll just take a second to change."

The caddie master held up his hand. "I'm not sending you out with a couple of our members when you have a black eye and a bloody lip. And what is wrong with your hand?" He indicated Tyler's right hand.

He'd been clenching and releasing it and every time with the same result—a dull, aching pain shot through his hand and up his forearm.

"It's nothing. Seriously, Mr. Rawlings. I need to work. I'm trying to help my mom with the bills and—"

"Tyler, I understand that. But if I send a caddie out there who looks like he just went four rounds with Mike Tyson, people are going to ask questions, questions neither of us want to answer."

Tyler hung his head. He knew at the bare minimum he'd make close to two hundred for carrying a couple of bags today. Now, it was like watching that money go up in smoke right before his eyes. The visual sucked the air out of his chest.

"Mr. Rawlings," he pleaded. "I really need that money."

"Tyler, I understand that. I do." His easy, Southern accent was sincere. "But I'm in a pickle here. There is no way I can send you out today."

Tyler's temporary fears swelled into a more foreboding one. *What if I lose my job? I can't make this kind of money working somewhere else.* He'd considered going into the food service industry, waiting tables as his side job. While the money doing that work could be good, especially on the weekends, he'd never get a chance to play this course again, and on top of that he'd have to work during times he would normally be playing golf.

Rawlings looked down at the floor and shook his head. "Not to mention what Mitchell's dad will say."

Mitchell's dad wasn't just a member of the club. He was a local businessman, and influential not only with the golf community but also with several city and state politicians.

"You know I wouldn't start a fight with anyone, Mr. Rawlings. Especially not here. This place is like a church to me."

"I know, Tyler. I know." The man sighed. "I guess we'll see what the fallout is from this, if any. You can bet Mitchell's father is going to have questions, though, when he sees the beating you put on his son. Then again, he might want to keep things quiet. It wouldn't do for people to know you took on Mitchell and two of his buddies and came out looking better than the three of them."

Tyler cracked a smile, but his body hurt. He kept clinching and unflinching his fist, grimacing each time. On top of that, the soreness in his gut seemed to worsen with each breath.

"Look, Tyler, go home. Get some rest. And put some ice on that eye. Or a frozen steak. You need to keep the swelling down. And I would get that hand looked at if I were you. You're going to need it in the tournament this weekend."

Tyler didn't need the caddie master to tell him that. It was the first thought that had zipped through his brain the second the pain started. He had no idea how it happened—if it was from throwing punches or if he'd landed on it funny when he hit the ground. Either way, the last thing he needed was a hand injury just a few days before the biggest tournament of his life.

"You're sure you can't let me go out there today?" Tyler deflected. "I could really use the—"

"You know I can't, Tyler. I'm sorry. But I'll let you pick up a couple of extra loops next week if that will help you and your mom out."

"It would. I'll skip class one day next week. I'm ahead on my assignments anyway."

The older man chuckled. "I don't know if I like the idea of you skipping classes to come out here, but I like your initiative. You're a good kid, Tyler. I know you didn't start that fight with those three knuckleheads." Rawlings glanced back at the door, then again at Tyler. "You ever seen those boys out here before?"

"No," Tyler shook his head.

"Yeah," Rawlings grumbled. "They said their parents aren't members. Mitchell must have brought them in. I knew that boy was no good from the moment they told me I had to hire him. Useless, if you ask me. He's not a good caddie. Slacks on all the other duties he has around here. Honestly, I don't know if he's good for anything."

Tyler tilted his head to the side and offered a wry, bloody-lipped grin. "Well, he's good for one thing."

Rawlings inclined his head a little. "Oh? What's that?"

"He makes for a pretty good punching bag."

The caddie master laughed. "Yeah, I guess it looks like he does."

17

CHARLESTON

Graham flattened the blazer as he stared at the man in the mirror. He looked good for his age. At least that's what he told himself. The skin on his face wasn't as tight as it had been thirty years before, and deep wrinkles curled out from the corners of his eyes from the years of sunlight he'd squinted against while hiking the fairways around the globe. His dark tan bore several freckles, each one a visa stamp from his uncountable rounds.

The navy-blue blazer contrasted with the white button-up shirt underneath, offset with tanned trousers. He mused that he would have fit in on a cruise ship in this outfit, working as the director of entertainment.

He liked the clothes, though. They made him look like he cared about his appearance, but just casual enough to not care too much.

He took a deep breath and looked down at the phone on the sink to his left and the piece of paper Alicia had given him with her phone number on it. There was no backing out now. He was supposed to pick her up in forty-five minutes.

Graham had texted her earlier to get her address so he could plan on a good time to leave. He didn't want to show up late for a first date. That wouldn't exactly make a great impression.

She'd sent him the address, which the map app on his phone estimated to be twenty minutes from his home. He had plenty of time but still felt the urge to leave and get there a little earlier than necessary.

Graham resisted that temptation. Showing up too early would make him look desperate. At least he thought it would. *Maybe I'm overthinking it.*

No, I'm definitely overthinking it.

It was his first date in a long time. How could he not overthink it?

Over the years since the divorce, he'd grappled with loneliness now and then but always managed to push himself deeper into the game, allowing it to absorb his entire being.

His psychiatrist hadn't entirely approved of that practice. While the doctor had encouraged him to continue working on his game, continuing to strive to be the best he could be in his profession, stuffing emotions away deep down inside was never a healthy way to handle them.

Graham blew it off for the most part. "I'm fine," he said every time the shrink recommended digging deeper into his past. But he was never sure about that.

Being alone all the time had taken its toll on him in ways he was only now beginning to realize. At first, after Linda had left, he was okay with it. Initially, he'd wanted to keep the house because of the memories it held with his son—the holidays of his childhood, seeing him grow up, all the firsts in his life. But those walls and floors and ceilings held just as much pain as they did joy, and when the hurt overtook the good times, Graham had to make the difficult decision to sell the place. It was that or drive himself crazy.

He'd moved to this neighborhood before the house sold. It was newer, and on one of the better golf courses in the region. There were other pros who lived there too, one of them just a few doors down. But they rarely bumped into each other here. Most of the interaction he had with those guys was at tournaments.

Graham lifted the phone and checked the time again. Only a couple of minutes had passed.

He didn't normally feel the urge to drink, but right now that bottle of bourbon sitting on his kitchen counter downstairs was calling his name.

His nerves were out of control and his stomach turned over, twisting itself into knots that would have impressed a sailboat captain.

He stuffed the phone into his pocket, switched off the lights to the vanity, and walked out of the room.

Graham made his way down the spiral staircase, his right hand sliding along the black iron rail.

At the bottom, he turned and walked into the living room, sat down on the big leather sofa, and turned on the television above the mantel. One of the golf channels came on. They were covering one of the women's tournaments in California.

He leaned back and tried to relax, watching the golfers swing and putt, largely ignoring the broadcasters' commentary. He usually tried to keep them out of his mind in case they somehow started talking about him.

Graham learned a long time ago to quiet that kind of noise. Letting those things in your head was never good. It caused people to lose focus in a game that required absolute control of emotions.

He'd largely remained off social media for that very reason, not that he had any desire to be on those outlets anyway. To him, those apps felt disingenuous, full of people posting images of themselves or their lives to make them appear like they were doing something cool or important. Others used social media as a way to be heard in a world full of billions of other people doing the same thing. Desperate to feel like they mattered—or that someone should care what they ate for breakfast, what they were wearing, or what errands they were running that day—those poor souls probably never realized they were grasping at straws that would snap the second they tried to bear the weight of their needs.

Social media, to Graham, was also a place full of negative energy. He refused to look at what people must have said after his epic tournament collapses, or even the comments referring to his recent retirement announcement.

He could imagine for himself what some haters probably posted. "Who cares?" Or "He hasn't been relevant in a decade anyway." That kind of stuff likely blew through the transom of what passed for the internet these days like an arctic wind, cold and unfeeling.

On the television, a blonde woman from Sweden hit an approach shot from 160 yards out. The camera zoomed in on the ball as it traveled through the air. Graham had always wondered how those cameramen did that. It was hard enough to track a golf ball with the human eye, especially on days where the glare from the sun was low in the sky. These people were able to pick out the ball in flight with a heavy piece of machinery. He wondered if they'd make good caddies.

He watched as the shot fell to the green, struck the surface, and then rolled to the left toward the hole.

Graham leaned forward, a string of hope pulling him toward the television. The ball stopped a foot away from the pin.

"An incredible shot," the announcer said, though Graham could barely hear it with the volume so low. The woman high-fived her caddie as both smiled.

Graham hadn't spoken to his caddie since the day of his announcement, but Eddie had taken it well. The two had been together for most of Graham's career, and the caddie had become one of Graham's few confidants.

They shared in the same misery and disappointment from all of Graham's close calls in the major tournaments and also in the wins. On top of that, Eddie had made a great living on Graham's bag. Tour caddies made 10 percent of their golfer's winnings from each tournament, but Graham always made sure to give his friend a little extra.

One of the more fun "tips" Graham surprised Eddie with was a new Cadillac Escalade. He could still remember the look on his caddie's face when he opened his eyes and saw the blacked-out ride with a big red bow on top.

"A caddie for my caddie," Graham had said when Eddie had

refused to believe it was his. "And you can fit several bags in the back of that thing."

The memory creased Graham's lips as he sat there watching the television. Eddie would be okay. He was a few years younger than Graham and would easily pick up work from another golfer if he wanted. Eddie had the magic eye, and everyone on the tour knew it. It had been Graham who'd failed to keep up his end.

Graham checked his phone again and noted the time. He'd killed ten minutes without realizing it, putting him closer to his departure than he'd anticipated.

He stood up, turned off the television, and walked over to the garage door where his keys hung from a hook. He tapped the phone, found the thread with Alicia, then typed out a quick message.

"Heading your way in a second," it said. Then he sent it, stuffed the phone in his pocket, and grabbed his keys.

He stood there for a moment, hesitating to leave the safe confines of his home. Here, he wouldn't experience rejection or disappointment. It was a comfortable place, his fortress of solitude.

But solitude hadn't done anything for him over the last ten years. Being alone here when all the cameras were off him, and all the media attention was turned elsewhere, he had nothing else to do but think about all the pain from the past.

On the outside, at media days, in interviews on television or with papers, he played it cool, acting like nothing from the past bothered him or caused him concern about his legacy.

Deep down, he did believe that too many people worried about that word—*legacy*. What did it mean anyway? Was anyone going to look him up on the internet two hundred years from now to learn about his life or career? He doubted it. And even if they did, what did that matter? He'd be dead!

Legacy was something that he always downplayed in every interview he'd ever done. But something still needled at him, pricking his skin like an annoying mosquito looking for a free meal.

His failures in the past were more personal to him than what the annals of golf might portray about his career. Just once, Graham wanted to know what it felt like to accomplish something truly magnificent. It wasn't for the glory or the attention. Heaven knew he didn't care for that. He'd spent most of his life trying to stay away from the limelight, avoiding situations where all eyes were focused on him, praising him for whatever remarkable feats he'd performed.

Now, thinking about that consciously, something stirred inside him. His next appointment with his psychiatrist was tomorrow morning. And now he had something specific he wanted to ask about.

That would have to wait, though. For the time being, he had something more important to attend to, a date with a barista he wasn't about to miss.

18

CHATTANOOGA

Tyler inserted the key into the door of his apartment, saying one last quick prayer that his mother was in the shower so he could go straight to his room, avoiding the line of questions that would ensue once she caught sight of him.

He hadn't seen her car in the parking lot, so it was possible she was out—maybe getting groceries. Then again, he was home earlier than usual, and it was possible she had worked a little later on her shift.

He'd left the golf course and stopped at a fast-food joint to get a bite to eat, even though he knew his mother would probably plan on making dinner like she did so many nights. But this afternoon, Tyler wanted a little comfort while he licked his wounds. And few things, at least that he could afford, fit that bill like a cheeseburger and fries.

If his mom asked what he wanted for dinner, he'd have to come clean about the fast food, but she'd understand the second she looked at his face.

Tyler turned the key, but even that effort sent a surge of pain through his hand and wrist. He winced, and a splinter of anxiety knifed through his chest.

"Come on. Not this week. Any week but this week."

He'd already noticed the pain when he opened his car door, and when he turned the key in the ignition.

Tyler switched to his left hand and twisted the key easily in the lock, then pushed the door open.

He poked his head through the opening and looked inside. The kitchen lights were off. That was a good sign. Maybe his mom wasn't home yet after all.

He stepped in and shut the door behind him, slumped his bag down onto the floor by the doorframe, and hung his keys on the hook.

"Tyler?"

The sound of his mother's voice sent a chill of worry through his body. "Yeah, Mom. It's me."

"You're home early," she said from somewhere in her bedroom.

"Yeah."

He ambled over to the kitchen and opened the fridge. There wasn't much in there; a few sports drinks, some leftovers, deli turkey for sandwiches, and condiments in the door racks. He took out one of the sports drinks and twisted the lid off, took a swig, and let out a satisfied sigh.

"I thought you were working at the course today," his mother said, appearing around the corner behind the sink's backsplash.

She wore a T-shirt and some pajama pants, comfortable clothes she couldn't wait to get into after a long day of working in the fulfillment center.

She looked tired, with dark circles under her eyes, and Tyler wasn't entirely sure she was over whatever illness she'd had before. Her skin was still pale, though it had more color to it than the previous night. Then again, that might have been due to her wearing makeup at the moment.

"What happened to your face?" she blurted, a look of motherly concern spraying across her.

Tyler tried to shrug it off as he closed the door to the fridge. "I... um, got in a fight?"

"A fight? With who?"

She walked around the counter and flipped on the kitchen light. She stopped next to him and looked up at his black eye, the swollen and cut lip, and a bruise on his cheek.

"One of the other caddies."

"Another caddie? How did this happen?"

"I don't know. I don't really want to talk about it."

He tried to slide past her, but she blocked his path. "Where do you think you're going?"

"To my room. I just want to lie down."

"You need to put some ice on that black eye."

"You sound like Mr. Rawlings," he huffed.

"Your boss knew about it?" Tyler saw his mom's concern grow, her eyes drawing down from their corners.

"He came in and stopped it."

She took a breath and shook her head, then stepped around him and pulled open the freezer drawer of the fridge. She reached into the bottom and pulled out a frozen bag of corn and handed it to him.

"Here. Put this on your eye. It will keep the swelling down. Now, come in here, and tell me what happened. Are you hurt anywhere else?"

He didn't want to mention anything about his hand, so he diverted to the other pain points. "Just what you see, for the most part. Pretty sure I'm going to have a bad bruise on my abs too."

She lifted his shirt and looked.

"Jeez, Mom. Come on. I'm not a baby."

His mother assessed the area in question within seconds. A dark bruise had formed just under his ribs. The mark was roughly the size of a fist.

"You definitely have a contusion there." She sighed. "Come in here. Sit down. Tell me what happened."

"Seriously, Mom. I don't want to talk about it."

He lowered his shirt and slipped past her, trying to make his escape.

"Tyler Logan Knox. Go in there, and sit down on the couch."

He stopped in his tracks with his back still to her. His shoulders slumped. Tyler knew, as did all children no matter how old, when a parent used their full name, they meant business.

"Fine." He surrendered and shuffled into the living room, where he plopped down on the sofa.

She took a seat and faced him, crossing one leg over the other. "So, what happened?"

"This kid Mitchell who works there," he began, "he and a couple of his buddies jumped me in the locker room. There isn't much to tell, honestly."

"They ganged up on you? Three of them?"

He nodded and pressed the bag of frozen corn against his face. He winced at the icy sting of plastic on his skin.

"Yep," he answered with a nod. "In the locker room of the caddie shack. No one else was in there at the time."

"Where was Justin? Is he working today?"

"He was already out on a loop."

"Honey, I'm so sorry."

"It's okay," he said. "You should have seen the other guys."

They both laughed quietly.

"I'm sorry I didn't make any money today. Mister Rawlings said I could work a double one day next week. I'm ahead on all my classwork, so I can skip the morning classes one day if I need to."

"Honey, don't worry about the money. We're fine. I promise. Your number-one job is school. Okay? You'll be graduating this year. Don't mess it up now that you're so close to the finish line."

He nodded absently, as if acquiescing to the order.

"You going to be okay? You hungry?"

"No, thanks. I ate something on the way home. I just wanted a burger."

"A little comfort food, huh? I understand that. Well, if you change your mind, let me know. I'll start making something in the next hour."

"Okay."

She peered over at him, hesitating to get up from the couch. "You're a good kid, Tyler. You're smart and a good golfer. You have a lot of things going for you, Son." The statement seemed to remind her of the upcoming tournament only a few days away. "You worried about the qualifier?"

He stared down at the wooden coffee table in front of him. She'd picked it up at a secondhand store. The stain had been sanded off but the wood had never been repainted, and Molly had just left it like that.

"A little," he admitted. "I mean, I know the chances of me winning it are pretty slim, but getting into the open could change everything for us."

"Oh, honey." She stretched out her hand and brushed his cheek. "You don't need to worry about me, or about us. We're going to be just fine, whether you win that tournament or not. You have to trust in that. Okay?"

He allowed a weak nod, but he doubted it did much to convince her that he believed what she was saying.

"Seriously, Son. Don't put that kind of pressure on yourself."

"Okay, Mom." He held the frozen bag with his injured hand. He couldn't tell if it was helping or not, but Tyler wasn't going to mention that one to her. Even as they spoke, he could think of nothing else. His mind locked in on whatever was wrong with his hand, and a single thought pummeled his mind like a boxer with a speed bag. *What if I can't swing a club?*

His phone started buzzing in his pocket, interrupting the conversation.

Tyler lowered the bag of corn and removed the device.

"Who's that? Lucy?" She asked the question with a playful grin.

He checked the screen. "No, it's Justin. He's probably wondering where I am."

Molly nodded and stood up. "I'll be back here if you need me."

She disappeared into the hall, leaving him alone on the couch.

Tyler answered the call and pressed the phone to his ear.

"What's up, man?" he said.

"Dude. What happened? I just finished my loop and heard you were in a fight with Mitchell."

"How did you hear that?"

"Word gets around."

"How? No one else was in there. Just Mitchell and his two buddies."

"Yeah, Mister Rawlings was furious. I guess Jeff overheard him reading the riot act to Mitchell. And you know Jeff. Once he found out, everyone found out."

"Great," Tyler sighed.

Jeff was a good kid, younger than him and Justin. But when there was a rumor to be shared, Jeff was all too happy to spill the tea.

He didn't mean anything malevolent by it, and he never talked about things that weren't true. He seemed to have everyone's best interest in mind while at the same time feeding off the energy of being the first one to know something.

"So, what happened?" Justin demanded.

Tyler didn't want to rehash it again, but that was unavoidable.

"Mitchell and his two pals jumped me in the locker room."

"They jumped you? Man, I'm sorry I wasn't there. I would have loved to get my hands on that little worm."

"I didn't want it to happen, J. I'm not even sure I'll have a job there next week."

He leaned forward and tried to look around the corner into the hallway. He heard his mother rummaging around somewhere in the back of the apartment.

When he spoke again, it was in a secretive, hushed tone. "Jeff didn't hear Rawlings saying anything about me being fired, did you?"

"No. I don't think so. From what I understand, he's mad at Mitchell. And I think he's going to ban the other two from coming out to the club again, although we'll see how far that gets past Mitchell's dad."

"Right."

"From what Jeff said, Mitchell looked like he took a pretty bad beating. I'm impressed, bro. Taking on three guys at once. You're my hero." Justin chuckled after the last line.

"You're hilarious."

"They didn't hurt you, did they?"

"Nah, nothing bad. Black eye. Bruise on my stomach." He intentionally left out the part about his hand but found himself trying to squeeze it.

"That's good. Don't need you getting injured before the big dance on Sunday."

"No. I'll be good to go," Tyler said, hoping that by merely speaking the words they would be true.

"Glad to hear it. Get some rest. And put some frozen peas on that eye. I know you don't have any steaks lying around."

He was right about that. Steak was a luxury item in Tyler's home, a rare treat he and his mom were only able to enjoy once every couple of months.

"I have a frozen bag of corn. That seems to be helping, I guess."

"Whatever you have to do, man. Has Lucy seen you yet?"

Tyler had forgotten about her in all the mayhem.

"No. She hasn't. Probably for the best. I don't think I look very attractive right now."

"You can't look worse than Mitchell. You really did a number on him and his buddies."

"I guess."

An awkward pause cut through the conversation.

"Look, man," Justin said, "rest up. I'll check around and see if I can find out anything else."

"Thanks. I'm worried that Mr. Rawlings is going to tell me I need to take tomorrow off too."

"Yeah. Well, to be perfectly honest, you probably should anyway. You need to recuperate for the big tournament this weekend."

"I can't do that, J. I already missed work today. I need the money. Missing two days is unacceptable."

Justin breathed audibly through the phone. "I'll see what I can do. But I doubt Rawlings will want you on a couple of bags tomorrow if you're banged up. He won't want the members wondering why their caddie looks like he was in a bar fight."

Tyler knew he was right. There was no way he could go into work tomorrow looking like this, and he doubted the bag of frozen corn would do much to help his appearance. He'd need a miracle, and so far in his life, those were in short supply.

He'd just have to go against his mother's wishes and skip class. There was no two ways about it. It was fine.

She'd mentioned him not falling short just before the finish line, but the last year was the easiest in many ways, and he already had everything lined up for the rest of the quarter. The winter months were lean for caddies, usually occupied by a lot of sitting around in the caddie shack and hoping a member showed up for a quick round before the early sunset.

Most of the golfers didn't play much in the winter, save for those rare days when the temperatures skyrocketed into the upper forties or low fifties.

As a result, money during that three-month window was hard to come by, so Tyler and the others needed to make as much as they could during the prime months.

He'd been wise with his earnings from the spring and summer, always careful to put enough back for emergencies, and to get him through the colder months. But he loathed dipping into those savings. Ever the hard worker, he didn't take many days off, and when he did, Tyler always felt like he should be working, building up that savings account just in case.

I guess this is one of those times I was waiting for, he resigned.

"Don't worry about it," Tyler said after thinking about it. "Can you tell Mister Rawlings I think I'm going to sit out tomorrow. I'm feeling pretty banged up, and like you said, I need to rest for the tournament on Sunday."

"That's the spirit."

Tyler snorted. "You're such an idiot."

"I know. That's why you love me. Okay, I gotta go. I'll talk to you later, man."

"Later."

Tyler ended the call and set the phone down on the cushion next to him. He took a long, deep breath, and stared at the blank television screen, trying to ignore the aching in his body.

He looked down at his injured hand and tried squeezing it into a fist again. Pain screamed through the nerves, and he had to release the tension.

"Perfect," he said. "Just perfect."

19

CHARLESTON

"This place is perfect," Graham said to the hostess, who stood next to a table for two in the back corner of the restaurant. "Thank you."

"Very good, sir," the hostess replied. Her dark brown hair was pulled back into a tight ponytail, and her white button-up blouse and black slacks looked like they'd just come from the cleaners. Her professional appearance reflected the elegance of the place, famous for its Jordanian cuisine.

She set a pair of menus on the table across from each other and nodded to the guests. "Malik will be your server. He should be with you shortly."

Graham and Alicia both thanked her and eased into their seats.

Alicia wore a lovely blue summer dress with gold trimming and Greek designs around the bottom and the waist. The neckline of the garment hung a few inches below her neck. Her hair flowed down over the right shoulder in a single, thick braid.

Graham thought she looked like a princess from some ancient Greek kingdom.

"You really do look beautiful," he said, hoping his compliment wasn't a venture too far.

"Thank you," she said, blushing. "And you look like a dashing gentleman."

He grinned sheepishly. "I don't know about the gentleman part, but thank you."

She smiled at the modesty and looked down at the menu. "I've always wanted to try this place," she said.

"It's excellent. The chef is from Jordan. He previously worked at another restaurant here in town. Interestingly, it was a Southern food sort of place. And I kid you not, that guy made the best buttermilk biscuits I've ever had in my life."

Alicia looked up from the menu in disbelief. "Seriously? A guy from Jordan? How is that possible?"

Graham shook his head and looked down at the menu. "I have no idea. But my grandmother is rolling over in her grave. I know that much."

Malik arrived at the table, a young man in his early twenties, dressed similarly to the hostess save for the black apron he wore tightly around his waist and neck.

"Can I get you two something to drink to get started, and perhaps an appetizer?"

"Sure," Graham answered, and motioned to his date. "Know what you'd like to drink?"

"I would love an old-fashioned," she said, looking up at the waiter.

"Great choice. Our old-fashioned is the best one in the city. And that's not my opinion. I've heard that from a lot of our customers." He turned to Graham. "And for you?"

"Sounds like I have to have one of those too," he said. "And can we get the hummus and pita bread to start?"

"Yes, sir. Sounds good. I'll put that in right away for you."

The server turned and walked over to a counter, where a touch screen sat on a counter.

"So," Graham said, turning his attention back to Alicia, "I really appreciate you coming out with me tonight. I have to admit, I wasn't sure you'd say yes."

"I wasn't sure you'd ever ask." Both her words and her smile disarmed him and dissolved a little of that ice that settled in his gut. He mirrored her expression, albeit meeker. "I'll be honest, I don't know why I did it."

Her eyebrows lifted. "Oh really?"

"No, not like that," he added quickly. "It's just that... I haven't asked a woman out in a long time. Much less a total stranger. It's just not my style."

"I'm sure you meet lots of women in your line of work. I bet women are throwing themselves at you."

He shifted uncomfortably. "They did when I was younger, when I was the next big thing in golf."

"Oh. I'm so sorry. I didn't mean it like that, Graham. I just meant that you meet a lot of people traveling around the world for tournaments. Dinners, parties, that sort of thing."

"It's okay. And you're right. I do meet a lot of people. I usually just show up for the planned stuff, have a polite drink, shake a few hands, and then make my exit quietly. I don't like being around all those people anymore. It was fun when I was in my twenties, but now, I just want some peace and quiet."

She nodded, and he thought he could see in her eyes that she understood.

"So," he said, changing the subject, "you said you spent some time abroad."

"I did. Took a little time off and traveled through Europe."

"Was it one of those backpacking deals I've seen people doing?"

Alicia laughed. "No. I'm not one of those types. I got enough steps in wandering through the different cities I visited."

"What was your favorite?"

"My favorite city?"

He nodded.

"I really loved Copenhagen. It was so clean, and the people were friendly. Everyone spoke English there. It was easy to get around. Good transportation system. And they have bicycles you can use to ride around and basically give yourself a tour."

"It sounds nice."

Malik returned with their drinks. He asked if they were ready to order entrées.

"Just a few more minutes, if that's okay," Graham said.

"Certainly, sir," Malik replied, and spun around to see to his other patrons.

"What about you?" Alicia asked, picking up her drink.

Graham raised his and they clinked the glasses together. "Cheers," he said.

"Cheers."

They both took a sip and set their glasses back down on the table.

"So, to answer your question, I think my favorite place to visit is the Florida panhandle along the Emerald Coast."

Her face turned a curious kind of sour. "But you live by the ocean here."

"Yeah. I know. But I'll probably retire over there. I like the sand better; the water is prettier. Don't get me wrong, I love Charleston. It's one of my favorite cities in America. But it's a little quieter over there on the panhandle, with the exception of spring break. In some of the smaller beach towns, though, it isn't so bad."

"What about your favorite place outside the United States?"

"You know, I really loved Germany. I enjoyed the cities, especially Berlin and Potsdam. But the countryside is so beautiful. And the people are real, authentic."

"And the beer doesn't suck."

He laughed. "No, it does not."

Their conversation fell silent for a minute, drowned in the ambient noises of the restaurant around them.

"So," she said, after taking another sip amid the pause, "you were married before?"

"Yeah," he answered with a nod. He knew that question was going to emerge at some point, partly because he'd been wondering the same thing about her. "You?"

"Yes. In my early twenties. It didn't last long." Graham thought he sensed pain in her words, and something that could have been a deep memory darkened her face. Graham wondered if she was returning to memories she hadn't wanted to revisit.

He knew the feeling. They were easy to recognize in her body language, so he quickly changed the subject to something more pleasant.

"So, you enjoy working at the coffee shop?" he asked.

The relieved smile that spread across her face told him she was glad he'd switched topics.

"Yeah. It's good for the most part. But it's not what I envisioned for a career when I was younger. You can't do many fun things when that's your main source of income."

"I would think not." He didn't like the direction this was heading. He'd seen it before on a few occasions after his divorce. A single woman, always younger, acts like she's interested in him, that he's attractive, someone she'd want to spend time with. But in the end, it was always about the money, the lifestyle. He'd feared she would go there when they first met, but she apparently saved it for the first date. That part disappointed him. At least most of the others had waited until the second date.

"Oh, it's fine," she added quickly. "I'm not complaining. I don't actually need much. I live a simple life on purpose. Sure, I would love to travel more again, but I'm not sure what I can do to make enough money to support that. Like I believe I said before, it seems like so many industries have left me behind."

"Yeah. I know what you mean. In my line of work, that happens in the blink of an eye. One day you're touted as the next big thing. Then the following day, some young gun is better than you."

"For me, I guess there were alternatives. I was in management. Maybe I could have picked up a role like that with some other company, but I wanted to do something different. I don't make as much money at the coffee shop as I did in retail, but I think that arena is looking for younger people than me."

"I see," Graham said, raising his glass to his lips.

"You think I should have tried to get my old job back? Maybe with another company?"

"No. I didn't say that. I was just listening. It sounds like you've lived an interesting life so far."

"I wouldn't say that." Her cheeks burned, and he couldn't tell if it was from embarrassment or from the compliment.

"How many countries have you visited?"

Alicia looked up at the ceiling as if it would reveal the number. After a quick recount, she said she'd been to twelve different countries.

"That's impressive," Graham said. "Probably more than me."

"I always wanted to see the world. I grew up in a small town." Her voice drifted into the distance. Her eyes locked onto something nonspecific along the wall to her left. "I met a guy while I was in college. Fell in love, or I thought I did. We got married a year later. Everything was great. For a while. Then I found out he'd been cheating on me with another woman in another town. Things started making sense—the abrupt business trips, the strange calls in the night, the random text messages he took in other rooms."

Graham saw how remembering all this was affecting her, even all these years later, and he was going to tell her to stop, but she kept going.

"Anyway," Alicia continued, "I spent the last few decades not really trusting men. My girlfriends told me I should take a leap of faith, that he was only one bad one out there. But it scarred me. And I never recovered from it."

"It's difficult to get over something like that, hard to trust again. After our son died, my wife left me and remarried shortly after. She gaslit me, telling me I hadn't been there for her after the death of our son."

"Oh, Graham. I'm so sorry. That is awful."

He shook it off. "It's okay. I mean, I deal with it as best I can. I've grieved, spoken to counselors, done all that. But some holes will always be there. It might be pain, or trust, or whatever. Personally, I'm tired of trying to look the other way. I guess that's why I decided to talk to you yesterday at the coffee shop. Normally, I would have just grabbed my order and sat down alone."

Malik returned to the table with a white plate of warm pita slices arranged in a circle around a white bowl of hummus in the center. The dip was garnished with fresh cilantro, paprika, minced garlic, and a dab of olive oil.

He looked at Graham, then to Alicia. "Are you ready?"

She glanced at Graham and nodded. "You know what? I think I am."

20

CHATTANOOGA

Tyler woke up Friday morning feeling worse than he had when he went to bed the night before.

His head hurt, his abdomen ached, and his eye, lip, and jaw, which were still swollen, were sore.

He struggled to get out of bed when his alarm went off, tempted to hit the snooze button and just lie there for the next year. But he had class in forty-five minutes, so staying in bed wasn't an option, especially if he was going to have to skip a session or two next week to make up for work.

He unplugged his phone, shuffled into the bathroom, and switched on the light. The first few seconds of the blinding glow were like jumping into a cold shower for his eyes. He winched, and blinked, eventually adjusting.

After putting on his deodorant and a T-shirt, he checked his phone for messages he might have missed after going to bed. It had been an early night for him, opting to take a couple of ibuprofen and a cup of chamomile tea before ten o'clock, and nodding off before 10:30.

He typically stayed up an hour later than that, but his body had demanded rest. It still did.

There were two messages from Justin and three from Lucy.

Tyler ignored the ones from his friend and tapped on the messages from her.

"OMG, Tyler. Are you okay? I heard what happened. I can't believe those idiots did that to you. Please text me when you get a chance." The next one read, "Hey, I know you might be worried about your caddie gig, but it's going to be okay. Promise."

Tyler huffed at that one. "I doubt that," he muttered.

He read the last one. "I guess maybe you're already in bed. I'm so sorry this happened, babe. I'll check in on you tomorrow morning to make sure you're all right."

He smiled. She called him babe. He'd never been called that by anyone before. He'd heard terms of endearment like that used by other people, but this was a first for him. He liked it.

Tyler brought his right hand up to the phone and started to type a reply, but the pain from the day before returned with just as much stabbing fury as he remembered.

He squinted his eyes against the agony, trying to move his thumb around the screen with the other as he always did, but now it was torture.

Tyler gasped and let go of the phone with his right hand, opting to go with the slow, methodical approach of only using his left thumb to send a reply to Lucy.

"Hey. I'm okay. Just a little sore. Went to bed early last night. Sorry for no reply." He tried to be as brief as possible since it seemed to take forever to send a message using only his left hand. "Going to class then coming home to rest."

He sent the message and placed the phone down on the counter next to the sink. The texts with Justin would have to wait, though he doubted they were that important.

Then a thought occurred to him.

What if they were about his job?

For a moment, Tyler hesitated. He stared down at the blank screen, uncertain if he wanted to look at the messages.

"You're going to have to at some point," he said.

He picked up the device again, tapped the screen, then he opened the thread from Justin and read the texts.

"Hey man. Just wanted you to know that Rawlings went to bat for you. Mitchell's dad was super pissed. Apparently, he was there playing a round when the fight happened. The nerve of that guy. With his dad on the premises no less. Anyway, I don't think you're going to be fired. So, rest up, and try to relax for the big tourney this weekend. You got this, bro."

Tyler scrolled with his eyes to the next message. "Oh, by the way, no funny business this weekend with your girlfriend. You need to lock it in. No distractions."

The message produced a snort from Tyler. He knew Justin wanted this just as badly as he did. Getting a chance to play in a pro tournament would showcase both of their skills. While Justin was a good golfer by any standard, he wasn't at Tyler's level, and certainly not up to the professional tours. But his caddying abilities were exceptional. Tyler had often said Justin was not only the best caddie at the club but the best in the city.

Like Tyler, Justin was in school, working on his degree, but both of them knew Justin's real aspirations were to become a professional caddie on the pro tour. Getting to that level could afford him a lifestyle he'd only been able to dream about up until then. And his text messages to Tyler reflected that deeply felt desire.

Tyler didn't respond to the texts, instead opting to let his friend dream for a little longer while he got ready for class.

He looked down at his right hand and tried to close his fingers and thumb again. It was no use. The pain was still there, as was the looming sense of dread.

If his hand didn't start feeling better soon, he'd be in real trouble for the qualifier on Sunday.

21

CHARLESTON

Graham woke up with a renewed sense of vigor he hadn't felt in a long time.

He rolled out of his bed after a quick glance at the clock and walked over to the windows. He threw open the light blue curtains and stared out at the scene. The dark ocean waves crested in foamy white caps. Light clouds drifted by to the east, dimming the light of the rising sun.

Graham took a deep breath and soaked it in.

The date with Alicia had gone much better than expected. Truth be told, he thought he would screw it up somehow, perhaps by saying something stupid, or just coming off as boring.

But she'd genuinely had a good time. He could see it in her eyes and body language.

The conversation over dinner took a lighter turn after the initial visit to their shadowy pasts. They discussed their desires for the future, what they'd like to do in their careers, and where they would like to be in life, generally.

He was surprised to learn that they had several things in common —including travel, which she seemed so addicted to. Visiting new places, seeing new cultures, new people, and trying new foods were some of the few things that took his mind off the past—his mistakes, failures, and regrets. Travel represented, to both of them, a chance to write a new life script.

Old doubts, however, still pestered him, riling the untrusting shadows that always lurked in the back of his mind. Alicia had run on some hard times financially, and who better to fix all that but a wealthy, professional golfer? She'd acted as though she had no idea who he was, which was both believable and not at the same time.

"No," he said quietly. "She's the real deal. Not everyone is like Linda."

Alicia hadn't asked for anything, and he convinced himself that she wouldn't. Living a life of suspicion and mistrust wasn't living at all. It was just existing, and he'd done that for far too long.

He let the doubts evaporate like clouds in a summer breeze.

Graham stared out at the ocean for a moment, feeling grateful for the view for the first time in as long as he could remember.

He'd always appreciated the place with its porch looking out to the ocean, the salty air blowing through his hair and filling his nostrils. But there'd been something missing that made the home feel empty, a hollow shell he didn't know how to fill.

Graham turned away from the window and walked over to the nightstand. He picked up his phone and looked at the last message from Alicia he'd received the night before.

"I can't tell you what a lovely time I had. Thank you so much. I hope we can do it again soon."

The smile that creased his lips felt like it stretched to both ears. He'd answered back with a simple, "Likewise. I look forward to it."

He hoped the brevity of his response hadn't been off putting, but that was the old him—the insecure version of a man he'd longed to put to bed for years now.

After dinner, he and Alicia had gone for a walk through the historic district of Charleston. They strolled lazily down to the battery and lingered there at the water's edge. They talked a little then stayed silent a little, neither forcing the conversation in any direction that felt unnatural.

When he took her home, he'd walked her to her door and thanked her for the good evening, then leaned in and gave her a kiss on the cheek.

She'd blushed at the gentlemanly gesture and waved to him after she entered the door to her home before he drove off.

He'd never believed in kissing on the first date. Maybe he was old-fashioned in that regard. But a polite peck on the cheek was an innocent, multilayered message to her that he had enjoyed her company and appreciated it on a deeper level.

"She likes me," he said, staring at the phone. Just saying it out loud warmed the center of his chest like a crackling fire in late fall.

He walked into the bathroom with a spring in his step, and when he turned on the light, he saw a different man in the mirror.

"Look who's back," he whispered, planting his hands on the counter.

As he stared into his reflection, Graham felt something he thought he'd never feel again—confidence.

22

CHATTANOOGA

Tyler barely heard a word any of his professors said that morning.

Once he was done with his last class of the day, he returned to his car and set a direct course for the nearest driving range.

He'd stowed his clubs in the trunk before going to campus, fully intent on getting in a little practice. However, there was a frightening thought underpinning those plans.

Could he even swing a club?

He could barely turn the steering wheel of the car with his right hand and was forced to put more effort onto the left.

He cursed Mitchell for starting the fight at the club. *Everything would have been fine if he'd just let me go to work as usual and not said a thing. Was it really so difficult for Mitchell to be a decent human being, or at least suppress his ire?*

Other dark thoughts penetrated Tyler's mind, taking him to a place he knew wouldn't fix anything. *What if the timing of Mitchell's attack wasn't a coincidence?*

He'd made no attempt to disguise his disdain for Tyler's success in navigating the previous qualification rounds. And he'd been dismissive of Tyler nearly tying the course record earlier that week.

The circumstances were beyond suspicious. What better way to keep Tyler from even coming close to sniffing a victory than to beat him up just a few days before the big event? Tyler gripped the wheel, and another bolt of pain shot through his right hand and wrist.

Still, Tyler fought the urge to feel like a victim. His parents taught him a long time ago that people who fell prey to a victim mindset would never experience great success. Admittedly, he'd met the type on many occasions, people who always complained about their bad luck, how things could never go their way. Or if life had started going well, something would inevitably turn against them. "I just can't seem to get ahead," was one of the more redundant quotes he'd heard.

Occasionally, Tyler felt the temptation to think that way. He did work hard, both at school and his job. At the latter, he strove to be the best at what he did and always gave the best possible experience to the players he caddied for.

He'd become one of the favorite caddies at the club, and the tips he received from the members reflected that. Still, every now and then he wondered if he was ever going to climb higher. He felt like the ladder was right there in front of him, waiting to be scaled. He just needed to grab the next rung and ascend.

Now, though, it seemed Mitchell had knocked all the rungs off the ladder, or tipped the whole thing over. There was no way he could swing a golf club with his hand feeling like this.

But he had to try.

He stewed over all of this for the fifteen minutes it took to drive from the university campus to the driving range he used in the suburbs.

At this time of day there were never many golfers out working on their game. It was more of an evening or weekend joint. Most of the true players were already out on the courses, some of them working business deals over cigars and beers, others living out their golden years of retirement.

He parked his car and walked around to the trunk. He popped the lid and took out the bag, wincing at a stabbing pain in his gut when he lifted it. The bag wasn't that heavy, but the muscles where Mitchell struck him in the abdomen were still extremely tender.

Tyler took a deep breath, grunted, and shouldered the bag.

He meandered across the lot and over to the window where the driving range owner always sat on an old metal stool, usually watching a small television he'd fixed to the corner.

Tyler liked the little shop. It smelled like golf—a mixture of tees, glove leather, golf ball boxes, club grips, and old carpet laced with a hint of stale cigarettes from a bygone era when smoking was allowed in a place like that. The wood-paneled walls inside completed the image. There weren't many places like that left in the world, other than in eighties movies.

The old man saw Tyler coming and slid the drive-thru-style window open. "Hey," he said through crooked teeth and cracked lips. How you doing, Tyler?"

"Doing all right, Mr. Crawford."

"I hear you're playing in the final round of the qualifier this weekend."

"Yeah? Who'd you hear that from?" Tyler asked dryly.

Crawford chuckled. "From you, my boy."

"Oh yeah." Tyler knew, but he played along. He liked Mr. Crawford. After all, it had been him who'd first given Tyler a chance to play the game at a price he and his parents could afford.

"Coming out here to iron out a few wrinkles in the old game, are ya?" Crawford's lips curled up to the right side. His face was as weathered as the faded and peeling white paint on the exterior of the shop. But unlike that old paint, Mr. Crawford was darkly tanned from years of manning the tractor that picked up the balls at the end of the day, and from using the same tractor to mow the grass. He couldn't run the range entirely by himself, though. While on the tractor, someone else would have to man the shop, not that there was a ton of foot traffic coming through here.

"Yeah," Tyler said, though he tried to be discreet about the real reason he was here. "Just a little tune-up before the big tournament."

"That's a good idea. Here." Crawford reached down and lifted the largest basket he offered at the range. "This one's on the house."

Tyler shook his head. "You always say that. One of these days you need to let me pay you, Mr. Crawford. It's not good for business."

The old man glowered at him as if his feelings were hurt. "Son, I've been in business running this driving range since before you were born. It ain't gone under yet. So, I think I know a thing or two. Besides, I know you and your mother work hard. Especially after your dad passed."

Tyler nodded his agreement, although begrudgingly. "Thanks, Mr. Crawford. If I make it to the open, I'll see what I can do about sending some more business your way."

"If?" Crawford looked appalled by the doubtful insinuation. "Boy, I'm counting on you to make it. I believe in you."

"Thanks, sir. I appreciate it."

"Now, get on out there, and run that tune-up. You need to be sharp this Sunday."

"Yes, sir. I will."

Tyler reached up and grabbed the basket handle and dragged it over the edge of the shelf jutting out from the window.

Out of habit, he used his right hand, but the second gravity tugged on the basket's weight, he nearly dropped it to the ground. The pain shot through his hand like lightning. A couple of the balls spilled off the mount atop the container, and bounced to a stop on the gravel.

"You okay?" Crawford asked.

"Yes, sir." Tyler lied. "I'm good. Just slipped. Thank you."

Tyler scooped up the loose balls and replaced them back atop the pile in the basket. Then he bent down and used his left hand to pick it up, his right still throbbing in pain.

At least the sunglasses didn't give away the black eye to Mr. Crawford, Tyler thought. His chrome-tinted aviators covered a decent circumference around his eyes, and Crawford must not have noticed the busted lip.

Carrying the bag and the basket over to a tee box proved harder than it should have been. The soreness in his gut made the short thirty-yard journey feel like a mile.

He propped his bag up next to a slot of fresh, mostly undisturbed turf and set the basket down, tipping it over to spill the balls out onto the ground.

Just as he always did when practicing, Tyler pulled the pitching wedge from his bag. He preferred to start with a few swings with the lighter club. Doing so also seemed to reconnect his muscle memory, helping establish the flow and tempo of the desired swing.

He held the club with his left hand and dragged a ball over to a thick patch of grass, then addressed the ball in his usual stance.

Tyler looked over his shoulder at the target downrange, then back down at the white ball with a black stripe across the middle. He wrapped his hands around the grip, wincing slightly at the pain in his right, then turned and took the club up until his hands were shoulder height.

It was only a three-quarters swing, which was how he always began to warm up. He was surprised at how little the motion hurt his right hand, but as he twisted his hips and began the downswing, the pain screamed through his nerves, nearly causing him to let go of the club completely.

He struck the ball on the heel of the club, and it skidded to the left, traveling fifty yards on the ground before it came to a stop.

Fear squeezed Tyler's chest with a terrible realization. *I can't swing.*

23

CHARLESTON

Graham swung the 5-iron in a smooth, steady rhythm. His tempo felt natural, effortless.

The clubface struck the ball dead center of the sweet spot, sending the white sphere into the air in a glorious, high trajectory.

He watched the ball land on the target green just a few feet from the pin, where it dug into the turf and came to a stop. The club slid down through the fingers of his left hand after he finished, stopping when the base of the face reached his thumb.

"Well, well, well," he said. "I haven't hit 'em like that in a long time."

He'd been there at the range for the last forty minutes, working on a selection of long and mid-irons. In his last few tournaments, those clubs had been particularly pesky, causing seemingly no end of trouble for him. Today, however, every shot he hit with them from the 4 up to the 7, were accurate and powerful.

He couldn't remember striking the ball so well, and half believed it was a fluke.

Graham found himself tempted to wish he could keep that kind of flow going in the open the next weekend, but that sort of thinking was folly. He wasn't necessarily superstitious, but few athletes didn't have a little habit or two they either consciously, or subconsciously, believed could turn the tides of luck in one way or another.

He stepped back over to his bag and replaced the club in its slot, then removed his glove and stuffed it in one of the pouches.

Graham removed the visor from his head, tousled his hair, and put the cap back on before picking up his bag and slugging it over his shoulder.

He walked back to his car, waving politely at the kid working the bag drop, and placed the clubs in the trunk of his sedan.

His stomach grumbled as he removed his cleats, reminding him he hadn't eaten yet. He checked the time on his watch. It was just after noon. He'd gotten to the range at 11:20 to run a quick session.

Something else gnawed at him besides hunger.

Graham wondered if Alicia was working today. He hadn't thought of asking on their date the night before. Then again, he wasn't sure if he should give it a few days before contacting her again or showing up at her workplace in what she now knew was not his usual time.

There were the text messages this morning, he reasoned. He'd heard that after a date, it was customary to allow two or three days before reaching out to the other person again—a practice he thought completely ridiculous.

Why, if you had a good time on a date with someone, would you simply ghost them on purpose for a couple of days just to play mind games, or try not to look desperate?

Maybe the last part was the reason. That was his best guess. And if he showed up at the coffee shop today, he might come off as looking a little too eager to see her again.

But he *was* eager to see her again. He couldn't help that.

Graham made up his mind. *Let the consequences fall where they may.*

The drive to the shop took less than fifteen minutes. As he drew closer, though, his heartbeat quickened with the anticipation of seeing her again. He hadn't felt this way in so long he could barely remember the last time.

He pulled into the parking lot and steered the car into a spot across the asphalt from the entrance. When he climbed out, he peered through the building's big windows but couldn't see through the glare.

So he closed the door and strolled across the lot to the entrance, opened the door, and stepped inside.

He quickly scanned the room, surveying the people working behind the counter, but there was no sign of Alicia.

Maybe she's on break, he thought.

Regret started chewing at his mind, its teeth grinding on the meat of his insecurities. *This was a bad idea,* he said to himself. *You look like a stalker. Just leave, Graham.*

He turned, pushed the door open, and walked back outside into the warm, humid air. "I shouldn't have come here," he said, hurrying quickly back across the parking lot to his car.

Once he was back inside behind the wheel, he let out a deep sigh. "This was a bad idea," he repeated the thought from a moment before.

A little voice in his head asked, "Why?"

He shook his head and gripped the steering wheel. She'd told him she enjoyed the evening, that she wanted to see him again. Everything had ended well.

But why isn't she at work today?

That was a silly, and once again, an insecure thing to wonder.

"Relax, Graham. She likes you. You're going to be fine. Just focus on getting ready for the open." Sometimes he found talking out loud to himself helped squelch the fires of doubt that sparked within him. "You had a good practice session today. Take that win and run with it."

He was supposed to meet his caddie for an hour of putting later. Before that, he'd need to eat, but he wasn't going to go back in the coffee shop. Not right now, anyway.

He turned on the ignition, and drove out of the parking lot, hoping he hadn't just made a mistake by coming here. Would Alicia's coworkers tell her?

24

CHATTANOOGA

S unday morning arrived before Tyler was ready—at least physically.

He'd mostly stayed in the house all day on Saturday, unwilling to venture out to do anything physically demanding.

Lucy had texted him multiple times, asking if he wanted her to come by, bring him something to eat, and maybe just hang out and watch television.

Tyler had steered her away at every turn. It wasn't that he didn't want to see her. But he wasn't in a presentable condition, and on top of that, he felt ashamed about where he lived.

Lucy's home was an actual mansion, and he lived in what a real estate agent would call a modest apartment. And on top of that, their furniture was old, and nothing matched.

Part of him felt bad for not seeing her since class the other day, and they hadn't spent any real time together since the night on the golf course fairway. He made sure to send a few reassuring messages to her to let her know that she hadn't done anything wrong, and that he wanted to see her, but at that moment he just needed some alone time.

She said she understood, but he doubted that. Maybe Lucy was more secure than he was giving her credit for. She wasn't just some delicate flower that could be blown over by the slightest breeze. She was strong, independent, and smart—three traits he found highly attractive about her.

He woke up early, though the truth was he'd barely slept through the night. A combination of the soreness in his abdomen and anxiety percolating in his brain allowed little room for rest.

The golfers were asked to be at the course by seven in the morning, which was a dreadful time for a college student to even be awake, much less ready to play in a massive tournament.

His mother had prepared a simple breakfast for him of bagels with egg and cheese along with a full pot of coffee. She still didn't look well, but despite his efforts to keep her home and rested for the day, his mom insisted that she wasn't about to miss the biggest tournament in her son's life.

She'd always been there to support him, through all the difficult times, and she wasn't about to stop now just because she felt a little under the weather.

They parked both their cars in the lot outside the clubhouse, and Tyler changed into his golf shoes while sitting on the edge of the trunk.

His mother watched him, smiling, as he tied the shoes. "Hey," she said once he was done. "No matter what happens today, I want you to know I'm proud of you. Okay?"

He nodded. "I know. And thanks for everything. Including coming out here today."

"Wouldn't miss it, sweetheart."

Tyler closed the trunk, and the two walked beside each other, crossing the parking area to the bag drop where Jeff stood. His eyes looked tired, as if he'd tried to sleep there at his podium the night before.

"Early day, huh, Jeff?" Tyler asked.

His younger counterpart nodded and yawned. "Yeah. Too early."

Tyler smiled and then looked to his mother. He pointed to a sign with an arrow that read Spectators.

"You'll have to go that direction. You shouldn't have any trouble getting in. I made sure you're on the list."

His mom narrowed her eyes and smiled again. "And I thought you wanted me to stay home today."

"Yeah, well," he shrugged, "I put you on the list just in case."

She leaned in and kissed him on the cheek. "Good luck."

Tyler watched her walk around the corner and disappear.

"So that was your mom, huh?" Jeff asked. "She seems nice."

Tyler continued looking in the direction she'd gone. "She's awesome."

"Well, best of luck to you today, Tyler. I'm pulling for you." He paused. "You feeling okay after that crap with Mitchell the other day?"

Tyler glanced around the parking lot, as if worried his nemesis might appear from nowhere.

"He's not here," Jeff said, sensing Tyler's concern. "He's not allowed on the premises until the committee decides what to do about all that. His dad was pretty pissed. Blamed you, obviously. Of course, he was probably getting fake news from Mitchell about what went on in the caddie shack. Even though it's his dad, you'd have to be an idiot to believe that one guy started a fight with three like that. Especially considering you've never done anything like that before."

"Thanks for the support, Jeff. I appreciate it."

"No problem."

"Is Justin here?"

"Yeah," Jeff answered with a point of his thumb toward the putting green. "He got here a while ago."

"Thanks. I'll see you after."

"Go win it, buddy."

Tyler shrugged the bag up higher onto his shoulder and marched away toward the putting green just beyond a grassy rise.

Off to the right, the sidewalk looped around to the side entrance of the clubhouse, where a registration table sat under an awning. A white-and-blue banner hung off the front edge of the table with the name of the tournament imprinted on it.

Tyler made his way over to it and got in line behind four other golfers. A woman in a pink long-sleeve golf shirt and white skirt sat behind the table, looking as if she was straight out of central casting. He waited patiently until it was his turn, then he stepped up and smiled down at the woman in the chair.

"Checking in?" she asked in a voice that was way too perky for this time of day.

"Yes, ma'am. Tyler Knox."

"I know who you are, Tyler," she said, dismissing the statement with a friendly wave of the hand.

"Just making sure, Mrs. Cochrane," he answered.

Tyler had caddied for her and her friends several times at the club. She was a good golfer, though not the best of the female members.

"Don't be silly. How you feeling today?" she asked as she scanned the sheet of entrants. She stopped at his name and pressed her finger to it, then made a check mark in an empty box beside it.

"I'm okay," he said, though that was a wish and not a fact. His hand still hurt when he tried to do anything with it, and he had no idea how to cope with that on the course.

He'd attempted to hit a few more balls at the range but ended up bailing on the idea. With his hand in such bad shape, there was no sense in exacerbating things. His hopes that he would wake up this morning and it be magically healed had proved nothing more than a foolhardy dream.

"Good to hear it." She looked up from the forms with a smile. "Your caddie is already checked in and waiting for you by the putting green. Best of luck today, Tyler. I'll be pulling for you."

"Thanks. I need all the luck I can get."

"Oh, hogwash. You got this. Just let go and play the game you love."

He nodded and walked away toward the practice green, but her words echoed in his head as he rounded the little knoll that brought the putting surface and a few dozen players into view. Caddies loitered on the fringe, watching their players putt. Through the trees beyond, the rest of the golfers warmed up on the driving range.

Justin spotted him as he stood with his arms crossed watching some of the other players. He hurried over to meet Tyler halfway and reached out for the bag.

"There you are," Justin said. "Cutting it a little close, aren't we?" He glanced at his watch.

"The tournament doesn't start for another hour."

"Yeah, but most of the field is already checked in and warming up."

Tyler set the bag down, relieved to be rid of the burden.

"You okay?" Justin asked, picking up the bag.

"Yeah. My eye is doing better, though it's still discolored."

"Let me see." Tyler guessed the order was more out of concern than mere curiosity.

Tyler pulled down his sunglasses to the brim of his nose, revealing the black eye.

"Ouch. That turd Mitchell. I can't stand that guy. I wish I had been in the locker room when they tried to jump you."

"It would have been good to have some backup. But then we might both be in trouble."

Justin slung the back strap over his shoulder and looked at his friend. "You're in trouble? Did Rawlings say something?"

"No. But I feel like it's only a matter of time. Mitchell's dad won't—"

"I know Mitchell's dad has influence," Justin interrupted, "but I get the feeling some of the other members are tired of his boy's antics. This isn't the first time he's caused trouble. Spoiled little brat."

Tyler had nearly forgotten some of the other instances that landed Mitchell on the naughty list in some of the members' minds. In one instance, he and some buddies snuck out onto the course at night to play with some glow balls. His father had bailed him out of that trouble, Tyler imagined, with a speech akin to the old "boys will be boys" line from the 1950s.

"Forget about it," Tyler said. "We need to focus."

"Right. Good point. Focus. No need to think about that, or Lucy, or anything else right now."

Tyler gave a sidelong glance over at his friend as they approached the green. "Lucy? What's she got to do with anything?"

Justin dismissed it with a quick head shake. "Nothing. It's just, women can be a distraction is all."

Tyler laughed. "My mom is going to be here. She's a woman."

"You know what I mean."

"Yeah, I guess. But Lucy said she's coming, so you better play nice."

Justin didn't answer at first. When they reached the fringe of the green, he set the bag down and pulled three balls out of the pouch. "Just lock in on your game and what you do best, and we'll be fine."

It didn't slip past Tyler how his friend worded it "we" instead of "you'll."

Tyler hadn't even attempted putting yet, and he wondered how that would go with his hand in the weakened state it had been in the last few days.

Justin passed the three balls to him then drew the putter like a sword from its sheath and handed it over.

"Thanks, J."

"You're welcome."

"It's definitely weird having you on my bag, though. Or anyone for that matter. I'm not used to being on this side of it."

Justin smiled. "Get used to it, buddy. You keep playing like you did the other day, you're gonna be working permanently on that side of the bag."

Tyler forced a grin then walked over to an empty patch of green and dropped his three balls twelve feet from an unused pin.

He stood over the first ball and swung the putter back and forth, gripping it gingerly with the right hand and letting the left do most of the work. That was simple enough to do, and he found there wasn't much pain when he employed that technique.

Mrs. Cochrane's words rang in his ears. "Just let go," she'd said.

Maybe her advice was more on point than she realized. Not only did he need to release the anxiety pent up inside him, but relaxing his grip on the club might help too.

He never thought he gripped it too tightly. That was something he'd learned a long time ago, that a loose grip could actually help add distance to the shot. Another key point he picked up during his early days in the sport was that the left hand was more important with the force of pulling the club through the swing, and the right more like a placeholder.

"How are they rolling today?" Tyler asked before he struck the ball.

"Fourteen," Justin said. "Really quick."

"Just the way I like 'em."

Tyler lined up the first ball, and swung through it. It didn't take much, just a tap and the follow-through. Physics did the rest.

The ball rolled, curling its run until it slowed just before dropping into the cup.

"Good way to start the morning," Justin said.

Tyler nodded with a satisfied smile stretching across his face. But underneath the veneer of satisfaction, troubled waters stirred. Putting was one thing. Taking a full swing with the other clubs wasn't going to be so easy.

25

L ucy finished getting dressed and stepped out of her bedroom into the hall.

The smell of freshly brewed coffee wafted all the way up to the second floor, impeded only by her bedroom door. But once that was open, the pleasant aroma filled her nostrils and excited her senses. She loved morning coffee, especially on the weekends, when the demands of her studies didn't require her time and attention.

Lucy had always been a good student, maintaining a high grade point average since it started being attached to her academic progress. She was studious, partly from intrinsic motivation but also due to the cultural demands that came with being of Korean descent.

Her parents expected high marks without exception.

They'd applied her to multiple Ivy League universities during her senior year in high school, but she'd made the decision to stay locally for college, a choice that had earned a heavy dose of disdain from her parents.

Both of them made their disappointment abundantly clear. While many parents would have been overjoyed to have their child stay home for another four years before moving away and starting their own lives, Lucy's mother and father were focused more on status, security, and achievement.

She'd never been certain, but Lucy always got the impression that perhaps her mother and father were living vicariously through her, even though both of them were successful in their career fields.

It was as if she were their doll, a plaything they propped up in front of their friends to show what great parents they were for guiding their child through life.

Her parents eventually came to accept her decision to stay in town, with the expectation that she would go on to graduate school and a more prestigious institution.

Lucy's studies in biology would demand that anyway since her university didn't offer the higher-level degree she would need.

Still, it bothered her that her parents pushed the narrative as if it were a hostage negotiation.

She bent down and greeted her cat that awaited outside her door. The orange-and-white tabby always stood there, waiting for her to wake up and come downstairs.

"Good morning, Mischi," she said, petting the animal on its fluffy head. "Did you get your breakfast yet?"

The cat responded with a meow and began purring, rubbing its flank up against Lucy's shin.

"Good boy."

She left the cat in her wake, making her way to the stairs. The feline quickly rushed past her, and descended the stairs as if running from a fire. His paws clattered loudly against the steps until it reached the bottom with a thump.

Lucy smiled at the animal, gracefully taking the stairs in a less-panicked fashion.

She found her mother in the kitchen making avocado toast, while her father sat at the counter holding a cup of coffee in one hand as he scanned the tablet propped up in front of him.

"Good morning," Lucy said. She smiled at her mother and wrapped her arm around her shoulders, leaning in to give her a kiss on the cheek.

'Good morning, dear," her mom said. "You're up early for a weekend."

"Morning," her dad added without looking away from his tablet.

Lucy nodded, stepping over to the black cabinet next to the sink. She opened the door and retrieved a white coffee mug that matched the color of the countertops, then picked up the pot and poured herself a cup of steaming-hot brew.

She raised the mug to her nose and inhaled deeply. This was one of her favorite moments of any day of the week. No pressures. No problems. Just her and a great cup of coffee.

And her parents.

"Where are you going?" Her mother asked the question in an almost accusatory tone.

"Green Mont," Lucy answered, sensing her mother's suspicion. "The open qualifier is there today. I told you about it."

"Oh yes." Her voice turned sour. "That boy is playing, isn't he?"

"Again, yes. We discussed that too, Mom."

"I don't want you hanging around him. He's bad news."

Lucy's face contorted into a scowl. "Mom, you don't even know him. He's a good guy."

"He doesn't come from our kind of people," her mother countered.

"She's right," her dad chimed in, still focused on something on his tablet screen.

"What's that supposed to mean? Our people? You mean Korean?"

"I mean he comes from a poor family. You are going places, Lucy. You have a plan for your life that can't involve slumming it with some boy just because you think he's cute."

Lucy couldn't believe what she was hearing, even though it wasn't the first time they'd said something like this. When she'd merely hinted at the notion of hanging out with Tyler, they'd pushed back against the idea, albeit with less vitriol than she was getting now.

"He is a nice guy," she defended, suddenly losing her appetite for breakfast.

"There are plenty of nice boys out there," her mother argued. "From better families."

"Better families? You mean families with money. Don't you? Because that's all that matters to you two, making sure that I keep up with the Joneses just like you both have your entire lives."

Her father looked up from the tablet. Lucy could almost feel the fires burning in his eyes. "Do not speak to your mother or me that way. That is highly disrespectful."

Lucy sighed. "I don't mean any disrespect. You both know I love you, and have tried to honor what you want me to do in life."

"Except the university you chose," her mother added in a snide voice.

"The boys from the families around here are jerks. Just like their parents. They're arrogant and materialistic. They have no substance. And honestly, most of them are so focused on themselves, I doubt they have time for anything other than trying to add another notch to their belts. Most of them aren't smart either, just so you know."

Her mother finished spreading smashed avocado on a second slice of toast and took it over to her dad.

"Thank you," he said, with a curt bob of his head.

"You're welcome, dear."

Lucy fought to keep the inferno in her chest from escaping and causing her to say something she might regret later. Part of her wondered if she'd already crossed that threshold.

"Come in. Sit down," her mother ordered in a matter-of-fact tone. There was no anger to it, almost as if the conversation from a few seconds ago had come to an abrupt end and she had accepted Lucy's unspoken surrender.

"Actually," Lucy said, setting down the mug on the counter. "I think I'll take my coffee to go. I don't want to miss anything."

She pulled open a drawer, removed a travel mug, and set it down next to the other.

"What? You need to eat. And your father and I haven't seen you much this week."

"Where were you two yesterday morning? I was here, drinking coffee alone."

"You know we had that brunch to attend at the club," her mother defended.

"Right. The brunch. That started at nine? That's breakfast, Mom. Not brunch. And it's fine. You guys do what you want. Just don't be mad at me when I do the same."

She carefully tipped the steaming mug of coffee over and poured the contents into the travel mug.

"I don't appreciate this disrespect, young lady."

"Nor do I," her father added, chewing his toast.

"I don't disrespect either of you," Lucy said. "But you can't control me like I'm a puppet my entire life. And I'm not an eight-year-old. I'm in college. I'm a woman now. The two of you are going to just have to square with that at some point."

She fit the lid onto the black travel mug, closed the flap, and picked it up. She walked to the archway leading out of the kitchen.

"Lucy," her mother said, her voice growing more stern with every syllable. "You are not to see that boy again. Are we clear?"

Lucy paused and looked back over her shoulder at her mother. A warning was written on the woman's face, one that Lucy knew came with very real consequences. She didn't know what that might entail, and she honestly didn't care.

Her parents had taken good care of her, given her everything she could ever want or need in life—except the freedom to make her own decisions, to forge her own path. Maybe that was one of the things she loved about Tyler. It wasn't just that he was a great guy—honest, caring, hard working. But he also represented a sort of freedom that she'd never experienced, and that she thirsted for deep down in her soul.

"I love you both," Lucy managed. "But I gotta go. I'll see you later."

She walked out the door, leaving her mother and father in stunned silence.

Lucy imagined the things her mother was trying to formulate in her mind to say, some of them possibly threatening to some degree. Lucy didn't care. She had a tournament to attend.

26

"The next time I see Mitchell, I'm going to kill him."

Justin's cheeks burned red. His eyes darted left to right, searching the grounds for the one who'd caused this calamity.

"J, take it easy," Tyler said, holding up a hand to steady his friend's boiling emotions. "He's not here." He didn't actually know if that was the case but figured telling his friend that might help him focus.

"Take it easy?" Justin's voice rose. A few of the other golfers within earshot on the driving range turned to see what the problem was. One of them miss-hit his shot and launched a scathing glare over at the two friends.

"Yes," Tyler said. "And could you keep it down? We're on a golf course, in case you hadn't noticed. Don't want to piss off the other golfers."

Justin looked at his friend with a forlorn expression, as if he might never feel joy again. "When were you going to tell me you hurt your hand?"

"Now."

Justin's head swiveled around, surveying the range for no one in particular, as if the very trees condemned them to doom. "Seriously?

That was your plan? You can barely swing a club, and you just thought it would be a good idea to tell me, your caddie and your best friend, forty-five minutes before the tournament starts?"

"When you say it like that, it doesn't sound like a good idea."

"No. No it doesn't," Justin hissed, drawing the ire of a tall, slender man in his mid-thirties wearing a pink golf shirt.

"Sorry," Tyler mouthed.

The man merely shook his head and went back to hitting practice balls with his 4-iron.

"Look," Tyler said in as calming a tone as he could find, "it's going to be okay."

"How? How is it going to be okay, Ty? You can't swing a club." It took every ounce of restraint within Justin to maintain a quiet tone. "Did you see a doctor about it?"

"No. I didn't see a doctor."

"Then how do you know it isn't broken? You can't play with a broken hand, Ty."

"I know that. But I don't think it's broken."

"How do you know that? You been taking medical school classes at night in your spare time?"

Tyler snorted a laugh. "No, but look. No discoloration. It's just really tender. But I can swing," Tyler corrected. "Just not the way I did before."

He had no idea the discoloration thing had any bearing on whether or not his hand might be broken, but at the moment he was just working damage control for his friend. He needed Justin's mind to be right today.

Justin sighed through his nose. His hands were planted on his hips like an angry schoolmarm who'd just caught a boy responsible for starting a food fight. "Great. That's just great. So, we have zero chance."

He took a step away and looked out into the forest, doing his best to breathe and stay calm. But there was no denying it. Justin knew they were done for. It was written on his face, in his slumping shoulders, his vacant stare.

Tyler shook his head and, ignoring his friend, pulled the pitching wedge from his bag.

At the range the day before, he'd given up trying to swing after hitting a single ball. It had just been too painful. He hoped that maybe one more day's rest would help the healing process for whatever injury his hand had taken. That, unfortunately, hadn't been the case. While it did feel a little better compared to two days ago, the pain in his hand still weakened his grip.

He dragged a ball off the top of a neatly stacked pyramid and pulled it over to a clean patch of grass.

Tyler set up his stance, addressed the ball, and loosened his grip in his right hand so that only his index finger and thumb were holding the rubber in place.

He'd seen something like this once before on social media with a guy he followed based in Japan. The video Tyler remembered featured the golfer swinging the club while only lightly gripping the club with his forefinger and thumb with both hands. The intent of the clip was to show that golfers often grip their handles too tightly, and by doing so reduce both distance and accuracy.

The general concept was one Tyler knew about, and had known for years, though he'd never seen it demonstrated to such an extreme.

Now, he felt like he had no choice but to try to implement it.

He twisted his body, raising the club back until his wrists were above his waist, then he shifted and brought the club down. The face struck the ball in the center, and lofted it into the air toward a target green fifty yards away.

The ball landed on the right side of the green, and trickled forward until it stopped fifteen feet from the pin.

"That wasn't too bad," Tyler mumbled.

The sound of the shot and the motion of Tyler's swing behind him dragged Justin out of the mental moat he'd wandered into. He turned, crossing his arms, to watch Tyler hit another one.

Tyler pulled several more balls off the pyramid and positioned one near the previous spot on the turf. Again, he repeated his motion, and swung the club.

This time, the chip shot sailed straight toward the pin, only veering off course by five feet. It landed, bounced, and rolled past the flag, stopping a mere ten feet from the target.

"Not bad," Justin said, still leery of getting his hopes up. "How are you doing that?"

Tyler held up the club so his caddie could see the way he was gripping the handle.

"Why are you doing that?" Curiosity furrowed Justin's eyebrows.

"I saw a guy in Japan hitting balls like this with both hands. I'm only using my right to do it. The left is still the same."

Justin didn't seem convinced. "That's all well and good for pitching or chipping. But what about the bigger clubs?"

"He hit every club in his bag this way," Tyler explained. "Let me take a few more with the wedge, and then we'll work our way up."

Justin watched as his friend finished with the pitching wedge and then progressed through the full gamut of irons in his bag.

Tyler took one last swing with his 4-iron and watched the ball fly down the range, beyond the target green far off to the right.

"Are you sure your hand is hurting?" Justin asked. He felt the tease of confidence tempting him, reeling him back into a positive mindset.

Tyler nodded. "Yeah, it is. But with this grip, it isn't so bad. I barely feel it."

"Doesn't seem like it's affecting your distance at all. Your accuracy is pretty good too."

"Pretty good?"

"I mean, it's not as tight as usual."

Tyler shook his head and laughed. "Dude, I'm barely missing the targets. We can work with this."

"Fine. But let's see how you do with the woods."

Tyler sheathed his 4-iron and removed the 3-wood from his bag. He nudged a ball over onto the turf and set up his stance, wagging the club back and forth to loosen up, and to test his hand again.

The bigger club's weight strained his injured hand a little, but it still didn't cause the weakening loss of grip he'd experienced when trying to use all his fingers at the range the day before.

He lowered the club head down to the ball and took a swing.

His tempo was perfect, and the club whipped around in a smooth, fluid motion. The ball launched into the air at a low trajectory as if fired out of a cannon. It bent slightly to the left, curling over a green downrange before landing and rolling another thirty yards.

"How was that?" Justin asked.

"Felt good. Not as good as the irons but still doable."

"It looked good. You even had a baby draw on it. That'll come in handy if you can keep it going like that all day. Let's see what the big dog does, though. You're going to need the driver today with this field."

Tyler knew he was right. He'd need all the distance he could get to compete against the lineup of players in the regional qualifier.

He hit a few more shots with the 3-wood, each similar to the first.

Justin took the driver out of the bag for him and traded it for the 3-wood, handing the big club to his friend.

"Let's see what you got, buddy."

Tyler pulled a long tee from under his baseball cap behind his right ear and bent down to pick up a ball. He cupped the white sphere with his palm while pressing the base of the tee against it as he'd done thousands of times before. He found a spot on the grass he liked and teed the ball up before stepping back and taking a few practice swings.

He made sure not to whip the club around too fast.

Justin inclined his head, pushing his sunglasses up closer to his eyes as he watched.

Tyler set up his stance, addressed the ball, and paused as he set the club head down behind it. He took a breath, exhaled, and turned.

He twisted his body until his left shoulder and left hip pointed down at the ball. His right knee tightened as it coiled with energy. At the top of the swing, the long club shaft pointed toward the target for a moment before Tyler shifted his weight, twisting his hips and driving forward off the right foot.

The club looped around in a smooth and dramatic arc. The clubface struck the ball true, echoing across the range with a loud pop.

Tyler finished the follow-through and held the club high as he watched the ball rocket through the air, straight down the middle of the range.

It landed out near the limit of the practice area and rolled to a fence at the edge of the forest.

Tyler looked back at his friend, who simply stood there with a grim expression on his face, unwilling to allow a smile to crack the moment.

"That'll work," Justin allowed.

Tyler raised both eyebrows and pulled his sunglasses down his nose so his friend could see the whites of his eyes. "That'll work?" He pointed the club downrange with his left hand. "That was three hundred-plus."

Justin nodded. "How did the hand feel?"

Tyler shrugged. "It felt okay, actually. I guess most of the pain comes from using the other three fingers."

"Well, whatever you're doing, keep it up. Hopefully, you won't need those other fingers because today is going to be a long one."

27

Thirty-six players stood around a stage set up just beyond the patio overlooking the 18th green. A banner hung over the stage with the name of the tournament printed on it. The official logo of the professional tour occupied a space on the bottom right of the vinyl sign.

The regional director for the tour stood behind a microphone. He wore a light blue suit with a pink tie. He had thick, grayish brown hair, and wore glasses that looked like they were twenty years old. His tan told of years spent outside on golf courses, but the ill-fitting suit suggested he spent more time now behind a desk than he might have preferred.

"I'd like to welcome y'all to the final regional qualifier for the White Oak National Open Championship," he said in a Southern drawl. He squinted against the sunlight, though it was still early morning, and the sun was at his back.

"I want to congratulate all the players who made it this far. As I'm sure all of you already know, the winner today qualifies to play in next week's tour event along with three other regional qualifiers."

The spectators surrounding the players applauded.

The director waited until they settled down. "This tournament, as you know, is a shotgun start. Your caddies have your starting hole assignment and pairing. I want to wish you all the best of luck. So, get out there, and show us what you got. Let the tournament begin."

The crowd applauded again before dispersing to allow the players to filter through and make their way out to their designated holes.

Dozens of multi-row golf carts waited on the path behind the 18th green to take the players and caddies out to their designated holes.

"What hole are we starting on?" Tyler asked, feeling silly that he hadn't asked the question before.

"Seven," Justin answered.

"A par three to start the day? Not sure how I feel about that."

"Nothing we can do about it," Justin said. "Luck of the draw. Besides, it's good to start off with a shorter club. Gets you in the flow."

"Not sure if you noticed how I was hitting the ball on the range, but most of the clubs seemed like they were in a good flow."

"Don't get cocky. You need to stay focused."

"Yeah, I know." The words had barely left his lips when he saw Lucy standing off to the side of the cart path next to his mother.

Tyler grinned and hurried over to them.

"Hey, you," Lucy said, stepping out to meet him. She hugged him and then inspected his face. "Are you okay?"

"I'm fine. Thank you. And thanks for coming out. I really appreciate it."

Justin watched from behind him, only sparing a casual wave to acknowledge Lucy's presence.

"She said I could walk with her," Molly chimed in.

"What hole are you starting out on?" Lucy asked.

"Number seven."

"Players," the starter's voice boomed from the loudspeakers on the stage, "please make your way to your designated starting hole."

Tyler looked back at the stage, then to Justin, who wore seeming irritation on his face like drapes over a window. Tyler quickly smothered his joy at seeing his girlfriend and strapped on a serious expression.

"Well, I better get going. I'll see you two out there."

"Good luck, babe," Lucy said. She leaned in and kissed him on the cheek.

"Thanks." Tyler blushed as he turned and walked back to his friend. Justin picked up the bag and slung it over his shoulder.

Tyler's golf bag was half the size of everyone else in the tournament. All the other participants boasted bags similar to the ones the pros carried—the aircraft carriers of golf gear. Tyler and Justin spent more than their share of time with those monstrosities hanging from their shoulders. By comparison, Tyler figured today would be much easier for his friend. Although the tip wouldn't be much more than a high-five at the end—he hoped.

The two made their way to where a cart driver held a sign with three hole numbers printed on it, one of which was the 7th.

"Which number are you headed to?" the driver asked. Two golfers and their caddies were already on board in the front seats.

"Number seven," Justin answered. "Tyler Knox."

The guy checked his list, noted the name, and nodded. "I'll put that bag on the back for you." He looked at the old, smallish bag with a modicum of disdain, but laid it on top of the others already in the cargo area in the back of the long cart. "Just have a seat, and we will depart in a moment."

Tyler and Justin sat down in the next-to-last empty row.

"You ready?" Tyler asked, with a tempered excitement in his voice. Anxiety blended with this emotion, but it was that time just before playing a round that he loved so much. It was like getting on an airplane to take off to a foreign country—something he'd only done once on a class trip in high school. How his parents had afforded to send him, he had no idea.

"Yeah," Justin said. "I'm ready. But are you?" His question was doused in a bitter tone.

"As ready as I can be. Why'd you say it like that? What's wrong with you?"

"Nothing. I'm fine. Just keep your head in the game."

"My head is in the game. What's the matter? A minute ago you were fine."

"I said I'm good," Justin answered. "Let's just get dialed in. We both have our work cut out for us today."

Tyler stared at his friend for a minute then turned away. He wasn't sure why Justin's mood had soured all of a sudden, but he hoped his attitude would change. The last thing Tyler needed was to be around a bunch of negative energy on the most important day of golf in his life.

He heard someone talking to the cart driver behind him and looked back over his shoulder.

"Who am I paired with?" Tyler asked, leaning close and talking in a hushed tone.

"Merritt Clifford," Justin answered. "Metro champion from Nashville. Really good."

Tyler continued staring at his friend.

"What?" Justin asked after he realized Tyler was still looking at him.

"Everyone here is really good, bro."

"Yeah, that's true." Justin reached into his pocket and pulled out a packet of gum. "Want some?"

Tyler shook his head as Merritt approached.

"Good morning, gents," he said in a cheerful tone. "Nice morning for a round of golf, isn't it?"

Merritt Clifford was a skinny guy. Around six feet tall and only 150 pounds, he didn't look like the kind of guy who could hit the ball a mile. But his reputation defied that logic.

Tyler didn't know much about him, other than he was a club pro up in Nashville and that he could crush his driver.

"Morning," Tyler and Justin said simultaneously.

"What are you guys' names?" Merrit asked.

"I'm Justin Bennett."

"I'm Tyler Knox."

Merritt shook hands with both of them.

"Tyler Knox. You're the one I'm paired with." He had a smoother, softer Southern accent when he spoke, his voice lilting as if he came from the Georgia low-country, someplace like Savannah. True to his gentlemanly speech and demeanor, Merritt had dressed the part: white pants with a black belt and a white polo, finished off with a black sort of mesh-and-wingtip combination. If he'd had a horse, he would have been the white knight of golf.

Neither Tyler nor Justin was sure how this interaction was going to go. The world of golf was full of two kinds of people, just like in the real world. There were nice folks, and then there were people like Mitchell.

"Nice to meet you, Merritt," Tyler offered.

"You look like you're still in college."

"I am. Graduating next spring. We both are."

Merritt nodded. "That's awesome. Congratulations. I have to admit, I saw your name on the list and didn't know who you were."

Here we go, Tyler thought. *Another one like Mitchell.*

"Do you play on your college team?"

"I did. But I haven't the last two seasons."

Merritt seemed confused. "Oh?"

"Life got too busy," Tyler said, unwilling to hang out all his laundry.

"I understand that. Well, you must be good to have made it to the regional qualifier. That's not easy."

"No, it isn't. But I have a good caddie." He winked at Justin, who rolled his eyes at the compliment.

"Always important to have one of those," Merritt said.

"I'm also a caddie," Tyler added. "We both work here when we're not in school."

Merritt looked surprised at the admission but also impressed. "Really? Man, then you're going to have a huge advantage today. You must walk this course all the time."

"We do."

"Wow. That is so cool. A caddie playing for a chance to get into the open. If I wasn't playing, I'd definitely be cheering for you. Best of luck today, guys. Here's hoping one of us wins it."

Merritt's friendly interaction calmed Tyler's nerves a little. He genuinely seemed like a nice guy.

As the cart driver sat behind the wheel and pressed on the gas pedal, Tyler squeezed his injured hand a few times, clenching his fingers to the palm.

Tyler knew the next several hours were going to be the most challenging of his golf life so far.

The driver stopped the cart at the number 7 tee, got out, and walked around to the back. He lifted Merritt's bag from the cargo bin and set it down in front of Merritt's caddie, a middle-aged man with a scruffy beard and matching long hair named Joe.

Justin received Tyler's modest bag from the driver before the man took off toward the next tee box with the rest of his players.

Tyler walked up to the back of the tee box and waited. Justin joined him and set the bag down on its bipod. Both of them stared down the slight hill to the green. A wide creek ran in front of it, with two white sand bunkers hugging the right and left. A third sand trap lurked in the back center, framed by rows of Encore Azaleas. Poplars and dogwoods stood behind the landscaping, casting early morning shadows across the face of the large, undulating green.

Merritt and Joe joined the other two on the tee box.

"You want to go first, or you want me?"

"Doesn't matter," Tyler answered. "I'll let you decide if you want."

Merritt grinned at the gesture. "Let the fates decide," he said, pulling a tee out of his front right pocket. He tossed it into the air and watched it flip end over end until the white object landed on the grass pointing at Tyler.

"Looks like those old Greek ladies want me to go."

Tyler nodded. "Good by me."

He looked back to the green again, leaning closer to Justin. "Did the devil choose that pin placement?"

Justin laughed. "Looks that way."

The flag stood in the back-right corner of the green just below a gentle slope that rolled down to the plateau. Anyone who missed the shot short would end up in the bunker on the front side, and for those going long, they'd be in a difficult lie in the pine straw mulch around the bushes. Of course, any players looking to land the ball in the dead center faced the challenge of the slope leading down to the water's edge, a deadly mistake Tyler and Justin had seen their charges make dozens of times over.

Merritt's caddie discussed their strategy for the hole as if they were conspiring to overthrow the government. Then Joe reached into the bag and pulled out a 6-iron and handed it to Merritt.

The club pro stepped up to the center of the tee box and planted a ball on the grass between the two markers. He took a step back and waited, swinging the club around to get his muscles loose before the starters gave the signal.

"What are you thinking?" Tyler asked Justin.

"For most people? I'd say a five-iron here."

"For me?"

Justin smirked. "Maybe a seven-wood?"

"You're an idiot," Tyler laughed with his friend.

"You should be good with a seven-iron."

The two didn't need to discuss the yardage. They'd seen this position before, or one close to it. They knew exactly how far it was to the front of the green, to the back, and to the center. From there, the nuance of their skills as caddies kicked in, giving them accurate measurements down to the foot.

Justin took the 7-iron out of Tyler's bag and handed it to his friend.

He swung the club around a few times, making sure not to put too much pressure on his right hand, or grip it too hard.

A splinter of pain eked from the bridge of his hand, but it was what he'd felt on the range before and had been able to gut his way through it.

He felt like a racehorse standing behind the gate, waiting to be unleashed on the track. But all the golfers had been instructed to wait until the horns blared around the course to give them the start signal.

Tyler looked down at the grass as he swept the iron across the tops of the dewy green blades. After four quick swings, he stood up straight and looked back over to the right. Lucy and his mother were walking their way, hurrying to get to the tee so they wouldn't miss a thing.

Tyler felt a nervous tickle in his stomach at the sight of his girlfriend. Normally, he was relaxed when he played the game, but he'd never had a girlfriend there to watch before, and the stakes had never been this high.

Lucy and Molly stopped on the edge of the cart path and waited eagerly for the tournament to begin.

Justin's expression darkened when he saw the two arrive. A smattering of other spectators arrived, including their coworker Jeff, and a few of the other caddies. Tyler was thankful to see no sign of Mitchell anywhere. The last thing Tyler needed was that bully heckling him.

The horns sounded around the course, signaling the start of the tournament.

"Hit a good one," Tyler said in a gentlemanly manner.

"Thanks," Merritt answered. "We'll see."

The club pro stepped up to the ball, positioned his feet, and lowered the clubface. A second later, he twisted and fired the shot. The ball towered into the early morning air before reaching its zenith and plummeting down toward the target.

It landed with a thud, bounced, and rolled to a stop in the center of the green.

The assembled spectators clapped their approval as Merritt grinned, pleased with the first shot of the day.

"Great shot, Merritt," Tyler said.

"Thanks, man. It felt good."

Merritt walked back over to his caddie and handed him the club.

Tyler felt his heart racing in his chest. Nerves gripped him like they never had before, except maybe for the other night when he and Lucy shared their first kiss on the fairway.

He took a ball out of his pocket and placed it between the tee markers. He backed away from the ball for a moment, turning away from Justin and everyone else who stood behind his friend.

In that moment, it was just him and the green. He zeroed in his focus on the pin in the back right.

Throughout his life, Tyler had played everything safe, never taking many chances that could jeopardize his safety, or his future. He didn't drink, didn't use drugs, and even tried not to go too much over the speed limit when driving.

He didn't take risks. Except on the golf course.

Here, he was free—free to run wild, free to express himself, free to create in ways other golfers could not.

Tyler closed his eyes, took a deep breath, and sighed.

As he expelled the air from his lungs, he let go of his worries, his concerns, the problems that life had thrown at him. He forgot about Lucy watching him, about his mother being there, and even about Justin's self-imposed pressure that winning would take them both to the next level.

In that moment, Tyler could only feel the club in his hands, smell the fresh-cut morning grass, and see the target.

He stepped up to the ball again, addressed it, and wiggled the club in his hands, maintaining the loose grip with his right thumb and index finger as he'd done on the range.

After only a moment of hesitation with the clubface behind the ball, Tyler reached back, and swung.

The white sphere sailed into the sky, touching the rays of sunlight that sprayed onto the course above the canopy beyond the green. Then, it dropped like a bomb.

"Come on," Justin said from behind him.

The ball hit the green less than ten feet from the pin, bounced once, and rolled to the left, narrowing the putt to under eight feet.

The small crowd roared at the marvelous shot.

Tyler lowered his head in a sign of humility then smiled.

"Outstanding," Merritt exclaimed with both a look of surprise and approval. "Somebody's closer!"

Tyler chuckled at the movie reference. "Thanks."

He turned and handed the club to Justin, who'd already taken a step toward him. "No guts, no glory, eh, Ty?"

"We didn't get here by playing it safe," Tyler answered.

"No. No we did not."

28

Tyler stood on the number 5 green, staring down a fifteen-foot putt for birdie. He knew this green like the top of his knees. He'd played it many times, and scoped it out for other golfers as a caddie more than that. He knew the angles, the bends and rolls of the green. He even knew which way the grains of grass flowed, all of which factored into the way he played the putt.

Now, though, his future was on the line.

Before, it had just been for bragging rights, or for the appreciation of whatever golfer he was carrying a bag for that day.

This time, he was the one who needed to make the putt, and for way more than mere gloating with the other caddies in the shack.

With two holes to play, Tyler found himself at a remarkable 6 under par, similar to his practice round the previous week.

He'd refused to look at the leaderboards that had been erected in various places around the course for the tournament, and he'd instructed Justin not to tell him where he stood as far as the rankings were concerned—a secret he wasn't sure Justin could contain for the entirety of the round.

Tyler knew there was nothing he could do about the other golfers or how they performed. And knowing where they stood versus his position on the leaderboard wouldn't change how he went about things. It wasn't as if merely being aware of the standings could make him drive a ball farther or putt a ball better. All he could do was focus on himself and his swing and control the things he could control.

He'd played remarkably, but doubt nagged at him, demanding his attention. He knew he was close to tying the course record for the second time in two weeks—an incredible feat by anyone's standards, but the field was full of great golfers, and fear taunted Tyler with visions of multiple other players breaking the long-standing low score.

"We've seen this putt before," Justin said quietly, standing behind his friend, looking over his shoulder.

"Yeah," Tyler agreed.

"It's going to bend hard to the left."

"Yep. I'm looking at a little mark over there." He pointed to a dry patch of green where an old ball mark had been repaired.

"That's pretty high," Justin said. "But if you get the speed right, it should be good. Won't take much. You know what to do. Let the green do the work. All you got to do is steer it."

Tyler knew his friend was correct. Just to be safe, he knelt down one more time and squatted behind the ball, eyeballing the lay of the green.

Merritt and his caddie stood off to the right, having already made par on the hole. Tyler knew the club pro he'd been paired with was around 3 under for the day, a respectable score by anyone's standards, but not good enough to catch Tyler on this day.

Tyler forced the distracting thoughts out of his mind and let them loose into the sky to float away on the white clouds drifting across the blue sea nearby.

He made his decision and stepped up to the ball while Justin took a step back to the fringe and watched, biting his lip.

Lucy and Molly stood amid a growing number of spectators who'd taken interest in Tyler's round. He'd smiled at the two a few times during the round, but hadn't spoken to them since teeing off on number 7.

Tyler positioned his feet, gave one last look over at the mark he'd set as his target, and swept the putter through the center of the sphere.

The ball rolled toward the mark, crossed it, then began to dip toward the hole.

Everyone watching held their collective breath except Tyler, who stood up straight and started walking toward the hole as if he knew the putt was already made.

The ball neared the cup, and for a second it appeared as though it would roll just past the outer edge of the right side. But it turned sharply a few inches before the hole and fell straight into its heart.

The crowd erupted, some shouting loudly at the incredible feat.

Tyler walked up to the hole, bent down, and removed the ball. As he stood, he smiled at the spectators and tipped his cap toward them. They reacted with more loud cheers.

He made his way back over to Justin and gave him a fist bump with his left hand.

"Great putt, buddy," Justin said. "How's the hand feeling?"

"It's okay," Tyler said.

"You keep playing like this, I'm thinking maybe you shouldn't go back to your old grip."

"Yeah. Maybe."

Merritt approached, shaking his head. He wore an admiring grin on his face, as if he already knew he was beaten and was just taking in the spectacle of the round like one of the people in the crowd.

"That was amazing," Merritt said. "That putter has been on fire today, Tyler. Keep it up."

"Thanks, Merritt. I appreciate it."

"One more to go. Let's finish in style, yeah?"

"Yes, sir."

They walked off the green together, followed by the caddies, and made their way through a path carved into the landscaping under the shade of twin oak trees.

The golfers arrived on the 6th tee box and waited for the caddies to set the bags down just off to the backside.

The pairing ahead of them stood on the fairway, one off to the right, and one dead center.

The par 4 bent to the left in a dogleg approach, threatening players with a thick peninsula of trees that jutted out from the forest. The guy on the right had obviously tried to open up the angle and pushed his drive too far to that side.

Being the farther man back, he'd been the first to take his shot once the green cleared of the players ahead.

Now, the man standing in the center of the fairway sized up his shot and let fly.

The ball took off like a rocket, curling right to left.

Tyler's group couldn't see where it landed through the trees on the left side, though they could see the shirts of the players walking to the next tee box.

A polite applause echoed from around the corner of the forest. The shot must have been a good one, though there was no way to tell just how good from the number 6 tee.

Tyler stood patiently, watching as the men ambled around the corner to the left, making their way to the green. He turned, just for a moment, and glanced over his shoulder at Lucy and his mother standing amid a hundred spectators.

Lucy blew him a kiss, which Justin happened to spot as he was drawing Tyler's driver from the bag.

"Hey," Justin said. "Stay focused. Last drive of the day." He knew better than to add further pressure to his friend's mind by saying something like "Make it count" or "Don't screw it up."

But he didn't hide his agitation.

He handed the driver over to Tyler, who teed up his ball and took a step back.

Just like he'd done all day, he purged the audience, along with all the other distractions, from his mind. He'd never played in front of spectators before, and now their numbers had swelled to nothing he could have imagined save for his daydreams about someday playing on the pro tour.

Tyler sensed Merritt's gaze on him and glanced over at his opponent.

The club pro didn't say anything, but he offered an encouraging nod—a gentleman's silent way of saying he was beaten, and good game.

Tyler stepped up to the ball. He planted his feet the way he'd done all day and waited for a second.

The sun burned bright in the sky now, more than halfway to its destination on the western horizon. It hung over the forest to the left of the fairway, and the one beyond that shadowed the slopes of the ridge rising up from the valley.

Tyler looked down the fairway across his left shoulder, taking in the scene for a moment that felt like an hour. In truth, he could have stayed there that long. He didn't want the moment to end. That was how he always felt on the golf course—like it was heaven on earth, a place where he didn't have to worry about bills, or his mother, or classes, or exams, or anything else. Here, everything made sense. He truly reaped what he sowed.

Life, it seemed, rarely offered such a place, or such just rewards. Out here, you couldn't blame anyone else but yourself for the things that went wrong. But even when it seemed all was going awry, all Tyler had to do was take a deep breath and appreciate the glorious setting around him.

He bent down and brushed his fingers across the grass, feeling the tiny blades against his skin. Then he stood, addressed the ball, and locked his focus on the point where he needed to strike it.

It seemed Mother Nature herself paused as he turned his hips, lifting the club in his backswing. Then, in Tyler's perfect, smooth tempo, he whipped the head around and smacked the ball deep down the fairway.

The trajectory started along the right edge where the first cut met the smooth fairway's surface. But as it carried, the flight bent to the left, drawing toward the corner where the trees blocked anyone's path who dared try to take a shortcut to the green.

"Hang in there," Justin prayed.

The ball hit the fairway like a fighter jet landing on the tarmac. The top spin carried it farther, speeding it along the ground until it came to a stop ten yards to the right of the corner.

The crowd roared at the marvelous drive, and there were more than a few people shouting his name the second the ball left the tee.

Tyler walked back to his bag and nodded at Merritt, who simply shook his head, smiling at the incredible shot.

"I just now noticed that grip you had on the handle," Merritt said, puzzled. "Never seen anyone do that before."

"I hurt my hand late last week." Tyler fumbled for the rest of the explanation but decided to leave it at that.

"Wow. You injured your hand just days before this tournament, and somehow you figured out a way to make it work." Merritt couldn't believe it. "I hope you win this thing, man. You've earned it. And done it with one hand."

"Thanks," Tyler managed, joining Justin at the back of the tee box next to Joe.

The other caddie nodded at Tyler and mumbled, "Great shot, kid. That's how you finish."

Tyler thanked him quietly as Merritt teed up his ball and took a few loose practice swings.

Justin patted his friend on the shoulder, his silent signal of approval.

Merritt lined up his shot and swung the driver one last time. The ball flew down the middle of the fairway, only peeling off slightly to the right, but still landing him in the fairway with a direct approach to the green.

The audience applauded the shot as the men marched forward down the little slope off the tee box and onto the fairway.

Merritt looked over at Tyler as they walked ahead of the two caddies. "You just hit that ball over three hundred yards. With one hand. Maybe I need to take lessons from you!"

Tyler laughed at the thought. "Just lucky on that one."

"Nonsense. Look, kid. I've seen a lot of golf. Played a lot of golf over the years too. You're one of the best I've seen in person. And better than some on television."

"Well, I appreciate that," Tyler said with a shrug. "Hit one up on the green here, Merritt."

"I'll see what I can do."

The two split away from each other, both heading toward their spots. Thirty yards separated the two, and Tyler's was at least fifteen yards farther down the fairway than Merritt's.

Justin set the bag down behind Tyler's ball, where they waited for the other players to clear the green.

Once they were gone, Tyler and Justin watched as Merritt took an iron and knocked his ball up onto the middle of the green, leaking it toward the hole until it stopped twelve feet from the pin.

Tyler clapped along with all the other people in attendance. Justin nudged him with his fist. "Great shot, Merritt," he shouted across the field tightly cut of Bermuda grass.

"Dude. What are you doing?" Justin asked.

"What do you mean? The clapping? It was a good shot."

"Listen, man. He's the competition. You need to stay focused."

"Uh, I am focused," Tyler corrected. "And in case you haven't noticed, I'm pretty sure Merritt is several strokes behind me. Even if he wasn't, there's not enough good sportsmanship in the game, or in any sports nowadays. If someone makes a great shot, you should appreciate that. Even if it means you might lose."

Justin shook his head. It was clear he didn't share the same sentiment, but he let it go and redirected his attention to the shot.

"Eight-iron in from here sounds about right," he said.

Tyler nodded. "Yeah, that's what I was thinking.

"Wind is right to left. Maybe five miles per hour above the canopy. Might knock it down a little if it swirls, which it seems to be doing."

"You thinking I should go for the right edge and let it fall back toward the hole?"

"It's a risky play," Justin said. "But we didn't get here—"

"By playing it safe," Tyler finished.

Justin grinned devilishly at him. "There's no hazard over there, so even if you miss it right, you can chip up and scramble for par."

They both knew the bunker on the right-front edge posed a problem for choosing that line of attack, but neither voiced concern for it. Even with the breeze, Tyler knew he could carry the green. It was all about how close to the pin he could get the shot.

"Okay," he said. "Let's go with the eight."

Justin unsheathed the 8-iron, handed it to his friend, then stepped back away to allow Tyler room to get a few warm-up swings.

"How's it feel," Justin asked.

"Feels good. Really good."

He positioned his feet, addressed the ball, lowered the face, and paused. Then he swung in the same steady tempo he had all day long.

The sound of the iron striking the ball echoed off the trees and the little hills around the fairway and in the rough.

The spectators watched in rapt silence as the ball soared high into the air.

"Come on," Tyler mumbled. "Be good."

"Looks good," Justin said. "Wind is playing with it."

The wind cooked the ball to the left, altering the flight slightly, just as they'd expected.

The white sphere reached the top of its arc and began its descent. It screamed downward to the pin.

"I love that line," Justin whispered. "I really love that line." A hint of excitement trickled through his voice.

Tyler couldn't say anything. He merely watched in mesmerized silence like the hundreds following him on either side of the fairway.

The ball landed on the green beyond the bunker, smashing into the tight surface with a thump. It rolled toward the pin, traveling left to right, using the slight embankment to garner momentum.

"Be good," Justin prayed. "That one's got a chance."

The seconds crawled forward as everyone held their breath.

Then the ball hit the pin, circled it once, and fell into the hole.

For another half second, it seemed like the air had been sucked out of the entire planet's atmosphere.

Then the fairway exploded in cheers.

People shouted and clapped from all around. Justin wrapped his arms around Tyler from the back and shook him violently.

"Yeah!" he yelled. "You did it! You did it, Ty! You just broke the course record with an eagle on the last hole!"

A tidal wave of emotions crashed into Tyler all at once. Tears brimmed in the corners of his eyes as he turned and hugged his friend, both jumping in tandem.

They let go of each other and gave a high-five. Then Tyler turned to the crowd to the right of the fairway where Lucy and his mother stood waving and screaming.

He took off his hat and tipped it to them in thanks.

Across the fairway, Merritt just shook his head in disbelief for a few seconds before he raised a finger to the bill of his cap and tipped it Tyler's way.

The two met in the middle of the fairway on their way up to the green, both caddies walking at their sides.

"Is there anything you can't do with a golf ball, kid?" Merritt raised his hand. Tyler clapped palms with him and gripped it tight.

Merritt shook it hard, wearing a proud grin on his face. "That was unreal, Tyler. I think you just broke the course record."

Tyler couldn't think of a word to say. It was all so much to take in. He could only muster a few deep breaths.

He didn't believe it himself.

They neared the fringe of the green, and Merritt motioned to the pin. "Now, if you don't mind, get your ball out of my way so I can putt." He laughed as he said it, and Tyler chuckled at the comment.

Tyler ambled over to the hole, looked inside it, and shook his head, still having trouble comprehending what just happened. The white sphere sat in the bottom of the cup, and for a moment, he just stood there appreciating the moment.

Then he bent down and pulled it out amid another roar of cheers from the crowd. He held the ball aloft over his shoulder, pumping his fist. For a second, he was tempted to toss the ball into the spectators as a souvenir, but he held off. To them, he was still a nobody. Just a local kid who'd broken the course record. They'd forget him in a few weeks. But his mother would never forget him. And that was who this ball was meant for.

Merritt finished out with a two-putt for par, and after he retrieved his ball from the cup, walked over to meet Tyler halfway. They shook hands with each other, then exchanged the same gentlemanly "good game" with the caddies.

As they walked off the green, Merritt pulled his scorecard from his back pocket to mark his par and looked over at his young counterpart. "You have a bright future in this game, Tyler. I don't think I've ever said that to anyone in my life."

"Thanks," Tyler mustered. "I appreciate it."

Lucy and Molly ran toward Tyler, both nearly tackling him as they wrapped their arms around him.

"That was amazing!" Molly exclaimed. "You holed it out to break the course record."

Tyler nodded. "Did I win the tournament?" he asked.

Merritt overheard the question from a few yards away and laughed. "Seriously? You haven't checked the leaderboard all day?"

"No. I didn't want to put more pressure on myself."

Molly grabbed her son by both cheeks and peered into his eyes. "Sweetie, the guy in second place was three strokes back going into this hole."

The realization hit Tyler, and he turned to look Merritt's way. "You're the runner-up?"

"Looks that way, kid. Go get 'em in the open next week."

Merritt turned and walked off the green with his caddie by his side.

"You seriously didn't know you just won the tournament?" Lucy asked.

"He just said he didn't," Justin cut in. "Come on, man. We have to turn in our scorecard."

Lucy seemed jolted by Justin's abrasive response, but she gave one last hug to Tyler then kissed him on the lips. "I'll see you after."

"We're going out to eat to celebrate," Molly announced, a pride-filled smile stretching across her face.

"You don't have to do that, Mom." Tyler resisted as Justin pulled him away.

"Oh, hush. It's happening. Might as well enjoy it, Son."

29

L ucy parked her car in the driveway of her home and turned off the engine.

It had been an amazing day. She'd watched Tyler dominate the qualifier to earn a spot in the open the following week, and a chance to showcase his talents to the world.

She knew he was a prodigy of sorts from the first time she went to a driving range with him. She'd been around enough golfers in her young life to know the good from the bad, and more importantly, the good guys from the jerks.

Her parents had generally tried to keep boys away from her in high school, though the guys always came around, pestering her about going out on dates. She even went on a few, ironically the sparse ones her parents suggested were good ideas.

Lucy could see right through their recommendations. They cared more about appearances and legacies than she did, and the squabble earlier that morning had only served to reinforce that truth.

While not entirely materialistic, her mom and dad seemed bent on establishing a powerful family that would last for generations. And that could only be done by establishing relationships with other influential, and usually wealthy, families in the area.

She stepped out of her car and closed the door. The stars hid behind a thick blanket of clouds, quite the opposite of the other night when she and Tyler lay out on the fairway, staring up into the twinkling heavens before their first kiss.

Some of the lights were still on in the house, which was unsurprising. It wasn't yet ten o'clock, which was when her parents typically began getting ready for bed.

Still, the glow coming from the windows troubled her.

She'd left angry earlier that morning, an emotion Lucy knew her parents shared at the time of her departure. She doubted they'd gotten over it yet.

Insolent was one of the words she imagined her mother would use the instant she walked through the door, but there were a few other choice adjectives in the woman's arsenal that could be loosed.

Lucy had never felt unloved by her family. Quite the contrary. She knew they wanted the best in life for her. But the constant refusal to let her make her own decisions, except begrudgingly on rare occasions, felt like she was in an ivory prison.

She locked her car and walked up the steps to the front door, bypassing the garage just in case her parents were already in bed. The sound of the garage door opening would signal her arrival and possibly stoke another, more heated argument. Then again, it probably wouldn't matter. They'd hear her at some point anyway. She'd have to face her problems again at some point. Might as well be now.

Lucy opened the front door and stepped inside. To her surprise, her parents were both in the living room to the right, each reading a book.

She closed the door, knowing there was no way she'd manage to slip out of this one.

Her parents looked over at her, both with heavy eyes and disapproving stares.

"Hey," Lucy managed with a feeble wave.

"Where have you been?" her dad asked.

"Out to dinner."

"With that boy?" her mother demanded.

Lucy took a deep breath, trying desperately to calm her irritation. "Yes. And his mother. And some of his friends. We all went out to eat after the tournament, and then we all went to an arcade after that to celebrate."

"Celebrate?" her dad asked, his curiosity barging his ire out of the way.

"Yeah," Lucy said. "Tyler won the tournament. Actually, he dominated it. Set the club record with an eagle on the last hole. The second-place finisher was like four strokes behind him. He's extremely talented. And if you two could see past your egos, maybe you would figure out there's a lot more to him. He'll be playing in the White Oak Open next week. With the professionals on the tour. And it will be on international television. But maybe that isn't good enough for you two. Personally, he's good enough for me whether he's great at golf or not. Because I know he's an amazing person. Whether he makes the pro tour someday, or goes into some nonglamorous line of work, I love him. And you're either going to support my decisions as a grown adult, or you are going to push me away."

She walked over to the staircase. Before she could begin her ascent, her mother stopped her.

"Lucy," her mom said.

Lucy looked over at her.

"We only want what's best for you. Because your father and I love you. We just don't want you to ever go without in life."

"If I go without, that's my choice, Mom. I appreciate everything you and Dad have ever done for me. Truly, I do. Now, what I want you to do is support my decisions. And I choose to be with Tyler."

She climbed the stairs without another word. When she reached the top, she felt a wall of emotions bearing down on her.

She'd just disrespected her parents again, for the second time that day. But beyond that, she also felt liberated, as if the bars of her prison had been ripped away by a bulldozer.

Lucy entered her bedroom and closed the door behind her, then walked into the bathroom and turned on the shower to allow the water to heat up.

She removed her phone from her pocket and opened the screen, tapping on the text messaging app. There, she found the last message from Tyler and typed out a reply.

"I am so proud of you. And I am so in love with you. Congratulations, babe. You deserve this."

30

CHARLESTON

Graham sat by the fireplace in his study, scrolling through the day's sporting events on his phone.

He'd watched the Braves beat the Phillies earlier and now was checking the other updates.

Doing so was a minefield for Graham. He loved sports and liked to keep up with everything from baseball to European soccer. But he also tried to avoid any news about himself he might stumble across.

Opinion pieces were all that would come out about him at this point in his career, and the thoughts shared were surely never going to be positive. He could have written the headlines for them if they'd asked.

"Washed-up Old Sullivan calls it quits. Does anyone care?"

That one was probably the most demeaning one he could conjure, but he wasn't a sportswriter. They could be devastatingly creative when it came to their criticisms of pro athletes.

Try as he might to avoid golf-related news, he accidentally skimmed across a headline that grabbed his attention and wouldn't let it go.

Fortunately, it wasn't about him.

"Twenty-year-old phenom holes out eagle to clinch regional qualifier," the line read.

His curiosity piqued, Graham tapped on the link. The screen blipped, then the article filled the page.

He read through the first few sentences about a kid named Tyler Knox out of Chattanooga, Tennessee, where the southeast regional qualifier was played.

Knox had obliterated the competition, beating out the runner-up by a whopping four strokes to qualify for the White Oak National Open Championship.

Graham raised his eyebrows at the result. "Impressive," he said. "And the kid isn't even old enough to celebrate with a drink."

He tapped on the highlight video at the top and waited while it loaded. A few seconds later, the video began.

From the looks of it, the footage was shot on someone's phone. The amateur camera person was standing off to the side of the green, recording Knox as he hit his approach. The ball was nearly impossible to spot once it went airborne, but the person shooting the video must have tracked it with their naked eye, right up to the point the ball reappeared in the footage and thumped onto the green.

Graham watched, his eyes wide as the ball rolled to the cup, hit the pin, spun around it, and fell into the hole.

The crowd went wild, and the camera started bouncing up and down as the holder joined in the raucous applause.

"Wow," Graham said. "That's a heck of a shot."

He scrolled down to the article again and read through it in a few minutes. Apparently, the kid who won the qualifier was a caddie at that course. "Kind of an unfair advantage," Graham thought humorously. But he knew you still had to make the shots, still had to sink the putts. Knowledge of the course could only take you so far.

It was a feel-good story. There was no denying that. Local caddie wins his way into one of the major tour events. It was the kind of stuff Hollywood couldn't get enough of.

Graham finished reading the story then switched his phone over to the text messaging app. He looked at the last text he'd received from Alicia a few nights before.

He'd asked her if she was interested in getting a drink this evening, but she'd declined, saying she had things she needed to do for the weekend. She'd offered no specifics, just a bland, vague excuse as to why she couldn't meet up with him.

His old doubts crept their way into his mind. Feelings from a long-dead past resurrected.

You're not good enough, Graham. You don't deserve a woman like her. Always the bridesmaid, Graham. In life, and in golf.

He decided to message her again and hoped he wasn't going too far.

"I hope you're having a good weekend. I'm heading out of town in a few days to go to the open. I know this is kind of a reach, but I would love it if you could join me. Maybe that's too much too soon. But I really enjoyed our evening. I felt like we really connected. I don't know. Maybe I'm crazy."

He contemplated not sending the text, not putting himself out there to have his heart ripped out.

"Screw it," he said, and sent the message.

"If she says no. Fine. I'm too old to sit around being afraid."

He set the phone down and turned on the television.

"Oh great," he said as a familiar face abruptly filled the screen.

Jamie Winthrop was talking at a press conference about the upcoming open.

Before Graham could mute the television, Jamie began talking. "No, I feel good. My back isn't hurting. I'm ready to go out there and give it my best shot."

He'd recently had some issues with his lower back, but that hadn't stopped him from already claiming a major tournament earlier in the year. Graham partly wondered if Winthrop actually had any real back pain or if he was simply using it to get a little more attention—something it seemed the man could never get enough of.

Winthrop loved the spotlight, and with his career presumably on the downslope, it wouldn't be long before he was replaced by the next press darling.

That day couldn't come soon enough.

Graham changed the channel to the weather and left it there as he spaced out, watching the radar and the predictions for the upcoming week and beyond.

He looked down at his phone, hoping for a reply that he may have missed from Alicia, but there was nothing. Just the last text he'd sent.

He wondered if she'd read it, and if so, why she was ghosting him.

You went too strong, his insecurities warned. *What were you thinking? Asking her to go on a trip out of town with you. You went on one date, genius.*

Graham decided to unsend the text. He hoped it wasn't too late and pressed on the message to open the submenu. Unfortunately, the Undo Send option wasn't there. Which he knew meant she'd already seen the text.

And had chosen not to respond.

"Maybe she's just really busy," he said, hoping that was the case. Deep down, though, he knew it wasn't. He'd moved too fast. Or maybe she hadn't had as good a time on their date as she'd said.

Either way, the rejection he felt burned his insides, and there was nothing he could do about it. Just like all the other failures in his life.

31

CHATTANOOGA

"Happy birthday, dear Tyler!" the group sang. "Happy birthday to you!"

Everyone cheered as Tyler stared down at the cake sitting on the table in front of him. A single candle burned on top of it, flickering in the teasing fall breeze.

He waited, closing his eyes for a second as he made the obligatory wish.

In his mind, several options flashed through his imagination. Winning the open was the grandest. A new car was a more basic option, but there was nothing wrong with his. Another wish, one that involved him taking Lucy away on a vacation, just the two of them, blinked in and out of his mind's eye for a second. Her parents wouldn't approve of that; at least he didn't think they would. But he could dream.

Instead of all those flashy, fun, or romantic things, he zeroed in on the same one he'd wished for since he first started working at the age of fifteen.

Tyler had always wanted to give his parents a better life, one where they were financially free from the worries of paying bills, buying groceries, surviving from one paycheck to the next. They'd never done anything fun, or had anything nice for themselves. Meanwhile, they always sacrificed to give him better opportunities than they'd ever been afforded.

Golf was one of those.

Now, his father was dead. He didn't blame himself for failing to do something incredible for his dad. He'd simply run out of time, and it was an exceedingly rare thing for a man of his age or younger to experience such levels of financial success that would allow him to do the extravagant for his parents.

He'd heard of a few soccer players in Europe who made it big at the age of sixteen, but they were massive outliers.

His mind made up, Tyler visualized the image of his mother in a new, fancy house, with a luxury SUV sitting in the driveway. He imagined her standing in the driveway, opening her eyes for the first time as he surprised her with the new life, one where she would never have to worry about anything ever again.

Then he opened his eyes and blew out the candle.

Everyone cheered, and then the conversations broke out among the attendees.

The party was nothing fancy. His mother had ordered an ice cream cake in his favorite flavor—cookies and cream. There were four pizzas and sodas to go with them, all spread out on the table in the gazebo next to the apartments' swimming pool.

This time of year was too cold for swimming, so Tyler's birthday party had the run of the place all to themselves.

Lucy stood next to him and leaned in to kiss him on the cheek. "Happy birthday, sweetie," she said, grabbing his waist firmly.

"Thanks," he said, blushing.

He still couldn't believe she was his girlfriend. It had all happened so suddenly. They'd gone from being good friends to this. Tyler didn't want that feeling to go away.

His mother hugged him around the shoulders from the other side.

Some of the caddies, including Justin, stood on the other side of the table, along with a few other friends from high school.

"Thank you all for coming," he said, looking down at the ice cream cake his mother had bought. "Let's cut this before it starts melting."

Molly offered to do it, but Tyler insisted, picking up a knife and slicing into the cake.

"Son, it's your birthday. You should get the first piece," she said.

"It's okay, Mom. I'll get a piece."

He cut slice after slice, passing them out until everyone had a piece. Then, he cut one for himself and placed it on a plate.

"Hey, Tyler," Jeff said with white ice cream smeared on the left corner of his lips. "You ready for the big dance?"

Tyler had been thinking about almost nothing else since winning the qualifier three days before.

He felt good about it. Sure, it would be a dream come true to be the first amateur to win a major tournament in nearly a hundred years—Omaha native, and orphan, Johnny Goodman had been the last way back in 1933—but the reality was his victory in the open was what scientists called a statistical improbability.

"As ready as I can be," Tyler answered. "Justin and I have to go to the course tomorrow for press day and to get registered."

Just saying it out loud seemed strange to Tyler, as if he'd just walked through a portal into a new dimension.

He'd already been called by the local news outlets and asked for interviews. Tyler told them all he would be happy to, but the television appearances would have to work around his class and caddying schedule. The people from the networks had been shocked at his reaction to their offers, but also sounded as if they admired his commitment to his education and to his work ethic.

Tyler had lived in the area his entire life but never once been able to enter the sacred grounds of White Oak National. He'd watched nearly every one of the opens held there for most of his life, but only on television.

Once, one of the members had offered him tickets to one of the practice rounds, but the timing didn't work out. His mother had needed some additional help with the bills that month, so Tyler couldn't afford to skip work to go watch the pros work on the finer points of their game leading up to the tournament.

Now, however, he would be one of the players in the open. No ticket required.

He'd been given four guest passes—one for Lucy, one for his mom, and two additional ones. He figured Jeff would like to attend and had offered it to him earlier that evening.

The younger guy had nearly fallen over at the offer and had hugged Tyler when he accepted the gift.

That left one other ticket.

Tyler regretted he couldn't give it to his father. He'd even considered leaving the ticket for him on his headstone at the cemetery. But that would be a waste, even if it was a poetic gesture.

He and those attending his party enjoyed the cake and casual conversation. They talked about doing something crazy like jumping in the pool, but no one did. Even though it was still warm out, the temperature had already started tilting toward the coming winter, with lows dipping into the forties after midnight.

Justin walked around the table with his empty plate and dropped it in the trash bin near the gazebo's railing. He made his way to Tyler's side and put his arm around his shoulders.

"Happy birthday, buddy," he said. "Finally twenty-one years old."

"You want me to buy beer for you. Don't you?" Tyler asked, half joking.

Justin laughed. "Of course I do. But beyond that, it's a big milestone in your life, man. And what a present, getting to play in the open. Right here in our hometown. That's a good birthday right there."

Tyler nodded. "Yeah. I just wish Dad were here to see it."

Justin sobered. "I know, man. I know. I wish he was here too."

"But hey. Look at all these people here for you. You got friends who love you, man." He glanced at Lucy, who was in the corner talking to Tyler's mom while they ate cake. "Just keep your eyes on the prize."

Tyler snorted at his friend's persistent focus on the big tournament. But deep down, it was starting to get old. "Relax, man. We made it into the open. I'll do my best. That's all I can do."

"I know. I know. And I don't mean to put any pressure on you. I just..." He faltered.

"Yes?" Tyler tried to pry it out of him.

"We don't need any distractions. That's all. You have a chance to do something in this tournament. You're not just another amateur who qualified, Ty. You're the real deal. You broke the course record at Green Mont."

"You and I know that course like the back of our hands," Tyler said. "We know all the breaks, all the angles. We've never played White Oak before, or even walked the grounds."

Justin nodded. "I know. That's what the practice rounds are for. You'll be fine. And I'll make sure to have all the reads by the time the first round starts."

"I appreciate it, man. You're a good friend. And a great caddie."

"I guess we'll both be put to the test."

"We definitely will."

32

CHARLESTON

G raham sat in the coffee shop, nibbling on his croissant. He'd chosen a seat in the old garage area to enjoy the fresh morning air.

Before heading here, Graham considered going to a different coffee joint. It had been several days since his date with Alicia, and he didn't want to look like a stalker, or at the very least, desperate.

His stubbornness, however, led him straight back to his usual coffee spot. That, and he decided to risk it since Alicia hadn't worked the morning shift before that fateful day. He'd been both relieved, and disappointed, when he arrived and saw she wasn't there. It was what he'd expected.

He took a sip of the hot coffee and stared out at the street. Cars drove by slowly until the stoplight halted them at the intersection. This time of day, there were more vehicles than pedestrians. Most people were on their way to work, commuting to their jobs around the city. Those on foot were mostly freelancers or those running online businesses of some kind.

No matter where everyone was going, they all needed coffee to get their day started, which pumped tons of money into the coffee shop on a daily basis.

None of the other customers seemed to recognize him, which was the norm when he came here. Few of them were golfers, and tucked away in the corner, he could enjoy his meal and coffee in peace.

Still, he wished one person would interrupt the morning routine. But as the minutes dragged on, he realized that wasn't going to happen.

He took another bite of the croissant and chewed on it for a moment, contemplating his next move. He'd be leaving for Chattanooga later that evening and knew that even if he wanted to book a flight for Alicia, that would be virtually impossible at this late notice.

What was he thinking? She wasn't coming. The sooner he squared with that, the better.

He reached over and picked up the paper coffee cup, raising it to his lips. "Oh well. I guess it's for the best."

Graham didn't believe that. But his whole life had been like this— one disappointment or tragedy after the other.

It was better to just not get his hopes up.

He took a sip of coffee as a woman appeared around the corner of the building in a light jacket, tight jeans, and a baseball gap.

Graham nearly spit out the brew, but managed to catch himself.

Alicia stood on the sidewalk, staring into the alcove at him. She looked as if she'd been crying. Her eyes were red, her face flushed.

Graham stood up out of instinct.

She rushed over to him and stopped at the other side of the table.

There were only a few other people out in the garage, and none paid any attention to them.

"Hey," he said, fumbling for the words he wanted to say.

"Hi," she answered, choking a little on the word.

"Listen, I didn't mean to—"

"No. I'm sorry. I had a great time with you the other night. And it scared me."

"Scared you?"

She nodded. "Yes." She stepped closer. He could smell the perfume lacing her neck, carried to him by the warm, humid air. "I wasn't sure I could trust anyone anymore. I didn't want to trust anyone, actually. But then, after our date, I found myself wanting to trust you. I really had a great time. And I'm sorry I haven't responded to your messages."

He grinned at her, hoping to disarm her fears.

"I wasn't sure either," he added. "I enjoyed spending the evening with you. I didn't want it to end, if I'm being honest. But I have trouble trusting too, after what happened before."

"I understand," Alicia said. "I'm sorry I can't go with you to your tournament this weekend. But I have to stay here and work. Just know that I want to go with you. And I would love to see you when you get back."

Graham felt tears pooling in the corners of his eyes. He smiled at her, this time with a goofy grin that spread across his face. "Thank you," he said. "I appreciate you being honest with me. And I'm not going to tell you that you can trust me just to set aside your fears. I know that won't do it. But I'll do my best. That's all I can offer."

"I know you will," she said, tears streaking down the sides of her cheeks.

"I, um, feel like I'm supposed to hug you right now. But I don't know how you—"

She stepped close and wrapped her arms around him. Graham squeezed her tight as he whispered in her ear. "Did you want to get a cup of coffee?"

Alicia shook, laughing at his question. "I hear this place is pretty good."

He tilted his head to the side, inhaling the scent of her hair, her perfume, even her laundry detergent.

"It is. But their best barista isn't working right now."

33

CHATTANOOGA

Tyler had never felt so nervous in his entire life.

The entire scene was surreal, from the moment he'd pulled up to the security gate that morning.

The guard at the gate had asked for his identification, even given him a suspicious look that paired with the awkward, judging once-over he gave Tyler's car.

"Oh, you're the local kid," the guard had said. "My apologies, Mr. Knox. Hey, we're pulling for you this week."

Tyler thanked the man and drove ahead down the winding, tree-shaded lane until he reached the parking area on the right. A parking attendant motioned him through, pointing toward another guy in uniform who directed the incoming cars to open spots.

Tyler left his vehicle parked next to an Aston Martin Vantage, which was parked next to a Ferrari. There were plenty of high-end SUVs in the lot as well, and a smattering of Bentleys.

A sinister part of him that resided in the back of his mind kept telling him he didn't belong here, that he was out of his league, that he should go get in his car and drive home.

"This is your place. You belong," he said to himself as he walked across the lot toward the clubhouse; a huge, white building with clap-board siding and cedar roofing.

Columns towered up to the second floor, supporting the portico over the entrance.

Tyler rechecked his shirt multiple times as he crossed the lot to make sure it was tucked in, and in doing so suddenly realized he only had three golf-appropriate shirts and only two pairs of pants that would pass the dress code.

He'd have to deal with that later. He had a little money in his savings account he could use to buy another shirt and two more pairs of pants. Then again, if he didn't make the cut, he would only need two outfits. That thought, for some reason, brought him a sliver of bitter comfort.

At the door, a young woman in a flower-print sundress and white heels greeted him with a practiced smile.

She held a tablet in one hand and had a radio piece attached to her right ear.

"Hello," she said. "Caddies will go that direction," she said, pointing to Tyler's left.

"Oh, I'm not here to caddie," he corrected as politely as he could manage.

"Oh, I'm sorry. Are you working the concessions?"

"No, ma'am," he said, feeling even more out of place than he thought possible. "I'm Tyler Knox. I'm one of the golfers."

The young woman's cheeks might have burst into flames had they turned any hotter. Her smile evaporated from embarrassment, and he immediately felt bad for her.

"I. Am. So. Sorry, Mr. Knox."

"Please, it's fine," he said, dismissing the mix-up. "Honest mistake. And you don't have to call me that. Just call me Tyler. You can't be older than me."

The color in her cheeks dimmed slightly. "Well, I am definitely. I heard you're only twenty years old."

"I just turned twenty-one."

"Oh, happy birthday." Her straight, dark brown hair shook back and forth as she turned her head, still in disbelief at her silly mistake. "I'm not sure how I didn't know what you look like. You're from here. I'm from here. We could bump into each other at any point in town."

"True. But I'm not a well-known person like some of the guys in this tournament. I'm just the local amateur."

"Hey, your score is the same as everyone else's right now. You got just as good a chance as anyone."

He smiled. She was pretty, in a high-society sort of way. Not his type, but he'd have to be blind not to notice. For what it was worth, she seemed like a nice person.

"So," she said, "you'll be going in through these doors. There are four press rooms. The main one is for the top seeds in the tournament. You'll be in room number four. Just go down the hall to the right, then you'll see it on the left. It's called the Magnolia Room. Can't miss it."

"Thanks. And your name is?"

"Emily. Emily Banks. Nice to meet you, Mr.... I mean, Tyler."

He shook her hand. It was delicate, and the skin was soft, as if it had been bathed in cocoa butter every night for her entire life. But the grip was strong, which he liked. Just from the handshake alone, he could see why she'd been given organizational responsibilities.

"Thanks again, Emily. I appreciate your help."

"You're welcome. And I'm so sorry for the misunderstanding."

"All good." He walked through the door and into another world.

The door closed behind him, sealing him off from the life he'd known for over twenty years.

A massive trophy case stood directly ahead, with names engraved on various cups and statues contained within the massive glass-and-oak frame.

To the left and right, old portraits hung on the walls, some of famous golfers, others of American presidents, and even a few of foreign dignitaries who'd either played here or were members.

Tyler knew about the membership roster here. There were celebrities, top-level professional athletes from every major sport, and several A-list politicians. That feeling of not belonging swelled in his chest. And he had to remind himself that he'd earned his spot here.

He turned right as prescribed by Emily and walked down the hall. The wooden floors, the paint on the walls—everything in this place felt like walking through a dream. A very expensive dream.

Several people stood in the hallway ahead of him. He recognized a few of the faces from the pro tour but didn't want to interrupt their conversations. Tyler was glad Justin wasn't with him. He probably would have stopped and asked for selfies.

Instead, Tyler simply eased by the men, gave a polite nod, and kept going.

He passed the first three doors to the press rooms and arrived at the last one on the left. A sign to the right of the double doors indicated it was the Magnolia Room.

A man in his mid-sixties with gray hair and a navy-blue blazer smiled at him. "How can I help you?" the man asked.

At least he didn't assume I was the help, Tyler thought.

"I'm Tyler Knox. I was told I had to be here for a press conference."

"Tyler," the man said excitedly. "So great to meet you." He shook Tyler's hand in a firm, vigorous grip. "Congratulations on qualifying for the open."

"Thank you, Mr...."

"Tompkins. Chester Tompkins. Your presser will be just through these doors here in twenty minutes. Have you ever been here before?"

"No, sir. I've always wanted to. This place is like my church."

Tompkins leaned in close and spoke in a conspiratorial, hushed tone. "I felt the same way the first time I set foot in here. And I'll tell you, after forty years, that feeling has never gone away. It's truly an honor to be able to come into this building for my job."

"I bet." Tyler glanced around at some of the furnishings.

"You can go in and get set up at the table in front if you like. Or the bar and restaurant are at the other end of this hall, to the left of where you came in the main entrance. They have coffee and breakfast food in there."

Tyler wanted a cup of coffee and to stuff his face with biscuits or whatever they were serving in the restaurant. But he decided to wait on that in case he threw up from being so nervous in front of a room full of journalists.

"I think I'll head down there after this is over," he said, trying to quell the anxiety trembling in his voice.

"No problem." Tompkins pulled open the heavy wooden door and held it. "I'll see you after you're done.

"Thanks again, Mr. Tompkins. I appreciate it."

"Sure thing, Tyler. Best of luck."

Tyler wasn't sure what he expected when he walked through the doors. But it wasn't a small ballroom full of chairs with a table up front on a foot-high stage.

Several cameras on tripods lined the side aisles, and a half-dozen reporters were already scattered around the room.

Tyler started rethinking the coffee and breakfast idea, but if he walked out now, he'd look like an idiot. So, he made his way to the front where another man, probably five years younger than Mr. Tompkins, stood next to the stage, wearing the same outfit as the man he'd just met at the doors.

"Good morning," Tyler greeted the guy. "I'm Tyler Knox."

"Tyler. Welcome. I'm Jerry Colton. Great to meet you. You need me to get you anything? Coffee? Water?"

Tyler noticed a few bottles of water sitting near the microphone in the center of the table. "Can I have one of those?"

"Sure. That's why they're there."

"Great." Tyler stepped up onto the stage, walked across, and grabbed one of the bottles before returning to Colton.

"You'll be on in just under twenty minutes. If you'd like to have a seat over here to the side, we'll wait until everyone's ready and begin the session." He indicated a couple of chairs positioned near the wall to the left of the stage. "You ever done one of these before?"

Tyler shook his head. "No, sir. And I'm a little nervous."

"You'll be fine. Anyone who can break the course record at Green Mont belongs on that stage."

Tyler's eyes lit up. "You heard about that?"

"Of course. I've played that course many times. Sadly, I was never able to get the best caddie out there." He winked at the insinuation.

"Well, I'm afraid my caddie for this weekend is the best we have at Green Mont. But thank you for the compliment. Maybe the next time you're out there I can be on your bag."

"Maybe. But not this weekend. This weekend, you're playing with the big boys. And from what I hear, you can give them a run for their money."

"I'll do my best, sir."

"I'm sure you will."

34

Tyler's nerves twisted in his gut.

He sat behind the table on the little stage, staring out at the room full of reporters. There were more people than he expected in the seats, but he figured that was due to some of the pros that would be entering the room to follow up his interview.

There was no way they could all be there for him.

He recognized a couple of the local news sports anchors, people he'd seen on television hundreds of times. Now, they were here for him.

It was weird, to say the least. Tyler just hoped he didn't say something stupid.

Mr. Colton stood up from his seat next to Tyler and settled down the murmurs in the room.

"Thank you all for coming out today. Welcome to White Oak National. First off, you all know the ground rules. Keep your questions concise, and please be polite to our guests. I'm looking at you, Erik." He pointed to a reporter with a shaved head in a gray cardigan off to the left.

Everyone in the room laughed, though Tyler didn't get the joke.

He guessed Erik must have been one of those journalists who asked the tough questions, the kind that made people uncomfortable both to answer and to read it in print after the fact.

"Now, our first guest of the day is Chattanooga's own Tyler Knox. And I can see from the turnout to this press conference that you all are just as curious about this young man as the rest of us."

Tyler frowned, unsure he deserved this kind of attention.

"Tyler, as many of you have heard, qualified for the open through the regional tournament here in town, at Green Mont, where he broke the course record in dramatic fashion. I'm sure most of you have seen the viral video of the eagle he holed out to clinch his spot here."

People around the room nodded, each wearing approving grins.

"So, without further delay, please welcome Mr. Tyler Knox."

A round of light applause echoed through the room before hands shot up.

There wasn't a reporter in the place who didn't have a hand raised. It was as surprising as it was daunting.

Mr. Colton called on the first reporter, a middled-aged man in front with a black vest that featured the White Oak National crest over the right breast.

"Go ahead, John. Kick things off."

"Thanks, Jerry. Tyler, is it true that you're a caddie over at Green Mont?"

Tyler glanced over at Colton, who gave a nod. Then, Tyler leaned into the mic and answered. "Yes, but not this week."

The audience laughed at the response, and their reaction sent a calming ripple through Tyler's body.

Colton called on another journalist, a blonde woman from one of the big golf magazines.

"Tyler, how does it feel to be here at the open?"

He smiled. So far, these were easy. "I don't mean to sound cliché," he said, "but it's quite literally a dream come true. I used to visualize this very thing when I would go to bed at night. The White Oak

National Open Championship is, in my opinion, the best tournament in golf, and played in the best setting in the world. Then again, I'm biased to my hometown."

"Are you nervous?" another reporter asked when called upon.

Tyler took a deep breath, exhaled, and nodded. "I think I'd be a fool not to be. The best golfers in the world are here. Just getting to walk the same greens, the same fairways as them, it's a tremendous honor."

"Do you have a favorite golfer?" a brunette woman asked from the front row.

"Graham Sullivan," Tyler answered without hesitation. "He's always been my favorite. I've followed his career since I got into the game when I was a kid. I tried to model my swing after his too."

"So, you know that this tournament is going to be Graham's final appearance in a major," the reporter followed up.

"Yeah. I saw that. I'm sure he has plenty of good golf left in him, but it's his life. I suppose we all have to face that decision at some point."

Colton called on another journalist near the back.

"How do you like your chances this weekend?"

It was a direct question, and one that Tyler hadn't anticipated. He supposed they asked every golfer that one, but he was just an amateur, a mouse among giants. That didn't change his response, though.

"Right now I think I have just as good a chance as anyone to win this thing. I wouldn't be here if I thought differently. I doubt there are any other golfers in this tournament who showed up thinking they're not good enough to win it all, or just to collect a paycheck from finishing thirtieth. You play to win, to beat yourself and the course. That's what I plan on doing."

"You realize that no amateur has won a major since the 1930s," the reporter followed.

"Yeah. I know," he said. "So, I guess it's overdue."

The room filled with a friendly laugh.

"Do you feel like you're out of place here?" Erik in the gray cardigan asked. "As an amateur among the professionals?"

Tyler thought about the question for a moment. He looked down at his hands folded in front of him. The right hand was feeling better than it had since the altercation with Mitchell, but the reporter's question brought that event back to the forefront of his mind. The things Mitchell had said, and others like him through the years, rang in Tyler's head.

"Yeah, I do," he said. "I grew up poor. My parents couldn't get me golf lessons or buy me new clubs. But they saw potential in me. They saw how much I loved the game, how dedicated I was to getting better at it. They sacrificed, scrounged, and figured out a way for me to learn, to practice, to play, and to develop. When I came here today, I parked my car next to an Aston Martin, and next to it was a Ferrari. I saw Bentleys in the lot too, as well as some other cars I didn't know existed. So, yes, I feel out of place in a setting like this, surrounded by a life I could only dream about before."

Some heads nodded. Through his honesty, Tyler was melting the reporters' normally chilly exteriors. Maybe one reason so few of them asked the tough questions was because the pros usually gave canned answers, something put together by an overpriced consultant.

"But I don't feel out of place on the course, with a club in my hand and a ball between my feet. There, everyone is on the same level. The cars. The houses. Where we came from. How we grew up. Who our parents were. None of that matters. The only thing that matters then is you and the ball. We are all equal off the first tee. And we have eighteen holes to show what we really are."

The long response left the room in stunned silence. No one else raised their hand.

Even Mr. Colton seemed taken aback by the young man's forthright yet provocative answer. He cleared his throat, and leaned forward to the microphone in front of him. "I think that wraps it up for this session. Thank you so much for your questions. I'm sure we'll all be following Tyler's tournament closely this weekend."

He stood and motioned for Tyler to do the same. They stepped off the side of the stage where Colton clapped him on the shoulder. He met Tyler's eyes with a proud grin. "That was terrific. One of the better opening pressers we've had here in a long time."

"Thanks. I wasn't sure if I did okay."

"You did great, son. Just great. They'll all be watching you with keen interest this week. That's for sure."

35

Graham walked through the entrance, offering a polite nod to Emily at the door. "Good morning, Emily," he said in a kind voice.

"Good morning, Mr. Sullivan," she replied. "I guess you know where you're going."

"Yeah. Looks like they tucked me back in the Magnolia Room this time."

"Yes, sir. Best of luck in your tournament."

The door closed behind him as he entered the building. He stared at the trophy case in front of him as if looking at it for the first, and last, time. One of those was undoubtedly true.

It was possible he might return to White Oak at some point, perhaps as a guest on one of the networks. But he doubted it. He had no interest in being a talking head.

He didn't have much of a plan in place yet for when he retired. As much thought as he'd given it, the future remained, as always, elusive and uncertain.

Graham walked down the corridor, passing several other golfers along the way. He greeted each of them in a friendly but disconnected manner, more out of the social convention of it than anything else.

It wasn't that he disliked them. He just wanted to do his interview and go get lunch.

He stopped at the open doors of the Magnolia Room and peered inside.

Another golfer, Antonio Garcia from Spain, walked by, exiting the room.

"Hey, Graham," Antonio said. "Good luck out there, old friend." He clapped Graham on the shoulder and offered a sincere, white toothy smile.

"Gracias, amigo," Graham answered. "Buena suerte."

Graham entered the room and walked toward the front.

There were only eight reporters in attendance, which was both disheartening and yet also a relief. He didn't feel like dealing with a room full of journalists asking him about his health, his mental state, his age, his disappointing finishes, his legacy.

He just wanted to talk about this weekend's event as if it were any other tournament, and then go back down the hall to get a chicken biscuit.

"Good to see you, Graham," Jerry Colton said as he neared the stage.

"Good to see you too, Jerry. You ready or do we need to wait?"

Graham surveyed the room again.

"It's time to start if you're okay with it."

Graham snorted a thoughtful laugh to himself. He'd been put in the last room, the place where the newbies did their interviews, or those whose careers were swirling the drain.

He'd expected this, though part of him believed there would be a few more people in attendance.

"Let's do it," he said.

Colton stepped up onto the stage with Graham following behind.

The two sat down at the table behind the microphones. Graham opened one of the bottles of water sitting in front of him while Colton introduced him.

"As many of you know, this will be Graham Sullivan's final major tournament appearance." He glanced over at Graham. "Unless he decides to change his mind."

The room chuckled, and Graham offered a humble smile in response as he shook his head.

"Graham Sullivan has had an incredible career, and it is our honor to play host to his final major event. So, we'll begin with questions now."

A few timid hands went up, which was just as striking as the lack of people wanting to ask questions.

"Graham," Erik in the gray cardigan began, "since you made your announcement, you've been asked why now? Why this tournament? Do you care to comment?"

Graham rolled his shoulders. "I think I've said it all before, but sure. There comes a time in everyone's career when they have to hang it up. Some do it later. Some sooner. This felt like the right time for me. Always do what feels right."

"Hey, Graham," the blonde in the back said.

"Hey, Jenny," he answered.

"How are you feeling going into the tournament this weekend?"

He nodded. "Actually, I feel really good. Better than I have in a long time." As he answered the question, it was as if the realization happened at the same time. He did feel better than he had in a long time, and he wasn't sure why. Something in his chest felt warmer, more positive, as if a long-dead belief had been revived. His thoughts drifted to the barista in Charleston, her kind face, sincere eyes, the smell of her hair. He wished she could be there. But they hadn't even been on a second date yet. Now that he was going to retire from golf, he'd have plenty of time to make sure that happened.

"So, you like your odds?" Jenny followed.

Graham hummed a laugh. "Well, I don't think anyone my age has ever won a major tournament. But I wouldn't be playing if I didn't think I had a chance to win."

"That's exactly what Tyler Knox said earlier this morning."

Graham leaned closer to the microphone. "Did he?"

"Yes. He's the local amateur that qualified through the tournament at Green Mont."

"Remarkable what he did there. I read about it. Eagle to break the course record, right? Incredible. I don't know much about him, but I'd say he definitely has as good a chance as any. "

The brunette woman on the front row raised her hand and spoke. "In his conference this morning, he said you were his favorite golfer. How does it feel to know you've had such an impact on the younger players of the game?"

"Well, first off, I'd say this Knox kid has poor taste in favorite golfers."

The room filled with laughter. After it settled down, Graham went on. "But that's cool, all kidding aside. It's always a good feeling to know that you're someone's favorite. Everyone likes to be picked."

"He said that he styled his game after yours. It would be interesting if the two of you were paired together at some point this weekend."

"Yeah. That would be fun." Graham wore a thoughtful expression, dipping into silence with the rest of the room. "I guess it would make for a good story for y'all. But look, we're all just golfers out here, trying to master a game that can't be tamed. You could play for a thousand years and never have the perfect round. That's what brings so many of us together on courses all around the country. On weekends with friends, or doing business on a Wednesday afternoon, golf is the ultimate challenge of both physics and your will. That, and there is nothing more addicting than catching that sweet spot. The sound, the feel of how the ball jumps off the face." He paused. "That's what keeps you coming back to the course, no matter how bad you may have played before. Or how much life might have beat you down."

The room fell into a deep silence. For a moment, Colton didn't know what to say either. After a prolonged five seconds of waiting for another reporter to raise their hand, he leaned forward and thanked them for coming out.

When the crowd began to disperse, Colton looked over at

Graham, who sat there gripping the water bottle with a fist so tight it might have burst.

"You okay, Graham?" he asked, making sure his voice didn't reach the microphones.

Graham nodded absently. He stared down at the table, his eyes locked on nothing in particular. "Yeah," Graham lied. "I'm good."

He waited until the room cleared before exiting back out into the hallway. He turned and made his way back toward the entrance, passing it to continue into the bar where the noise of several indistinct conversations filled the air.

Graham was mentally prepared for the scene he expected to find in the bar area, and wasn't disappointed when he rounded the corner.

Dozens of golfers stood around, sharing stories from their travels, their home lives, and even a little about the parts of their game they'd been working on leading up to the open.

Graham made his way over to the bar and ordered a glass of sweet tea as he sat down. He wasn't in the mood to mingle, but he also knew he needed to spend a little time there for posterity. It was customary to make an appearance. Just like it would be at the pre-tournament dinner tomorrow evening.

The bartender, a cute blonde with her hair pulled back in a ponytail, brought him his glass of iced tea and set it on top of a square napkin.

"Would you like anything else?" she asked.

"No, thanks. Just the tea for now."

"Let me know if you change your mind."

He acknowledged with a nod then turned in his stool to survey the room.

Graham recognized nearly everyone in there, save for a few newcomers to the tour he hadn't met yet. Just as he finished sweeping the room, his eyes fell on the one face he didn't want to see.

Jamie Winthrop was twenty feet away, standing with three other guys next to an empty table.

Graham hoped he hadn't been spotted and immediately regretted coming in here.

"Hey, Sully," a voice said from behind him.

He turned the other direction and found a friendly face staring back at him.

"Hey, Bobby," Graham said. "I didn't see you there."

Bobby Anderson grinned back at him. "That's because I'm a ninja, son. I'm a sneaking son of a gun."

"I don't know about the ninja part, but you are a sneaky cuss."

The two shared a laugh, and the tension Graham felt from the sight of Jamie eased.

Bobby Anderson was a few years older than Graham, slightly taller, and much heavier. His blond hair had faded over the years to nearly white, but he still had a youthful look in his eyes, full of mischief and fun. And he seemed to always have a can of beer in his hand.

"How you been, old-timer?" Bobby asked. "I heard you're retiring. Say it ain't so."

"That's one of my favorite songs," Graham said. "But yeah, I decided to hang it up. Time to take the next step in life."

"The next step is into the grave, buddy. You don't want to take that one." Bobby's laugh thundered through the room.

"You're right about that," Graham agreed. "And who are you calling old-timer? You're two years older than me, old man."

Bobby huffed. "I was hoping you'd forgotten that little detail." He looked around the room for a second before lowering his voice to a secretive level. "Seriously, brother. What's going on? You feeling okay? You're not sick, are you?"

Graham put on a grim face. "There's no getting anything past you, is there?"

"Oh, Sully. I'm so sorry. How bad is it?"

Graham leaned closer. "I'm dying, Bobby." He paused for effect. "Dying to whip your butt this weekend."

It took Bobby a second to realize Graham was messing with him. But when it hit him, a few choice curse words escaped to go along with a friendly punch to the shoulder.

"You son of a gun," Bobby exclaimed. "Don't do that to me. I thought you were serious."

Graham smiled and raised his glass of tea. "No, I'm fine, Bobby. But I do appreciate your concern."

"So, what's the story? You're younger than me, and I ain't quittin' anytime soon."

"I don't know. I guess it just feels like I'm spinning my wheels out there. Been a long time since I won a tournament. So, what am I doing if I'm not competing?"

"You're living, man. Look around." He waved his hand at the gathering in the room. "Every week we get to be in a different place, drinking, having a good time with other golfers. It's like a guys' trip every weekend."

"I know. And it was fun for a while. But I'm tired."

Bobby frowned at the response. "You know what you need, my friend?"

"Don't say a woman."

"A woman."

"I said not to say that."

"Yeah, but I chose to ignore you."

Graham looked dubiously at his friend. "Bobby, you've been divorced four times. And every time I see you, you're with a different woman. The last one was like fifteen years younger than you."

"Twenty." Bobby's eyes glazed over as he recalled. "Yeah, she was a fun one. That's what you need, my man. There are plenty of those types at these events. Especially the majors. Always looking for a sugar daddy to show them a good time for a while. And the best part is they aren't in it for the long haul."

Graham chuckled as he shook his head. "I'm glad you haven't changed in the thirty years I've known you."

"If it ain't broke."

Graham took a sip of tea.

"What are you drinking?" Bobby asked. "Is that tea?"

"It is. I'm not in the mood for booze right now. Besides, I need to walk the course with my caddie here in a bit. I prefer to strategize with my head on straight."

"Not me. I find a little nip helps me see things better."

"That's not what your last few finishes would suggest."

Bobby pretended to be hurt. "Hey, I got unlucky."

"Let's call it that." Graham set his drink down. "But back to the topic of ladies, I actually met one."

Bobby looked around, suddenly excited at the prospect. "Is she here? How old is she? In her thirties?"

"No. Goodness no."

"Twenties? You're dipping that low? Impressive."

"No, definitely not. She's in her early fifties. And no, she's not here. She's in Charleston. Couldn't make it up for the tournament. We just started talking last week, so it's nothing serious. But—"

"Nothing serious, huh? You have that look in your eyes that says differently. You like this one."

"I have no idea what you're talking about." Whatever look Bobby was talking about quickly morphed into one of disgust. "Oh, great."

Graham followed his stare and saw Jamie Winthrop approaching like a tiger, stalking through the undergrowth of the jungle, eyes locked on its prey.

"Well, well, well," Winthrop said as he neared. He made no attempt to suppress his voice, which didn't surprise Graham in the least. Winthrop seemingly loved to hear himself speak, something he did constantly to monopolize conversations with just about anyone. "If it isn't Sully and his pal Bobby. What is this, the runner-up area of the bar?"

Winthrop looked around as if expecting laughter from the rest of the room, but no one was paying attention.

He laughed, forcibly, then shook his head. "I'm just kidding, guys. Lighten up."

Graham knew he wasn't joking. Not at all. Winthrop had been like this ever since they met. And he'd only grown more agitating since his big comeback victory a decade ago, in this very place.

It hadn't been so much of a comeback due to Winthrop's skills, so much as it was a total collapse by Graham. He'd held a firm grip on the lead for the better half of the tournament, but a series of unfortunate events wrecked his score, and the lead he had evaporated.

It was impossible not to relive that fateful day. Graham had done so over and over again, no matter how many times he claimed to have put it in the past where it belonged.

Choking was what he did with devastating consistency. It was his legacy, and men like Winthrop were all too happy to let Graham know about it.

"Don't you have a photo shoot to go to?" Bobby fired back. "I heard you're modeling for a new underwear commercial. Calvin Swine, is it?"

"Stay up all night working on that one, Bobby?" Winthrop replied. "Clever, in a fifth-grade sort of way."

Bobby glowered at him, but Winthrop's vapid expression reflected the emotionless, uncaring soul that dwelled within.

He turned his attention to Graham, who sat calmly, sipping his sweet tea.

"What about you? Got anything witty for me?"

"No. I'm good."

"You're okay. I wouldn't say good."

"What's your problem, man?" Bobby demanded. More than a few people turned their heads toward the escalating situation at the bar.

"No problem. I've won this tournament twice. Along with three other majors. Not that I need to tell you two that."

"Then why are you wasting your time with us losers?" Graham asked. "Like you said, this is the runner-up area. You should be where the winners are, and leave us to our drinks."

Winthrop cracked his neck, tilting his head side to side.

Graham knew he was getting under his skin by not reacting, but simply deflecting the man's desire for a fight of words. Graham had been around long enough to know when someone was trying to get in his head. Normally, he would have simply let it go from there and watched Winthrop skulk away in search of another, more game victim. But it was his last time here as a player, so he figured he'd have some fun with it.

"Guys like you shouldn't try to play mind games, Jamie," Graham said. "Not with men like us."

"What?"

"Psychology is a tricky business. You can't get in the heads of those who won't let you. Besides, like you said, we're just a couple of runners-up for life. We're no threat to you. You're still one of the top players on the tour."

"The number-one-ranked player in the world."

"There you go. See? Why would you slum it over here with us? Why don't you go on back to your pals over there and work on getting in their skulls? They're the ones you have to worry about anyway. Or is it because you know you have to worry about them, and they won't be bullied by your weak mind-games?"

Winthrop looked indignant, both from being called "Jamie" and because he realized he was getting called out.

Before he could say anything, Graham pressed further. "Yeah. That's right. See, I've known bullies like you all my life. Guys who are making up for something, if you know what I mean." He let his eyes flick toward Winthrop's belt for a nanosecond. "But there's nothing you can say that will unnerve me, boy. I've been through hell and back. More times than I can count. So, if you're trying to mess with me, you're wasting your time."

Winthrop's eyes flamed, which matched the heat radiating from his chest. But he couldn't think of anything to say to counter Graham's words.

"Good luck in the tournament," he managed. "I guess that's all you two can hope for."

He spun around, happy with having gotten in the last word, and walked back across the room to some of the other players he'd been talking with.

"I really don't like that guy," Bobby said. "The nerve. And here of all places. This clubhouse is holy ground. You don't come in here acting that way. I guess he never heard of being a good sport."

"Guys like him didn't ever hear of that concept," Graham offered. "If I had to guess, he's probably carrying around some deep-seated issues from his past. Maybe he could never live up to his parents' expectations or something like that. But that's not our concern, is it?"

"What are you, a shrink now?"

Graham chuckled. "No. Just been around the block enough to have picked up a few things along the way."

"I've been around longer than you, and you don't hear me talking like that."

"That's what you have me for," Graham said.

36

Cameras flashed in the back of the ballroom as Jamie Winthrop entered. His agent, dressed in a white Italian suit, walked behind him.

Winthrop forced a smile onto his face as he passed the reporters lining the rows of seats, eager to get a glimpse of the best golfer on the planet.

He walked up to the stage and shook hands with the man in the blue blazer standing next to it.

"Good morning, Jamie," the older man said, pushing his glasses up higher on his nose. "How you feeling?"

"I feel good, Billy. Thanks for asking." Jamie looked out at the crowd. Only seven of the fifty seats were empty. "I guess not a sellout crowd today, huh?"

He turned back to Billy, who immediately put on an apologetic face. "I'm sure they'll filter in any second now." He checked his watch. "We should get started, though. We're on a tight schedule."

"Sure. Whatever. Let's get it over with."

"Right."

Billy led the way up onto the stage, but Winthrop lingered on the floor for a second. He leaned in close to his agent and lowered his voice to a whisper.

"Why is the room not full, Greg?"

"Relax, man. They're more people here than any of the other pressers. And there have been cutbacks at a lot of the media outlets. Lot of people got laid off in the last year. Just try to have fun with it."

Winthrop stiffened his spine, flattened his shirt, and took a deep breath. "I'm the best golfer of all time. There should never be an empty seat where I speak."

He left it at that and stepped up onto the stage, immediately replacing his irritation with another fake, patronizing smile.

He sat down as Billy introduced him. The room filled with applause, which Winthrop waved off with a practiced false modesty.

"Thank you," he said. "I appreciate you all coming out this morning. Let's get started." He looked at a man in the front row whom he recognized from one of the largest sports media outlets. They'd done this for years, and both knew the routine.

"Solomon, you want to lead off?"

The middle-aged man grinned and nodded even as other hands shot up around the room.

"Thanks, Jamie. How are you feeling going into this tournament? There were some rumors that maybe you had tweaked your back in the last one."

Winthrop shook his head. "I feel better than ever. You should check your sources." He winked at the reporter, and laughter echoed through the room. Solomon laughed too and made a quick note on his phone.

Winthrop called on a redheaded woman in the back. She looked to be in her mid-thirties, and wore a red dress with a low-cut V-neck in the front and a short, black skirt.

He caught himself admiring her for a few seconds as she spoke.

"Amanda Burnett. As I'm sure you know, a win here this weekend would tie you for the most ever open titles," she said. "That would be an incredible achievement. Does that add any pressure, and if so, how do you deal with that?"

"Good question, Amanda," he said with a flattering grin. She smiled back, and he knew she was hooked. "I try to treat every round, every shot the same way. If you get too much in your own head, you'll make a mess of everything. So, I take it one shot at a time. But I've never really felt a sense of pressure, to be honest. I know what I can do on the course, what I can do with the ball. I constantly work on being the best in the world. That's my focus, from the time I get up to when I go to bed at night. I expect to win. In some ways, I guess I just assume I will. When you go about things in that way, pressure doesn't have any impact."

She seemed to like the confident answer, as evidenced by the sultry smirk on her lips.

Winthrop stared at her for another second before turning his attention to another reporter, an older man in the middle of the right-hand side.

"Yeah," he said, pointing at the man. "Go ahead, Larry."

"Thanks, Jamie. What do you think about the field this year?"

"It's a solid field, as always. I mean, it's the tour, so it would be weird if the competition wasn't fierce. You go up against the best players in the world every single week. And I have a target on my back. But that's okay. I'm good with it."

Winthrop called on another reporter, a man in his late twenties on the left side.

"What do you think about the local amateur playing in this event?" the journalist asked.

Winthrop's brow furrowed, and he glanced over at Billy to his left before answering. "I honestly don't know who you're talking about."

"His name is Tyler Knox. He's a caddie from another course here in town. He qualified through the regional event. Holed out for eagle on the last green."

Winthrop shook his head. "Sorry, I don't know anything about it. Sounds like a cool story, though."

He raised his finger, ready to call on another reporter, but the same guy pressed on. "The video of the shot went viral. It hit over ten million views within forty-eight hours. You think there's any chance someone like that could challenge for the title here this weekend?"

It took every ounce of effort Winthrop could muster to not look annoyed, and even then he wasn't sure he pulled it off. "Hey, anything is possible. But I don't think an amateur has won a major tournament in a long time."

"Since the 1930s," the irritating journalist said.

"Right. The 1930s. So there you go. Pretty long odds. I guess you never know, though."

"It would be an incredible story," a blonde woman in her mid-twenties chirped from the right-hand side in the third row. "A home-town kid being the first amateur to win a major in almost a hundred years."

"Yeah. I'm sure that would make for a great fairy tale." Winthrop was losing all restraint now. "Any other questions for me? No? Okay. Thanks for coming out. I'll see you all soon."

He stood up, ignoring the bewildered look on the MC's face, and walked off the stage amid murmurs and whispers.

His agent looked uncomfortable and desperate at the same time. "Jamie, I am so sorry. I didn't know—"

"Didn't know what? That they were going to start talking about some amateur during my press conference? How could you have known that? Although you might have shared the video with me so I could have known what they were talking about."

"It won't happen again."

"Oh, I know it won't. After I destroy the field this weekend, and that kid misses the cut, they won't even remember his name come Monday."

37

T yler pulled up to Lucy's driveway and parked along the curb near the mailbox.

The day had been weird, surreal, basically every adjective he could think of that was the opposite of normal. He wanted it to be his normal, though. He wanted to belong there, at that club, in that tournament, on that tour.

After the press conference, he found his way into the bar and restaurant area of the club where three lines of buffet tables held all sorts of Southern breakfast treats. Grits, biscuits and gravy, scrambled eggs, sausages, oatmeal, fresh fruit, waffles, and some of the best coffee Tyler thought he'd ever tasted.

He had a huge appetite after the nerve-wracking interview and devoured everything on his plate.

While he was in the clubhouse, he met several of the pros from the tour and did his best to pretend he was one of them, even though they all knew his story.

One pro, Gill McElroy, had made a big deal about the eagle on 7 that Tyler made to clinch his spot in the tournament. He took out his phone and replayed the video for everyone around to see.

As the ball fell into the cup, the men nodded approvingly at the incredible shot.

"You keep hitting 'em like that this weekend, kid, and you'll be fine," Gill told him.

Tyler spent the rest of the afternoon walking the course with Justin, picking their angles of attack, making notes on how each green would roll if the pin was placed in certain spots.

Justin had asked what Tyler was up to afterward, and the answer "I'm meeting Lucy," had soured Justin's face.

"Dude. You need to lock it in this week. Okay? No distractions. That means girls too."

Tyler reassured his friend that he was, indeed, focused on the tournament, but that he wasn't going to simply ignore his girlfriend either.

There was no way Tyler was going to let his friend dampen his mood today. He felt like a winner, like a real golfer. He didn't know how long that feeling would last, or any of this, but he was going to enjoy it while he could.

He stepped out of his car and breathed in the fresh, evening air. The sun was already behind the trees on the hill behind Lucy's house, and the sky's bright light drained by the second.

Tyler closed the door to his car and walked up the driveway, passing Lucy's vehicle on his way to the front steps.

He stopped at the front door and reached out to ring the doorbell. Before he could press the button, the door opened.

Lucy's father stood in the doorway like a dragon blocking an ancient path to a treasure trove.

"Good evening, Mr. Park. How are you?"

The man inclined his head, peering down at Tyler as if judging him from some lofty courtroom seat.

"Lucy isn't here," he said, his tone cold and unwelcoming.

"Oh." Tyler looked back at the car in the driveway. "Sorry, I thought she was here because her car is."

"She went somewhere with her mother. I don't know when they'll be back."

Tyler sensed something amiss, but he didn't want to push it with Lucy's father. The polite thing to do would have been to invite him in to hang out for a while, maybe talk about golf or school or whatever was on his mind.

But Mr. Park didn't invite him in.

"I don't actually think we've met, Mr. Park. I'm Tyler."

"I know who you are. My daughter told me all about you."

"Only good things, I hope," Tyler half joked. Taking on a room full of reporters had seemed like child's play compared to this inquisition.

"She told me enough. You're studying at the university. And you work as a caddie."

"Yep. That's pretty much it. I did just qualify for the White Oak National Open Championship." He tried not to sound boastful, but he got the distinct sense that maybe he needed to impress the guy.

"Yes. I am aware of your win at Green Mont. Impressive. But what will you do once the tournament is over? You want to date my daughter, but you two come from different backgrounds and are on very different career tracks."

A lump the size of a kettle bell dropped into Tyler's stomach. It wasn't the way he wanted the nervous tension to leave. He'd hoped the man would ask him to come in, sit down in the living room and have a nice conversation. But now it was clear that wasn't going to happen. It was never going to happen.

"I'm sorry," Tyler said. "You're right, sir. Your daughter is too good for me. I know that. She's extremely intelligent, beautiful, funny, and a fun person. Maybe I'll never have enough money to support the lifestyle you expect for her, or the social standing. But no one would ever treat Lucy better than me. She's a great girl. You and Mrs. Park did a good job raising her."

His words apparently struck Mr. Park, but only caused the slightest twitch from his eyelids.

Tyler turned and walked down the steps to the sidewalk. He paused for a second, tempted to look back, or fire another comment at Lucy's father, but instead he left it as it was and continued down the driveway to his car.

He climbed into the seat, slammed the door shut, and sat there for a minute, squeezing the steering wheel with both hands as if he were going to rip it out of the mount.

Tyler's eyes watered with tears.

He started the car, stepped on the gas, and drove around the cul-de-sac and back out to the next street. He stopped at the stop sign, trying to calm himself down by breathing steadily. It wasn't working, but he managed to accelerate out onto the street without squealing his tires and drove away without looking back.

Nothing had changed. He'd broken a course record at a difficult golf course. He'd qualified to be in a professional tournament. Been interviewed by reporters he'd only seen on television or on social media.

None of it made any difference.

Lucy's dad, and presumably her mother, saw him the same way Mitchell did. As an outsider. Someone who didn't belong in their world.

38

Graham smiled.

The sound of Alicia's voice was like Haydn playing through the speaker of the phone.

"So, you're feeling good about all of it?" she asked.

"Yeah," he answered, but his gruff tone couldn't hide the truth behind the words.

"Are you sure?"

"Yeah. I'm sure."

"Because you don't sound so sure."

He grumbled something unintelligible.

Graham had been irritated ever since he left the press conference. Something itched at him, a clawing annoyance that he hadn't felt in a long time.

"What is it?" she asked. "You can talk to me."

"No, I know. It's nothing. I'm fine."

"Graham?" Alicia said in a motherly tone. "What's going on? Are you having second thoughts about... seeing me?"

"No," he said quickly. "Absolutely not. In fact, I wish I could see you right now. You're pretty much all I've been able to think about for the last several days." He paused then added, "I'm sorry. That sounded obsessive."

"It didn't. You're being sweet and honest. I like it when a man can be vulnerable."

"When and where I came from, a guy being vulnerable was a big no-no. But thanks."

"Any time. So, you going to tell me what's on your mind, or are you just going to keep showering me with compliments and poetry?"

He chuckled. "I didn't realize I'd done any of that."

"You haven't. Not yet, anyway. But I feel like there's the heart of a poet inside that chest of yours."

No one had ever said that to him before, and it sent warmth radiating through his torso.

"I don't know about all that. But thank you." He looked out the window of the hotel. The silhouette of Lookout Mountain loomed against the evening sky. The mountain was partially dimmed by the city lights of downtown, which also muted the glimmer of the stars above.

"I'm waiting," she said.

"I don't know. It's weird. I know I made the announcement to retire, and I'm still planning on doing that, but—"

"You're having second thoughts?"

"I guess. I'm not sure. I think it's just—walking into that clubhouse today—that will be the last time I go in there for a press conference as a professional golfer. Every time I go in that building this week will be the last time I do it for the practice round, the first round, and so on. It's just the finality of it all, I suppose. It all sounded reasonable and like the right thing to do before. But now, it feels like I'm cutting out a part of my life. The biggest part of my life for the last four decades."

"Do you think you should change your mind? Professional athletes do it all the time. They retire then make a comeback."

"No," he shook his head. "I don't go back on my word. And besides, I don't need the money. I'm probably not going to win another tournament. Heck, I haven't won one on the senior tour. If I can't cut it there, what am I doing with my life?"

"Playing the game you love?"

Her question hit him like someone was flicking the back of his head. It was annoyingly on point.

"Yeah. I don't know. I think the other thing is my pride. It's really messing with me right now. Like I'm giving up before my time is over. You know?"

"Sure. I understand. Pride goes before a fall. It can make us do things, irrational things, that we normally wouldn't do otherwise. Acting on emotions, especially negative ones, often leads to bigger problems."

"That's the game of golf right there. You have to take emotions out of the equation. Otherwise, you'll be out of control."

He paced back toward the bathroom, then pivoted, and returned to the window before he continued.

"It's just... I feel like I still have something to prove. That I can be better than I have been. For the last decade, I've just been a middle-of-the road golfer. I made good money, had a few respectable finishes, but I never really felt like I played up to my capability."

"And why do you think that is?" Alicia asked.

He'd pondered that question for more hours than he could possibly know. It haunted him. If he could have figured that out, there was no telling how much better his performance might have been.

"I'm not sure," he admitted. "I've been trying to figure that out. I guess I eventually accepted that maybe I'm not as good as I thought I was, or at least as good as the experts thought I was going to be way back when."

"You were a highly touted player when you were younger. Weren't you?"

"Yeah. How'd you know that?"

"I may or may not have done a little independent research on you."

Graham grinned at the confession. "You've been stalking me online?"

"Researching. I've been researching you online. You never know what kind of whack jobs you might meet out there."

They both laughed, and for a moment everything didn't seem as serious.

"Well, I'm flattered," he said. "And yes, I was a highly touted prospect back in the day. They all thought I was going to be the next Palmer or Nicklaus or Player. But it never worked out. Just a long series of disappointments."

She listened silently and when he was done, didn't speak immediately. When she did, her tone sounded comforting, sincere to Graham. "It sounds like you played with a lot of pressure on your shoulders for your entire career, Graham."

"Yeah. It does, doesn't it?"

"When we put pressure on ourselves to achieve anything, to do anything, it makes doing that thing all the more difficult. On top of that, we place expectations on a pedestal as if they must be attained. This sort of attachment is a dangerous thing for creating the reality we want in life, or achieving goals we may have set. You have to let go of that pressure, Graham. You have to realize that you are good enough, no matter the results."

Graham stayed quiet; in silent awe of the wisdom she was laying down on him.

"And you have to go out there and play the game you loved as a kid. Swing those clubs like you did when you were twenty, without a care about the result. The swing is the point. Being there on the course is the point. Just control that. Appreciate that you're there, in such a special place. Smell the grass, the flowers, the trees. And when you swing the club, don't worry about where the ball is heading. You can't control that once it's gone. Just like the past. All you can do is focus on the moment. Not the future. Not what has already happened. The moment."

He stood there for a moment, stunned by every word.

"You still there?" she asked after twenty seconds of silence.

"Yeah. I'm here. I just didn't realize I was talking to a self-help guru. I thought you said you were in retail before."

She giggled. "I was."

"I think maybe you missed your calling."

"I do like that kind of stuff. Mindfulness has really helped me through the years. Especially when things don't go the way you want them to."

He nodded although she couldn't see him. "I'll give it a try," he said. "You've given me a lot to think about it, and I need to sit with it for a bit. I'll talk to you tomorrow? I need to get to bed soon."

"Sure," she answered. "I like talking with you. Hard to believe this is only our third conversation. Feels like I've known you so much longer."

"It does, doesn't it?"

"Good luck in your practice round. I'm sure you'll do great."

"Thanks. And thank you for talking with me. I appreciate it."

She hummed at the comment.

"What?" he asked.

"You're such an interesting person, Graham. I've never met a guy like you."

"What do you mean?"

"I've never had a man thank me just for talking to him before. And I can tell you mean it."

"I do. I enjoy our conversations. Or just the sound of your voice."

"And see? You say sweet things like that. Now I really wish I could make it up there to see you."

"I'll leave a ticket for you at the gate just in case your plans change," he said.

"No, please don't waste that on me. I'm sure there's someone else you—"

"There isn't," he interrupted quickly. "And besides, I get a couple of passes for free. It would just go unused anyway."

"Well, it's a very sweet gesture. Thank you."

"Have a good night, Alicia. I'll talk with you soon."

"Okay. Goodnight."

He ended the call and lowered the phone down to waist level, staring at the now blank call screen with the words *Call Ended* at the top.

He smiled and set the phone down, then walked into the bathroom, turned, and faced the man in the mirror.

"She likes you," he said. "Now just don't screw it up." Graham froze. His gut tightened, and the warmth in his chest left over from the conversation waned.

He'd said those words before. Many times throughout his life. Before he got married. Before most of the major tournaments he'd played. And now it hit him that he'd said the same words the morning before his biggest collapse, here, at the White Oak National Open Championship.

His entire life, those words had rung through his mind whenever something important was on the line, something that he wanted or even felt like he needed.

For the first time, he actually heard the words coming out of his mouth. And it took him back to when he was a kid. He'd heard it before, out of his father's mouth at a little league baseball game. He'd heard it from other kids too, all of them putting pressure on him not to mess up in the big moment. And not just at baseball games, but from friends when he was about to go on a date with a girl he liked, or from his ex-wife on numerous occasions.

The realization that hit him could have knocked down the entire hotel, even leveled the city with the atomic-like power behind it.

His entire life, he'd been playing not to lose—playing scared. Those words, "Don't screw it up, Graham," had been programmed into his subconscious so deeply that he didn't even realize they were there all along, guiding him without his awareness.

But now he was aware. Now he could see clearly. The epic choke here a decade ago at White Oak. His failed marriage, and all the other relationships that came before it. Everything he'd screwed up in his life had come from one simple phrase begging him not to screw it up.

That negative sentiment had created all of the disappointments, all of the monumental failures he'd suffered.

That knowledge unclasped the two-ton yoke that had been strapped to his neck for decades, and for the first time in his life, Graham felt something new, something lighter, even optimistic.

He didn't know why, but he felt happier than he had since he could remember, and for a second wondered if he was losing his mind. But there was nothing wrong with him. Not anymore.

He stared back at the smiling, goofy guy in the mirror. "Took you long enough to figure that out," he muttered. "But better late than never." Graham nodded as the pain from the past melted away. "Go out there and play the best you can," he said. "Show the world what you can do."

39

Tyler stood at the back of the tee box, staring down at the grass in front of him. He kept his arms crossed, mirroring Justin's stance.

While Justin wore a blank, emotionless expression, Tyler's face was set in a grim, angry stare.

His jaw clenched, as it had a hundred times throughout the morning.

He thought being here, in his fortress of solitude on the golf course, that he would feel better about the conversation he'd had with Mr. Park the night before.

But a restless night of little sleep, and a heavy dose of bitterness, had done little to calm his emotions.

"You sure you're okay?" Justin asked, leaning in close as the other golfer, a Japanese player, swung his driver to loosen up before teeing off.

"I'm fine, I said," Tyler answered, and added nothing else.

"Okay," Justin lowered his voice to a whisper. "It just doesn't seem like you're okay."

"Drop it," Tyler replied, louder than he intended.

The player who was warming up looked back at him. So did the guy's caddie, as well as the third player and his caddie, who stood waiting to Tyler's left.

"Sorry," Justin offered for his friend.

They watched the first two guys tee off before it was Tyler's turn.

Tyler had gone home after the visit to Lucy's house and tried to go to bed early. But he'd been unable to fall asleep until well after midnight, and even then he kept waking up throughout the night until his alarm went off in the morning.

Throughout the dark hours, his mind kept taking him back to the conversation with Lucy's father, how it made him feel, how it reminded him that he didn't belong in this world of the rich and famous, or even in the world of the upper-middle class.

No matter how much he tried to consciously fight those thoughts, they kept coming like an endless army, swarming over his kingdom.

Tyler took the driver from his friend and found a spot on the grass he liked in the tee box. He set the ball on the tee and stepped back, swinging the club twice before addressing the ball.

He reared back and swung, striking the ball hard with the driver's face.

The ball launched into the air, but it veered hard to the right and into a patch of forest beyond the fairway and rough. It stopped behind a pine tree, effectively cutting off a direct approach to the green.

Justin stared at the ball for a second, then looked to his friend, whose gaze remained fixed ahead.

The other caddies picked up their bags and followed their golfers off the tee box without saying a word.

A few dozen fans stood around the tee box and had clapped for each of the shots, including Tyler's, though for his, the applause was significantly less inspiring.

He turned and handed the driver to Justin, who sheathed it in his bag and hurried to catch up with his friend as he stalked ahead and onto the fairway.

"It's all good," Justin said. "Shake it off. Just some nerves."

"Sure," Tyler said, leaving Justin to wonder what was going on.

GRAHAM STOOD over the ball and swung. His hips drove forward and through the target, striking it true in the center of the clubface. The swing was effortless, smooth, and easy, yet produced immense power.

The ball soared down the middle of the fairway before landing and rolling another twenty yards.

The smattering of spectators around the tee box clapped politely.

Graham grinned and returned to his caddie, a guy with long gray hair named Mike. He handed him the driver and adjusted his belt as he turned to watch the other two guys hit.

"Great shot, Sully," Mike said.

Graham nodded. "Yeah. Not a bad way to start with a fairway hit."

"Always a good thing."

"I feel good today. Not sure what it is. But there's something different. I guess we'll see if that translates into a good round."

"Can't hurt, chief."

"Nice one, Sully," one of the other golfers offered in a Swedish accent. Markus Larsson had been one of the up-and-comers on the tour when he was in his early twenties, but he'd never come close to winning a major tournament and only had two wins on tour in the last six years. But he'd made a good living as a professional golfer, usually finishing in the middle of the pack and almost always making the cut. The one thing he was known for on the tour was his eclectic selection of clothing, seemingly always wearing bright colors.

Today's choice was a pair of bright pink pants and a lime-green shirt with a pink hat.

"Thanks, Markus," Sully said.

"You keep hitting them like that, you're going to have a fun round," added the other golfer, a middle-aged man named Terrell Dawkins.

"I guess we'll see. It's only one shot, boys. Long way to go."

Graham waited for the other two men to hit their shots, but he kept thinking about his own, how pure it felt. Like he said, it was only one shot.

Still, he didn't remember hitting the ball in such a way, not recently. He was still a great golfer by most standards, as were any professionals. But the last decade had felt labored, difficult, as if there were some kind of resistance holding him back.

Still, doubt dug at his chest like a mole burrowing into the ground. He took a deep breath and sighed, trying to let go of the old nemesis.

Just have fun, he thought to himself. *You have no pressure. Play the game.*

40

Tyler was in a nightmare.

He stood in the bunker, staring at a wall of sand that towered over his head. He could barely see the flag behind it.

He'd heard about the sand traps at White Oak many times. They were internationally famous for making wayward golfers pay the toll of extra strokes if their shots went off target.

This was the third one Tyler had found on the day, and his score reflected not only the additional strokes they added but his complete loss of focus.

Initially, Justin had tried to encourage him, telling him that it was just some rust he needed to knock off and not to worry about it. That's what practice rounds were for, he'd said.

But as the day progressed, and the hours ticked by without mercy, Tyler's score continued to climb, and he had no answers.

He'd been tempted to look at his phone during the down moments when he had to wait for the threesome ahead of his group to finish their shots, but he'd refrained. He didn't know if Lucy had texted him or not, and he wasn't sure he wanted her to.

The conversation with her father had taken him from the pinnacle of hope to the depths of despair. And now, the one thing he had going for him in life was flying off the rails.

He lowered his sand wedge and swung through it, catching the bottom of the ball. A blast of sand sprayed up into the air as the ball carried up and over the ridge at the top of the bunker. But he'd struck it too hard, and the ball sailed over the pin, landing somewhere beyond it.

Justin watched from the left edge of the green and rubbed the back of his neck as he watched the ball roll away from the target.

Tyler stepped out of the bunker, handed the sand wedge to his friend, and held out his hand for the putter.

"What's the matter with you today?" Justin asked. He'd likely been wanting to ask the question for the last seventeen holes but had managed to keep his thoughts to himself.

"Just give me the putter and rake the sand," Tyler ordered, his expression somber.

"What?"

"Give me the putter, Justin."

"You haven't even seen where the ball went."

"It doesn't matter. Just give me the putter, man."

Justin shook his head. "I don't know what is going on with you, but you need to get your head right. I've never seen you play like this before. It's like you've never swung a club in your life."

Tyler reached for the putter in the bag, but Justin turned away, blocking it with his body. "I'm your friend, Ty. You can talk to me. What's going on with you? You're not playing well; you don't seem like yourself. What happened?"

"Let it go and give me the putter, Justin."

"No. This is the biggest moment of your life, man. And I'm not going to watch you just throw it away."

Tyler leveled his gaze with his friend's. "You mean the biggest moment of our lives?"

"What's that supposed to mean?"

"I know how bad you want to make it on the tour as a caddie. Those guys make the big bucks. No more working for tips at Green Mont if I perform well here this weekend."

"Is that what you think this is about?"

"Tell me I'm wrong, then."

"You are wrong. You're my best friend. I want this for you more than anything. Sure, I would love to be on the tour someday. But I would prefer to be on your bag than anyone else's." Justin paused. The tone in his voice echoed the pain of Tyler's words. "Did something happen with you and Lucy? Did she dump you?"

"No. And I don't want to talk about it. So give me my putter, and go rake the sand."

Justin shook his head and set the bag down on its bipod. "You can rake your own sand. I'm done."

"Oh. That's it? You're just going to quit?"

Justin took a step backward, still staring at his friend as he threw his arms out wide. "Seems like you have. I might as well while I can."

"You don't want me with Lucy anyway," Tyler snarled, unaware that the other golfers and the spectators were still there to witness the argument. "You can't stand that I'm with her, always telling me to stay focused."

Justin cocked his head to the side, as though staring at a mouse with two heads. He took one step closer to his friend and raised his finger. "I was happy for you to be with her. In fact, I think it's been way too long coming that you two got together. I don't care that you two got together. I just didn't want you to be distracted for the biggest stage of your life. I don't know what happened between you and her, but whatever it was has messed with your head. I was just trying to help you clear it and get back to what you're great at."

"That's all I am. A good golfer from the wrong side of the tracks who will never fit in."

Justin shook his head and stepped away again. "Only if you chose to be." He turned and walked off, leaving Tyler alone next to the green with everyone watching.

"Fine," he said, anger fueling his voice. He stormed over to the nearest rake, picked it up, and stepped back into the sand, where he pulled the loose grains over where he'd stood and where he'd hit the ball until it was as though he'd never been there, then left the sand and dropped the rake next to it.

Then he yanked the putter out of his bag and stalked up onto the green to look for his ball.

The other two golfers and their caddies did their best to act like they'd not been paying attention to the extremely awkward exchange and focused instead on where their balls sat.

A third ball lay off to the left on the backside of the green, just on the fringe. Tyler had been lucky it hadn't rolled off and into the bunker looming on the back.

He walked over to his ball and stood behind it for a second, holding up his putter to let it dangle in a line behind the white sphere.

His was the farthest ball from the hole, so he had to hit first.

He took less than three seconds to size up the line, then stepped up to the ball, and uncaringly struck it.

The ball rolled quickly, up over a slight rise to the left, and then back down, curling fifteen feet past the hole.

It was a careless, poorly judged putt. And Tyler didn't care. He walked over to the ball, placed his mark, and picked it up before turning away. He looked toward the clubhouse, where Justin was headed, kicking grass every other step.

Some of the spectators mumbled among themselves. They wore confused expressions, and even a few disapproving ones.

A sharp pain stabbed at Tyler's chest, and his gut tore at his senses.

What am I doing?

He returned his attention to the green and the other players as they took their turns putting. One of the guys sank a birdie from seventeen feet out to finish strong. The other put his within a foot, and with Tyler's permission finished out the hole with a par.

Tyler walked over to his ball, stood behind it for a moment to analyze the line, and then stepped up to it.

He lowered the putter to the surface, took one last glance at the hole, and drew the putter back. The stroke was smooth and rhythmic as it struck the ball. But his line was off, and it rolled six inches past the cup.

A collective groan escaped the spectators. Tyler sighed, not believing what he'd just done. He could make that putt in his sleep. This entire round had been cataclysmic to his confidence, and now the one place he felt like he belonged had turned into a desolate wasteland of doubt.

Tyler ambled over to the ball, put most of his weight on his right foot, and tapped it in for a double bogey.

The people gathered around the green offered a consolation golf clap, but to Tyler it felt like pity.

He took the ball out of the cup then shook hands with the other players.

"Great playing with you guys," he offered, fighting through the agony in his heart.

They exchanged the usual pleasantries and then made their way off the green. No one said anything about Justin's disappearance, or about the tension between them.

Tyler picked up his bag, slung it over his shoulder, and trudged down the slope behind the green, making his way toward the clubhouse.

He didn't want to stay here any longer. There was a dinner to attend that evening, and he'd planned on going. But things had changed. If he didn't belong here, where did he belong?

Tyler felt everything he'd ever dreamed of slipping away, and he didn't know how to rein it in.

GRAHAM WATCHED from the edge of the 18th green as Markus tapped in for par. Terrell had already birdied the hole with an incredible putt from twenty feet away.

Graham's ball had been the closest to the hole after a spectacular approach from 140 yards out. Now he was left with a nine-foot putt for birdie to finish a surprisingly solid round.

He roughly knew what his score was, as did most golfers when playing. He'd given up a long time ago on trying not to think about it. Marking his score on the card imprinted the result in his mind, and he'd never figured out a way to prevent that.

"A little right to left," Mike whispered to him as Graham and his caddie stared down at the putting surface. "Two cups outside the hole."

"Yeah, I think you're right."

"Slight uphill. Give it enough gas to go two feet beyond, and you should be good."

Graham nodded. "You're the boss."

Mike chuffed quietly at the comment.

Graham stepped up to the ball and positioned his feet.

The spectators around the green watched in hushed silence. A few dozen of them had been following the group all day, but most had been parked in the stadium seating or on fold-up chairs they'd brought with them.

Graham wasn't bothered by the audience. He'd played in front of thousands of people for decades, and that didn't include the millions watching on television. The first few times had made him nervous, but that faded over time, and now it was as if they weren't even there.

He turned his head to the left, studying the line one last time, then lowered the putter to the surface and tapped it forward.

The ball climbed toward the hole, turning slightly every inch it traveled. The spectators held their breath. Some of them stood up from their seats to get a better view.

A few shouted encouragement. One guy even yelled, "You da man, Sully!"

The ball curved, and Graham knew it was perfect even before it hit the back of the cup and dropped in.

The crowd roared at the putt.

Graham merely smiled, almost surprised at having hit it so true, then took off his hat and waved to the crowd in appreciation.

He walked over to the hole and took out the ball, while Mike brought the flag back over and stuck it back in the cup.

He and Graham exchanged a high-five that came with a "Great putt, Sully" from the caddie.

"Terrific round," Terrell said as he stepped forward and shook Graham's hand.

"Thanks, Terrell. You too."

"Outstanding," Markus added with his handshake. "You play like that this weekend, and you'll be at the top of the leaderboard."

"I don't know about that, but it was a good day. Pleasure playing with you, fellas."

The crowd clapped and hollered as the group walked off the green and made their way to the clubhouse.

"I'll see you in a few minutes, chief," Mike said, veering away with the other caddies.

"Okay, thanks, Mike," Graham offered. "You were great today."

"Hey, you did all the work. I haven't seen you hit the ball like that in a long time. You got this."

"I guess we'll see."

Graham continued up the hill toward the clubhouse, passing between rows of fans standing behind ropes on either side. He waved to the crowds in the stadium seating and nodded at those along the walkway.

Some extended their hands toward him, shouting encouragement.

It wasn't his normal thing to do it, but Graham slapped hands with some of them as he passed, giving out high-fives on his way to the clubhouse.

He hadn't felt like this before. Not that he could remember. It was like being a rock star.

He'd made this long walk up to the cabin many times in his career, and others like it on courses all over the world. But today something felt different, lighter, better. Just like his swing had.

His mind flashed to the face of the barista, and he found himself wishing she was there. His imagination took off on its own and offered visions of him wrapping his arms around her and kissing her as he finished the final round on Sunday.

But those were daydreams, wishes that deep down he knew couldn't be fulfilled. Even if he had just shot a remarkable 4 under par for the day.

41

Tyler parked his car outside the apartment and sat there staring at the steering wheel.

He'd just shot an abysmal 9 over par. It wasn't an easy course, but the course wasn't the issue.

"Nine over," he muttered. "Unreal."

He felt embarrassed, both by the performance and because people had been there to see things fall apart with Justin.

Tyler hadn't checked his phone since leaving the course. Now, he looked at the screen and saw several missed calls from Lucy, along with dozens of messages. But there was nothing from Justin.

Tyler let out a heavy sigh. He should have known better than to get his hopes up.

He climbed out of the car, removed his clubs from the trunk, and made the difficult journey up the stairs to his apartment. When he made the turn at the top of the steps, he froze.

Lucy was standing in front of his door, her eyes swollen from crying, her face streaked with tears.

"Tyler," she gushed and rushed toward him. "Tyler, I am so sorry."

"For what?" he asked, marching forward as if to pass her and go to the door.

"Tyler, my dad told me you came over. He told me what he said. I felt so awful. I called. I texted. But you didn't answer, so I decided to come here."

He looked into her pleading eyes, but his defenses wouldn't let him feel bad for her. "Your dad made it clear where I stand. And where I'm supposed to be in life."

"Tyler, don't say that. You are an amazing guy, and you have a bright future ahead of you."

"Do I? I just shot nine over, Lucy. I'm a fraud. Okay? Your dad was right. I don't belong in your world."

"Babe, my dad was not right, and I told him as much. Don't worry about today's round. It was just practice. You'll do better in the real thing. I know you will. I wanted to come watch you today, but you didn't respond to any of my—"

"It's better that you weren't there," he said, his voice cold and distant. "That would have only made things worse."

"What do you mean?"

He didn't answer right away.

"Are you saying you don't want to be with me?"

"I don't know," he said.

"What?" The tears brimming in her eyes burst through whatever weak dam she'd built, and they flowed down over her cheeks. "Babe, you don't mean that. Please, my dad was wrong about you. I just want to—"

"I'm tired, Lucy. I just want to go lie down."

"But aren't we going to the dinner tonight?"

"I really want to go now."

"Tyler, you don't know what you're saying. The tournament organizers expect you to be there. It's part of the deal."

He shook his head. "No one will miss me there. And I'm tired of being everyone's pity party. I don't need their pity. Or yours."

Tyler slipped past her and stopped at his door.

"Is that what you think this is? You think I'm with you because I feel sorry for you?" Her sadness quickly transformed into anger. "The only one it seems feeling sorry for you is you, Tyler. If you're going to let things people say have such an impact on you and your emotions, then maybe you're not the guy I fell for."

She turned away and hurried to the edge of the steps.

He stood at the entrance to his apartment, staring at the door. A voice inside him told him to stop her, to run over to her and hold her tight, to tell her that he was sorry. That he'd been wrong. But instead, he merely stood there, unable to move, unable to speak—paralyzed by the events of the last twenty-four hours.

He saw her out of the corner of his eye, waiting at the landing as if silently begging him to stop her.

Then, with a loud sob, she took off down the stairs and disappeared.

His heart ached, and his stomach turned somersaults.

Tyler leaned forward and knocked his head against the door three times. "What are you doing?" he mumbled.

42

Tyler reluctantly walked through the entrance of the White Oak clubhouse.

He'd put on his best shirt and tie, which still felt like they weren't good enough for this place and this crowd.

A man in a suit held the door open for him as he entered, giving Tyler a welcoming nod as he passed.

Tyler thanked him and stepped into another world.

In the hallway, dozens of people in expensive outfits stood around holding drinks, conversing about vacation homes, new luxury cars, vacations, and yachts. One of their watches cost more than three of his old car.

The women were dressed in lavish, colorful dresses, huge hats, and fascinators similar to the ones donned at Churchill Downs on the first Saturday of May.

Yep. I am definitely underdressed.

For a moment, Tyler considered turning around and walking back to his car, but he knew he had to be there. It was compulsory. At least that's what he'd been told. He wondered if anyone was actually taking attendance.

An older gentleman in the iconic blue blazer with the club's crest on it, stood in front of the trophy case across from the doors and greeted Tyler while looking him up and down as if judging his appearance. It was easy to see the man's displeasure, but it was the best Tyler had in his closet.

"Welcome, Mr. Knox. I'm glad you could make it." The man's accent was deep Southern, and betrayed a long lineage of family ties in the region.

"You... know my name?"

"Of course," the man said, wiping away his initial reaction with a pleasant smile. "You're all the talk around here this week. Although I heard you had a rough outing today during the practice round."

Tyler nodded, and there was no hiding the shame he felt. "Yeah, I just couldn't get it going today."

"Well, that's why they call it a practice round, son. My name's Clark, by the way. Clark Fletcher."

Tyler shook the man's hand. The old guy had a strong grip, like he'd worked on a farm his entire life, and his skin was rougher than that of most golfers he'd met.

"Nice to meet you, Mr. Fletcher."

"The pleasure is all mine, Tyler. I'm pulling for you this weekend. From what I hear, you could have a real shot at winning this thing. Of course, you wouldn't get the prize money since you're an amateur."

Tyler was well aware of the prize money and his amateur status. But he was surprised to hear the man suggest he might have a chance at winning the tournament, especially given how poorly he performed earlier that day.

"I don't know about winning it, but I appreciate the support."

"Hey, any kid who worked their way up like you did is my kind of player. That's how I got into the game too."

"Really?" Tyler looked around at all the people milling about in the corridor. He saw some going in and out of one of the ballrooms down the hall where the press conferences had been held earlier.

"Sure. I started doing yard work when I was fifteen years old to help my parents out. They hit on some rough times when I was a kid, and I wanted to do my part."

That explained the man's firm grip.

Mr. Fletcher leaned in closer, speaking in a secretive tone. "I also know what it's like to feel like you don't belong in a place like this."

"How did you know?" Tyler asked, glancing around as insecurity squeezed him.

"I can tell. Not to worry. I've got you covered. This is a suit jacket kind of party. And it just so happens we have a few spares here in the back." He turned to a young man standing near the entrance to the bar area. He looked about Tyler's age, with thick black hair and a white button-up shirt with a black bow tie. "Logan?" He motioned for him to come over.

Logan immediately walked over to where Fletcher stood and awaited orders. "Yes, sir?"

"Go look in the coat room for a jacket for our young friend here. Seems he left his at home."

"Yes, sir. I'll be right back." Logan looked over Tyler to assess his size and then disappeared around the corner into a corridor that ran behind the bar.

"Logan's a good kid," Mr. Fletcher went on. "Hard worker. Not unlike yourself from what I hear."

Tyler wanted to ask how the man knew so much about him. His work life wouldn't have been featured in any of the papers or local media. Would it? Sports writing had changed since Tyler had first started following it a decade ago. Reporters today were hungry for any morsel, any facet of a player's life—golf-related or not—to fill the twenty-four-hour news cycle.

"I'm sorry," Tyler offered. "I didn't realize I had to wear a jacket. No one told me. Honestly, I don't even own a suit."

The confession didn't seem to bother Fletcher in the least.

"Not a problem. I've got you covered. And they probably assume everyone knows it's that kind of an occasion. You aren't the first one to show up without a jacket."

That relieved Tyler a little.

"So, what happened out there today?" Fletcher pressed as they waited for Logan to return.

Tyler shrugged with a sigh. "I don't really know. Everything just felt off." He wasn't sure how much he should share with the man he'd just met, no matter how kind Fletcher was being.

"Well, we all have our off days. I'm sure you'll pull it together for the tournament."

"I hope so."

Logan reappeared around the corner carrying a light blue blazer that went perfectly with Tyler's dark gray pants and dark blue tie.

"Here you go," he said, handing the jacket over. "Give that a try."

Tyler slipped his arms into the blazer and then snugged it up on his shoulders. It fit perfectly.

"Looks like it belongs to you," Mr. Fletcher said. "Good work, Logan. Thank you."

"Yes, sir. Happy to help. Good luck in the tournament, Mr. Knox."

"Thanks. And call me Tyler. You're like my age, dude."

The two laughed, and Logan nodded. "I'm one year younger. But a big fan. I hope you crush it out there. Good luck." He turned and walked back to his station by the bar entrance.

"Good kid, Logan. Good golfer too. Needs to work on his short game, but he'll get there."

Tyler shook his head. "It's definitely weird being known here."

"You'll get used to it, my boy. Now get in there and grab yourself something to eat. They already made the announcements, but you didn't miss anything. You can find your start time and pairings for Thursday's round one on a board in the ballroom."

"Thank you, sir," Tyler said. "For everything."

"Happy to."

Tyler shook the man's hand again and made his way through the minefield of elites hovering around in the corridor and then walked through the entrance into the main ballroom door. Inside, he found that the walls adjacent to two other ballrooms had been folded to create one enormous dining hall.

Hundreds of people sat at round tables, eating, drinking, and conversing.

Two long buffet tables stood at the front of the room just in front of the stage. Several workers in white chef's outfits waited behind the tables in case they needed to swap out some of the pans as they emptied. Two guys in the center of the lines were busy cutting slices of rib roast and turkey.

It was a feast unlike anything Tyler had ever experienced before.

He hesitated but then walked ahead through the center of the room, hoping he wasn't drawing any attention. He quickly realized no one seemed to notice him, which made him a little more comfortable as he approached the buffet lines.

He stood behind a guy he recognized as a pro, and the man's wife, but tried not to make eye contact. Tyler just wanted to get some food, find a seat, and eat his meal quietly before checking his start time for round one.

The food looked amazing, and he had to remind himself to keep his lips sealed while his mouth watered.

He picked out some buttery roasted potatoes, mixed veggies, macaroni and cheese, and a slice of the rib roast with a dollop of horseradish sauce on the side.

Then he turned and started scanning the room for a table. One off to the left near the far wall had several empty seats, with only one other person sitting there. Tyler's eyes widened when he realized who it was.

Graham Sullivan.

He stepped away from the buffet line, debating in his mind whether or not he should go over and sit down. Sullivan clearly didn't want to be sociable, hence the seat away from everyone else.

But this might be Tyler's only chance to meet his hero.

That last bit pushed him over the edge. He didn't want to sit with anyone else either, and at the very least, he and Sullivan could eat their food quietly without being bothered by the rest of the people at the party.

He made his way through the array of tables and people walking to the food line or to one of the four bars positioned on each corner.

Tyler finally made it to the table and picked out a chair opposite of Sullivan. "Is it okay if I sit over here?" he asked, nerves tickling his words.

Sullivan looked up from his half-eaten plate and nodded. For a second, he studied Tyler's face to see if he recognized him, then grinned. "By all means."

"Thanks," Tyler said.

He set his plate down on a dark blue mat between a glass of iced tea and a glass of water, then eased into the seat, doing his best not to knock anything over and look like a clumsy idiot.

Graham picked up a yeast roll and held it near his mouth but didn't take a bite. "What's your name?" he asked.

Tyler couldn't believe Graham Sullivan was asking his name.

"Tyler," he nearly choked. "Tyler Knox."

"Tyler Knox. I've heard of you."

Tyler had lifted a forkful of macaroni and nearly dropped it. "You have?"

"Sure. Heard you broke the course record at Green Mont to get into the open. That's quite the achievement."

Tyler cleared his throat, trying to banish the nerves strangling it. "I got lucky."

"You don't break course records without some skill. Maybe a few lucky shots here and there don't hurt. But don't sell yourself short. I hear you're really good."

He finally took that bite of his yeast roll.

"I didn't play so well in the practice round today." Dejection took over his tone, and wiped away the nerves he'd felt.

He took a bite of the macaroni.

"It happens, kid. I'm Graham Sullivan, by the way. Nice to meet you."

Tyler couldn't believe this was happening. "Nice to meet you too, sir. I don't mean to sound like a fan boy, but you were the reason I got into golf. I'm a big fan."

Graham smiled at the sentiment. "We're all just people playing a game, Tyler. Everyone in this room is in the same career field. We're all peers. And now that includes you."

The statement left Tyler speechless for a moment. He couldn't find the words to say other than a humble "Thank you."

"No problem." Graham sliced a piece of rib roast on his plate and stabbed it with his fork. "So, what's a good-looking young man like yourself doing here without a date? I'm surprised you don't have a girlfriend."

"I do." Tyler's eyes lowered to the plate. "Well I did. Now, I'm not so sure."

Graham tilted his head to the side, studying his young counterpart. "That sounds confusing."

"It is."

"Why is it confusing? Did you break up?" Graham stuffed the piece of roast in his mouth and chewed.

"No. But I said some things I regret earlier."

"Oh. That does sound complicated. Regret is a tricky thing. Plays mind games with us."

Tyler didn't know why, but he felt comfortable enough to say more. "I just started officially dating this girl. Her name is Lucy. She's beautiful, and fun to hang out with. And so sweet. We've been friends a long time but just decided to date recently."

"So, what's the problem?"

Tyler exhaled the demons. "Her father doesn't like me. Says I don't fit in because I don't come from a family with money."

"I see. Seems like a story I've heard before."

"On top of that, I had a fight with my best friend, Justin, who is also my caddie. He walked off the green on eighteen. I said some things I shouldn't have. I wasn't even upset at him. I was just mad about what Lucy's dad said to me about not belonging." Tyler looked up from his plate and waved his hand around, indicating the setting. "Like I don't belong here."

Graham looked like a man who hadn't expected to be thrown into a deep conversation with a young stranger, but he also didn't seem to be bothered by it. Tyler saw a sincerity in his eyes, framed by the wrinkles of experience. There was what looked like a distant pain in them but also an apparent kindness that pushed out those shadows to the deepest corners.

"We all make mistakes, kid," Graham said. "Say stuff we don't mean to the people we care about most. Life is hard like that. It pushes us to our breaking point, gives us things we think aren't fair, or that we don't deserve."

Tyler knew all about his story, and not just the golf part of it. He knew about the tragedy with Graham's son, and his wife leaving him. He'd had a rough go. And yet here he was, still churning along.

"The reality is, though," Graham continued, "everything in our world is mental. Our subconscious mind creates this," he waved a hand around, "based on programming from our earliest years on earth. So in a weird way, every unfortunate thing that happens, or what we deem unfortunate, was created by us. That's an empowering thing to understand."

Tyler had never considered it that way before. But the idea still confused him. "But I don't want to lose Lucy. I don't want to lose my best friend. I want Lucy's dad to accept me for who I am and who I can be. And I want my mom to have a better life." He looked down at his plate again, dejected. "My dad died before I was able to do that for him."

Graham nodded, and for a second, he allowed Tyler to have his thoughts to himself. "It tests us, kid. Usually to see if we're ready for the next level. It's all a game, just like golf. You start off, and you suck at it. Then you practice, play more, and get better. All we can do is control how we react to what is given to us. You get angry at something you don't like, you'll just get more of it. I won't get too religious, but there are a lot of ancient scriptures that teach that stuff. The point is, just like in the game of golf, sometimes things don't go the way you planned or wanted. If you react poorly, or in anger, you'll only make things worse."

Tyler nodded. "Yeah. I definitely did that in the practice round."

"What did you shoot?"

"Nine over."

Graham shrugged. "That's not so bad. In fact, I've done worse than that before when I was upset about something. Try eleven over on for size when you're a professional. And that was just one round."

"Yeah, I saw that one."

"You did?"

"Of course. I always tried to keep up with your tournaments when I could, if I wasn't working."

Graham smiled and scooped up a heap of mashed potatoes on his fork. He took a bite and thought for a moment while he chewed. Tyler took the cue and also ate another forkful of the macaroni.

"I'm sorry to dump all this on you," Tyler said. "That's not what I intended when I sat down. I just came over here because I didn't want to be around anyone else, and your table was the most empty."

"It's fine. I was just sitting here ignoring everyone too." He chuckled, and the laugh disarmed Tyler's concerns. "You have a promising career ahead of you, kid. And it sounds like you have good people around you. If I was you, I'd call that young lady, and your friend, and set things right. It might take a while for them to get over it, but that's okay. It'll all work out. You just have to remember in every moment, in golf and in life, that the only thing you can control is how you react to whatever comes your way."

Graham was right. Tyler thought he'd reacted well to most things that happened in his life, but now he wasn't so sure. He ate quietly for a minute before speaking again.

"Thanks for talking to me, Mr. Sullivan. I really appreciate it."

"We're peers now. You can call me Sully like everyone else here."

Tyler wasn't sure he felt comfortable with that, but he nodded. "Okay. Well, thank you."

"Happy to. Who knows? Maybe you and I will get paired together. Though for your sake, I hope that's not the case since I'm not usually at the top of the leaderboard." Graham laughed.

Tyler smiled at the joke. "Well, I still think you're great."

"I appreciate that."

"You mind me asking why you're calling it quits? I know lots of other people probably asked that question."

"Nah, it's okay. You can't play forever, Tyler. I don't want to be one of those guys who can barely swing but is out there taking up a spot on the tour when someone better is waiting in the wings for their shot."

"I see." Tyler finished eating and then took a drink of the iced tea.

"You going to go back for seconds?"

Tyler grinned. "Maybe. That was really good."

"I can't tell seeing how you cleaned your plate." Graham laughed again.

Tyler was about to stand up when he felt his phone vibrating in his pocket. His heart raced, wondering if it was Lucy or not, and if so, what would she say. He felt his nerves tighten in his gut as he looked at the screen.

It was a number he didn't recognize, but the identification at the top said it was one of the local hospitals.

He frowned, wondering if he should answer the call or not. Usually, if it was something like that, he'd just let it ring. It was probably a wrong number. But he'd never gotten a call from the hospital before.

Something inside him told him to answer the call.

Tyler tapped the green button on the screen and held the device to his head. "Hello?"

Graham watched Tyler's face darken with concern as he listened to whoever was on the other end of the call.

"Oh no," Tyler said. "I'll be right there."

He ended the call and slid the phone back in his pocket.

"Is everything okay?" Graham asked.

"No," Tyler said. "My mom was taken to the hospital."

43

Tyler sat in the waiting room of the hospital with his elbows on his knees, hands folded, leaning forward in the seat as he kept repeating the same silent prayer.

He'd been there for thirty minutes, and the only thing the doctors had told him was that his mother had passed out at work. Luckily, she hadn't sustained any external injuries.

Every possible negative emotion ran through his mind, blasting worst-case scenarios through his imagination so fast he couldn't dispel them no matter how hard he tried.

He'd texted Lucy and Justin before he left the golf course to let them know, and both had replied that they would be right over.

He tried to tell them that wasn't necessary, but the truth was, Tyler wanted both of them to be there. Outside of his mother, they were the two most important people in his life.

Tyler looked up as he saw movement through the glass windows of the waiting room walls. It was Justin.

His friend pushed through the door and hurried over to Tyler, who stood as his friend approached.

"I'm so sorry, Justin," Tyler said. "I didn't mean to lash out at you. That wasn't fair."

"Dude," Justin said, embracing his friend. "Forget that. How's your mom?"

They stepped back, and Tyler wiped a tear from his cheek. "I don't know. They were going to run some tests. She passed out at work, and an ambulance brought her here. I have no idea what's going on."

He looked over Justin's shoulder and saw Lucy through the windows. Justin turned and saw her too.

She walked in through the door wearing a look of sympathy on her face to go with a gray jacket and black leggings.

They locked eyes, and for a second, she hesitated before crossing the room.

"Lucy, I am so—"

"Stop," she said, wrapping her arms around him. "It's okay."

"It's not. I should never talk to you like that. It wasn't your fault."

"It was my dad's, I know. I was so mad at him when I got home."

"No," Tyler insisted. "I have to control my emotions better. With both of you, and with everything. I know that now. I'm so sorry."

She pulled back, looked him in the eyes and kissed him on the lips.

Justin turned away at the display of affection.

Lucy retreated a step. "How is your mom? What happened?"

"I don't know," Tyler said. "They told me she passed out at work. Then she was brought here."

"Someone has to know something," Justin said. "I'm going to go talk to the head nurse."

"No. I already tried that," Tyler said. "She doesn't know anything yet either."

"Sit down," Lucy said. "You've had a long day."

Tyler shook his head as he slumped back into the chair. Lucy sat next to him on the right, and Justin on the left.

"It's going to be okay, man," Justin said. "I'm sure your mom is fine."

Twenty minutes passed without a word being said. The day had gone from bad, to meeting Graham Sullivan, to worse.

The conversation with Sully had given Tyler a glimmer of hope, and maybe a way for dealing with adversity that he so badly needed. But all that washed away when he got the call from the hospital.

Or had it?

This, like so many other things in his life—including the death of his father, the lack of financial security he'd experienced as a child, and even the ridicule and self-loathing for not belonging in the elite class—had all been a test. Every step of his life had been one trial after another. And this was perhaps the greatest of them all.

But he didn't want to lose his mom. And he hadn't wanted any of those bad things to happen in the past either. Still, Sully's words echoed in his mind. "You can't control what happens. Only how you react to it."

Tyler recalled how Sully said that if he got upset, and put that negativity out into the world, that's exactly what he'd get back.

Right then, Tyler refused to be sad. He refused to be angry about the circumstances, and he chose to focus on what he had right there in front of him—two people who cared about him, and who'd dropped whatever they'd been doing to rush over to the hospital to comfort him.

"Thank you, guys, for coming," Tyler said, wiping another tear from his cheek. "I really appreciate it."

"Of course," they both said, almost simultaneously.

"I'm really grateful both of you are in my life," Tyler added. "Seriously. I'm sorry I lost it earlier today."

"It's all good, man," Justin said. "You're my boy."

"And you're my boyfriend," Lucy added with a smile. She glanced at Justin, who grinned at her and bobbed his head once in approval.

A female doctor in light blue scrubs appeared in the doorway and entered the room. She met Tyler's gaze. The moment sent a shiver down Tyler's spine, and he couldn't tell from the woman's expression whether or not the news was going to be good or bad.

The doctor stuffed her hands in her pockets and walked over to the group.

"You Tyler Knox?" she asked in an even tone.

Tyler stood up and nodded.

The doctor looked like she was in her mid-forties, stood four inches shorter than him, a slender frame, and kind, brown eyes. She looked like the kind of woman who did this job to help people, not for the money some physicians obsessively chased.

"So, your mother had a brain bleed."

Tyler felt his knees go weak.

"But thankfully, we were able to get to it in time. She's out of surgery now, and in recovery. We'll have her in a regular room in an hour or so. We'll need to keep her here for a few days for observation, but I think she's going to be okay. She was lucky."

"Any idea what caused this?" he asked.

"These things can have many causes, often head trauma is a cause. In her case, it's high blood pressure. She's going to need to alter her diet, and definitely lower her stress levels. Getting some exercise every day would be good too, at least six days a week for twenty to thirty minutes. Has she been under more stress than usual lately, perhaps with her job?"

Tyler knew his mother had been under loads of stress for most of her life. Nothing had ever come easy for her. But as far as he knew, it hadn't gotten worse recently.

"No," he said. "I don't think anything has changed, not that I know of."

"Well, before we discharge her, we'll talk about ways to improve her health going forward, how to get that blood pressure down— including some medications that will help. But stress is the number one killer. It's the cause of most health problems. We just see how it manifests in disease or other conditions such as hers. She's going to be okay, though. She got here in time. That's what matters."

Relief cascaded down from Tyler's head all the way to his toes. "Oh, thank you, Doctor. Thank you so much."

"You're welcome. We will let you know when she's been moved into a room."

"Can I see her right now?"

"No. She's sleeping, and we don't allow anyone in the recovery room while the patient recuperates. I'm sorry. But like I said, when she's in a regular room, someone will let you know."

Tyler didn't like the answer, but he knew there was nothing he could do but sit here and wait.

"Okay. Thank you again, Doctor. Thank you so much."

"You're welcome. Your mom is a tough lady."

"She is," Tyler agreed.

The doctor turned and walked out of the room.

"You guys can go home if you want," Tyler said. "Looks like she's going to be okay."

"Are you kidding?" Justin asked. "I'm not going anywhere."

"Me either," Lucy added.

"I appreciate it. Seriously. But you both have classes in the morning. And you can't stay here all night."

"I'm ahead in all my classes."

"And I don't mind skipping," Justin said.

"I know," Tyler insisted, "but it could be a while before they move her into a room. Seriously. It's okay. Go home and get some rest. I'll be fine."

"You know, you're a great golfer, but you don't listen very well. We're not leaving. So, you might as well get used to that."

"Yep. We're not going anywhere," Lucy agreed.

Tyler could see there was no getting around it. They were going to stay whether he wanted them to or not. Deep down, he knew he did want them there. He didn't want to be alone.

"Thank you," he said, accepting defeat. "I appreciate it."

As he sat there between them, Tyler thought a lot more about what Graham had said. And he thought about how lucky he was to have Justin and Lucy in his life. They clearly cared for him, and he promised himself he'd never again lose his composure, or his temper, around them, no matter what came next.

44

Graham couldn't stop thinking about Tyler's abrupt exit. He'd finished his meal alone and then quickly left the clubhouse, doing his best to avoid any social interaction on his way out.

A few people caught his eye, which required a few awkward exchanges of pleasantries before excusing himself. But he managed to get out of the building and to his car in a relatively short amount of time.

Once behind the wheel of his sedan, he sat there thinking, wondering what he should do.

He'd only just met Tyler, and had no reason for his unfortunate circumstance to bother him so much. But it did.

He needed to do something. But what could he do?

The idea of driving over to the hospital kept popping into his head, but that would just be awkward. Again, he'd just met the kid.

So instead, Graham drove out of the parking lot and headed toward his hotel.

Back in his room, he set down his keys and wallet and sat on the edge of the bed.

He folded his hands between his knees for a moment, thinking about Tyler, about his past, and about Alicia.

He took out his phone, found the last message to her, and typed out a quick text. "Are you free to talk?"

He set the phone down next to him on the bed and waited. It wasn't late yet, so he figured she would still be awake.

He waited for five minutes, then checked his phone to make sure she hadn't replied without him knowing, but there was nothing.

Graham stood and paced over to the window. He looked out at the darkened sky, lit by the moon hovering over the mountains and hills.

Why is she so flaky? he wondered.

The more he thought about it, the more old worries piled up in his mind. Linda, his ex-wife, had been this way before she left him. Of course, she'd been seeing someone else, taking comfort in the arms of another man and blaming him for never being there emotionally for her after the death of their son.

Was that what was going on with Alicia? Had she just been playing him, playing his emotions to earn his trust all the while fooling around with someone else?

"Why should you care?" Graham asked out loud. "It's not like we're in a committed relationship or anything. She can do what she wants. She's a grown woman."

Temptations slipped through his defenses. He could go back to the party. There were several women there who would be happy to comfort him for the night. Gold diggers? Sure. But what did that matter anymore? He had money.

He was tired of being alone. And Alicia, as great as she seemed, wasn't helping with that problem.

He stalked back over to the bed and picked up the phone. Still nothing from her. He went to the bar and poured a tall glass of whiskey into an empty tumbler, then held the cup to his lips.

The scent of oak barrels and spicy caramel drifted into his nostrils.

"What are you doing?" he asked.

Graham knew the answer. He was going to have a tall drink to numb his emotions, and maybe give him enough courage to get a ride back to the party to put himself out there for whoever would take him.

Doubts riddled his mind next as he stood there holding the cup. Should he retire? Or should he keep playing, potentially opening the field to more women, and more options.

It was what many of the other pros did on tour. Some of them were even married. He didn't have that burden to bear.

And to think he'd fallen so head-over-heels for Alicia.

If she truly cared about him, wouldn't she be more responsive?

His past failures loomed like apparitions, ghostly memories of his colossal collapse at the open ten years before, of all the other cataclysmic losses he'd suffered both on and off the course.

"You aren't meant to win," he said. "No matter what you believe or what you think you believe, you are and always will be a loser."

He was about to take the drink when something else in his head halted the tumbler just as the rim touched his lips.

The image of his son appeared in his mind's eye. He was full of energy and joy. It was the last time they'd spoken face to face. Graham had told his son he loved him.

"I love you too, Dad," his son had said.

They'd hugged, just like they always had. Then he had gotten in his car and driven off, heading to meet a friend.

Remember what you said to Tyler? a voice in Graham's head asked, as if the memory of his son somehow linked to the young man he met earlier that evening.

Graham did remember. He'd told the kid not to let his emotions dictate his reactions to things, and now, here he was doing that exact thing. He was getting angry over Alicia not responding immediately to his message. And the conclusion he'd jumped to was that she was sleeping with someone else.

He lowered the glass and set it on the bar.

"Don't react with emotions," Graham said to himself. "Everything is fine. No. Everything is great."

It didn't matter how many times he repeated the affirmation, the burning knots in his stomach continued to swell.

The world seemed to shrink around him, tightening his entire body in a vise grip. He tried to breathe, using exercises he'd learned before to calm his nerves, but nothing helped.

The overwhelming anxiety wrapped its arms around his chest and gripped his lungs, making deep breaths nearly impossible.

Graham hurried over to the bed, worried for a moment that he might pass out and hit his head on the floor.

He sat down on the edge of the mattress and leaned forward, putting his head between his knees as he'd done before when panic attacks hit him.

The room continued to close in around him, and for a minute, he considered calling for help.

"Come on," he said, trying to grit his way through it. "Don't be a wuss."

The blood moving to his head seemed to help a little, but breathing remained a difficult endeavor.

He tried to shorten his breath, taking in little bursts then exhaling more slowly. But his chest continued to tighten.

This wasn't the first time he'd experienced an acute level of anxiety. The worst of the attacks had come before final rounds of major tournaments when he was in the lead. These emotions, he knew, were fear based.

Before, he feared blowing the lead in those events, and as if by some magic, that was exactly what happened. The stress wasn't as bad in minor tournaments, or in major events where he was in the middle of the pack.

He'd spent years trying to figure out how to deal with this, how to douse the burning storm inside him. But nothing had truly eliminated the anxiety.

He thought he'd made a breakthrough when he found a guy on YouTube talking about the endgame of anxiety, and how we shouldn't look at it as if it were a foreign invader but as a way our body is trying to heal itself, to expel something bad from our past.

The speaker likened it to having a fever. Even though the natural tendency is to try to get rid of the fever, what that is actually a symptom of is your body defending itself against something bad, and its attempt to get rid of whatever thing is making it ill.

"What is it?" Graham asked himself, trying to sort out what bad thing was trying to escape his body. "What are you holding on to?"

You're not worthy, something said in his head. *You don't deserve to be happy. You don't deserve her. That's why she's not calling you back. She knows you're a loser.*

"I am not a loser!" he shouted as he rocked back and forth, desperate to rid himself of the demons. "I am worthy! I am worthy of winning. I am worthy of Alicia. And I don't have to let you control me anymore."

The voice inside him quieted. But the anxiety still held a firm grip on his entire body. He felt paralyzed, unable to stand, unable to take full breaths.

Graham recalled something else he'd read regarding dreams, desires, and goals. "I release my attachment to the outcome. I release my attachment to the outcome," he repeated. "I want to make a run at this with Alicia. And if it doesn't work out, I am okay. I am always okay. I am enough. I have enough. And I will always be enough, and have enough."

He felt his vision fading, and he leaned back onto the bed, curled up, and surrendered to the darkness.

45

"Good morning, sleepyhead."

Tyler heard the familiar voice through the charcoal-gray haze of slumber.

His eyelids peeled open, blinking rapidly against the daylight streaming in from the half-open curtain over the window.

For a moment, he struggled to remember where he was. Then the hospital room revealed itself through the fog. He rubbed his eyes and sat up on the couch in the corner of the room opposite a bed.

"Mom," he said, his senses finally seizing where he was and what had happened.

Molly smiled at him as he stood and rushed over to her side. She looked tired and weak, and her skin was paler than usual.

Tyler looked at the tube running into her arm from a bag hanging on a mobile rack. Machines on the other side of the bed beeped in a steady rhythm. Lights blinked, and a display of her heartbeat bounced along on a digital screen.

"How are you feeling?" Tyler asked.

"I'm okay," she said. "I'm really tired. I feel like gravity is working double on me right now."

"I'll get the doctor," he said.

"No, don't do that. I've been awake for a little while now. Besides, the doctor and nurses have already been by to check on me."

Tyler peered into her eyes. Of all the people for this to happen to, he wondered why it had to be her. She deserved so much in life, and perfect health was one of those good things.

"Do you know what happened?" Tyler asked.

"They told me I had a brain bleed, and that I passed out at work. But they say I'll make a full recovery. I guess they got to it in time. It could have been so much worse."

Tyler shuddered to think of that worst-case scenario. He'd already lost so much in life, and he hadn't had much to lose to begin with.

"You slept here last night?" she asked.

"Of course. I wasn't going to leave you here by yourself. You're my mom."

She smiled feebly at him. Her eyes drifted over his clothes. "You look like you were dressed for the occasion last night?"

In his hurry to get to the hospital, he'd not been able to change out of his dress clothes. "The food was good," he said with a smile. "I got to meet Graham Sullivan."

"Really?" She looked and sounded happy at the statement.

"Yeah. He was really nice. We ate at a table together before... before I got the call from the hospital."

"Oh, Son. I'm so sorry."

"What? Stop. Don't be. I love you, Mom. You're the most important person in my life. None of that other stuff matters now."

A look of concern filled her eyes. "Shouldn't you be in your second practice round today? The tournament starts tomorrow, doesn't it?"

"It does. But it's more important that I be here."

"Oh, Tyler. I'll be fine. You need to go play. This is a big moment for you. You can't miss it."

"You are more important than golf, Mom. I need to be here with you. I am withdrawing from the tournament. I already told Justin to let the organizers know I wouldn't be there today. But I'm going to have him tell them I'm pulling out."

"No, you are not," Molly countered, her voice turning stern with sudden renewed strength. "Tyler, I am going to be fine. The doctors said so. You are not going to miss the chance of a lifetime just so you can sit around here and babysit me."

"How am I supposed to go out there and play knowing that you're here hooked up to all these machines?"

Her expression softened with her voice. "Son, I'm fine. Let the doctors and nurses do their jobs. You go do yours."

He glanced at his watch and shook his head. "I already missed my slot for the practice round."

"Then go hit balls at the range. Do whatever you need to do to prepare for tomorrow. I'm sorry I can't be there in person to watch it. But I'll definitely be watching it on television. I can promise you that."

He still wasn't sure. "I don't know. What if something happens?"

"I'll be in good hands. But nothing is going to happen, Son. I'm fine. You go out there and show them what you got. I know you'll do great."

Tyler shook his head. "I didn't do so great in yesterday's practice round."

"No?"

"My head wasn't clear. I shot nine over par."

"That doesn't sound so bad," she said. "You're still alive. Still breathing. Still functioning."

He allowed a snort of a laugh. "Yeah. I guess."

"That's right. And nine over is still better than most people will ever dream of shooting, on a professional course no less."

He knew she was right, even though it didn't help him feel much better. Tyler had higher standards he'd set for himself, and playing below those felt unacceptable.

"Clear your mind," she offered. "Let go of all the pressure you've put on yourself. Play it like you would any other day on any other course."

"Easy to say when millions of people aren't watching."

"You don't know any of those people. Well, you know me. And

maybe some of the members of Green Mont. I'm sure they'll be watching too."

"Great," he joked. "That makes me feel better."

She grinned at him. "You just go out and have fun. Play free. And you'll be fine."

"Okay, Mom. But I don't like it."

"Doesn't matter if you like it. That's an order, Mister."

He leaned down and kissed her on the forehead. "I love you, Mom. I love you so much."

"I love you too, sweetheart. Good luck in the tournament."

"I'll be back this evening to check on you."

She shook her head. "You're going to have too much going on, Son. I have my phone over here," she motioned to a nightstand. "You can text me or call me. But I want you to focus on the tournament."

"Fine," he said. "But I'm not going to promise I won't check on you in person when I can."

She shook her head. "Stubborn just like your father." Tears formed in her eyes. "You look like him, you know. Like he did when he was your age."

Tyler fought his own tears. "I wish he was here right now."

"I do too, honey. But he is always in our hearts. And that can keep us going. Now get out of here before I start crying. You have a tournament to get to."

46

Graham rolled over in the hotel bed and checked the clock. It was six in the morning. Dim gray light peeked through the crack in the curtains over the window.

He took a deep breath and planted his feet on the floor, sitting up straight.

For a second, he struggled to remember how he got here, or what had happened. He was still in his clothes from the night before.

Then it all came flooding back. He'd started overthinking things, anxiety had taken over, and he couldn't push it out.

I must have passed out.

Looking around, he thought everything seemed to be in order. He felt oddly good, too, as if a terrible weight had been taken off him after yoking him for most of his life. He felt free.

He stood up slowly, just to make sure he wasn't wrong, but the room didn't spin, and he felt remarkably stable.

His phone sat on the edge of the bed, where he'd left it the night before after texting Alicia.

Graham wondered if she'd responded, but instead of a sense of paranoia or insecurity, he was unusually okay with either way.

He bent down and picked up the device and tapped the screen. It remained black.

Battery must be dead, he realized. *Better charge that before I head to the course.*

He reached over to the charging cord on the nightstand and plugged in the phone, then went to the bathroom, turned on the shower, and brushed his teeth while it warmed up.

Twelve minutes later, clean and refreshed, Graham put on a clean set of clothes and slipped into his shoes.

He leaned over to his phone and tapped the screen again. This time, it bloomed to life and displayed a lightning icon over the battery in the top corner. It also showed him a message preview in the center.

There were three messages from Alicia.

He tapped on the preview, which opened the texting app, and the thread between the two of them.

"Hey, you. I'm so sorry I was late responding to your texts. I ended up working a double shift last night, so I didn't get done until late. Gotta pay the bills. I hope everything is okay. I really wish I could be there to watch you play this weekend. You never know. I might be able to make it up there if something changes. Good luck. I know you'll do great."

Graham smiled at the messages. They sent a warm feeling through his chest, and filled him with a sense of calm unlike anything he'd ever felt before.

"She likes me," he said. "Good job, Graham."

He unplugged the phone and brought the cord with him to finish charging it in his car, then with a newfound energy in his step, walked out of the hotel room and headed for the elevator.

47

T he television hanging on the far wall of the hospital room displayed a close-up view of the clubhouse at White Oak National.

Molly watched as the scene transitioned to an overhead view of the course with the mountains and hills in the background.

"Welcome to the 105th White Oak National Open Championship," the male announcer said in a velvety smooth voice. "It's a spectacular day here in Southeastern Tennessee. The weather is absolutely perfect for golf, and it looks like it will be all weekend long. I'm Troy Fallon, along with two-time major champion Steve Watson and an all-star broadcast team covering every hole, every shot of the tournament for you. Steve, how you doing this morning?"

The camera focused on the two men sitting in a broadcast booth with a row of double-knockout roses behind them and a mountain rising beyond that.

Both men wore suit jackets with the channel logo on them. Troy, a man in his mid-fifties, had covered this tournament for the last eight years, and his name and voice had grown synonymous with it. His partner, Steve, was older, in his mid-sixties, with gray hair and a high forehead baked permanently tan from his decades on the links.

"I'm doing great, Troy, and you're right: This weather is absolutely perfect for golf. It'll be cool in the mornings and warm and dry in the afternoons. So if these guys want to stick the landings on the greens, they'll have to be careful in the later parts of the day. We could see a lot of balls take off and run away from the hole as the course dries out."

"Good point, Steve. Lot of stories coming into today's first round, including the number-one golfer in the world, Jamie Winthrop, who's the odds-on favorite to win it again."

"Yeah, Troy. Jamie is still, remarkably, at the top of his game even as he nears fifty years of age. And he hasn't shown any signs of slowing down yet. You keep thinking maybe the next time he goes out will be the day we see him drop off, but his resilience is unlike anything we've witnessed in the game of golf for a long time."

"That's right, and he's won here before so he's no stranger to how the course plays."

"Absolutely," Steve agreed. "He's a stone-cold killer out there, and he showed it in the two practice rounds, shooting a stellar three under yesterday."

"Indeed," Troy said. "And another interesting storyline on the docket is the cagey veteran Graham Sullivan, who recently announced that this would be his final tournament as a professional."

"Yeah, it's sad to see that Sully is hanging it up. He's been a great competitor through the years. Unfortunately, he has a string of close seconds attached to his name, which is unfair in a lot of ways. But he had a strong couple of practice rounds, shooting one under yesterday in the second one. So who knows? Maybe he's going to give us one more look at the greatness we all expected from him years ago."

"Would be incredible, wouldn't it? What an amazing story that would be if he could somehow find himself near the top of the leaderboard."

Troy paused for a second and then continued. "There are a ton of great storylines brewing here at White Oak, but none more capti-vating than the local kid who qualified as an amateur. Tyler Knox grew up here in the area and is a caddie at another course in town, where he recently broke the course record."

"Yes, quite the talent, but he faltered in the first practice round the other day, shooting a nine over par. Maybe it was the pressure of playing in front of an audience. Or just the fact that this course is so difficult compared to probably anything else he's played in his life."

"Right you are, Steve. And he's also battling some personal issues. We received word that his mother was taken to the hospital the day of the first practice round. From what we understand, she is recovering from surgery and doing well, but as a result, Tyler missed the second practice round, which he probably needed after doing so poorly during the first one."

"Yeah, it's unfortunate, and honestly I don't know how the kid will stay focused with all of that going on in the background."

Molly shook her head. "You don't know my Tyler," she said, defiance pulsing through her.

"Well, I'm sure we'll keep a close watch on him one way or the other," Troy said. "He'll be teeing off here momentarily in one of the early groups, paired with two seasoned professionals in Matt Carlson and Tom Pitchford."

48

"How you feeling?" Justin asked, setting Tyler's bag down in the tee box.

"I feel good," Tyler said, glancing at his friend with a smirk. "Better, actually. I still feel bad for the other—"

"Water under the bridge, bro. Stop thinking about that. I have."

"I know. But—"

"Tyler." Justin stopped what he was doing and looked straight into his friend's eyes. "Let it go."

Tyler nodded. He looked to the left at the crowd of people surrounding the 1st tee and spotted Lucy in the front row wearing a white visor that matched her golf skirt. She had a pink golf shirt on with the top button undone so her silver necklace was visible. He knew she'd dressed cute just for him, although he doubted she knew it was more than a little distracting. Still, her outfit, her smile, all of it told him how she felt about him, and it caused his heart to skip a beat.

She beamed at him, and as their eyes met, he felt a rush of emotions sweep through him.

He wanted to tell her he loved her but wondered if it was too soon for that. They'd been friends for years, and even though their official dating status hadn't been for long, his feelings for her had been forged through time.

The starter interrupted his thoughts.

"Please welcome to the tee, Matt Carlson."

Tyler stole one more glance at Lucy amid hundreds of crowded onlookers. He'd apologized profusely to her, and to Justin. Both had accepted his apology without hesitation, which surprised him a little. He'd been a jerk to them both, and he wasn't so sure he would have been so quick to forgive.

Matt Carlson, a slender guy in his thirties, planted his ball on a tee, took a few practice swings, and then stepped up to the ball.

Tournament workers held up signs that said Quiet, Please on them, and the crowd's already low murmur died into total silence, leaving only the sounds of the birds to interrupt the moment.

Carlson swung the driver, and the ball launched into the air, soaring down the fairway along the right edge.

The spectators applauded the shot as it flew and landed, rolling close to the rough along the right side.

Carlson picked up his tee, gave a quick wave to the crowd, and walked back to where Tyler and the other golfer stood.

"Great shot," Tyler said to Carlson as he returned.

"Thanks. Felt good."

"Perfect placement over there too. Terrific angle for the approach."

"Please welcome Tom Pitchford," the starter announced.

Tom, a slightly heavier guy stepped into the tee box to a round of applause. He repeated the same process as Carlson and then addressed the ball, paused a second, then swung.

His swing was quicker, snappier than Carlson's. It was a violent assault on the ball, which resulted in a powerful drive down the middle of the fairway, but with a slight draw to the left.

The crowd cheered the shot even though it curled dangerously close to the left side of the fairway, cutting off a direct approach to the green due to the trees lining the second cut.

He thanked the audience with a wave, but Pitchford couldn't hide the irritation on his face. The reality was, this hole was one of the easier ones on the course, and starting off in a bad position from the first drive added unnecessary pressure.

"Good shot," Tyler offered.

"Would have preferred to be where Matt is," Pitchford said in a joking tone.

"Please welcome Tyler Knox," the starter announced.

The spectators applauded, and Tyler took another glance over at Lucy, who was clapping excitedly. She smiled at him as he stepped into the box.

"Ty?" Justin said, stopping him.

Tyler turned around and saw his friend holding out the driver for him.

"You might need this."

Tyler's face burned red with embarrassment, and the audience laughed at the gaff.

Shaking his head, Tyler took the driver. "Thanks. Yeah, probably do better with a club."

Justin laughed at his buddy then propped up the bag on its end and watched as Tyler placed the ball on a tee and stepped back for a few practice swings.

Then he addressed the ball, looked down the fairway one more time, and swung.

His swing was poetically smooth, the tempo absolute perfection.

The driver's face smacked the ball and lifted it into the air. Tyler held his pose as he watched the sphere carry dead center down the fairway. The crowd roared their approval at the shot and continued clapping as it landed and rolled to a stop along the right middle, passing Carlson's shot by ten yards.

He turned and found both pros staring at him, nodding simultaneously. "Great shot, kid," Pitchford offered. "Want to trade?"

"Outstanding," Carlson said. "Keep hitting like that all weekend."

"Thanks," Tyler said, humbled by the praise. He handed the club back to Justin while the other two golfers and their caddies took off down the fairway.

"Great shot, buddy," Justin said. "Looks like someone found their groove again."

"It's only one shot."

"That's right. One shot. Just focus on one shot. All day. You got this."

GRAHAM STOOD next to his caddie and waited for the starter to announce his name. As the eldest of the three, he was given the honor of hitting first. Graham wondered if that had to do with the fact that it would be the last time he teed off on the first hole of any tournament. If the tour loved anything, it was drama. Drama produced ratings, which grew the game.

He knew there wasn't any drama to be had with him. Just an old golfer on his last legs, trying to get in one more tournament.

Of course, there were older men than him playing in the tournament, and would continue playing until they couldn't swing anymore. But he wasn't going to go out like that.

"Feeling good?" his caddie, Mike, interrupted his thoughts.

"You've asked me that like four times this morning," Graham said with a laugh. "Do I not look good?"

Mike chuckled. "You look great, chief. Just taking care of my guy."

"You always have, Mike. And I appreciate it."

"You're gonna miss all this."

The two stared down the fairway, waiting for the golfers ahead of them to clear out of the way and move ahead.

Graham nodded. "Yeah. I definitely will."

He didn't add anything else to it. There was nothing else to say. Golf had been his life for four decades. Something like that didn't just go away.

The men in front of them moved ahead and out of range.

Graham took one last look around at the spectators, searching the crowd of faces for one he recognized, one he hoped had surprised him by showing up even though she'd said she couldn't.

He'd left a ticket for Alicia at the gate, a pass that would allow her entry for the entire weekend. But there was no sign of her in the mass of people.

You knew she wasn't coming, he reminded himself. While he wished she could be there, he also understood. She had a life of her own. Alicia worked hard and was an independent woman. He liked that about her. She was different from so many of the women he'd met on tour since Linda left him. And Alicia was exponentially better than her.

"Ladies and gentlemen," the starter said, interrupting his train of thought. "Please welcome, in his farewell tournament, Graham Sullivan."

Graham resisted the urge to roll his eyes at the introduction. He just wanted to play. But the crowd surrounding the tee box cheered wildly for him, with chants of "Sully! Sully! Sully!" echoing through the valley.

He grinned at the reception, waving as he stepped into the tee box. The cheering dwindled, and he planted his ball on the tee, pushing it into the turf in a spot he liked.

He moved back and squared up, facing the fairway to visualize the area where he wanted to aim as he held the driver out like a two-handed broadsword.

Then he addressed the ball and lowered the clubface behind it.

One last ride, he thought to himself. *Let's make it a good one.*

Graham turned, lifting the club up over his shoulders, and then twisted, whipping the club through in a perfect arc, striking the ball true in the center of the driver's face.

49

Molly stared at the television, unwilling to blink until the commercial interruptions. She'd done little else in the last four hours, not that there was anything she'd rather do, or could do, from the hospital bed.

"And we're back," the announcer said as the shampoo commercial gave way to an aerial scene of the clubhouse at White Oak. Peaceful piano music played in the background.

"What a day it's been so far in round one of the open here at White Oak National. Some interesting scores are coming in already, and one of the early headlines here is the veteran Graham Sullivan, playing in his last tournament and sitting at two under par through twelve."

"It's been quite the show Sully has put on for the crowds here today, Troy. He's been steady with the putter, hasn't made any mistakes except for an approach on seven that went awry, and even then he scrambled for par. It just seems like he's swinging free today, more relaxed. And it's working."

"It sure is, Steve. Let's go over to Allen on thirteen."

The camera shot changed to a wide green surrounded by bunkers on three sides and a creek running past it in the front. Graham Sullivan stood over his ball, ready to putt.

"Graham Sullivan has this one for birdie," Allen said in his English accent. "He's looking at about twenty-three feet, right to left. There's a hump he needs to get over if he wants to have a chance to roll this one in. Not an easy putt."

Graham struck the ball. It rolled toward the hole, the line bending as it cleared the hump the announcer mentioned.

"That's a great line he's taken there," Allen said. "This one has a chance."

At the last second, it dove slightly more to the right than Graham had anticipated, and narrowly missed the cup by an inch, stopping less than a foot away.

The crowd around the par 3 let out a disappointed groan then immediately replaced it with applause at the skillful shot.

Graham appeared unaffected by the miss and walked over to tap his ball in and get out of the others' way.

"Well, that was a close one," Troy cut in over Allen's broadcast. "So Graham Sullivan will remain at two under heading to fourteen."

"Not sure that will be the low score for the day," Steve said, "but it puts him easily in range to make the cut for the weekend if he can hold there. And he still has holes to play, with a few of them presenting decent chances at birdie."

"Right. Let's go to eighteen, where the local kid, amateur Tyler Knox, is lining up a putt for par to finish the day at an incredible four under par."

Molly sat up a little higher in the bed and clapped excitedly.

"This one is pretty straight forward, Troy," Steve said. "Ever-so-slight bend from right to left. If he makes this, he'll be the low score of the day so far going into the house. We'll see how long that holds, especially with a lot of good players still coming up behind him, including the favorite, Jamie Winthrop, who is already three under through nine."

"Oh shut up," Molly said at the television, loud enough to draw the attention of a passing nurse.

The man in blue scrubs ducked his head in, a look of concern on his face. "You okay, ma'am?" he asked.

"I'll be a lot better if my kid makes this putt," she said, refusing to take her eyes off the television.

The nurse glanced at the television, confused, and nodded. "Okay, then. Just wanted to make sure you were fine."

She didn't respond, her eyes still locked on the television.

Obviously not understanding what was going on, he retreated back through the door.

"Knox, for par and four under on the day."

"Come on, Tyler," Molly said, holding her fists up to her chin.

Tyler eased the putter back then brought it forward in a smooth stroke.

The ball ran toward the hole on a dead line for the heart.

"This one looks good," the announcer said. "Yes!"

The crowd roared as the ball disappeared into the cup. The camera zoomed in on Tyler, who smiled as he looked back over at his caddie as if to say, "Great read."

"Incredible," Troy said. "A four under sixty-eight at White Oak National, on national television, with a huge crowd watching."

"He probably hasn't played in an environment like this, on a course this difficult," Steve said. "And yet it doesn't seem too big for him. But we all know doing this on day one is a lot different from doing it on Sunday. This old course has a way of punishing the most intrepid of golfers on the last day."

"Right you are, Steve."

"Oh shut it, Steve," Molly said over the television.

50

Tyler shook hands with Pitchford first after making par on 18.

"Outstanding round, man," Pitchford said. "Well done."

"Yeah, that's a heck of a way to introduce yourself to the world," Carlson added. "Best of luck the rest of the tournament, not that you need it."

The man smirked at him and walked off with his caddie, followed by Pitchford and his guy.

Justin arched his right eyebrow at his friend. "Wow. That was amazing."

Tyler lowered his head for a second, heading toward the gap between the stands where thousands of onlookers watched.

"Yeah, it was a good round."

"Good round?" Justin asked, glaring at his friend as they marched up the hill. "Dude, you just shot four under on one of the toughest courses on the pro tour." He leaned closer, lowering his voice so neither the spectators nor the other golfers could hear. "And you blew those two out of the water."

"I had some things go my way today," Tyler reasoned. "But I'll take it."

"You are so humble. Keep it that way. Okay?"

Tyler laughed. "Sure, whatever. Lot of work to do yet if we want to win this thing."

Justin nodded in approval. "That's what I like to hear."

Lucy approached them, ushered by a couple of the security guys working the event in the standard blue blazers.

She rushed toward Tyler and threw her arms around him, then kissed him on the lips. "Great round, babe," she said, brimming with pride.

"Thanks." He squeezed her tight for a second before letting go as Justin slowed down, lingering awkwardly nearby. "My caddie was on point today."

"Yeah, you were," she agreed, nudging him on the shoulder with a fist. "You both did great out there."

"I can line him up all day," Justin said, "but he's the one who has to make the shots. Proud of you, Ty. I'll see you on the other side. Go turn that scorecard in before you lose it."

They shared a laugh, and then Tyler looked at his girlfriend. "I gotta go turn this in. See you in a few minutes."

"Okay," she said, nodding.

Tyler walked up the hill between the throngs of cheering fans. People reached their hands over the security ropes, egging him on. Some chanted his name, "Tyler! Tyler! Tyler!"

It felt like nothing he'd ever experienced before. It was exhilarating, and filled him with an energy that made him feel as if he could run through a brick wall.

He high fived some of the fans as he passed and waved at others in appreciation. With every step, the feeling of excitement waned, and he felt something else. He'd compartmentalized the crowds, the television cameras, the leaderboards, all of the distractions, until that moment. Then, suddenly, it all hit him. He stumbled but caught his balance and hurried forward toward the clubhouse, where a doorman stood by the back door, holding it open for him to enter.

As the pressure mounted, all he wanted to do was get inside and hide.

GRAHAM STOOD over the ball on 18.

The sun hung high over the trees to the west on its way to the horizon.

Graham and Mike had discussed the putt, a fourteen-foot leaner to the left. He didn't have to look at the leaderboard to know his score.

He'd played well today and was sitting at a respectable 2 under par with this putt for birdie.

The crowd watched intently, all of them leaning forward either in their chairs or on their toes.

He'd always known that while he could never win a tournament on the first day, he could certainly lose it. Graham had done well in keeping himself in it, though he also knew that tomorrow would pose new challenges, just as life did every single day.

"You've come this far," he mumbled. "May as well make this one."

He pulled the putter back then swept it through the ball.

The white sphere rolled directly over the line he'd drawn in his mind. Some of the people clapped, and others cheered, willing the ball to disappear.

It reached the left edge of the cup, and for a second he thought he'd missed it. But the ball dipped to the right and fell in, accompanied by the roar of the crowd.

Graham relaxed his shoulders, relief filling him one instant and then adrenaline the next. He pumped his fist in a way he hadn't done in a long time.

Mike walked over and high-fived him before he stepped over to the hole and removed the ball.

The spectators went wild, hundreds of them chanting, "Sully! Sully! Sully!"

"Not bad for an old-timer," Mike joked as he clapped him on the shoulder.

Graham shook his head as he walked out of the way to allow the other two men to putt. "No," he agreed. "Not too bad at all."

51

Tyler gently pushed open the door to the hospital room. He craned his neck to look inside, making sure his mother wasn't sleeping.

"Come in," Molly said, looking his way.

A female nurse in blue scrubs was checking the IV bag hanging next to the bed.

"Hey, Mom," Tyler said. "I brought a few friends along to say hi."

He stepped into the room, followed by Justin and Lucy.

"Hey, guys," Molly said. Genuine happiness filled her face despite the tubes and machines attached to her.

"Hey, Mrs. Knox," Justin said.

"Hello, Mrs. Knox," Lucy added.

Molly's grin brightened the dimly lit room. "What are you three doing here? Isn't there some kind of a party going on at the club for all the players?"

"We wanted to check on you," Tyler said. "Besides. We're college kids. We have our fair share of parties."

His mother's right eyebrow lifted slightly. "Uh-huh."

Tyler walked in and stood by his mother's side while the other two waited at the foot of the bed.

"Everything is looking good," the nurse said, completing her check. She looked at Tyler. "Your mom is doing great. She should be out of here in a few days. At this point we're just keeping her for observation."

Tyler nodded his understanding. "Thank you. I appreciate it."

"You're welcome."

The nurse walked over to the door, paused, and looked back over her shoulder. "I'll be back in a few minutes with supper."

"Okay, thank you." Molly waited until she left the room and then threw a serious mask over her face. "Please tell me you brought me something to eat that isn't hospital food."

Tyler laughed. "No. But I will tomorrow. I didn't know I could do that."

"Technically, you're not supposed to," Lucy interrupted. "But everyone does it."

"Yeah, and besides," Tyler went on, "I wasn't sure if they had you on some kind of dietary restriction after the surgery. You had a pretty serious issue, Mom. We gotta watch what we eat from now on."

"I know. I know. Enough about that. You were amazing today, honey!"

Tyler hung his head humbly. "Thanks. So you watched it?"

"Seriously?" She tilted her head to the side, staring at him as if his hair was made of snakes. "Of course I watched it. I saw every second. I wasn't going to miss my baby boy playing in his first professional tournament. Hospital or not."

"Aww, you did so great today, baby boy," Justin teased.

"And you were good too, young man," Molly said to him. "I know that having a good caddie is crucial. So, good job to you too."

"Thanks, Mrs. Knox."

"So, how do you feel? Was it everything you imagined it to be?"

"Yeah," Tyler answered with a timid nod. "I think so."

"You think so? I didn't expect that answer."

Tyler shrugged and looked over at his friends. "Would you guys mind if I spoke to her alone for a minute?"

"No, of course not," Lucy said. "We'll come back in when you're ready."

Justin bowed his head at Molly, and followed Lucy back out into the hall, closing the door quietly behind them.

Tyler sat down in the chair next to the bed and sighed.

"Yeah, I mean, it was awesome. But all of it is kind of overwhelming. You know? Thousands of people watching, not to mention the television cameras and everyone watching through that. I never realized how crazy it all was."

Molly nodded. "I bet. But here you are. You handled it all. And look at you. You're near the top of the leaderboard, one stroke back from the leader."

Tyler knew where he stood. In truth, he couldn't believe it. He was one stroke back from Jamie Winthrop, who'd posted a stellar 5 under for the first round.

"All the experts are saying the next few days will be much harder. Pin placements will be more challenging. Scores shouldn't be as low."

"Tyler, look at me."

He picked his head up and met her solemn gaze.

"You can handle it. You can handle anything life throws at you."

Tyler recalled the things she'd taught him when he was younger, spiritual teachings from many ancient religions and beliefs she'd imprinted on his mind.

The Bible was at the core of it all, and one verse kept coming back to him through every rough moment, every seemingly untamable challenge he encountered. "I won't be tested above what I'm able to handle," he muttered.

"That's right," she confirmed. "We are built to handle whatever situation is given to us. There is nothing you can't overcome, Son."

"But what if I choke? What if I can't keep playing at the same level I played today, or when I broke the course record at Green Mont?"

"What if you can't?" She let the question hang in the room, accompanied by the beeping of the machines behind her.

"I just—"

"You have enough, Son," she interrupted. "You have always had enough. And always will. And you are enough. Winning or losing doesn't change that."

He nodded, though it was obvious he still wasn't sure. "I... I just always wanted to give you and Dad a better life. You both sacrificed so much, worked so hard. I'll never be able to do it for Dad now. But I hoped I could for you. I still want that."

"Sweetie. You are such a good boy. And you're so unselfish. That is the best thing you could have given to us. I'm proud of who you have become. And your father would be too. I am fine. I have a good life. I'm thankful for everything that I have. Every single day I thank God for you, for our apartment, my car, my job, all of it. I couldn't ask for anything more."

Tyler had a feeling she would say that. He knew she was right. He'd tried his best to model that sentiment, to be grateful for all the little things in life. But it was hard when he saw guys like Mitchell and others who had nice cars, big homes, amazing vacations.

"I guess you're right," he surrendered.

"Of course I'm right. I'm your mother. As far as you're concerned, I'm always right. So, don't put any pressure on yourself. And as for the fans in attendance, and those watching on television... give them something they've never seen before. A golfer who's out there having the time of his life."

GRAHAM HELD the phone to his ear, looking out at the dying light of the sun in the faint orange sky to the west. Above and to the east, stars glittered in the black heavens.

"It was a fun day," he said.

"That's the most important thing, isn't it?" Alicia asked.

"It should be. It was a long time ago."

"What changed?"

Graham inhaled and exhaled deeply. He turned and looked out at the number 18 green beyond the bushes at the back corner of the clubhouse.

The sounds of the forest around him mingled with the gathering inside the building where golfers and their guests ate and drank and talked about the day's events and what tomorrow might hold.

He knew around half of the players in there were feeling the pressure of missing the cut the next day, having posted poor scores during round one.

After tomorrow, the wheat would be pared from the chaff, and only the best would remain.

Graham had surprised himself today and put himself in a good position to easily make the cut barring some sort of catastrophic collapse. He'd endured several of those, but none so bad that it would take him below the cutoff in this tournament.

He sat only two strokes back of the leader, his nemesis, Jamie Winthrop. Well within striking distance.

Graham didn't kid himself. He had no misgivings about storming to the top of the leaderboard. Not at his age. Not at this time in his career. Would he love to? Sure. But a round like today was probably the best he could manage at this point.

Still, his imagination toyed with him, teasing him with visions of holding the cup at the end of the tournament.

"Graham? You there?"

"Sorry. Yeah. Just a lot going on in the clubhouse. People sound like they're having a good time."

"You need me to let you go?"

"No," he said quickly. "No. I would rather be out here talking to you than in there glad-handing all those folks."

"You going to answer my question?"

"Yeah." He paused, reflecting on the way he'd played when he was a kid just learning the game. "Once it became about making money, I guess that's when it all changed. My dad pushed me hard, not only for the financial security, but he was big on legacy. He wanted me to have a legacy of greatness, probably because his name would be attached to it too. So in a way, I was his legacy. And my legacy reflected on him."

Now that he said it out loud, Graham felt as if he'd just sliced through the last piece of the jungle with a machete to discover a lost treasure hidden within.

Saying it out loud sent a tingle of relief through him.

"So, today you didn't put all that pressure on yourself, huh?" Alicia clarified.

"No. I honestly didn't even think about it. I just went out there and played the best I could. And had fun doing it."

"I wish I could be there," she said. "I saw some of the highlights. You looked good in that green shirt."

He grinned. "You saw that?"

"Uh, yeah. Of course. I wanted to watch it on my phone while I was working, but we were pretty busy today."

A twinge of disappointment taunted him. "That pass I left at the gate for you is still there in case you can make it up this weekend."

"Graham, don't waste that on me. Let someone else have it."

He shook his head. "There is no one else, Alicia. Besides, it's complimentary from the club. We each get so many guests. So don't worry about it."

"Okay." She hesitated for a moment. "Well, I'll talk to you tomorrow. Okay?"

"Sounds good."

"Keep swinging like you did today. Just have the time of your life out there."

Graham nodded as a sense of peace unlike any he'd ever felt settled over him. "I will."

52

M olly stared at the television screen as it panned over the number 18 green at White Oak National, then cut to a close-up of a cluster of double-knockout roses hugging a hill behind the par-3 number 8 hole.

"What a gorgeous day it is here for the third round of the White Oak National Open Championship," Troy said with that same melodic piano playing in the background, just beneath his voice. Half the field is gone after yesterday's tense day of golf. And now, only the best remain."

A digital display of the leaderboard filled the screen, overlapping a shot of the clubhouse.

"And boy, do we have something special happening at the top of the leaderboard going into moving day. It's no surprise that world number one Jamie Winthrop tops the rest of the field at a stunning eight under par. But the real storyline is right below him. Local amateur Tyler Knox is sitting only two strokes back at six under par."

"Woo-hoo!" Molly cheered. "Go, Tyler!" The hospital bed shook as she pumped her fist.

"Mrs. Knox, please. Try to take it easy," the nurse standing next to her requested.

"That's my son they're talking about," she insisted.

The announcer continued on the television. "Meanwhile, the old pro Graham Sullivan, playing in his final tournament, is playing like a man possessed. He's only one stroke back of the leader at seven under par, after weathering a tricky round two yesterday.

"I'm Troy Fallon here with my partner and two-time major champion, Steve Watson. Welcome to White Oak National for round three of the open."

The camera view switched to the two men in their network blazers, and another row of roses blooming behind them filled the backdrop with pink and green against the partly cloudy sky beyond.

"Steve, what a tournament it's been so far, and I have to say, while no one is surprised by who's in the top spot right now, something is building in the second- and third-place positions."

"Yeah, you're right about that, Troy," Steve said. "Lot of drama simmering below first place. I don't think anyone expected Winthrop to be anywhere else on the leaderboard than where he is right now. But no one saw this coming from a fifty-eight-year-old Sullivan and an amateur who just turned twenty-one last week. The kid couldn't legally buy a drink when he qualified for this event. And now here he is, sitting in prime position going into moving day."

"Yes, and of course, an amateur hasn't won a major event since 1933, and Knox has everyone thinking it right now: Is it possible?"

"It is," Steve said as if it was a matter of fact. "At this point, anything is possible. This kid has an absolutely gorgeous swing." As he continued talking, the screen switched to a slow-motion highlight of Tyler hitting a drive. "Here is yesterday on number five. His back swing is steady, takes the club up high over his shoulders. Notice the point of his hips and his shoulders, the bend of that right knee coiling a massive amount of energy. Now watch as he starts with his hips, generating all that power as he drives through and stacks up on the ball. And what's remarkable is how easy he makes it look. I've played with guys who swing twice that hard and hit it thirty yards shorter than this kid. It's smooth. It's fluid. And right now he's making it look easy."

"You're right about that, Steve. But we all know that today is where the real test begins. There are still plenty of players within striking distance, with three at five under, three at four under, and a collection of golfers sitting at two under par. So, as well as Winthrop has played, it's still anyone's tournament to win."

"Let's cut to some of the highlights from yesterday's compelling round two."

Molly watched as the network showed cuts of the players making putts from the second round, including some that featured her son. They showed one of Tyler's remarkable shots on a par three over water that landed mere feet away from the pin and nearly rolled in for a hole in one.

"And this one by Knox," Troy was saying, "had all of us thinking hole in one. Alas, he had to settle for birdie."

"Not an easy hole to birdie, so setting up with an easy putt like that—I'm sure the kid was grateful for a gimme on that one. Only forty-eight percent of the field birdied the hole in the first two rounds. It's just an extremely difficult green."

The highlights continued, featuring several other golfers and their best shots from round two. Then the screen cut back to the two announcers.

"It's all lining up for a dramatic finish here tomorrow at White Oak National in Chattanooga. But for today, we have some delicious pairings for you to enjoy."

"Yes, we do, Troy," Steve agreed. "In the final pairing of the day, we have two old rivals going head-to-head with Jamie Winthrop and the old dog Graham Sullivan."

"And of course," Troy added, "everyone knows the history of these two that started here ten years ago on this course, in this tournament. In the second pairing just in front of them, we have an interesting setup with Japanese sensation Miho Nakamura, who is only one stroke back of the local kid, and his partner for today's matchup, Tyler Knox."

GRAHAM SWUNG his 5-iron and cleaned the ball off the tee. It took off into the sky over the driving range, flying toward the pin he'd aimed for a moment ago.

It landed on the right edge and bounced left into the right half of the green.

"That's a good one to end on, boss," Mike said, watching from behind while supporting Graham's bag with his right hand.

"Thanks," Graham said. He stepped back over to the bag and grabbed the blue towel hanging off the side.

Mike extended his hand to take the club, but Graham shook him off. "I can do it. You'll be busy enough today."

"Not a lot of pros like you, Sully. I'm going to miss working with you."

Graham noted how the man said "with" instead of "for."

That's how it was supposed to be, at least as far as Graham understood it. There were some players here and there who considered their caddies to be more like an employee, but the best had forged a friendship and trust over time.

"Yeah, I'll miss taking long walks in the grass with you too, Mikey."

The two laughed as Graham finished cleaning off the iron's face and slid it back in the bag.

"So, that's why you're retiring?" A new and unwelcome voice entered the conversation from Graham's right.

He turned and saw Winthrop approaching, wearing the same smug, crap-eating grin that might as well have been his trademark.

"Going to start cleaning clubs at the local course in Charleston?" Winthrop egged on. "Sounds about right. Or are you learning the caddie trade?"

Graham wasn't going to let the jerk get to him. "Just not afraid to get my hands dirty," he said, glancing down at Winthrop's left hand. "I guess you wouldn't want to ruin your manicure."

Winthrop's eyelids narrowed. "You think that's funny?" he fumed.

"That you get manicures? Yeah. A little."

Mike giggled from behind him.

"Well," Winthrop said, trying to calm his anger. "I guess we'll see who's laughing tomorrow when I lift the cup. Again. Then again, you know what that's like, right Sully? Oh wait. You don't. Because you've—"

"Never won a major?" Graham interrupted. "No, I'm well aware of that. The whole world is aware of that. You know, Jamie? I used to care about it. I obsessed over it. And every time I lost one, it felt worse and worse. Now, I just don't care anymore. So, I'm just going to go out there and play and have the time of my life playing on a course that the rest of golfers around the world can only dream of walking."

"Fine speech," Jamie countered. "But we both know it's eating you up inside. I guess the good news for you is, since you're one stroke behind me, you can't blow the lead this time."

Graham allowed a humble smile to creep across his face as he exhaled through his nose in a short sigh.

"No, you're right about that, Jamie. I can't blow the lead this time. Not today, anyway. But at least I don't have to worry about moisturizing my hands or chipping a nail during the round."

Winthrop stewed, clenching his teeth as he tried to conjure a witty comeback. "You're going to lose again, Sully. Just like you always do. Because that's what you are. A loser."

The words seemed to bounce off Graham like tiny pebbles off a boulder.

He merely nodded. "That may be true, but at least I don't get my nails done."

Winthrop fired one last glare at Graham. "See you on the tee box. I'm going to miss beating you, but hey, one more for old time's sake." He stormed off with his caddie trying to catch up.

Graham sighed, releasing any pent-up anger that tried to build inside him.

"Don't worry about him," Mike said, glancing back over his shoulder. "Just focus on your game, Sully."

"Oh, I'm not worried about Jamie," Graham said, staring at his opponent as he marched past the photographers and television crews. "Guys like him don't end up winning in the long run, no matter how many trophies they may cling to."

———

TYLER SQUATTED behind his ball on the number 6 green, staring down the long birdie putt. Justin crouched behind him, looking over his shoulder at the line.

His partner, Miho Nakamura, had already tapped in for bogey after missing a twenty-five-foot putt for par. The mistake had been his second of the day and dropped him further away from Tyler, who'd already made birdie on number 3 and had yet to make a mistake, parring the other four holes.

As usual, Tyler refused to check the leaderboard to see where he stood. And with Winthrop and Sully right behind him on the course, they were playing with a hole in hand.

He didn't think about any of that. He'd banished that kind of stuff from his mind, as well as the throngs of people in the stands and surrounding the green. It was just him, his friend, and the game.

"I love this putt," Tyler said. "Challenging bend from right to left."

"You're sadistic. You know that, right?" Justin countered.

Tyler laughed quietly. "Yeah, I know. But these kinds of putts make the game fun."

"I prefer the easy, straight-into-the-cup sort of putts with a one-inch uphill to them. But whatever floats your boat."

"The only question is, how much is it going to bend?"

The cup was straight ahead of him, a daunting twenty feet from his ball, but the green tilted hard from right to left and dropped two inches along the way. The putt would have been difficult even if it had been a straight line.

"You see that mark over there?" Justin asked, pointing at a discoloration in the green so faint it was unlikely anyone else noticed.

"Yeah?"

"That's your line."

"That much, huh?"

Justin stood up and took a step back. "I mean, you can go lower than that, but you'll blow past the hole underneath it."

Tyler knew he was right. He'd been considering a similar tack, although a little higher on the slope than his friend suggested.

"Okay," Tyler said, standing. "But if I miss this, you owe me a Coke at the caddie shack next week."

"If you miss it, it's because you missed the line," Justin joked before he turned and walked over to the fringe.

Tyler grinned at his friend's barb and stepped up to the ball. He lowered the putter behind it then checked his mark one last time. He took a breath, exhaled, and swept the putter back then forward.

MOLLY LEANED FORWARD in the bed; her fingernails curled under her lips as Tyler hit the putt.

"He's gone with a high line here, Troy," the announcer said. "Pretty aggressive."

The ball rolled up the slope then began to turn. It picked up speed on its way toward the target.

"This one is going to be close," the announcer said. "He may have the line."

"Come on," Molly urged. "Get in the hole!"

The crowd stood from their seats to join the rest who were already on their feet. Some of them coaxed the ball on with cheers of their own.

Molly watched as the ball neared the cup, rolling hard toward it.

"It's going to need to slow down a little," the announcer said.

Then the ball hit the back of the hole, popped up an inch into the air, and fell in.

"Or not!"

The crowd surrounding the green erupted into a cacophony of applause.

"Yes! Yes! Yes!" Molly shouted, forgetting any worries that the nurse would come in to tell her to be quiet.

Tyler pumped his fist as he stalked over to the hole and picked up the ball. He waved to the crowd, taking off his white cap to give them an appreciative salute. Then high-fived his caddie as Justin brought the flag over to put it back in the hole.

"An absolute stunner of a putt right there, Troy," the announcer said. "This kid is on fire, and I don't see any signs of him cooling off."

The camera zoomed in on Tyler's face as he walked off the green, his smile beaming as he continued to wave at the spectators.

"He's become a fan favorite here, that's for sure," Troy said. "And why not? He lives with his mother about fifteen minutes from here. And we'd like to take a moment to say, Molly Knox, if you're watching this, we're all praying for a quick recovery and hope you can make it out here tomorrow to see your boy play in the final round. Whatever happens the rest of the way today."

Tears streaked down Molly's cheeks. The doctor told her she could be released tomorrow at noon if things continued to improve. She was sick of being here in this bed, in this room. But more than that, she wanted to be there for her son. This was his moment. She wished she could have been there for more of his events in the past, but her job had kept her out of more than she would like to admit.

She closed her eyes and prayed that the doctors would let her out tomorrow at noon. That would still give her just enough time to get over to the course for the start of the final round.

The television screen switched to another golfer who was putting for par on number 12.

"Simpson here for par," a female announcer said. "Left edge should be good here."

The man hit the putt, and the ball covered the eight feet, resulting in it dropping into the hole.

"Steady as she goes," the announcer said. "Simpson remains at three under for the tournament, and still has an outside chance to get to the top for the final round."

"Right you are, Jenny," Troy said.

The screen focused in on Graham Sullivan standing on the fairway behind his ball as he lined up the approach onto the green.

"We're back here at number five, and Sully has a decent approach to the green from here. He's going to have to carry that water in the front."

"That's right, Troy," Steve agreed. "And we've seen plenty of guys this weekend leave the ball on the front of the green and roll it back into the water."

"Indeed."

"The safe play is to go for the right middle and then hope to hit a long putt for birdie, or at the very least to salvage par here."

GRAHAM STARED at the the pin on the number 6 green, holding the iron in his right hand. He stood 158 yards out, with a slight drop to the green. The water hazard loomed on the front-left side, directly in front of the pin. He'd known the pin placements would only get tougher as the weekend progressed, and the guys in charge of deciding where to put them hadn't disappointed.

The crowd surrounding the green on their feet and in the stands had gone wild as Tyler Knox sank a long putt for birdie, moving the kid to the top the leaderboard.

Graham grinned when Knox made the putt. "That boy has got it," he'd muttered to himself as Tyler walked to the cup and removed the ball.

Now, it was Graham's turn.

"Wind is probably five miles per hour up above the tree line," his caddie said in a hushed tone. "Right to left. You want to play it safe, or you going at the stick?"

"I'm too old to play it safe, Mikey," Graham answered. "Might as well have some fun with it."

"I like the aggression." The caddie grinned, baring his teeth.

"Then you want to hit the shot at the right edge of that big bunker. Don't take anything off the shot. You've got the right club to carry it. Full swing. Let the dip in elevation get you there."

Graham nodded without looking over at Mike. "Sounds good."

Winthrop and his caddie watched from behind and to the left, where he'd already hit his approach after getting outdriven by his senior counterpart.

The ball sat in the middle of the right side of the green, about thirty feet from the hole. He'd gone the safe route to eliminate the risk of hitting his ball into the bunker in front of the pin and now sat with a long putt for birdie.

So far, both men had posted one birdie and three pars, going shot for shot through the first four holes without either being able to gain a foothold.

Graham stepped up to the ball, took one last look at the green, and hit the shot.

The onlookers along the sides of the fairway shouted their encouragement the instant the ball left the grass.

It towered into the air; its line true to Graham's aim at the right edge of the bunker.

"Carry it," Graham whispered. "Get there."

The ball veered slightly as the wind above the canopy caught it and pushed it to the left. Graham knew it was going to be close.

Everyone held their breath as they watched the ball descend toward the pin.

"Be there," Graham urged.

The little white sphere dropped onto the green behind the bunker, then rolled toward the hole, stopping a mere three inches away.

The crowd erupted, sending a roar across the course that echoed through the trees.

Graham smiled and walked back to his bag, where Mike waited with a high-five.

"Why didn't you just knock it in?" the caddie teased.

"I think you had the distance wrong," Graham joked.

The two laughed as they marched down the fairway, merging with Jamie and his caddie.

"Looks like you're out, Jamie," Graham jibed. "I'll finish up unless you want me to mark my ball."

Winthrop could only offer an irritated grumble for a reply.

53

Tyler looked back from the number 7 tee box as the crowd on the other side of the trees cheered.

He couldn't see what happened, or who'd done it, but it must have been spectacular.

Tyler's opponent and the two caddies also turned their heads at the cacophony from the hole behind them.

Tyler hoped Graham had been the one to rouse the spectators, but there was no way to know yet.

He was 2 under on the day; that much he knew. And he'd played well up to this point, only narrowly missing a long birdie on number 2 as his lone mistake. If it could be called that. He doubted many people would have actually made the putt.

Nakamura smiled over at Tyler after the noise subsided. They were both still waiting for the pair in front of them to move out of range.

"I wonder who caused that," Nakamura said.

Tyler squinted with his grin. "I don't know, but it must have been pretty special."

"I am most impressed with your abilities. Your swing is very good."

"Thank you," Tyler said, bowing his head slightly. "I appreciate it."

"You keep playing like this, and I may have to ask you for some pointers."

The two chuckled.

Tyler could hardly believe it. He was standing here on a tee box in a major tournament, cutting up with one of the top pros on tour.

"Surreal, isn't it?" Justin whispered, leaning close to his friend. "You and me, here in this event, with these players. Crazy."

"I was just thinking the same thing."

GRAHAM STOOD on the edge of the green next to Mike as Winthrop stalked the green, taking in every possible angle with his caddie.

Graham had already tapped in for birdie, putting him in at the top of the leaderboard, something he was keenly aware of.

He'd spent much of his career avoiding eye contact with the leaderboard of tournaments, a sort of superstition he clung to out of fear that by gazing upon the scores, he might jinx his own round and end up failing miserably.

The opposite had proved itself true in every major he'd played—always falling short and failing to win the title.

This weekend, however, he'd done things the other way, checking the scores of his opponents every chance he could, treating it like a horse race. And he was one of the horses.

He crossed his arms and watched Winthrop retrace his steps, trying to determine which line to take for the long birdie putt.

Graham wasn't the sort to cheer against an opponent. It was a gentleman's game, one in which you applauded a competitor for their skills. In this case, that sportsmanship was pushed to the brink, the ultimate test of character for Graham.

Winthrop finally made up his mind after a third quick discussion with his caddie, then stood over the ball. He turned his head and gazed down the line he'd chosen before looking back down again.

He visibly relaxed, then struck the ball up the slope to the right, playing a hard bend on the surface.

It was a slight downhill roll from there, and an extremely difficult line.

The ball picked up speed, and as it neared the cup, Winthrop begged it to slow down. "No. No. No. Ease up."

Instead, the ball continued past the hole and finally rolled to a stop eight feet beyond it.

The crowd groaned at the bad miss.

Even so, the second putt was one Winthrop could make in his sleep. It was a straight uphill line and would keep him tied at the top of the leaderboard.

Graham watched Winthrop shake his head and look back at his caddie as if he was the one to blame for the miss.

Then he walked over to the ball and assessed the green.

His caddie joined him, hovering over his shoulder.

"Looks straight in from here," the caddie said.

"Yeah, no kidding, Sherlock," Winthrop replied, loud enough for Graham and Mike to hear, as well as some of the closest spectators to the green.

Several murmurs swept through the crowd, but Winthrop either didn't care or pretended not to.

He stepped up to the ball, positioned his feet, and gave one last check to the hole before focusing on the white sphere again. He swung the putter, striking the ball firmly in the center, and watched it climb the slight rise to the cup.

Molly watched with rapt attention as Winthrop's ball neared the hole, but pushed just to the right of it, touching the lip before it stopped mere inches beyond.

"Oh my," Troy said through television speakers. "Winthrop misses an important one there to stay level atop the leaderboard."

"Shocking," Steve added. "He's probably made that putt a million times in his life. And now when he needs it most, he pushes it to the right."

The replay showed the putt again, this time in slow motion.

"You can see here, Troy, it just comes off a little to the right as he hits it. No doubt he's going to want that one back."

"Absolutely," Troy agreed. "You can see the look of utter astonishment on Jamie's face there. He can't believe he's just missed that one."

"Yessss!" Molly hissed. "Keep missing them."

Winthrop walked over to the ball, leaned over on one foot, and tapped it in.

"Tap in for bogey for Jamie Winthrop," Troy announced. "And that drops him out of the lead for the first time in a while. So, we have a pair of new leaders on the top of the board. The old pro, Graham Sullivan, and the young amateur, Tyler Knox. What a storyline we have brewing here, folks."

"Could you imagine if those two end up in the final pairing tomorrow, Troy?"

"It would be a story for the ages, but there's a lot of golf left here to play on moving day, round three, at White Oak National."

54

"It's been a wild third round so far," Troy said as the television screen returned from the commercial break. "And we have a pair of plots going right now that I don't think anyone saw coming."

"I know I didn't," Steve added. "That's for sure."

"Jamie Winthrop started the day in the lead at eight under par but has fallen apart after the missed par on number six. Since then, he's posted two additional bogeys and no birdies, seeing his place at the top of the leaderboard evaporate.

"Meanwhile, two of the most unlikely golfers to be in the top spot are now running neck and neck. The local kid, amateur Tyler Knox, and the cagey veteran, Graham Sullivan—playing in his final tournament—find themselves tied for the lead at a remarkable ten under par with a five-stroke lead over Winthrop, who is locked in third with two other golfers."

"It's been an incredible turn of events," Steve said. "No doubt about it."

The screen zoomed in on Tyler's partner for the day as he stood over the ball with a putt for birdie from sixteen feet out on the 18th green.

"Miho Nakamura here for birdie and a seventy-one for the day," Troy said.

Nakamura hit the putt and the camera zoomed in on the ball as it neared the cup. It rolled by, missing by two inches to the outside of the hole, and stopped a foot away.

"Just hasn't been Nakamura's day," Troy said as the camera focused on the man, who looked up to the sky as if it might have answers.

"He's struggled all day with the putter, Troy. And too many mistakes on the front nine had him pressing on the back."

"Nakamura for par and a seventy-two on the day."

Nakamura walked over to his ball, checked the line, and tapped the putt in.

The crowd applauded, and he waved as he took the ball out of the cup.

"It could have been much worse," Troy said. "Give him credit for gutting it out and staying alive, though now it would take something spectacular to win it tomorrow."

"Yeah, his chances are slim now, especially considering how well his partner is doing today, and with Sullivan still behind them on the fairway."

"That's right. Sullivan and Winthrop are both in the middle of the fairway awaiting their turn to hit. Now it's Tyler Knox, the local caddie with a chance to take sole possession of the lead going into the final round at White Oak."

"It's a twelve-footer, left to right, Troy. I'm guessing his caddie is telling him to aim a half cup out to the left. It's not going to bend a lot, but he can't go straight at the hole here either."

Molly sat up higher in the bed, leaning forward with her elbows on her knees.

"Well, Mrs. Knox," the doctor's voice interrupted her as the man entered the room. He held a tablet and wore a white lab coat over his blue scrubs. "It looks like you're doing much better. So, you may be able to see that tournament in person tomorrow. Just take it easy and get lots of rest. Don't push yourself too hard."

"Shhh," she hissed at him, never taking her eyes off the screen.

The doctor scrunched his face in confusion, then looked over at the television.

"My son is about to putt for birdie on eighteen," she explained to him.

"Oh, how's he—"

"He's winning. And this putt could put him all alone at the top."

"Wow." The doctor turned and stared at the television, momentarily forgetting why he came into the room in the first place.

Tyler stepped up to the ball and rechecked his line one last time.

"Tyler Knox for birdie and to go five under for the day, and eleven under for the tournament."

"Come on, Ty," Molly prayed.

Tyler stroked the ball toward the hole with a smooth, even swing.

It rolled gently along the grassy green surface, bending slightly toward the end.

"Oh, he's got this one, Troy," Steve said, cutting into the temporary silence.

"Yes!" Troy shouted as the ball fell into the hole amid the roars of thousands of people surrounding the green. "He's done it! Five under par by the amateur, and for the moment, he stands alone on top of the golfing world here at White Oak National."

"Yeah!" Molly screamed, nearly scaring the doctor out of his pants.

The physician laughed and looked back at her. "That is amazing," he said.

Tears clung to the sides of her eyelids. She beamed with pride, her hands folded in front of her face as she watched her son shake hands with Nakamura and his caddie, then put his arm around Justin's shoulders before walking off the green toward the clubhouse.

"An incredible round for the young amateur," Troy said. "When this thing started on Thursday, who had him at the top of the leaderboard going into Sunday here at White Oak?"

"I know I didn't," Steve admitted. "But this kid is turning heads, and he's putting the golf world on notice."

"He sure is, Steve. Now we go to Jamie Winthrop, who has just had a monumental collapse today after the bogey on number five."

"Yeah, I don't think I've ever seen Jamie like this before. Usually, he's an assassin out there, just taking care of business. But that miss on number five seems to have gotten in his head, and the mistakes just kept compounding throughout the day."

The screen showed highlights from earlier holes, including a penalty in the water on number 8, and another ball that landed in the woods on number 14.

The screen switched back to Winthrop as he lined up his shot and swung. The ball sailed off his club, high above the fairway but moving left the entire way.

"Come on. Straighten out," Winthrop said audibly through the screen as the camera zoomed in on him for a second.

Then the view switched back to the ball just before it plummeted into the bunker on the left-hand side.

"Oh no," Troy said. "He's in the sand, and that is not going to be an easy out for Jamie there."

The camera closed in on the ball, half-buried in the soft, white sand.

"Yeah, that one is half-buried like my kids used to do to me at the beach. Plus, he'll need to get it up over that tall embankment. And let me tell you, Troy, I've been in that sand one time, and it took me two shots to get out."

Winthrop looked furious as he walked back to his caddie and slammed the club down in the bag.

"Now, Graham Sullivan, fifty-eight years young, playing in his final tournament, with the approach on eighteen. Sitting one stroke behind the local kid, Tyler Knox, who is in the clubhouse at eleven under for the tournament."

Graham spoke briefly to his caddie, discussing the shot, the wind, and the angle, then took an iron and walked up to the ball.

"Looks like he's going with the seven-iron here, Troy," Steve said. "He's been deadly with that club all day."

"Yes, he has. And this marks the third time he's outdriven his playing partner today as well, which is just one more layer to the drama of this magical tournament round by Sully."

"If you had asked anyone prior to today if they thought Graham Sullivan would outdrive Jamie Winthrop even once, I doubt you'd have any takers on that bet."

Graham positioned his feet and set the clubface down on the grass, then hit the ball high into the air.

"This one looks good," Troy said.

The camera tracked the ball into the clear, afternoon sky.

"He's taken a direct route to the pin," Steve added.

The ball landed on the green, sixteen feet from the hole, bounced once, then rolled back toward the flag.

"Look at the backspin on that," Troy said. "He's going to like that one."

The ball kept rolling until it stopped a mere five feet from the pin.

The crowd exploded in raucous applause.

The camera zeroed in on Graham who lowered his club and smiled, then turned and handed the iron to his caddie.

"This man is on a mission, ladies and gentlemen," Troy said. "Graham Sullivan has a makable putt for birdie here on number eighteen to go eleven under for the tournament, and be tied at the top of the leaderboard with young Tyler Knox. I'll tell you what, it doesn't get any better than this right now."

"No, it really doesn't, Troy. What we've seen here so far is a fairy tale. Two of the longer shots when it came to winning it all, and now they're both set to face off in tomorrow's final round here at White Oak National."

"It's a story that is truly captivating," Troy agreed. "But first things first. Graham needs to make that putt, and for mortals it's anything but a gimme. Meanwhile, his partner, Jamie Winthrop, is in real trouble with that sand."

Winthrop walked up to the edge of the bunker and placed his hands on his hips. He stared at the half-buried ball, shaking his head while he spoke to his caddie.

"You have to wonder what's going through Jamie's head right

now," Troy said. "How he let it all slip away so quickly after having such a firm grip on the tournament."

"It's so uncharacteristic of him, too, Troy. We've been watching him for a long time now, and it seemed as if he was bulletproof, especially in major events. But today has been a monumental collapse."

"Something his playing partner knows all too well."

"Right. Sully has been through this before, although usually on the last day."

Winthrop took a sand wedge from his caddie and stepped into the bunker. He sized up the shot one more time before planting his feet, digging in for the shot.

"If he can manage to get this up and on, and somehow par the hole, Winthrop would still have an outside shot going into tomorrow."

"He's going to really have to dig this one out," Steve said. "A shovel might be the better club here."

Winthrop lowered the club to just above the surface behind the ball then swung. A wave of sand blasted fifteen feet up into the air, and for a second, the ball wasn't visible.

Molly watched the screen as the sand cleared and Winthrop looked toward the pin.

"Oh, my," Troy said. "That's what you were talking about right there, Steve."

The ball hit the top of the bunker on the last few inches of sand before the fringe, then rolled back down the hill, stopping eight inches behind Winthrop's previous position.

Furious, Winthrop said something the microphones didn't pick up.

"Probably best if you don't read his lips there for those of you watching at home," Troy said.

Steve chuckled. "Yeah, he's really frustrated with himself, but that's the danger of that bunker, Troy. There wasn't much anyone could have done with that shot. Winthrop is the number-one player in the world, but that bunker is designed to punish mistakes, and it doesn't care who makes them."

"Now, Winthrop, who started the day with a two-stroke lead, finds himself in damage control mode at this point."

"Yeah," Steve agreed. "He's going to need a good one here to maybe save bogey. I can't believe I'm saying that, but it's a must now. His tournament life is on the line with this shot here."

"Third-easiest hole on the course according to the rankings," Troy added. "For him to make that mistake is really unthinkable."

Winthrop set up in his stance again and swung. This time, the clubface lifted the ball high out of the sand, pushed by another blast of the white grain.

The ball carried over the lip of the sand trap, landed on the green, then rolled off to the right.

"Well, he's out of one kind of trouble and into another," Troy said as the ball slowed down in a dip on the right edge of the green.

"Yeah, he'll be glad to get out of the sand there, Troy, but that spot where his ball ended up is really the worst place to be on this green, given the pin placement. Difficult to get a read out of that."

"Just an astonishing turn of events here on day three at the open. Jamie Winthrop, number-one player in the world, coming in with a two-stroke lead off the first tee, now seeing his title hopes vanishing before his eyes."

Winthrop took the putter from his caddie while shaking his head angrily. The caddie raked the sand as Winthrop trudged around the bunker and onto the green toward his ball.

Graham marked his ball and slipped it into his pocket before walking back to the side where his caddie stood waiting, peering at the line to the hole.

Winthrop stood behind his ball, trying to decide what angle to take. He waited until his caddie joined him then discussed the putt. Both of the men pointed at different spots on the putting surface, weighing the possibilities.

"This is a tricky read here, Troy," Steve said. "It's going to start left, then bend back to the right. If anyone can make this putt it's Winthrop. Historically, his putter has been extremely accurate."

"But today has been a different story. He's struggled to make putts, especially birdies, and now stands on eighteen needing a bogey just to have an outside chance at winning tomorrow."

Winthrop paced around to the right to get one more look before glancing at his caddie and asking him something. The caddie responded with his suggestion, and Winthrop nodded as the caddie stepped back off the green.

"Looks like he has his line here," Troy said. "Jamie Winthrop, for a bogey on eighteen and a stunning four over for the day."

Winthrop hit the putt up the slope toward the pin. It bent one way, then the other before straightening out. It slowed to a crawl and stopped inches short and to the right of the hole.

"He's missed it!" Troy announced with the groan of the crowd. "Incredible turn of events here for Jamie Winthrop. I can't recall seeing a collapse like this."

"Yeah, not even from Graham Sullivan. Granted, the leads he lost were on the final day, but numbers wise, this is much worse."

Winthrop looked up at the sky then hung his head in total dejection. He stood there for a few seconds in disbelief before walking over and tapping the ball in.

"Winthrop with a double bogey on eighteen for five over par on the day, and three under for the tournament."

"It would take a miracle for him to win it now, Troy," Steve said. "Eight strokes back of the leader going into the final round, and the way Sullivan and Knox have been playing, I don't know if they're going to slow down at this point."

"Right you are, Steve. And Winthrop finds himself now in a dead lock for fifth place in the tournament with two other golfers at eight strokes back. Not only will he not be in the final pairing, but this will put him in a much earlier round for the day."

Graham walked over to his ball with putter in hand.

"Now, the old veteran, Graham Sullivan, with a chance for bird here on eighteen, and to tie the unlikely leader, local young phenom Tyler Knox, going into the final round here at White Oak National."

Graham set up in his stance, stole one quick look across his shoulder at the hole, and stroked the ball smoothly with the putter.

The spectators in the background stood. Some shouted "Sully!"

Then the ball disappeared in the heart of the cup, and the place came unglued.

"He's got it!" Troy boomed. "Unbelievable. Four under by Graham Sullivan here at White Oak on day three to put him tied for the lead at eleven under for the tournament."

"Smooth as you like on that one," Steve said.

Graham took the ball out of the cup and then waved to the cheering crowd. He took off his hat and wiped his brow as he high-fived his caddie, then walked over to Winthrop to shake his hand.

The disgruntled Winthrop only shook hands for a brief moment, said something to Graham, and then turned and walked off the green while the caddies exchanged handshakes.

"What a day three to remember here at White Oak," Troy said. "Graham Sullivan and Tyler Knox will be paired in the final round tomorrow. And I have a feeling it's going to be one for the ages. You are not going to want to miss it."

Molly sat back against the pillows piled up behind her and exhaled for what felt like the first time in half an hour. The pride she felt for her son was dimmed by the realization that Tyler was going to have to face his childhood hero, a man he'd rooted for through all of his devastating losses.

Now, it was Tyler's job to add to that tally. And she had no idea how he would have the stomach to do it.

55

The reporters filled the press room to overflowing. Cameras snapped pictures while others recorded the interview.

Tyler Knox sat behind the table with an orange sports drink and microphone in front of him. He squeezed his right hand, gripping then releasing. The pain he'd felt earlier in the week was almost gone. Still, he tested it out of habit now.

"How do you feel sitting at the top of the leaderboard going into the final round of your first major?" a female reporter asked near the front of the room.

"Um... well, I guess it hasn't really sunk in yet," Tyler answered. "It's all pretty overwhelming. And to be honest, I didn't look at the leaderboard today until the round was over."

"How are you able to stay so calm out there in the face of such a difficult course, and surrounded by the world's best golfers?"

"It doesn't feel calm on the inside; I can tell you that," he said.

The room filled with laughter.

"I don't know, though. I just try to play my game. You know? I don't try to go outside of what I know I can do, and just take what the course gives me. If that makes sense."

Nods around the room told him it did.

"What's it like playing in front of so many people for the first time?" a man in a suit asked in the back.

"That part was initially pretty unnerving," Tyler admitted. "And then you pile everyone watching on television onto the people here on the grounds. It's daunting when you think about it. So I try not to."

"You've said that Graham Sullivan is your favorite golfer," a blonde female in a white dress said. "Now you're going to be paired with him in the final round here at White Oak for a shot at the title. What does that feel like?"

Tyler nodded and looked down at his hands for a second. "It's a lot of things. I mean, I'm excited to get to play with my idol. I've been a fan of his for a long time, so to get to play with him in a major event, much more the final round, is beyond a dream come true. On the other hand, we're both competitors. I know Mr. Sullivan is going to give it everything he's got. So, I have to do the same. And we'll see what happens. The best golfer will win."

More heads bobbed around the room.

"You know the history," an older gentleman said from the left side of the room. "No amateur has won a major title since 1933. Is that in the back of your mind?"

"It wasn't," Tyler said. "But it is now." He paused for a second and shook his head. "I'm just kidding."

The room filled with laughter. "No, seriously. Of course it's in the back of my mind. But I'm not trying to make history or anything like that. I'm just trying to do the best I can with every shot. Luckily for me, I have a great caddie, and the love and support of my mom, and my girlfriend, Lucy."

His eyes wandered to the back of the room where Lucy stood in the corner, watching with a proud smile on her face.

"I couldn't have even qualified if not for the support of those around me."

"Tyler," a bald guy in the middle of the room said. "You mentioned your mother. We all heard the reports about her being hospitalized. How is she doing?"

"She's recovering well. Thanks for asking. I believe she will be released tomorrow, so that's good."

"Any chance she might make it out here to watch you?"

Tyler smiled. It was a humble, hopeful gesture. "I sure hope so."

JAMIE WINTHROP STARED out at a half-empty room of reporters. His anger from the poor performance in round three had not subsided in the hour since finishing, and the grim frown on his face showed it.

"Jamie, what do you think happened out there today?" a man in a white shirt and black tie asked from the front row.

Winthrop took a deep breath, exhaled, and shook his head. "I don't know. The bogey on five kind of set the tone for the day. After that, I think I just got in my own head."

"This was really uncharacteristic of you," a young woman on the right side said. "What do you need to do to get back to Jamie Winthrop's signature style of golf?"

"If I knew that, I would have done it earlier. Usually, I stay composed, as you said. But something came unglued today. That's all I can say. I'm not a robot."

"It was a sort of role reversal today with you and Sullivan," another guy stated from the back row. "In the past he was the one who—"

"Choked? Is that what you're saying? I choked?" Winthrop lost the frail grip on his emotions. "I don't choke," he stated. "Let's get that clear right now." His voice grew angrier by the word. "I had one bad day. I've won more major titles than anyone playing on tour right now."

The room sat in stunned silence for several seconds before another female reporter decided to risk speaking up.

"You're eight strokes back," she said.

"Do you have a question, or are you just here to state the obvious?"

From the side of the room, Winthrop's agent blushed bright red. His client wasn't doing himself any favors.

The reporter, to her credit, kept her cool. "Yes. What do you think you need to do to get back in this tournament and have a shot at winning?"

"Well, I just have to go out there and do what I know I can do. I'm the number-one player in the world for a reason. I can go out there and be number one tomorrow. And then we'll see what happens. But we know Sully's history. He struggles in the final rounds when the chips are on the table. And his partner tomorrow is a kid who couldn't buy a beer until last week. I just have to play my game and see what happens."

He let the statement hang in the air, along with the insinuation that his opponents would crumble under the pressure.

But to everyone in the room, he came off as pompous, anything but a good sport, and that reflected on each face.

"Anyone else got anything to say?" Winthrop asked, arrogance filling his voice.

No one said a thing. So he stood and walked off the stage without so much as a thank-you.

"GRAHAM, you have been nothing short of incredible this weekend," a male reporter in his sixties said from the second row. "I'm wondering where the fountain of youth is, and if you'd mind sharing it with us."

The room burst into laughter, and Graham joined in. He gripped the water bottle in front of him and peered around the burgeoning room.

"If I did find the fountain, it sure hasn't helped me look any younger."

More laughter erupted.

"You haven't played this well in a long time. How can you explain your performance this weekend?" a woman in her forties asked from the third row.

He smiled. "Thanks for pointing out how poorly I've been recently," he joked. Again, everyone chuckled. "But yeah, I don't know. I have just felt freer this weekend. I'm going out there playing like it doesn't matter, I guess. That's the only way I can explain it. I don't feel like I'm putting any pressure on myself like I used to."

"Do you think that's because it's your final tournament?" another guy asked.

"Maybe. Sure. I can't definitively say that isn't a part of it. But I don't know. I just feel different this time. And it isn't just the aches and pains that come with age."

More laughter echoed off the walls and ceiling.

"You're going to be paired with the local kid, Tyler Knox, tomorrow. He's a big fan of yours and has a chance to be the first amateur to win since the 1930s. How are you going to approach tomorrow's round with him?" The woman sat back and waited for the answer, as did everyone in the room.

Graham pined over the question. It twisted his stomach into knots. "To be honest, I hadn't really thought about it until you mentioned it. I mean, obviously I saw his name at the top, so I knew we'd be together. But yeah, that's a heck of a storyline. I'm sure all of you will be soaking this one up."

He paused for a second before continuing. "I had the chance to meet Tyler the other night at the banquet. We sat together at a table. Really nice young man. If anyone is going to beat me at this tournament, then it should be him. One of these days, another amateur is going to win a major event. And he's got as good a shot as any. For me, I just have to go out there and keep swinging free, like a friend of mine said to me last week. Let the chips fall where they may."

56

A million thoughts raced through Tyler's head.

Lucy leaned against his car in the parking lot of White Oak National, illuminated by the lights on poles staggered every fifty feet around the asphalt's outer edge. She wore a cute, flirty expression on her face.

Justin stood a few feet away with his arms crossed, trying to look unhappy but failing miserably.

"Well, well, well," he said. "If it isn't the rock star finally coming out to join the commoners."

Tyler grinned and shook his head. "I'd hardly say the lead guitarist is a commoner."

Justin's frown cracked, and he clapped his hand together with his friend and gave him a hug.

"Amazing round again today, bro," Justin said. "Just incredible."

"Justin. Credible? I see what you did there."

The three laughed.

Tyler turned to Lucy and wrapped his arms around her, giving her a kiss on the cheek. "Thanks for coming out again," he said.

She looked him in the eyes and shook her head. "Yeah, like I would miss my boyfriend playing here."

"Ugh. Great. You two going to get matching air brushed T-shirts in Gatlinburg next?" Justin drawled.

They let go of each other and grinned at him, happy to have made him uncomfortable for a few seconds.

"So," Justin went on, "thanks for the shout-out in the interview. That was really cool, man."

"Of course," Tyler said. "I couldn't have done this without you two."

"I'm just the cheering section. Justin is the one who sets it up for you."

Justin blushed. In that moment, Tyler saw that his friend realized he'd misjudged Lucy before. Maybe that epiphany had hit him earlier, but Tyler was glad they seemed to be getting along.

Tyler looked down at the ground and leaned against his car. Emotions swirled in him like a vortex that seemed to leak out of his body and stir the leaves and debris on the asphalt. Even the leaves in the trees rustled from it.

"You okay?" Justin asked, noting the troubled expression on his friend's face.

"Yeah. It's just a lot, you know?"

"What? Being tied for the lead at the preeminent major tournament in the world going into the final round? And being paired with your hero?" He dismissed the notion with his hand. "Child's play for you, brother. You're the guy who eagled out on number seven to lock up the qualifier."

"Beyond that," Lucy added, "you've overcome so many bigger obstacles in your life than a round of golf. No matter what the title, whatever the course, whoever the competition, your life has prepared you for this by giving you much more difficult challenges than this. Golf, compared to all that, is easy, like Justin said. It's what you're great at. So, don't worry about all the spotlights or the interviews, or some kind of perceived pressure."

"She's right," Justin said. "And on top of all that, no one expected you to win. I mean, right now, you're already winning just by being in the top ten, much less tied for the lead. So, go to the hospital. See your mom. And get some rest. We have an afternoon tee time tomorrow, buddy."

He grinned at the statement, and Tyler's stoic wall collapsed. He smiled back at both of them. "Only the best get the later tee times," he said.

"Exactly. I'll see you tomorrow."

Justin clapped his friend on the shoulder then walked down the row of cars toward his.

"You want me to go with you to the hospital?" Lucy asked, shuffling closer to him.

He stared down into her dark eyes. They gleamed in the bright hue of the parking lot lights.

"No, but thank you. That's really sweet of you to offer. I think this time I want to see her by myself."

"I understand," she said with a smile. "I'll see you here tomorrow. Okay?"

He nodded.

Then she stood up on her tiptoes and kissed him. Her lips were warm, like the breeze dancing around them. And he didn't want it to stop.

But she pulled away and let her hands slip out of his as she turned and walked toward her car.

"Sleep well."

"Good night," he said, watching her walk away down the row of cars. He lingered for a moment, unashamedly enjoying the view. Then, with a goofy grin and a shake of the head, he willed himself to open his car door and climb inside.

GRAHAM STOOD next to the 18th green.

The moon hung over the valley in a dark sky that only painted a few wispy cirrus clouds over the backdrop.

Most people weren't allowed out on the course after hours, but Graham wasn't most people. He rarely used his standing in the golf community for any sort of perks, but in this case, he knew no one was going to say a thing to him about it.

The dry, cool air embraced him, hinting that winter lurked only a few months away.

He'd spoken to Alicia on the phone after his press conference, and the conversation still lingered in his mind.

She truly was unlike any woman he'd ever met.

Most of the women who interacted with him knew who he was—a big-time professional golfer with a big house on an elite course, and tons of money in the bank. Usually, that was all they were interested in.

He'd gotten used to it over the years and could always tell their ulterior motives behind the kind words and the obvious flirtations.

They'd talk about all the things they could do together, the trips they could take, and the things she would do to him and for him, all with the underscored motive of living a lavish lifestyle.

Graham never fell for it, of course. He was too old to be that kind of sucker. And the last thing he needed was another divorce. One was enough for him.

He'd actually sworn off the idea of ever getting married again, but now Alicia had him thinking maybe he should never say never.

It was crazy. He knew that.

He'd spent almost no time with the woman other than on the phone, but there was something about her.

She'd never once mentioned taking an expensive vacation to an exotic place, or pressed him for dinner at an exclusive restaurant in town. On top of all that, she had refused his offer to come up for the tournament so she could work her shifts.

After his experience with women over the last few decades, she wasn't just a breath of fresh air—she was a jet stream.

He stared out at the fairway leading up to the green, the thought of Alicia waning like sunlight at dusk.

He couldn't wait to see her when he got back to Charleston, and she'd promised to take him out for dinner when he returned.

Her. Take him out for dinner.

Graham was living in an upside-down world.

Only one world felt familiar to him.

The green and fairway in front of him.

Thick forests of pine, oak, and poplar funneled the fairway up the slight hill to where he stood. For an average golfer, that narrow corridor would punish any wayward shots to the left and right.

This hole held so many bad memories for him. It stood as a reminder of all his past failures, and not just for this tournament, or golf in general.

It tormented him with visions of all the errant shots that preceded this final hole, the missed putts he wished he could have back, and the marriage he probably should have never had.

The one good thing he'd gotten out of that shipwreck was his son, but he was gone. Still, the fact that he'd been in Graham's life for two decades gave him cause for gratitude. Despite the sadness, he knew that someday he would see his son again, when he finished life's final round.

Birds chirped and sang, blending their voices with the frogs that lived in the creek just on the other side of the stretch of woods to the right.

He inhaled the air deeply, taking in the smell of the forest, the cut grass, nature.

Graham used to think he was cursed. That like so many teams throughout history, or athletes who came up short in big moments, he was doomed to failure—a lovable loser.

He'd been in this position before, with a big lead over the man behind him. But never had he been in a spot like this where he was tied for the lead, and with an amateur no less.

Graham liked the kid. He seemed like a good person, with a strong head on his shoulders. Part of him wanted Tyler to win the tournament, to be the first amateur in nearly a century to win a major. It was hard not to root for him. But Graham wasn't a spectator. He was here to win. And for the first time in years, he actually had a legitimate shot.

Still, that didn't mute the conflict within him.

He only knew a little about Tyler's backstory, about how his father had passed away a few years ago, how Tyler worked as a caddie at a course in town to help support his mother. Winning this tournament wouldn't do him financial good since he couldn't collect the prize purse. But it would lead to fortune as soon as he went pro.

In the past, Graham would have never felt this way. He wouldn't have entertained such emotions, such sentimental thoughts.

"Maybe you can teach an old dog," he said, letting the rest of the adage fall unspoken into a warm breeze.

He gazed at the flag still standing upright in the hole. It would be in a different position tomorrow. The groundskeepers would be by early the next morning and move all the pins to new locations.

Graham felt the finality of standing there, looking out across the green and the fairway beyond.

It was the last time he would stand here the night before a final round as a player. He knew he would be welcomed back here for the rest of his life, but after tomorrow it would be as a spectator.

He crouched down and ran his fingers on the tightly cut Bermuda. It was cool to the touch.

"Thank you," he whispered. "It's been an honor to play here so many times." He stood again and swept his gaze across the valley. "You have been a worthy opponent."

He kept the next thought to himself as he took one last look at the darkened splendor laid out before him.

I sure would like to be the worthy one just once.

57

"I don't know if I can do it, Mom," Tyler said, pain darkening his face.

He looked as though he were on the brink of crying. His tired eyes filled with tears that didn't escape and run down his cheeks.

"Oh, honey," Molly said from the hospital bed. "You can do anything you—"

"No, it's not that," he interrupted. "I know I CAN do it."

She studied his face for a moment, in the way only a mother could. She'd raised him since he was a baby, knew more about him than he probably realized—including some of the things he'd tried to keep secret from her when he made the occasional bad decision.

"Ah," she said, realizing what was going on. "You don't know if you can beat the guy you grew up idolizing, the one you looked up to."

"It's not just that he's my favorite golfer, Mom. I met him the other night. He seems like a good person."

"Didn't you always suspect that?"

He offered a weak smile and shrugged. "Yeah, but you know what people say about meeting your heroes."

"Never do it?"

"But in his case, I'm glad I met him. It was so surreal, sitting there at a table with him. And now, here I am, paired with him in the final round of the open. The only thing that stands between him and his first title... is me."

His mother nodded that she understood. Pride radiated from her face. "Oh, Son. You're such a good person. But you have to go out there and give it your best shot." She leaned forward. "Or shots, as it were."

He smiled at the wordplay.

"But you used to tell me winning isn't everything."

"It isn't. But that doesn't mean we don't give it everything we have. And that applies to all things."

Tyler sighed and looked down at the floor. "If I beat Sully—in his last tournament—it could break him. I don't want to be responsible for that."

"Son, you have a good heart. But you have to ask yourself, what would Sully tell you?"

"He'd probably tell me not to go easy on him," Tyler said, lifting his head again. "And then he'd laugh."

"Right," Molly said with a shrug. "But here's the other thing, honey. Graham is playing really well right now. He may just go out there and beat the brakes off you tomorrow."

His brow crinkled, and he scowled at her, feigning offense. "Hey."

She laughed, and after a second he joined her.

"And don't forget, there are four golfers within striking distance going into tomorrow's round," she reminded. "You know better than me how the positions change on the leaderboard on the last day."

Tyler did know that. He'd watched this tournament, and all of the majors, since he was a kid, almost never missing one except recently when he had to work. The last day often held drama-filled twists and turns that shook up the leaderboard, and often wrecked scores that seemed to be unbreakable.

"Yeah. I guess you're right. I can't take my foot off the gas."

"Nope. And besides, let's say you did, and Sully won the whole thing. How would you feel, knowing that your favorite golfer and a man you admire, was a fraud of a champion? I don't think he would like that. Nor would you."

Tyler knew she was right, even though he still didn't feel great about it. The idea of beating a guy he'd rooted for his entire life, who'd been beaten up by the game and by circumstances beyond his control, turned Tyler's stomach.

He decided to change the subject.

"You think they're going to let you out of here tomorrow?"

"Honey, there's no way I'm going to miss my baby boy playing the final round of one of the biggest tournaments in the world. If they don't let me go, I will sneak out of this jail cell myself."

58

Tyler yawned as he shifted his car into park and turned off the engine.

He barely slept in the dark hours leading up to the alarm on his phone cruelly sounding its reminder to wake up. At least he didn't have to be up as early as he did on the first two days of the tournament.

He spent most of the night tossing and turning, twisting the sheets and covers around his legs until the bedding was a tangled mess.

He tried to meditate, listened to some sleep hypnosis videos on YouTube, and even tried visualizing himself on a sandy beach along the Gulf Coast of Florida, listening to the waves wash in while the sun warmed his skin.

But it was no use.

Sleep evaded him.

It had, for the most part, the previous three nights too. Tyler wondered if all the players struggled with the same issue, or if, over time, that went away as experience piled up and normalized the moment.

He hoped that was the case because if he did end up making it on the pro tour, those kinds of sleepless nights were something he'd rather not have to endure for the next thirty to forty years.

Tyler killed the engine and picked up his phone out of the cup holder. He'd received so many text messages over the last few days from his caddie buddies at Green Mont, along with a few other friends and relatives in the area.

For the most part, he'd tried to keep the noise to a minimum. He didn't need distractions.

He looked at the screen and saw he had a message from a number he didn't recognize.

Tyler tapped on the preview, and the text app opened.

His mouth dropped open as he read the message.

"Hey, Tyler. I'm sorry about the fight at the shack. I was wrong about you. Good luck in the final round today, man. Mitchell."

Tyler blinked slowly, rereading the text twice to make sure it wasn't some kind of joke. He started to shove the phone into his pocket, but instead typed out a quick message. "Thanks, man. I appreciate it."

He hit Send and then pocketed the phone before walking around to the trunk of his car.

He opened the lid and took out the clubs as one of the many uniformed attendants in a blue polo and gray pants trotted toward him. It was a younger guy this time, with red hair and freckles sprayed across his pale face. He looked maybe seventeen years old.

"I'll take your bag for you, Mr. Knox," the boy said as he slowed down nearing the car.

Tyler offered an appreciative yet exhausted smile. He wasn't accustomed to people calling him Mr. Knox and didn't believe he deserved that title yet. He was only three or four years older than the attendant and had only just turned twenty-one.

"Tyler" he said. "Call me Tyler."

"Okay," the boy said.

Tyler felt uncomfortable allowing the kid to take his bag for him. That too was something he wasn't used to. Usually, he was on the other end of the golf service spectrum.

But he also knew it was customary, and wouldn't make the boy look bad by carrying his own bag.

He took the bag out of his car and set it down on the bipod. "What's your name?"

"Ethan," the boy said as he picked up the bag and slung the strap over his right shoulder.

"Nice to meet you, Ethan," Tyler reached out his hand.

The boy looked surprised, then shook it timidly. "Nice to meet you too."

Tyler closed the trunk and started walking toward the clubhouse with Ethan by his side. "How long you been working here?" Tyler asked.

"Um, for about a year."

"Mostly work the bag drop?"

"Yeah, but I'm hoping to be a caddie. You're a caddie at Green Mont, aren't you? Or I guess you were."

Tyler grinned at the question. "I still am. Just not this weekend. I'm also finishing up college."

"If you win today, you won't have to go back to either of those things."

"True. But I will anyway. Always finish what you start." It was a lesson he remembered from his dad during a conversation they'd had a few months before his father passed.

Now, those words seemed more important than ever.

They walked through the lot then turned down the path toward the driving range. The morning pairings were well into their rounds, while Tyler still had a few hours before he and Sullivan teed off.

The first person Tyler noticed as they approached the range was Justin. He stood at the back of the tee area, watching the other golfers swinging irons and woods, warming up for their rounds.

"You can leave that with Justin," Tyler said to Ethan.

Justin turned and raised an eyebrow. "Sleep in this morning?"

"Not hardly," Tyler said.

"I'm surprised you got any sleep at all. I know I didn't and I'm not even playing."

Tyler turned to Ethan. "Thanks. Maybe I'll see you after the tournament."

"I hope so, Mr.... I mean... Tyler."

The boy set the bag down and walked away.

"Looks like you have another fan," Justin teased.

"Seems like a nice guy."

"Yeah, well, I hope you haven't been paying attention to social media. Seems you have a lot more fans out there now. Particularly of the female variety."

Tyler hummed a short laugh. "I don't really get on social much. Probably best not to mention that last part to Lucy, though."

"Oh, I'm sure she knows."

"Great. I hope she knows she doesn't have anything to worry about."

"With how goofy you are, I'm sure she's fine."

"What's that supposed to mean?" Tyler asked, pretending to be hurt.

"Means you got no game, my man." Justin nodded to an empty slot on the range. "Except the game of golf." He picked up the bag and lugged it toward the opening.

Tyler stood there for a few seconds. "I have game," he muttered, then followed his friend.

He followed Justin to the empty tee box then stopped and looked down the row. Sullivan was already warming up five spots down.

Tyler felt the urge to go talk to him, but he didn't. Now was the time to get focused. None of the other golfers were talking to each other. The only sounds came from the clubs whipping through the air and sending golf balls down the range.

Everyone was locked in, preparing for the final round of the tournament.

Justin pulled the pitching wedge out of Tyler's bag and handed it over.

"Time to go to work," Justin said.

Tyler nodded. "Yeah. Time to go to work."

59

Tyler stood waiting just outside the clubhouse on the path leading out to the 1st tee. Spectators surrounded the walkway ahead, loitering behind ropes as they waited to catch a close-up glimpse, or maybe a high-five, from the final pairing.

It was unlike anything Tyler had ever experienced, not even in his wildest imagination. After day one, he'd grown more accustomed to the throngs of people watching him, but that was before he was tied for the lead. And those rounds hadn't been on a Sunday at White Oak.

They'd watched him, he guessed, as they would a novelty, a cool story, but an unlikely champion—at least as an amateur.

But as every hole passed, word about Tyler's play spread. It was slow at first, like the trickle of a dry creek in late summer. But it soon turned into a flood, raging through every media outlet, and on the lips of everyone in attendance.

Now, they weren't looking at him as merely a feel-good story but as one of the best golfers in the world.

While Tyler wasn't sure he was that, he'd done enough to be one of the best in the world over the last three days. He just needed to do it one more time.

Behind him, the door to the clubhouse opened, and Graham stepped out, passing the doorman and thanking him before joining Tyler and the two caddies on the path.

A chill swept over Tyler.

He'd felt it when he sat down next to Sullivan at the dinner, and again when he found out they would be paired together. But now, it was happening. He was going to play a round of golf with his all-time favorite golfer.

For Tyler, that meant just as much as a shot at winning the open, and what it would do for his future.

"Morning, Tyler," Graham said, extending his hand to the young player.

Tyler shook it firmly but nervously.

"Good morning, Mr.... I mean Sully."

Graham smiled at him. "You feeling okay today?"

"Yes, sir. I mean, I feel a little like throwing up, but other than that..."

Graham burst out laughing. "Yeah, I remember my first final round here too. Of course, I wasn't tied for the lead. Heck of a weekend you've had."

"I've had some things go my way."

"Maybe. But no one gets to the top of the leaderboard in any tournament through luck alone. And usually, you need a few lucky bounces to win. That's true in any sport."

"Yeah, I guess you're right."

Graham looked out at the crowd surrounding the path. People took pictures and video on their phones. Some merely stood there, staring at them with wide eyes.

"How'd you sleep last night?" Graham asked.

"Not great."

Graham chuckled. "That's normal."

"Does it ever go away?" Tyler asked, looking over at him.

"Yeah. Eventually. I think for me it was in year two. You get used to all the spectators, the television viewers, the talk shows, the interviews, all that. But really, the nerves come from the pressure we put on ourselves. Doesn't matter what anyone else thinks or says. All that hype comes from within. Once you let that go, and just do what you were meant to do, you'll be fine."

"What I'm meant to do," Tyler muttered.

Graham glanced over at him. "Yes. In case you didn't notice, you're a fantastic golfer, kid. You've got what it takes."

"Thanks, Sully," Tyler said. "It's an honor to play with you today. Good luck."

"It's an honor to play with you too, Tyler. And best of luck to you too."

A man in a blue blazer stood atop the knoll in the pathway. He had a radio earpiece in his right ear and a tablet in his hands. He nodded and motioned for the final group to make their way up the hill toward the tee box.

"Here we go," Graham said. He motioned to Tyler as though he wanted him to go first.

"No, sir. You have the honors."

Graham squinted with a subtle, appreciative grin. "Well, all right then."

He started up the hill to a round of cheering with Tyler right behind him.

They marched along the path, both occasionally reaching out to high-five a fan who stuck their hands out over the ropes.

Tyler felt goosebumps tickle his skin. People were shouting his name, cheering him on. He waved at the crowd as he passed, doing his best to mimic Graham's responses to the support.

They made their way down the other side of the rise toward the 1st tee box.

Tyler searched the mass of people for familiar faces, but he knew if his mother was there, she would be off to the right where most of the other golfers' families waited behind the 18th green. She and Lucy were over there somewhere, probably watching on one of the televisions the tournament provided in a big white tent.

This round, it would only be him and Justin. The way it began more than a month ago with the first qualifying round.

Graham and his caddie stopped at the edge of the tee box. Tyler and Justin caught up and stood next to them, waiting for the starter to announce them.

"Ladies and gentlemen," a man in his sixties wearing the signature blue blazer said into a microphone, "the final pairing for the one hundred and fifth White Oak Open Championship."

The spectators cheered. When the applause died down, the starter spoke again. "Please welcome to the tee, from Charleston, South Carolina, Graham Sullivan."

Graham waved to the people as they clapped and hollered, then took a driver from his caddie and walked over to a spot between the tee markers.

He teed up a ball, took a few practice swings behind it, then stepped into position.

The crowd descended into utter silence. The only sounds came from birds and insects in the trees and bushes, and a few distant cheers from other points on the course.

Graham settled into his stance, then twisted back and drove the ball.

People in the crowd shouted, "Sully!" More clapped as the ball continued far into the distance before landing and rolling to a stop on the right middle of the fairway.

Graham smiled at the result then turned and walked back to his caddie, handing the club over to him.

"Great shot," Tyler said.

"Thanks. It felt really clean."

"Looked it."

"Good drive, Mr. Sullivan," Justin added.

"Thank you. Your turn, kid."

Justin took the driver out of Tyler's bag and handed it over to his friend.

"Please welcome, from Chattanooga, Tennessee, Tyler Knox."

The crowd cheered wildly for the local kid. Even Graham clapped for him as he walked onto the tee box and waved to the spectators.

Tyler stuck a tee in the ground with the ball atop it and stepped back to look down the fairway.

Graham's ball was perched in a perfect spot a little over three hundred yards away.

The sun beamed down between white clouds, casting a bright light onto the lush green grass and the dense tree foliage. A warm, dry breeze washed over him as he held his driver out in front of him, staring at the spectacular setting.

For a moment, he just took it all in, breathing the rarefied air that most golfers would never get to inhale—not from where he was standing.

"Thank you," he whispered the silent prayer. Then bent down, brushed his fingers across the grass as a show of appreciation to the hallowed grounds. The crowd fell silent as he moved behind the ball, whipping the club back and forth to loosen up his shoulders and back.

Tyler addressed the ball, positioning his feet wide apart. He lowered the club and paused. He felt thousands of eyes on him, and millions more through the cameras positioned around the area. His heart pounded in his chest. Doubts tried to force themselves into his mind, making him question if he could do this or not.

He blinked and inhaled slowly, reminding himself that it was just another round and no one was watching him. *It's just you and the ball,* he thought.

Tyler turned, raising the club high over his shoulders, and swung. The face of the driver hit the ball hard with a thunderous smack.

The crowd erupted in applause as the white sphere flew through the air. It landed fifteen feet short of Graham's ball, then rolled past it, stopping ten yards beyond.

He held his finishing stance for a few extra seconds then turned to find Justin walking up behind him with a big grin on his face and right hand extended.

"Great shot, buddy," Justin said, taking the club from Tyler.

"Outstanding," Graham said as he walked by, nodding his approval.

Tyler felt his cheeks blush. "Thanks, guys."

He turned and started down the fairway as a tepid relief smothered the tension in his chest.

"That's one," he whispered.

60

Ten television screens displayed the tournament in high definition for the families and friends of the players gathered in the enormous white hospitality tent outside the clubhouse, behind the hill that led to the number 18 green.

Molly Knox sat in a white chair next to a round table with a white cloth draped over it. Glasses of iced tea and water sat on the surface, along with plates of finger food for the guests.

Lucy stood next to her, both with their eyes glued to the television nearest them.

They both wanted to be out there in the crowd, following Tyler through every hole of the final round, but it was customary for friends and family to hang out here to greet the golfers after they finished.

Molly had arrived only forty-five minutes before Tyler was scheduled to tee off, but thanks to Lucy's help had navigated the security and been brought here by a nice man in a blue blazer.

Now, she leaned forward in her chair, her eyes stuck to the television as her son stood on the 3rd green, about to putt for birdie.

The volume on the televisions was turned down to a level she could barely hear above the conversation going on in the tent. Thankfully, everyone else in there was just as interested in watching their players as they were chatting to people they only knew as golf friends, or acquaintances.

"Knox is off to a good start here, going shot for shot with Sullivan," the announcer said. "And here he has a chance to make the first statement of the day with this birdie putt."

"Yeah, you said it, Troy," Steve agreed. "And this is a makable putt for Knox. Fourteen feet, slight left to right. Uphill. We've seen him bury these all weekend."

Molly nearly slid out of her chair as she inched forward, resting on the very edge of it as she watched her son reach back and stroke the ball toward the cup.

"Looks like he has the line," Troy said. "Does it have enough?"

"Come on. Get in there," Molly demanded.

Lucy stood on the tips of her toes, as if it would will the ball into the cup.

"It's going to be close," Troy teased.

Then the ball fell out of sight into the hole.

"He's got it!"

The crowd surrounding the green roared through the television.

Molly started to scream but tempered her excitement with rapid clapping and a loud "Yes!"

Lucy turned to her and they slapped palms.

"Easy as you like," Steve said on the television. "Knox's putter has been lights out the last three days, and so far here in the final round, he hasn't disappointed."

"Now it's Graham Sullivan's turn. His putt is significantly different."

"Yeah, Troy, he's got a slight downhill, and a sharp bender to the right. He's going to have to be careful here. He only needs to breathe on it to get the ball close to the hole. Then it's all a matter of the line."

"Sullivan and Knox both parred the first two holes of the day after trading missed birdie opportunities. But only eleven percent of the field ahead of them had birdies on those two holes."

"They are playing extremely difficult today, and there's more danger ahead after this," Steve added.

Graham finished assessing the line with his caddie, and walked over to the ball. He set up, stared down the path one more time, and then struck the ball.

It rolled easily down the slope, bending hard to the right.

"He's picked a really high line here, Troy," Steve said. "And he needed to with that hump."

"This one might have a chance," Troy said, his voice rising. "Can it? Yes!"

The spectators exploded again in raucous cheering.

Graham pumped his fist and smiled, then walked over and retrieved the ball from the cup.

"The two leaders go birdie here on three and stay neck and neck while extending their lead over the next position."

Molly leaned back in the chair while she watched her son walk over to Sullivan and give him a high-five.

She never saw competitors do that in tournaments, but she'd not watched as much golf as her son or her late husband.

"Do they always do that?" she asked Lucy.

"No," Lucy shook her head. "I've never seen anyone do that before." She looked down at Molly. "Your son is an amazing person."

Molly beamed. "I know. He really is."

61

Tyler stared down the green of the number 8 par 3. Graham's ball was already parked eight feet from the hole after a spectacular tee shot that sent the crowd into a frenzy.

Tyler had to remind himself that he wasn't just a fan watching his favorite player. He was a competitor. But he found it impossible to turn off the admiration and ignore the thrill that pulsed through him at such an awesome shot by his idol.

Now, he had to drown that sentiment, and try to match his opponent.

They were both 2 under par on the front nine, with two holes to play before they made the turn. Tyler still maintained his practice of not checking the leaderboard, but he knew where he and Graham stood as far as their scores were concerned. If someone below them on the leaderboard was making a run, Tyler didn't know about it.

Tyler banked as a gnat buzzed around his face. Rays of sunlight streaked through the trees on a hill behind the green and onto the putting surface as if casting heaven's blessings on the place. Roses lined the slope, mulched with pine straw down to a strip of thick Bermuda that ran along the back edge of a narrow bunker.

In front of the green, a pond hugged the left side, fed by a creek that divided a patch of fairway and rough from the target.

A stand full of spectators stood to the right of the green, and thousands more wrapped around the fairway. A narrow, stone bridge crossed the creek for the golfers to walk over.

Tyler couldn't imagine a more picturesque setting for a hole. He'd seen it on television more times than he recalled, but it was truly one of his favorites of all the tournament locations on the tour. Now, for the fourth time, he was standing here as a player.

He thought that, even if he played here a thousand times, this view would never get old, and he would never cease to appreciate it.

He'd birdied the hole twice, and parred it once so far. But today's pin location was near the front, and hitting it to the back of the green would present a challenging downhill putt that could easily roll off the front edge, and potentially down to the creek.

It was a delicate task to get the ball as close as Graham had.

He'd managed to attack the right side, keeping the pond to the left out of play, and with a slight draw pulled his shot back to the left, where it landed on the right side of the green and rolled to a stop in a perfect position.

Tyler knew he needed to approach it the same way. He'd hit that kind of shot before hundreds of times, maybe thousands. But never with so much on the line.

"No wind right now," Justin said, gazing at the treetops beyond the green. "You saw the line of attack with Graham's shot. No need to reinvent the wheel. Yardage will play true."

Tyler nodded. His friend was right. Now he just had to hit the shot.

He stepped up to the ball he'd placed on the surface and cleared his mind. He took another glance at the green.

The thousands of spectators remained perfectly silent amid the sounds of birds and bugs in the forest.

Tyler reared back and swung, striking the ball with the sweet spot of the iron.

The sphere towered into the air, climbing high just above the canopy. It started on the right edge, then veered slightly left.

The second he hit the shot, the crowd cheered some then fell silent as they held their breath to see what would happen.

"Come on," Tyler prayed. "Be there."

A lump caught in his throat. He'd hit the ball cleanly, but a bad feeling told him he hadn't struck it hard enough.

He watched as the ball fell from the sky and landed on the front lip of the green. For a second, no one moved. None of the fans, the caddies, or the players said or did anything.

They merely stared as the ball sat for a second, teetering on the edge of danger, just short of the green. Then the white orb started trickling down the slope. It was slow at first, barely rolling away from the pin. But it quickly picked up speed, and Tyler knew he'd messed it up.

The ball tumbled down the embankment and plopped into the water. A loud groan sounded from the crowd.

Tyler's shoulders slumped. He let out a frustrated sigh.

It was the first big mistake he'd made the entire tournament. And it was a costly one.

Now he'd have to drop and chip up and hope to make bogey. Meanwhile, Graham had a legitimate chance at birdie.

A two-stroke swing hung in the balance.

"Shake it off, kid," Graham said as he walked by. "You're fine."

Tyler nodded, but he didn't feel fine. He felt sick to his stomach.

How far back were the other players?

More doubts and worries flooded his mind.

"Hey," Justin said, walking up beside his friend. "It's okay. On to the next shot. That one's in the past."

For a second, Tyler watched as Graham and his caddie made their way toward the bridge 150 yards away. Then, he exhaled, handed his friend the iron, and bobbed his head.

"Yep," Tyler said. "Next shot."

He and Justin walked down to the edge of the creek amid appreciative applause, but now most of the cheering was for Graham.

Tyler didn't resent that. While he was disappointed in himself, he was glad Graham was doing well and hoped he could continue the pace even though the desire to win still pumped through Tyler's blood.

Winning this tournament would change his life.

But he had to force those kinds of thoughts out of his mind. They added unnecessary pressure and did nothing to help him.

He stopped at the drop area marked out in front of the creek and looked across at the pin.

It wasn't far, but again, the shot to get it there would be tricky. If Tyler shorted the chip, the ball would roll into the water again, and his chances of winning the tournament, or even finishing in the top three would be in serious jeopardy.

He'd have to play it long and let the slope behind the flag roll the ball back toward the cup.

"Get it close," Justin said. "Take your bogey. And regroup on the next one. Lot of golf left to play, buddy."

"Yeah. Or I could just knock it in for par here," Tyler said with a wry grin.

"True. I've seen you do it before. I mean, not in these circumstances. You know, the biggest stage possible."

"You trying to help or make me feel worse?"

Justin laughed. "Just loosening you up, bro. You got this. Park it close. Let the hill do the work." Justin handed his friend a shiny new ball and a utility wedge.

Tyler didn't like using gap wedges, found them difficult to manage, and often hit them inconsistently.

He dropped the ball into the marked area and took a step back as he flipped the club back and forth, loosening his hands and wrists.

Graham and his caddie watched from the other side of the bridge near the pond.

Tyler steadied his breathing and lined up the shot, planting his feet firmly in position. He looked at the pin, picked a spot eight feet beyond it, then focused on the ball.

He took the club up just above his waist and brought it down cleanly through the sphere. Grass and dirt flew from the divot as the ball took off. It peaked around twenty feet in the air, just over the top of the flag stick before falling to the green beyond.

MOLLY STOOD UP, squeezing her hands together as she and the others in the tent watched the ball go over the pin and hit the green.

"Oh wow. He's going to like this," Troy said through the speakers.

The ball started rolling down the slope toward the pin.

The crowd started cheering, as if their voices and applause would coax it into the cup.

"It's got a chance!"

"Get in the hole!" Lucy said loudly.

The ball picked up speed as it descended the slope. It hit the pin with a clank then dropped out of sight.

"Yeah!" Lucy and Molly screamed.

"You've got to be kidding me!" Troy shouted through the television. "Who is this kid?"

"That's my son!" Molly answered, pointing at the screen.

Everyone in the room cheered along with the roaring mass of people on the course.

The sounds echoed through the valley all the way to the clubhouse, surely causing the rest of the players to wonder what just happened.

"Tyler Knox, chipping it in to save par there, Steve. Just incredible."

The camera focused on Tyler, who held a fist in the air then pumped it several times before high fiving his caddie.

"What we're seeing here is the birth of a star unlike any we've ever seen before," Steve said.

"We sure are. And now, if you're Graham Sullivan, you need to make this to take sole possession of the lead. But instead of two strokes, it will only be one. Let's go over to Jamie Winthrop on number eleven. Jodie, what's going on there?"

"Well, Troy," the female announcer said, "Winthrop's struggles have continued since the debacle yesterday on number five. He's two over par on the day now, and needs this sixteen-foot birdie to stop the bleeding. He's lost any shot at taking the title, and now he's in damage control mode to remain in the top ten."

Winthrop stood over the ball for a second then hit it toward the hole.

The ball rolled steadily, curling at the end near the cup, but hit the lip and twisted out to the right.

Winthrop looked up at the sky, shaking his head in utter frustration.

"So close," Jodie said. "But that's just how it's been for him here since yesterday. It's been a strange thing to see. That's for sure. Very unlike him to lose his composure."

The television coverage switched back to Graham standing on the green at number 8.

"Here's Sullivan for birdie on eight," Troy said.

"On television, it looks easy," Steve commented. "But there are no easy putts here the rest of the way."

Graham took one last look at the putt with his caddie then stepped over the ball.

"Sullivan... for birdie and sole possession of the lead here at White Oak."

Graham struck the ball with smooth precision.

It rolled straight toward the cup and fell into the center.

"He's got it!"

The crowd erupted, losing their minds at the display by the two golfers.

"Three under par on the front nine by Graham Sullivan. Fifty-eight years young. Leading the field on Sunday at White Oak."

"It doesn't get better than this, Troy," Steve said. "There is something magical happening between the roses here today."

Graham walked over to the hole, removed the ball, and tipped his cap to the crowd, who continued cheering as he strode off the green.

62

The television cut away from the commercial break, and the aerial view of the golf course filled the screen again as the camera descended until the sun disappeared behind the treetops to the west.

"Welcome back to the final round of the White Oak National Open Championship," Troy said. "Such a beautiful place. And the perfect setting for the drama that is unfolding here today."

The digital leaderboard overlaid the scene on the television.

Sullivan was at the top, with Knox just below him in second place.

"And then there were two," Troy went on. "Graham Sullivan is on top of the mountain all alone at an astonishing fourteen under par. But the local amateur, Tyler Knox, hasn't folded yet, and is only one stroke behind at thirteen under. The rest of the field has fallen away now with only two holes to play. And it all comes down to this. The young amateur against his childhood hero, the veteran who has never won a major tournament, falling painfully short so many times before."

The screen switched to highlights of the previous holes.

"Neither man has flinched since Knox's penalty on number eight.

They've been locked in a stalemate, matching shots in a battle of attrition."

"No, Troy, this has truly been a battle of the ages. As you said, the one mistake by Knox on eight has been the only thing separating the two."

The highlights changed to the shot Tyler hit into the water on the 8th hole. Then switched again to his follow-up shot from the drop zone that sent the crowd into a frenzy.

"But even that mistake had a silver lining," Troy said. "Knox chipped in for par in dramatic fashion, keeping Sullivan's lead to only one stroke. And so, here we stand after sixteen, with only the thinnest of margins between them."

"Yeah, Troy, and this hole has been a nightmare for Sullivan in the past. He's done well here so far this week, with three pars, but you have to wonder if his history here is going through his mind right now with two to play and a one-stroke lead."

The screen filled with highlights of Graham's mistakes on 17 through the years. One he hit into the woods to the left. Another into a bunker. And one that splashed into the water on the right edge of the fairway.

"Will this finally be the year that Graham Sullivan gets his first major, in his last professional tournament? Or will the local kid, Tyler Knox, play the spoiler this time and be the first amateur to win a major in nearly a century? We go now to the seventeenth tee box, where Graham Sullivan has the honors, and the lead, with two holes to play."

The camera zoomed in on Graham as he stared down the par-5 fairway.

Molly and Lucy stood next to an older man in a blue blazer as they watched the television.

"After this hole, you'll need to come up to eighteen. We have an area blocked off for you there."

Most of the other friends and family had already departed and gone with the same guy to greet their players as they finished the round. Only the wives and kids of the men in the next-to-last pairing lingered in the tent, and they were about to leave.

There was one other woman in the tent. She'd kept quiet during most of the round and stayed at a table alone near the back, avoiding social interaction with everyone else.

Lucy and Molly had both noticed her and wondered who she was, but decided to leave her alone. She may have been the wife or girlfriend of one of the golfers and not wanted to be bothered.

"Ma'am," the man in the blazer said to the woman.

She turned toward him as if frightened by the sound of his voice, or concerned she'd done something wrong.

She wore a pale orange sundress and a necklace with a turquoise pendant dangling from a silver chain.

"You'll need to come with these two after they finish seventeen."

The woman nodded.

The realization hit Lucy first, and she smiled at the woman. "Are you here for Mr. Sullivan?"

The woman nodded as she stood up from her chair. "Yes. I don't think he knows I'm here. I wanted it to be a surprise."

The epiphany sent a smile across Molly's face. "Oh my goodness. Are you and Graham—"

"I honestly don't know." She walked over to the two and extended her hand. "I'm Alicia."

Molly and Lucy introduced themselves.

"I'm Tyler's mother," Molly said. "He is such a big fan of Graham. Always has been."

Alicia grinned proudly. "I'm becoming a fan myself."

"So," Lucy cut in, "are you two dating?"

"We've gone out, but I really like him. I just don't know for sure how he feels. We've talked. He's such a sweet guy. But I don't know much about golf. So, all this is pretty new to me."

"Well, sis," Molly said, "stick with us. Looks like our boys are going to take this to the wire."

———

GRAHAM STARED out across the narrow fairway. He always tried to focus on the place he wanted the ball to go, not the danger around that target. A peninsula of trees and shrubs cut into it from the left-hand side, and a long pond lined the right just beyond fifteen yards of rough.

It was a tight shot, and one that he'd gotten wrong before at the worst possible times. So far this week, he'd navigated the treacherous waters, but now he stood there again, facing the looming threat and the demons of his past head-on.

"Breeze is slight," Mike said to Graham from a few feet away. "Right to left. Shouldn't impact the drive much."

Graham agreed with his caddie's assessment. They'd been on this course, and this hole, many times throughout Graham's career, and both men knew exactly how to approach it.

Unfortunately, that hadn't resulted in positive outcomes in the past, not on Sunday at least.

Graham rolled his left shoulder as Mike handed him the driver. The muscles around the joint were sore, but in thirty or so minutes, he wouldn't have to swing a golf club again except for the sheer fun of it.

In the past, he'd managed the stiffness and pain with over-the-counter meds like ibuprofen, and with an ice pack in the evenings. So far this weekend, he'd been fortunate the issues hadn't gotten worse.

He'd come into the tournament with no problems and thought everything felt good through the first three rounds, but after the 11th hole today, he noticed the shoulder flaring up.

"You okay?" Mike asked.

"Yeah. I'm good. Just a little stiff."

The caddie dropped the topic and watched as Graham walked onto the box and teed up a ball.

Tyler and Justin stood on the edge of the tee area, both remaining silent as Graham took another look down the fairway before addressing the ball.

Graham set the club head down on the ground, turned, loaded up on his right knee, and twisted.

As his wrists pulled the club down, he felt something pop in his left shoulder. The driver's face crushed the ball, powering it into the air. The shot initially started on the right edge of the fairway where Graham aimed, but it quickly hooked left.

"No," Graham breathed as he lowered the club and rolled his shoulder again.

He watched the ball curl toward the woods on the left where thousands of onlookers lined the fairway behind a rope. It landed on the left side of the fairway and rolled ahead, finally coming to a stop behind the trees that jutted out from the forest, effectively cutting off a direct path to the green.

Graham dropped his head, dejected at the mistake.

The audience clapped politely, but it was a timid, hopeful gesture born more of etiquette than admiration.

"It's okay," Mike said, taking the club and sliding it back into the bag. "You're fine."

Graham inhaled deeply and sighed. "Yeah. I guess we'll see. Could have been worse. I could have been in the trees like twelve years ago."

"Don't think about that. Just think about the next shot."

Tyler walked past him without saying a word. He held his driver in his left hand and the ball and tee in his right.

He crouched down and planted the tee in the ground, then stepped back for one last assessment.

Tyler and Justin knew the plan of attack. The right edge of the fairway around 280 yards out would give a perfect line of attack for the second shot. Hit that true, and the approach into the green would be straightforward. The challenge of this hole was off the tee.

He'd seen where Graham hit his shot, and half of his heart sank for the man, while the other half skipped a beat with the realization that the door had just been opened. All he had to do was walk through it.

Tyler stepped up to the ball, set his feet, and whipped the club around a few times before settling it to the ground.

The crowd watched silently as he turned, taking the club up over his shoulders, then drove it through the ball in a fluid, smooth swing.

The sound cracked through the valley as the ball took flight, soaring straight as a javelin down the fairway only a few feet left of where Tyler aimed.

The spectators cheered the shot and then the sound waned as they waited to see where the ball would end up.

It landed 285 yards away, and rolled to a stop a little beyond three hundred.

A cacophony of applause filled his ears, and he slowly lowered the club and turned back to his caddie.

Justin beamed at him. "Atta baby!" he said, taking the driver from his friend and stuffing it back in the bag.

Graham walked by, and Tyler glanced at him for a second, not wanting to say anything.

Instead, Graham said, "Great drive, kid. You want to swap with me?"

The joke disarmed Tyler's reluctance. "Thanks."

He wanted to offer some kind of advice or encouragement to the man, but he was just an amateur, and it might come off sounding patronizing.

So, he simply left the conversation where it was and made his way onto the fairway, walking side by side until Graham split off to go to his ball.

Graham walked over to his ball and stopped, looking up at the patch of trees blocking his path a mere twenty yards away.

There was no way through them, and at that proximity, he could try to go over but at the cost of distance. The other option was to go around, to chip the ball out to the right beyond Tyler's ball, and play it from there. While that was the safer of the two options, it would cost him even more distance, and he would end up essentially putting himself a stroke behind as they headed to the green.

Mike set the bag down ten feet behind the ball.

"What do you think, Mike?" Graham asked.

Mike cocked his head to the side for a second. "I think you should have hit the drive straight."

Graham looked over at him, and the smug grin on his caddie's face melted the stress in an instant. He laughed and shook his head.

"You're an idiot."

Mike smiled back at him. "I know. So, you know your only options here. You play it safe and punch out over there to get around the trees. Or you go more aggressive over the top, but that'll be a high loft club, and won't get you that much closer to the green. Either way, you're going to basically lose one. The risk of going over the top is if you miss it low, you're talking more than a stroke."

"Well, that makes it easy. Give me the five."

Graham wasn't about to take the risk for such a small reward. In his younger years, he'd failed that test multiple times, forgoing course management to go for the home run. It had cost him, and those mistakes made this decision easy.

Mike took a few more steps back with the bag as Graham moved to the ball. He flicked the club a few times as he would if he were chipping and then took his stance.

Tyler and Justin stood off to the side of the fairway near the water hazard as Graham hit the ball up and around the last tree in his way.

The crowd applauded as the ball rolled clear of the barrier, stopping on the right edge of the fairway seventy yards from where Graham stood.

He walked back to Mike and handed him the iron. "Well, I guess we'll see."

"Smart play," Mike said. "I know that didn't feel good. Shoulder okay?"

"It is for now. We'll see about that too. Only one more to go after this."

63

Molly, Alicia, and Lucy watched the television as the camera zoomed in on Graham stalking around his ball on the number 17 green.

"Well, Steve, just when you thought this tournament couldn't get more intriguing, here we are on seventeen with Graham Sullivan... in the lead, with a putt for par, while Tyler Knox is on the green with a birdie putt to tie it up heading into the last hole."

"I tell you what, Troy, you couldn't write it any better than this. Graham really needs to make this, or else he could find himself one stroke back going into the final hole."

"Right you are. And after a nearly flawless tournament by Sullivan, another mistake here on seventeen would be absolutely devastating."

"He did the right thing after that errant drive. Made the safe play to give himself a chance at par while his counterpart had no trouble getting down the fairway and into position for a beautiful approach that's left him eleven feet from a tying birdie."

Graham spoke to his caddie for a moment, nodded a few times, then walked over to the ball.

"Sinister little putt, this, Troy. It's going to tip hard to the left at the beginning and then straighten out. Ever-so-slight downhill. Graham really has to get the line right here."

The camera focused on Graham as he crouched down one more time to make sure he had his mark. Then he stood and set up over the ball. He took a few practice swings to get the tempo right, then lowered the putter, paused, and hit the ball.

A few guys in the audience shouted "Graham!" after it left his putter and rolled toward the cup.

"It's going to be tight," Troy said. "I'm not sure it has the line."

Alicia clasped her hands together. Her knuckles turned white as she stared at the screen.

The camera zeroed in on the ball as it neared the cup and touched the outer edge. It stopped for a second, the logo of the ball clearly displayed on the screen. Then, as if kissed by the wind, tipped over and fell into the hole.

"Yes, sir!" Troy blared as the crowd went bonkers in the background. "Incredible par by Sullivan to bail himself out of trouble on seventeen."

Molly touched Alicia on the shoulder in a kind show of support.

"I had no idea this was so stressful," Alicia confessed.

"Yeah, funny how a leisure activity does that."

Troy spoke up again as Graham plucked his ball from the hole and tipped his hat to the crowd as he always did.

"Now the pressure falls squarely on Tyler Knox's young shoulders. The amateur, playing in his hometown, with a chance to tie for the lead going into the final hole here on Sunday at White Oak National."

"I had enough trouble doing this as a seasoned pro," Steve admitted. "I couldn't imagine what he must be feeling right now."

It was Molly's and Lucy's turn to hold their breath as Tyler discussed the putt with Justin, then made his decision and ambled over to the ball.

He hovered for a second, staring down the hole with a determined look in his eyes. Then he set his feet in, took two practice swings, and then paused with the putter behind the ball.

"Tyler Knox, for birdie."

He hit the putt, and the spectators stood from their seats. The ones who were already standing leaned in for a better look.

The ball curled left into the cup and vanished to the sounds of raucous cheers.

"The kid has ice in his veins," Troy exclaimed. "Birdie for Tyler Knox. And we are all tied at the top of the leaderboard going into the final hole."

"If it ends in a tie here," Steve said, "we will go to sudden death holes. But the way these two have been going at it, this tournament could go until Judgment Day."

Troy laughed. "No kidding. Wow, what an incredible display by these two. A tournament for the ages here at White Oak National. And it all comes down to this on eighteen. Will either of these guys crack? Or will we keep going into a playoff?"

The man in the blue blazer stood at the edge of the tent beside the opening. "Ladies?" he said. "It's time."

Lucy, Molly, and Alicia exchanged excited and nervous expressions.

"Good luck," Molly offered.

"You too," Alicia replied. "After you. I have no idea where I'm going."

Molly followed the man up the hill and over the top. They were surrounded by throngs of people on both sides, all eager to get a close look at the players as they passed by after their rounds.

Once over the slight rise, the full display of the hordes of spectators came into full view. People lined the fairway and wrapped around the green. The three stands of seats were packed.

"You can stand right over here," the man in the blazer said, pointing to a roped-off area under the leaderboard. A few other families stood there waiting for their husbands and fathers to finish."

Alicia felt severely underdressed compared to the women wearing expensive dresses from Lily Pulitzer, Chanel, Prada, and others she didn't even recognize.

The man held back the rope for the three as they passed by and then closed it again.

The viewing area offered a clear line of sight onto the green and all the way to the tee box more than four hundred yards away.

Two other players were walking up the hill toward the green to finish their rounds.

"Okay," Lucy said. "This is it."

"Yep," Molly chirped. "I can't watch. But I can't look away either."

Lucy reached out and grabbed her hand.

Molly looked over at her and smiled. "I'm glad you're with my son."

"Thanks. Me too."

Tyler walked up onto the tee box and stopped as Justin set his bag down and pulled out the driver.

"Okay, buddy," Justin said. "You know what to do. Last hole."

Tyler nodded. "Yeah. Last hole."

He looked over at Graham, who stood eight feet away with his caddie.

A tornado of emotions stormed through Tyler's mind. Graham had played almost perfectly the entire tournament. And his mistake on 17 hadn't even cost him that much. But it was enough of a window for Tyler to slip through and knot things up.

He looked back up the fairway, hedged on both sides by huge trees that cast shadows over the first 150 yards.

The narrow corridor opened up around 180 yards, widening the landing zone and the fairway leading up to the green.

Tyler took a deep breath and walked over to the middle of the tee box.

He placed his ball on a tee and stepped back to take a couple of loose swings.

"Just another drive," he whispered to himself.

He wished his father could be there to see it. To witness this entire experience.

Tyler knew his father would be proud, and probably a little overwhelmed by it all. He imagined his father smiling at him at the top of the knoll behind the 18th green as he finished, whether he won the tournament or not. His dad would have been ecstatic either way.

A tear tried to make its way out of his right eye, but Tyler choked it away and focused on the next shot.

He moved closer to the ball, setting his feet as he always did, lining up the ball with his left heel.

Tyler dropped the club head slowly to the ground, paused for a second, and exhaled.

He swung the same way he had all weekend—free, easy, rhythmic.

The ball carried high into the air, breaking through the shadows cast by the trees, flying straight down the middle of the fairway.

The crowd surrounding the tee box cheered as the ball landed and rolled up the hill, into the sunlit grass.

Tyler held the finishing pose for a few seconds before letting the driver slide down through his palm until the hilt hit his hand.

It felt good—the impact of the ball on the clubface. The sound of it. The applause of the crowd. It was like nothing he'd ever experienced. And he didn't want it to end.

He turned and started back toward Justin. But Graham had already grabbed his driver and was walking his way.

Before the two passed, Graham grinned at him. "I guess you're not going to take it easy on me, huh, kid?"

Tyler blushed and smiled. "No, sir. The Sully I pull for wouldn't want it any other way."

Graham nodded. "You got that right."

Tyler returned to Justin, who gave him a fist bump as he took the club from his friend. "Great drive, Ty. Outstanding."

"Thanks, man. You've been on point all day."

"Just doing what the second-best caddie at the club does."

Tyler chuckled as Graham set up his ball. The crowd fell silent, watching Graham take his practice swings.

Tyler noticed him wince as he whipped the club forward and wondered if he would be able to swing like he wanted. He looked as if he was in some pain and realized that must have been why he hooked the previous drive so badly.

Graham finished his warm-up and addressed the ball to the sounds of nature all around them. He flicked the driver head up once, bouncing it in the air to loosen his grip, then lowered it to the ball.

He swung the way Tyler had watched him swing for most of his life. Except now, he was seeing it in person, from the best seat in the house.

Graham grunted as the clubface blasted the ball into the air.

He followed through but cut it short at the top, leaning forward over the tee as he watched the ball fly through the shadows.

The crowd's voices and clapping echoed through the forests and filled the ears of the golfers and their caddies.

Tyler never took his eye off the ball as it flew true, right down the middle of the fairway, splitting the trees on both sides.

It landed and rolled to a stop fifteen yards short of Tyler's ball, but in a great position to attack the green.

Graham turned as Mike approached with the bag. The caddie took the driver from him and slid it into the slot.

Tyler noticed Graham rolling his shoulder a little as if trying not to let anyone see.

"He looks like he's hurting," Justin said, noting what Tyler was thinking.

"Yeah," Tyler agreed but added nothing more.

The rows of spectators lining the fairway applauded the two men as they marched up the fairway with their caddies in tow.

Tyler had dreamed of something like this. But he'd never expected it to come so soon, much less with his favorite golfer, the man he'd tried to model his game after.

"Looks like I'm out," Graham said with a touch of snark in his voice. He grinned at Tyler, who chuckled.

"It's been an honor to play with you today. No matter what happens. I will never forget this for the rest of my life."

"Yeah, I don't think I will either, Tyler."

Graham and Mike stopped ten feet behind the first ball, and the caddie dropped the bag on the ground.

Tyler and Justin moved out of the way to the right to wait while Graham hit his approach.

"You gonna be okay?" Mike asked.

"Yeah. Nothing a couple of ibuprofen and a shoulder scope can't fix."

The caddie snorted a laugh.

"You want the eight-iron here? Or you want to go lower?"

"Pin's at the front, yeah?"

Mike nodded. "Yep. A medium seven puts it safely in the center of the green. Gives you an easy par."

"Yeah, but eight is the club for that distance."

"Yep. Just giving you your options, my friend. An eight will park it close."

"Or leave it short off the green."

The caddie shrugged. "So? Then you just chip in for birdie." He drew the 8-iron out of the bag and handed it over.

"I'd rather putt," Graham said with a wink.

He walked over to the ball and whipped the club around. It hurt much less than the big driver, and he felt confident he could get one more good swing out of that shoulder with the lighter iron.

He addressed the ball on the slight uphill lie.

No one dared whisper a sound as he lined up the iron and took his swing.

A clean divot chased the ball off the ground as the white orb shot up into the sky. Graham watched it sail toward the green, the line of flight just right of the flag that blew gently in the late afternoon breeze.

"Get there," Graham said. "Be enough."

The word hung in his mind and took him back to the last few

weeks—the conflict within him that forced him to face the insecurities rooted in his past.

The ball dropped out of the air, thumped hard into the putting surface, and rolled to a stop.

From that vantage point, Graham couldn't tell how far from the hole it was, but the cacophony of noise from the crowd told him he'd done well.

Mike walked up behind him with the bag as Graham turned and passed the iron to him. "Not a bad final approach there, old man."

"I guess not."

They stayed there on the fairway and waited while Tyler and his caddie walked over to the ball fifteen yards ahead.

Graham removed his glove and passed it to Mike, pausing to reflect on the moment. "Last time I'll be handing you this, Mike."

"Don't get all nostalgic on me now, Sully."

The two men shared a quiet laugh.

Justin set Tyler's bag on the ground and looked up the hill to the green.

"What are you thinking here?" Tyler asked. He knew what he needed out of the bag but wanted Justin to confirm it.

"Pitching wedge. You know that as well as I do. But it's cute you keep asking me."

"Hey," Tyler said with a smile. "If you can't trust the second-best caddie, who can you trust?"

"Funny," Justin said, removing the wedge from the bag. "Knock it close, buddy."

Tyler grabbed the club from his friend. "Thanks, Justin. I wouldn't have wanted to go on this ride with anyone else."

"Same, bro. Same."

Tyler stepped up to his ball, flicking the club around a few times to stay loose. His shoulders and back were tired. He hadn't played golf four days in a row—well, ever. But he still had enough for one last shot.

He set up in his stance, looked over his shoulder at the green at the top of the slight rise, and then stared at the ball.

This one's for you, Mom, he thought.

Tyler swung and struck the ball true, clipping a chunk of turf up with it.

The sphere rocketed into the air on a line with a pin.

"That looks real good," Justin said from behind him.

As he watched the ball flight, Tyler's mind went back to the clinching hole of the qualifier and how he'd holed it out for eagle. Could that happen again?

The ball reached its peak and began its descent, bombing out of the partly cloudy blue tapestry overhead.

It landed on the green, but how far from the pin he didn't know. The crowd in the stands and surrounding the hole cheered, so it must have been a good one.

"Great shot," Justin said as he approached.

"Thanks," Tyler answered. "It felt really good."

"I don't think you knocked it in, but it should be a nice setup."

They joined Graham and Mike in the middle of the fairway as the crowd cheered them on, two gladiators dueling in the round of a lifetime.

Tyler and Graham smiled as they removed their hats and waved appreciatively to the spectators lining the fairway.

More filed in behind them, following the men as the hiked the famous path up to the 18th green.

When they reached the top of the rise, they saw the two balls nearly equidistant from the hole, each roughly fifteen feet away, separated by ten feet. Tyler's ball had gone past the pin, while Graham's was to the right on the shorter side.

The caddies planted their bags on the fringe and took cards out of their pockets to check their notes.

Graham looked over at Tyler. "They look about the same. You want me to go first, or do you want to?"

"You're the headliner, Sully. I'll go if that's okay with you."

"Well, all right then. Hit a good one, kid."

Tyler bobbed his head then turned to Justin, who was studying his notes. He stuffed the card back in his pocket and motioned to the ball. "It's a straight shot, right to the hole. Mostly flat."

Tyler crouched down and eyeballed the line. Justin was right. There wasn't much to it. Just a straight putt for birdie to either be the first amateur to win a major in nearly a hundred years, or to send it to a playoff.

No big deal.

Justin handed him the putter, and he walked over to the ball, inspecting the green between it and the hole for any irregularities he might have missed. The surface was immaculate, like walking on hard carpet.

Tyler moved into position as the thousands of people in attendance murmured their hushed conversations. The volunteers with the Quiet, Please signs raised them high, and the spectators silenced their voices.

Tyler felt the weight of the moment hanging around his neck. So many people. The cameras. Lucy. His mother. All of them were watching.

You've come this far, he thought. *Just a little more.*

Tyler set up his stance and took a few smooth practice strokes before setting the putter behind the ball.

He exhaled, pulled the club back, and swept it forward.

The ball clicked against the putter's face and rolled toward the hole.

Those who sat in the crowds stood up on their tiptoes to get a better view. Everyone held their collective breath as the ball neared the cup then crawled to a stop one inch to the right.

A massive groan swept over the green. Tyler's heart sank into his stomach. He'd missed it.

Then the audience began clapping. He'd given them a show. And he'd done the best he could. He walked over to the ball, glanced up at Graham, who nodded at him, and then tapped the ball in for par.

Tyler reached into the hole and removed the ball as the crowd continued to cheer. He stood up again and removed his hat, waving to the spectators all around the green before walking over to where Justin stood on the edge rubbing his forehead.

He offered a consolation fist bump to his friend and took the putter.

"Stupid straight putts," Tyler muttered.

"You made par, buddy. On a pro course. On Sunday. In front of millions of people. And you shot four under."

"Yeah. Pretty crazy, huh."

"Not bad for a caddie."

The two shared a grin as Graham took his putter and walked over to the last ball on the green.

He tilted his head to the side for a moment, then crouched to get one more look at the line.

Tyler knew his putt was the same as his, just from a different angle. And Graham knew this green like the tops of his knees. He'd been here so many times before but never walked away a champion.

This putt would change all that. It would change a lifetime of bad luck, of catastrophic mistakes.

Tyler thought he felt pressure when he stepped up to hit his putt, but now he realized it was nothing compared to what that man must be feeling.

Graham finished his assessment and moved up to the ball, tapping his feet gently on the surface until he felt comfortable.

He took a warm-up swing. Then another, getting the tempo the way he thought it should be for this distance.

Tyler watched his chest swell with a deep breath then shrink again as he let it out and lowered the putter to the green. Tyler couldn't keep the fan inside him quiet anymore. "Come on, Sully," he breathed.

Graham swept his putter through.

The throngs of people leaned forward as the ball rolled toward the cup. And for a moment, it felt like the air had been sucked out of the entire planet.

64

The pause seemed like it lasted a lifetime. And for Graham, his entire career, his life, flashed before his eyes in the single second before the ball hit the back of the cup and fell in.

In an instant, the roar that filled the air shook the very ground under his feet.

For a moment, he could only stare at the hole as if it were some foreign object fallen from an alien world.

Then, his knees gave out. Tears that hadn't been there mere seconds before broke through and poured down his face.

He dropped to the firm, green surface, running his hands up through his hair and knocking his hat off behind him.

His ears filled with wild chants of "Sully! Sully! Sully! Sully!"

The first person that should have been there to congratulate him was Mike, his caddie and loyal friend for most of his career.

But as Graham opened his eyes and tilted, he found Tyler Knox rushing toward him on one side, and Mike by his side.

"You did it, Sully!" Tyler screamed. "You did it!"

Graham trembled, tears streaming down his face. This kid, this boy who had a chance to make history, was genuinely happy for him to the point that he too was crying.

Mike's eyes were red with tears too as he wrapped his arms around Graham and embraced him in a hard hug.

The caddie shook him, finally releasing him after a few seconds. Then Tyler extended his hand and smiled. "Congratulations, Sully! I knew you could do it!"

Graham took the boy's hand and pulled him in for a hug.

"Tyler, I'm sorry."

Tyler pulled back away from him, and the two looked each other in the eyes.

"Don't be. I gotta do better. You earned this. And I have the rest of my life for this."

Graham couldn't believe the maturity, the humility, the sincere joy the young man expressed in that moment.

"Tyler," Graham said, choking back the tears, "I've never played with anyone like you. And I can tell you, you are going to take the golf world by storm, kid. Just keep swinging free."

"Yes, sir," Tyler said and backed away to allow the man to have the moment he'd waited a lifetime for.

Mike bent over and picked up the cap Graham dropped and handed it to his friend. Graham took it with an appreciative nod and walked over to the cup.

He hovered over it, staring down at the white ball in the center. Ghosts from the past evaporated in the dying afternoon light as he bent down and picked up the ball.

The crowd roared again, and he held it up while waving his cap to them.

Then he looked toward the path leading up over the knoll toward the club house.

A familiar face hurried forward, escorted by a man in a blue blazer.

"Alicia?" he said out loud.

Graham started walking toward her, his feet carrying him on clouds.

He picked up his speed to a near jog.

"You did it!" she shouted. "You did it!"

They met and threw their arms around each other.

Graham let go and kissed her in front of the entire world.

He held her there for seconds that felt like years, and finally pulled away to look into her eyes. "I thought you said you had to work?"

She smiled at him through the tears running down her face.

"And miss the biggest moment of your life? Not a chance."

He kissed her again and then grabbed her by the hand. "Walk me to the clubhouse?"

"I wouldn't miss it."

Tyler watched as the tournament champion hiked up the hill, surrounded by a frenzied applause from the onlookers.

He smiled.

Justin patted him on the shoulder. "Well, the good news is we automatically qualified for the tournament here next year."

"That's right," Tyler realized. "I forgot about that."

"And next year, you'll be eligible for the prize purse."

"Yeah, let's hope so."

"Hope? Dude, you just finished second at White Oak. You got this."

Tyler saw his mother and Lucy walking down the pathway.

"Hey, do you mind if I—"

"Go to your ladies," Justin said.

"Thanks, Justin." He clapped his friend on the shoulder and hurried off the green.

Justin looked out into the crowd and locked eyes with a pretty blonde in a pink sundress who kept staring at him. For a second, he looked around, wondering if she was looking at him. She nodded, and he grinned and nodded back.

"It's good to be the caddie," he muttered.

Tyler met his mom and Lucy off the backside of the green, and the three embraced in a group hug.

"Oh, sweetie, I am so proud of you," his mom said.

"Yeah, babe. You were so great," Lucy added.

Tyler looked into his mother's eyes, and then his girlfriend's. "I'm just happy for Graham. He waited his whole life for this."

"I know, honey," his mom said. "And I'm sorry you didn't win. But you did amazing."

"It's okay," Tyler said. "I didn't win the tournament this time. But I'll be back. And besides, I have the two best women in the world in my life. I'm already a winner."

65

Tyler stood alone on the number 18 green. The moon hung over the hills toward the city, and stars poked through the inky sky above as the dying light of day faded to the west. The only sounds echoing through the valley were the frogs chirping in the creeks, and the evening songs of birds in the darkness of the forest.

All the spectators were gone. The players had departed, heading back to their hotels or the houses they'd rented for the week. The television crews had left, heading to their next stop. Tomorrow, the leaderboards would be taken down, and the temporary suites and stadium seats would be removed.

Lucy, Justin, and his mother were some of the last to leave, planning on meeting Tyler for a celebration at their apartment.

It would be the first time Lucy set foot in his unremarkable home. That would have made him nervous only a few days before. But now, he felt like he could stare a rabid tiger in the face without flinching.

His mind raced through the last few days—the shots he'd made, and especially that one on 18 he'd missed.

That one didn't plague him as it might have every other golfer on the planet. Instead, Tyler smiled as he stared down the fairway toward the 18 tee box. He felt genuinely happy for Graham, his hero, the golfer he'd followed so closely for so long.

Every devastating loss Graham suffered broke Tyler's heart too.

Tyler's miss on 18 opened the door for Graham to finally get the one thing he'd never been able to grasp—a major tournament victory.

"I watched the replay of that putt," a familiar voice said from somewhere behind Tyler.

He spun around and saw Graham ambling up the slope of the green toward him.

Tyler smiled at him. "Yeah?"

Graham nodded. He stopped next to Tyler, a mere two feet away. They faced the fairway together.

"Yeah. I've seen a lot of your highlights from this week. And I don't think I saw one where you missed a putt like that. You were automatic from that range, and beyond, for the entire tournament."

Tyler rolled his shoulders. "I guess I just froze up," he admitted. "I've never had to make a putt in front of an international television audience for a chance to win a major."

Graham pouted his lips and bobbed his head. "I guess."

Tyler's forehead wrinkled and looked over at his hero. "What do you mean?"

Graham kept his gaze down the fairway. "I just hope you didn't miss that on purpose."

For a moment, Tyler felt like the air around him instantly got heavier, weighing down on him like some all-encompassing yoke.

He chuckled. "No, sir. I seem to recall my favorite golfer once saying titles are never given. They're always earned."

Graham grinned. "So you watched my press conferences back in the day too, huh?"

"If you were going to beat me, it had to be because you were the better golfer. Yeah, sure, I couldn't win the prize money, and everyone is talking about how I have my entire career ahead of me, that I'm going to be the one to watch for the next two decades. But I wouldn't miss a putt on purpose. That's not how Graham Sullivan would play the game. And he's the most honorable golfer I've ever met."

A tear formed in Graham's right eye. Tyler barely noticed, and quickly returned his gaze to the fairway.

"You have the opportunity to be one of the greats, Tyler," Graham said. "Not just as a player, but as an ambassador of the game. That's how I tried to do it my entire career. Live honestly, honorably. Do right by people. For a long time, I wondered what difference any of that made. When things got hard, after so many near misses, after losing my wife, my son, my world, I was tempted to say screw it. To live by my own rules, to do it the way so many others were. What did it matter if all life gave me was disappointment?"

Graham faced Tyler. "I'm here to tell you, it does matter, son. It's the only thing that matters. What happens in our lives has nothing to do with our past good deeds or bad. All of that is gone. There is no past. There is no future. There is only now. Always try to do what is right in this moment. Trophies, cars, houses, vacations, all of those things are gone the moment we take our last breath, when we play the real final round."

He turned away and looked into the distance. "The great P. G. Wodehouse called golf the infallible test, and that the ideal player is one who plays like he knows God is watching him, who always plays the ball as it lies. That's why golf is the greatest mirror of life. There are so many ups and downs, so many obstacles, challenges, difficulties for us to sort through. And it seems no matter how much you work at it, how hard you try, nothing ever changes."

"Just like with golf, you'll never reach perfection," Tyler said.

"That's right." Graham inched closer and patted Tyler on the back. "Perfection is in the trying, it's in the effort, Tyler. So, never stop trying. Do that, and you'll pass the infallible test. And when that real final round comes, you can face that number eighteen with a smile on your face, and the pride in knowing you gave it your best."

Graham took his hand back. "I'll be watching your career with great interest, my boy. I have a feeling you're going to give the world of golf a spectacular show."

"Thanks, Sully," Tyler said, tears forming in his eyes now. "I appreciate that."

"See you around, kid."

The older man turned and walked off the green, leaving Tyler alone again. He knew he needed to get going, to get back to the apartment and the people he cared most about in the world. But he lingered, just for two more minutes.

Even though he lived in another place, his real home was here, on the fairways, on the greens, in the bunkers, in the rough, on the fringes, between the trees. Everything life could throw at him, the triumphs and the struggles, all happened here.

And if he could do great things here, in the most challenging of environments, he could do the same in life.

Tyler inhaled the scent of cut grass, and exhaled slowly one more time before turning, and walking toward the life that awaited him.

THANK YOU

Thanks so much for reading this story.

Writing it was a far cry from the normal books I've created in the past.

People have asked why I wrote this, why get out of my lane to do something so different. The answer is simple. This idea came to me one night, and I knew I had to write it.

I wanted to share this story with the world, to share the emotions, the challenges, and the triumphs that these characters experienced. Because they are us.

We go through trials and challenges, and must meet them with resilience, belief, and persistence.

I hope that you enjoyed this story, and I appreciate you taking the time to read it.

Your friendly neighborhood author,

Ernest

OTHER BOOKS BY ERNEST DEMPSEY

Sean Wyatt Archaeological Thrillers:

The Secret of the Stones

The Cleric's Vault

The Last Chamber

The Grecian Manifesto

The Norse Directive

Game of Shadows

The Jerusalem Creed

The Samurai Cipher

The Cairo Vendetta

The Uluru Code

The Excalibur Key

The Denali Deception

The Sahara Legacy

The Fourth Prophecy

The Templar Curse

The Forbidden Temple

The Omega Project

The Napoleon Affair

The Second Sign

The Milestone Protocol

Where Horizons End

Poseidon's Fury

The Florentine Pursuit

The Inventor's Tomb

Adriana Villa Adventures:

War of Thieves Box Set

When Shadows Call

Shadows Rising

Shadow Hour

The Relic Runner - A Dak Harper Series:

The Relic Runner Origin Story

The Courier

Two Nights In Mumbai

Country Roads

Heavy Lies the Crown

Moscow Sky

The Adventure Guild (ALL AGES):

The Caesar Secret: Books 1-3

The Carolina Caper

Beta Force:

Operation Zulu

London Calling

Paranormal Archaeology Division:

Hell's Gate

Guardians of Earth:

Emergence: Gideon Wolf Book 1

Righteous Dawn: Gideon Wolf Book 2

Crimson Winter: Gideon Wolf Book 3

ACKNOWLEDGMENTS

As always, I would like to thank my terrific editors, Anne and Jason, for their hard work. What they do makes my stories so much better for readers all over the world. Anne Storer and Jason Whited are the best editorial team a writer could hope for and I appreciate everything they do.

I also want to thank Elena at Lı Graphics for her tremendous work on my book covers and for always overdelivering. Elena definitely rocks.

A big thank you has to go out to my friend James Slater for his proofing work. James has added another layer of quality control to these stories, and I can't thank him enough.

Last but not least, I need to thank all my wonderful fans and especially the advance reader team. Their feedback and reviews are always so helpful and I can't say enough good things about all of them.